THE
DISTANCE
HOME

THE
DISTANCE
HOME

Orly Konig

FORGE

A TOM DOHERTY ASSOCIATES BOOK
New York

THE DISTANCE HOME

Copyright © 2017 by Orly Konig-Lopez

A Forge Book
Published by Tom Doherty Associates
175 Fifth Avenue
New York, NY 10010

www.tor-forge.com

Forge® is a registered trademark of Macmillan Publishing Group, LLC.

The Library of Congress Cataloging-in-Publication Data is available upon request.

ISBN 978-0-7653-9041-7 (hardcover)
ISBN 978-0-7653-9043-1 (e-book)

Our books may be purchased in bulk for promotional, educational, or business use. Please contact your local bookseller or the Macmillan Corporate and Premium Sales Department at 1-800-221-7945, extension 5442, or by e-mail at MacmillanSpecialMarkets@macmillan.com.

First Edition: May 2017

Printed in the United States of America

0 9 8 7 6 5 4 3 2 1

For Lea and Peter—My inspiration

For Philippe—My motivation

For Alex—My heart

ACKNOWLEDGMENTS

As a writer, one of my favorite parts of a novel is the acknowledgments page. I always fantasized about writing one for my own novel and here I am. Dream come true! I will say, however, that it's so much more daunting to write the acknowledgments page than writing the actual novel. This story may have been born in my over-caffeinated brain, but it came to life with the support and encouragement of so many amazing people. A huge, blanket thanks and hug to everyone who supported and encouraged me along the way.

But there are a few people I do need to call out by name.

First, my agent, Marlene Stringer. Since that first babbling pitch session at a writers' event, you've been a supportive online friend. So perfect then that, three years later, you'd become my champion. Your enthusiasm, guidance, and friendship are the best gifts an author could ask for.

Dream editor Kristin Sevick. I'm so lucky that you fell in love with Emma, Jack, and Jukebox. Thank you for knowing what I wanted to say and showing me the way to actually say it. Big thanks to Bess Cozby and everyone at Forge, for taking such great care of me and my book baby.

I'm privileged to have met so many fabulous authors on this journey and am continuously awed at the generosity of the writing community. Forever thanks to Erika Marks, Amy Sue

Nathan, Lori Nelson Spielman, Julie Lawson Timmer, and Barbara Claypole White, for answering newbie questions and cheering me on. This story would never have made it out of the messy first-draft phase without kick-ass crit partner and friend Laura Drake. Awesome readers Kerry Lonsdale, Jamie Raintree, Jessica Strawser, Kimberley Troutte, and Vicki Wilson—thank you! This manuscript wouldn't be what it is without you. The support of the Badasses, writing pals at Writers in the Storm, Tall Poppy Writers, and last but dear in my heart, the Women's Fiction Writers Association, has meant the world to me.

To dear friends Vicky Gresham, Kim and Scott McWilliams, and Barbie Underwood, who asked enthusiastic questions about my story and the writing process, poured wine when it was needed (and more wine when doubly needed), and never doubted that this would someday happen—thank you.

My husband, Philippe, who so wisely suggested I try a new creative outlet such as, oh, maybe writing, before committing to a Ph.D. program, and then supported me every step of this crazy journey. Thank you for giving me the time and opportunity to pursue my dream.

To my parents, Lea and Peter, for the sacrifices you made so I could ride all those many years ago (including walking my horses at horse shows despite being deathly afraid of the beasts) and giving me the confidence to pursue anything I wanted. For reading early and revised and re-revised drafts and never wavering in your belief that my story would one day become a published novel, thank you for being the best role models a girl could hope for!

And finally, to my number-one fan, the guy who cheered loudest when this book sold, and whose unconditional love fuels everything I do—my son, Alex.

The real voyage of discovery consists not in
seeking new landscapes, but in having new eyes.

—PROUST

THE
DISTANCE
HOME

1

JUMPING FROG FARM

The first time I saw that sign I was eight, and believed, with the certainty that allows reindeer to fly and little girls to heal, that this place would save me.

And for eight years it did.

For eight years, I spent most of my waking and many of my sleeping hours at the farm, thankful for the friendship from the horses and grateful for the escape from my home.

Until the accident. Until I was sent away.

Now here I am, thirty-two years old, staring at the same sign, praying that the eight-year-old who once believed isn't completely lost. Praying that the horrific tangle of deceit and heartbreak that kept me away is mostly forgiven.

But reindeer don't fly.

And time hasn't healed me.

A horse whinnies, setting off a chorus from the barn. A tractor rumbles to life, sputtering and groaning at the call to duty. A dog barks, letting loose a stampede of dogs and cats.

The sounds of my past life are muffled by the heavy air. It's mid-September and as hot today as any stifling Maryland summer day.

"Toad." A gravely voice skids across the gravel parking lot. "Is that really you? No bloody way."

I turn and I'm face-to-chest with the man I adopted to be my grandfather.

"Simon." I look up into the brown eyes that had given a timid girl the confidence to conquer her fears.

And in that heartbeat of a moment, I'm lost. Will the Emma he knew hug him? Or will the Emma standing in front of him shake his hand?

"Put that damn hand down, girl." Simon pulls me into a bear hug. With a final squeeze that knocks a gasp out of me, he pushes me to arm's length. "Let me look at you. Well. Well. Emma Metz."

My nerves crackle like a sputtering fire and my face flames. Each day of the past sixteen years settles between us. I'm no longer that shy girl who desperately wanted to fit in.

"You're not dressed for riding." He smirks at my maxi dress, the hem grazing the top of overpriced, custom-designed red-and-white-striped Converses.

"True." The word sounds more apologetic then acknowledgment. I run the fingers of my left hand over the sign's green lettering. "Actually, I didn't even realize I was coming out here until I found myself staring at this."

The corners of Simon's eyes pinch and his head juts forward to peer closer at my face. "But you are here."

I nod. "But I am here."

Simon squeezes my shoulders. "I'm so sorry, Toad."

Toad. The first time Simon saw me, eight years old and all arms and legs, he'd called me that. Tears swell my throat and all I can do is force a wobbly smile.

"Later. Right now, I'm just happy you're here. Come, Rena will be tickled to see you. And there's another old man in the barn you need to say hello to." Simon grabs my hand and pulls me forward.

Jack. He's still alive. My heart stutters.

Then clenches. "Jillian?"

"She's not here today. Come."

I take a step to follow but the bottom of my sneakers feel like they've melted into the hot gravel of the driveway, each step a slogging effort obvious even to Simon, because he gives my hand a reassuring squeeze.

I close my eyes and breathe in the tingle of freshly mowed fields, the tickle of sawdust, and the sweet smell of horses. "I've missed this."

"You didn't have to stay away."

"Yes, I did."

Another squeeze. I allow him to lead me to the barn with a gentle tug. We're greeted with nickers and whinnies as heads pop over the top of stall doors along the outside wall of the barn. Big brown eyes blink into the sun. Simon releases my hand and reaches into a pocket of his baggy jeans, pulling out a handful of treats. He walks to the large black head with the lightning-bolt blaze poking out of the stall closest to the barn door and offers the palm of his hand. The horse's pink muzzle twitches along Simon's palm and the treats that were there a blink ago are gone. The horse crunches his snack and pushes his head into an old friend's chest.

Simon rubs behind the horse's right ear and braces his legs as the horse pushes deeper into his chest. I feel the pressure against my body and rub at my breastbone.

Why did I come? What's the point of looking back?

There's a clang of wood on metal as someone adjusts a jump. "One more time, Laura. This time, dammit, wait for the distance. Don't let him dictate the speed. You're in charge. You. Not him."

A smile cracks through my apprehension. "Has she changed at all?"

Simon chuckles. "Nope. Still scaring the shit out of little kids and big horses."

He walks through the large double doors into the barn, tossing a "Go say hi to her" over his shoulder. He disappears into the dark of the barn, leaving me rooted in indecision.

I walk the perimeter of the barn toward the outdoor arena. A few curious faces stick their noses toward me, hoping for a walk-by snack. I stay just out of their reach. At the edge of the barn, I stop and suck in a deep gulp of dusty air.

Am I about to make a horrible mistake?

Or was the mistake my slinking away in shame all those years ago? Shame for something I didn't do.

But what choice did I have? We were best friends, "horse-and-heart sisters," we called ourselves. Without Jillian, I was no one.

Turns out I was no one even with Jillian.

I make the turn and stop when the outdoor arena comes into view. I inch closer to the aluminum siding and lean into the corner. One step back and I'll be hidden from view. One step forward and I'm committed.

"One. Two. Three. Better. Leg. LEG," Rena bellows. "Don't let him slow down. You know he hates going away from the in-gate. Kick him." The horse scoots forward as his rider gives him a solid kick.

My head bobs as horse and rider canter around the ring and pop over another jump.

"Well, well."

The butterflies in my stomach freeze. She's staring at me.

It's impossible to read her expression under the shadow of her straw hat, suspiciously similar to the hat she wore all those years ago. She crosses her arms over her chest and shifts her weight to the right. I remember that stance. I'm expected to move and say something or turn and run. I don't do either.

My gut flops and I fight the bubbling urge to throw up. I shouldn't be here.

And yet, here you are.

My right arm starts a slow ascent, pulled upward by a force stronger than my weakening resolve. Rena's head tilts in a semi-acknowledgment of my pathetic hello.

Behind me I hear the clomp of horseshoes on gravel. A tall man with a disheveled shock of black hair leads a huge gray to the arena. He smiles and nods as they walk by. His arrival releases me from the grip of Rena's attention. She asks the man, towering over her by at least a foot, a question and they both squat to look at the horse's left front leg.

The flopping in my stomach wins and I slink back, away from the reunion I'm obviously not ready for.

There's only one head hanging over the outside stall doors this time. I stop a few feet from the big black horse, just out of his reach. If I were able to unlock my arm from my side, open my palm, and lift my hand, I'd feel his warm breath and soft muzzle. The same soft muzzle that eased my fears so many times over the years. I clench my fist, digging fingernails into my palm. I don't deserve his comfort.

"Hi, Jack."

The horse tosses his head and snorts a hello. The afternoon sun casts a spastic shadow dance with each movement.

"Remember the day he was born?" Simon wraps his arm around my shoulder, barricading my escape route.

My head bobs. Jillian and I had persuaded Simon and Rena to let us sleep in the stable and keep an eye on Cassie, who, we were convinced, would go into labor that night. At three twenty-three in the morning, Jack Flash was born. It was the day before my tenth birthday, one day after Jilli's eleventh birthday. The best birthday present any horse-crazy girl could ask for. He was going to be ours. Together we'd train him, show him. Together we'd make the Olympic team.

Together, we almost killed him.

The truth of that memory lodges in my throat like a jagged chicken bone.

"I shouldn't be here." I stiffen, and Simon tightens his hold on me.

"But you are. And it's not just because you missed my charming sense of humor or Rena's bubbly personality."

My lips curl to a sad smile. "I did miss you guys. Every day."

Hands accustomed to maneuvering large animals and farm equipment grab my shoulders and turn me around. "It's been long enough, Emma."

The words carry a punch to my gut. My body caves in and I wrench free of Simon's hold.

Only to find my way blocked by Rena. Solid and daunting, all five feet two inches of her.

Her gray eyes spear through what self-assurance I've gained in the years since college. *You're an adult, a professional.* That pep talk works with the board of directors, with presidents of international companies. It doesn't work against Rena Winn.

"You finally decided to show up again. Why now?" Her tone is soft, not welcoming, not accusing, not any of the greetings I'd run through my head over the years.

"I was feeling restless at the inn. The meeting with my father's lawyer isn't until tomorrow. Next thing I know, I'm here." I'm rambling. I shrug and my shoulders get stuck by my ears.

Rena scans my spotless shoes, my out-of-place dress, my fancy salon highlights. So drastically different from the girl she used to know. "I'm sorry for your loss. It appears you've done well for yourself. Your father must have been proud."

Before I can respond, she turns and marches to the lounge, the screen door slapping shut behind her.

"I'm sorry," Simon says, the words falling flat in the aftershock.

Jack nickers and tosses his head, his long black forelock flopping in a come-on-you-can-do-it encouragement. I look into his soft eyes and will myself back sixteen years. Would I have done it differently?

Where would I be now if I had?

"What will you do now?"

"Keep going." Two simple words, words I've been saying to myself for as long as I can remember.

Simon releases a sigh and Jack snorts a horse's equivalent.

"Sometimes, Toad, you have to change direction."

The rumbling of the tractor unsettles a few birds from the trees along the front of the stable. The gears grind as the driver makes his way to the fields where the manure is spread every morning and afternoon. How many summers did I spend cleaning stalls and riding that godforsaken old tractor as it bounced and jolted along the fields? Or cleaning tack for the riding school and borders who were too busy to take care of their own equipment? Or leading horses for the therapeutic riding program?

Simon studies my face. "We visited you at the hospital, you know. Your dad wouldn't allow anyone to see you. Maybe he thought we'd press charges. Ridiculous."

I swallow hard, not sure if I'm making room for the words to come out or trying to push them back down. "Did Jilli come?"

Simon releases a growling sigh. "No."

I nod.

Had I expected her to come? Yes. We were H&H sisters. We looked out for each other.

No, you looked out for her. She left you twisting in the blame.

"Does she ever mention me?" My voice is no more than a shiver of a breeze, almost overpowered by the chatter of an agitated squirrel and the fading rumble of the tractor.

Simon's brown eyes darken and he slaps his thigh, dislodging a puff of sawdust. "No."

The squirrel shakes his bushy tail at us.

"Rena didn't seem very happy to see me."

He chews the inside of his lip, his eyes looking for an answer in the shimmering reflection from the lounge windows.

"You know Rena, she's a tough one. Doesn't let go of things easily. She'll come around."

"I don't think I'll be here long enough for that."

Our eyes meet in the reflection of the window. "Give her a chance."

"I need to go." I take a hesitant step backward, then, when Simon doesn't react, another.

"Emma?" My name feels familiar in his deep voice, the slightest hint of his childhood in England giving it a soft elegance, and foreign in the scratched pitch that comes with age, a painful reminder of the years stretched between us. "I don't know exactly what happened. Only that it was awful. It tore our hearts to pieces seeing the two of you broken."

My left hand fidgets with the car keys. The jingle triggers a glare from Simon and I squeeze my hand into a fist, hiding my nails. Instinct. He used to fuss at me for chewing the skin at the edge of my nail to the point where I'd draw blood. I haven't done that in years, but under his knowing eyes, I feel the sting of ripping skin.

At what point does a past mistake become so ingrained in who you've become that there's no going back? For sixteen years I've lived in the shadow of this mistake. I've let it take my dreams and stain my self-worth. I've replayed the day in my mind, wondering if I could have done something different. Replayed the following days in the hospital, tumbling the words I should have said until they were smooth in my mind. Yet each replay only sharpened the pain. I learned to shut my brain against those thoughts. With each success—school, job, promotions—I shuttered that pain deeper into the past.

"Did you ever question Jillian about what happened? What really happened?" I meet Simon's eyes and blink at the sadness reflected in them.

"Of course."

"And?"

"Her story never changed. And you never challenged what she said."

"Would it have mattered?"

Our gazes do a clumsy two-step around each other. It wouldn't have mattered, even though we both would like to believe otherwise. My side of the story would have raised questions neither family wanted out in the public. So I buried my truth and my father made sure the grave remained unmarked.

A white pickup lumbers up the driveway and pulls into a parking slot next to my rental. A slight woman with a tight ponytail slips out of the cab, followed by a panting golden retriever. Simon and the woman exchange hellos while the dog pokes a twitching snout at each pocket of Simon's jeans.

The woman strides to the barn, her black riding boots stamping a familiar beat. My insides clench and I turn away before I have to label the feeling.

"It was good seeing you, Simon." I feel his eyes on me as I walk to the car. I watch the toes of my Converses emerge and disappear with each step. Without turning around, I open the car door, then melt into the oppressive air inside the car.

The road away from the stable dips and turns, with only a few farmhouses dotting the green pastures. A sign cautions a ninety-degree turn and a blind driveway entrance.

A long-suppressed ghost takes control of the car. My foot slams on the brakes. My hands tighten on the wheel, knuckles threatening to pop out of my skin. Sparks shatter in my vision and my breath racks in my ears as pain splinters my ribs. The shrill grating of steel on pavement. The screaming of humans and horses. The slow-motion roller coaster of the truck flipping. Jilli's head slamming into the steering wheel. The flashing lights and yelling voices. The utter silence of lives shattering.

Through the distance of sixteen years I hear a honk, then two quick, then a very long one. I blink my surroundings back into the present. A head pokes from the window of the truck behind me and a man's voice yells for me to move.

Flipping on the hazards, I release the brake enough for the car to coast to the edge of the road. The driver of the truck revs the engine and lunges past, waving his left hand out the window in what most likely wasn't a good-bye.

I close my eyes, waiting for my heart to settle back into my chest. A sedan comes from behind and the driver gives me a curious look as he slides past. I wave him on. Nothing to see here.

I force my foot to lift, allowing the car to creep through the sharp turn, my hands in a stranglehold on the wheel. The sedan must have turned into the driveway on the right because I see dust swirling.

The field on the left side of the road looks like every field I've passed so far, browning after a hot, dry summer. No skid marks. No mangled steel. No broken lives.

"Oh my god." The dark irony slams into my chest. An accident sent me away sixteen years ago. And an accident is responsible for bringing me back.

The sun envelops the mountain in a soft hug and the fields glow. A magical, peaceful setting for my worst nightmare.

2

The morning drive is far more peaceful than the one the night before. Granted, the drive to downtown Emmitsville is the opposite direction from Jumping Frog Farm.

Downtown has matured since I lived here. There's a new strip mall with a Subway and a Starbucks, a karate studio nestled between them. A bank sits at the end, its front door facing the other side, like the buttoned-up kid who doesn't get called for the kick-ball teams.

I take a right at the Stop sign my father used to complain was a waste of time and pull up to an old Victorian flanked by two older Victorians, one a coffee shop, the other a used bookstore.

The door to Crème Café opens, releasing the stomach-gurgling aroma of fresh-baked bread and strong coffee. I'd declined breakfast at the Mountain Inn this morning. Now I wish I hadn't.

A woman in a jewel-toned gypsy skirt bumps the door wider with her hip, her hands trying to keep three paper cups and a white paper bag from falling. She negotiates the three steps down, judging each out of the corner of her eye. She looks frazzled already and I wonder if that's how bystanders saw me on Friday mornings on the way to work—worn by the week, exhausted by the sheer thought of the day ahead. She passes in front of my car, then takes the steps to the bookstore. The sign says they open at 10 A.M. I glance at the clock on the rental's dash. It's 8:56.

We're both early. My appointment with Thomas Adler is at 9. I'm always early though.

Punctuality, Emma, is a sign of professionalism and respect.

"See, Dad, you taught me well."

Even though the digital clock still shows 8:58, I get out of the car.

The steps of the old building creak a welcome. A small blue sign by the door confirms I'm in the right location.

ADLER LAW
SINCE 1953

Before I have a chance to knock, a man pushes the screen door open.

"You must be Emma Metz. You look just like Edward. And you obviously inherited his promptness."

I shake off the urge to protest. I'm nothing like my father. I never wanted to be like my father. And yet everything about me seems to be a copy of him.

"Yes, I am. You're Thomas Adler?"

"That's me. Please come in." He steps to the side, propping the screen door open with his body while his hands gesture me ahead.

He's younger than I expected. Not much older than I. He's wearing khakis and a button-down shirt, one button open at the throat and folded at the wrists. On his left wrist are two braided yarn bracelets. Friendship bracelets. No fancy watch. A wide band of various metals gleams on the ring finger of his left hand as he waves me into the house. A woodsy cologne pricks at my nose.

Inside, the old house is remarkably modern. Instead of tiny dark rooms, I'm standing in an open floor plan with sleek desks in the middle, chest-height bookshelves providing partitions between the workspaces. The whirring of a copy machine rattles from the back of the house and a phone rings on an empty desk. A woman in a gray pencil skirt and crisp white blouse swivels her chair between a sleek computer screen and a laptop on the perpendicular surface of an L-shaped desk. I resist the urge to tell her it's not an efficient setup.

Thomas Adler gestures me into a room where burgundy leather couches create a striking accent to the light wood floor and lighter beige walls. Two of the walls are covered with whimsical paintings of men playing cards and boules, a man on a bike with a baguette sticking out of a pouch on his back, and a woman reading a book on a park bench. He takes in my surprised expression. "Not what you were expecting?"

"Not exactly."

"My dad knew the artist. They lived in the same apartment building in Paris when they were in their early twenties."

A third wall boasts an impressive selection of diplomas. Those I expected.

He points to one of the minimalist leather couches and folds his lanky frame onto a matching one, pulling at his pant legs as he settles. He crosses his right leg over his left and weaves his fingers together, cupping his right kneecap. He's not exactly what I imagined, although I'm not honestly sure what I imagined.

"Have you had a chance to review the documents I sent?"

I push deeper into the square couch, uncomfortable under his direct gaze and direct approach. "Some. There's a lot to take in."

"Your father was meticulous. He made sure everything was accounted for."

That would be Edward Metz. Everything in his life was controlled. It's what made him a successful psychiatrist. And it's what made him a failure in his personal life. But maybe I'm the only one who saw it that way.

He traveled all over the world, lecturing at medical conferences. His articles appeared in prestigious medical journals. He worked endless hours seeing patients.

Because of his travels, we never went on vacation. Because of those endless hours helping strangers, he was never around to see what was happening in his own house.

"Ms. Metz?" He's watching me, a pen poised midair as though waiting for my thoughts.

I look around the room, stalling, until I've made a full sweep and land back on my father's attorney.

A week ago I was in my office, on the tenth floor, windows overlooking busy Chicago. I had dinner reservations at a fancy Italian restaurant with a handsome lawyer from the fifteenth floor. And I was blatantly ignoring the e-mail from my father with details on his business trip the following month. *We need to talk*, he'd said. *Please save an evening for me.*

I hadn't gotten around to answering.

The last time he'd sent me a "we need to talk" e-mail had led to four months of not speaking to each other. It had started as a rare father-daughter bonding discussion in a cozy French restaurant. He'd inquired about my job, asking questions even if he hadn't been overly enthusiastic in his responses.

At some point the conversation shifted to my then live-in boyfriend. Gavin, my father thought, was using me. I was being naïve and gullible and he was here to make sure Gavin was moved out of my life.

The irony was that I'd already planned on kicking Gavin out. My father's parental declaration bought Gavin another two months. It was another two months before I started speaking to my father again. And a few weeks beyond that before I let it slip that the go-nowhere boyfriend was gone.

Another "we need to talk" e-mail stank of crispy feelings. So no, I hadn't answered. And yes, I was carrying that extra poundage of guilt. My left thumb picks at the cuticle on the ring finger. *Don't do it. Don't chew on it.*

A week ago, my ghosts were safely tucked several states away, and under years of emotional baggage.

Then someone popped the lock on the suitcase of my past.

The phone call had come while I was in a meeting. An unfamiliar Maryland number. I'd let it go to voice mail. Another thing I'd learned from my father—answer the phone only when you can give the caller your full attention. I guess that's why he usually let calls fall into voice mail.

My return call was answered immediately. Thomas Adler's

voice stutters through my mind. "I'm sorry to tell you . . . car crash . . . so sorry . . . dead . . . instant . . . nothing they could do . . . so sorry . . . I've arranged a flight and hotel . . . if I can help . . . so sorry." He'd said "sorry" more times than was necessary.

My father had left strict instructions that I was to come to Maryland in the event of his death. But why? He'd orchestrated every get-together as far from here as possible. *Now that he's dead I'm summoned back?*

"Why am I here, Mr. Adler? This could have been taken care of without me having to upturn my schedule."

"I don't know his motivation. Maybe he hoped that making peace with the past would help you move forward?"

"I moved forward. My life is in Chicago. There's nothing for me here. This," I gesture at the papers on the low table between us, "could have been handled by mail."

"It's not just about signing a few papers."

"Then what? You're taking care of the practice. And I could have hired someone to clean out his condo."

He pulls his lips into a tight circle and I wait for him to release the words he seems to be tasting. "The service?"

I tighten the distance between my shoulder blades and pluck at a thread in the throw pillow by my elbow.

"What service, Mr. Adler? You read his instructions to me over the phone. I heard his words in your voice, 'There is to be no public service. My body is to be donated to Johns Hopkins University Hospital. My daughter, Emma Metz, is to have a private moment at the grave of her mother, my wife.'" I wince, equally horrified at the explicit instructions he'd left and at my brain for memorizing those instructions verbatim.

We fall into an uncomfortable silence, office sounds suddenly too loud in the adjoining rooms where Mr. Adler's colleagues are talking on phones and photocopying papers.

"How long will you be in town?"

"A week. Why? How long do you expect this to take?"

"The paperwork part won't take long."

The paperwork part.

"What other part is there?" The private moment at mom's grave is nothing more than a moment on my drive back to the airport. I square my shoulders against the mounting dread that even from the grave my father is controlling my future.

Thomas pulls in a long breath, his fingers fussing over the stacks of papers on the coffee table between us.

"I think you should take the time to go through your father's things. I've taken the liberty of pulling some of the personal effects from his office. The extra keys to the condo are in here, too." Thomas taps the top of a box on the floor next to his feet.

After a long moment of listening to muffled office sounds and my own breathing, I look up and make eye contact. What I see knocks me into the back of the couch.

"What are you not telling me, Mr. Adler?"

A shadow darkens his green eyes and in his voice I hear sadness.

"I'm sorry, Emma. The answer isn't with me. But please do as he asked. I think you will find it beneficial."

The Mountain Inn is at the base of a "hill," but the locals call it a mountain. The drawing on the sign at the foot of the long driveway depicts the house with a not-to-scale mountain behind it. Although I suppose if you're lying on the ground, looking up with one eye closed, it looks about right.

For the second time in twenty-four hours, I wonder why Thomas booked me here, instead of a hotel in DC or Bethesda or any of the larger cities for that matter. And for the fiftieth time in twenty-four hours, I wonder why I haven't moved myself.

The quiet here is suffocating. I've been away from Chicago for one day and I already crave the sound of traffic, the grunts of buses, the muttering of commuters.

The sign for the inn boasts "an idyllic country setting that will restore your sense of well-being." I snort at the idea. My well-being just needs to get back where it belongs. My well-being is in desperate need of a double-shot, low-fat, hazelnut latte.

I push the door open and startle at the loud intrusion of the bell above the door. My heart hammers and my hand white-knuckles the door handle. This is not helping my well-being.

The young lady who checked me in yesterday steps out of a back room and smiles when she sees me. I force a smile and silently vow to find a hotel where I'm just another body moving through.

"Welcome back, Ms. Metz. Please let me know if I can be of any help. We have menus for nearby restaurants if you're looking for ideas, or we have a few open tables here if you'd like to join us."

"Thanks. I haven't thought that far ahead yet." Which isn't exactly true since the smell of something baking has my stomach performing aerial acrobatics.

The young lady, whose name is floating in a hazy cloud at the back of my mind, smiles, says I should be free to call on her if I need anything, then returns to the room she came from, leaving me alone with the quiet.

Quiet is good. I'm used to quiet back home. After all, I live alone, and since I'm rarely in my apartment, I generally forget to turn on the TV or radio when I am there. And my apartment building has the hushed acoustics of music-practice rooms.

The music department was my favorite place to study in college. I'd walk down the hall, peeking through the small glass windows in the doors until I found an unoccupied room. Room 6 was usually open. In room 7, there was almost always a dark-haired girl practicing cello. I'd stand outside watching through that small window. Regardless of the season she'd wear a colorful wool scarf loosely wrapped around her neck. She played with her eyes closed, releasing herself to the movement of her hands. She never acknowledged that I was standing there and we never spoke. Once I saw her walking across the quad, wool scarf waving behind her. I'd been tempted to chase her down, ask her name, ask the name of the music that so captivated her. But I hadn't. Then one day she wasn't in room 7 and I never saw her again. I wonder what became of her.

But even in the halls of the music department and the halls of my apartment building you can hear muffled sounds of life. I take the steps to the bedrooms and stop on the landing, listening for a whisper of noise. Nothing. Not even an air-conditioning unit or the mumbling of a television set. This isn't quiet. This is floating in uninhabited space.

My room is large, with french doors opening to a small balcony overlooking an open field that ends at the base of the mountain. I set the box on the small table in front of the french doors and shake out my arms. It's not heavy yet feels like it weighs a ton.

I lift the top and flip through the envelopes. Each has a white label at the top-right corner, the contents cataloged in 12-point Times New Roman. The top one contains his death certificate. He died three days short of his sixty-fourth birthday.

"Oh god." The words echo in the room. I hadn't even remembered his birthday was coming up. That's not exactly true, the date was in the back of my mind and marked in blue ink in my calendar. But I was busy and the timing slipped behind all the meetings and deadlines and the comfort of the standing order with Godiva. Did the box of chocolates arrive before he died, or will I find it neatly wrapped with the message typed in whatever font the Godiva store uses?

I don't think I can stomach looking at the box of chocolates and knowing that was the last time my father may have thought of me. It's because of him that I started sending them. He had a standing order with Tiffany for my birthday. Except he still knew what they sent each time. I only knew it was a box of chocolate.

When was the last time I handpicked a birthday gift for him?

When was the last time we celebrated a birthday together?

I squeeze my eyes shut, trying to capture the memory. Thirteen. It was my thirteenth birthday. I was home sick with strep throat and Dad had canceled his afternoon patients to take me to the doctor. On the way home he stopped to buy me a soft-serve ice cream from Joe's Cones. *Happy birthday, Emma.*

The chair closest to me is turned away from the table, just enough for an easy landing.

When I turned sixteen? No, there'd been a box waiting for me on the table when I came home from school. Inside was a key on a shiny Tiffany keychain. A typed note read, "Happy sixteenth. May it take you to all the places you dream." In the garage was a shiny new silver Jeep. Just like the one on my "wish board" in my room. He came home late that night, after I was already in bed. I pretended to be asleep. It was easier than pretending I was okay with his absence.

That birthday, like so many before, had been celebrated with my wish-you-were-mine family. Rena had baked a carrot cake in the shape of a carrot. Jilli had given me a bracelet braided from Jack's tail hairs.

My fingers brush at my left wrist where I'd put the bracelet, where it had stayed for five months. They'd cut it off in the hospital and thrown it away with my bloody clothes.

Most birthdays after that were celebrated with my friends. At the boarding school, then in my dorm at college, and with roommates during grad school. There was the year right after graduation that Dad had paid for a trip to France. He was to meet me in Toulouse and we were going to spend four days touring the Loire Valley.

He'd canceled at the last minute.

I slip the death certificate back into the envelope. It won't tell me more than I already know, which is nothing.

I reach for another envelope with my father's home address on the label. The envelope bulges and jingles. House keys. A card for a realtor named T. J. Ross. A sheet of paper with the name and number of the cleaning person.

The box contains several more envelopes, one full of labeled receipts, another with itineraries from various business trips, yet another with what looks like several years of medical reports.

Five years' worth of black agenda books and several sketch pads anchor the bottom of the box.

I flip through the top agenda. Doctor's appointments, concerts at the Kennedy Center, dinner engagements. Typical stuff.

I open the top sketch pad and I'm transported into the lives of people I've never met. Sad people, lonely people, old people, young people. People deep in thought or in the throes of anguish. People enjoying a happy thought or laughing at a joke. I flip to the end, then start over at the beginning, mouth open, eyes wanting to close and shut out the assault. Each drawing is alive in details and emotion. Each drawing is signed by my father.

"These can't be yours. They're amazing."

I leaf through the sketch pad again, slower this time.

"Were these your clients or random people?"

How did I not know he could draw like this?

Why am I so surprised that there's something about my father I didn't know?

Except it's not really his secret talent that's rattling my nerves. It's the intimacy in that talent, the raw emotion that he saw and captured.

More than that, it's as though he opened himself to these people, allowed them to touch his heart. A heart he never opened to me.

3

After a sleepless night haunted by the faces my father had brought to life, I need a dose of familiar. Work. I need work.

Like an addict desperate for a fix, I chew the rough skin at the edge of my thumbnail while the laptop comes to life.

A full day without checking in was twenty-eight hours more than I can handle. I've never been good at boundaries between work time and personal time. Awake time is open season and even sleep hours often become equal opportunity. Despite all my rantings that I'd never be like him, there's no denying how very much like him I've turned out. Would I be different if my mom hadn't died when I was so young? If she hadn't been sick those last years and been a stronger influence?

I tap at a voice message on my cell phone and groan as Howard's pouty voice puffs through the distance. "Em, I've been trying to reach you. The proofs for the corporate brochure are in and Bruce is boiling PO'ed. Claims we used the wrong photo of him. Says he gave specific instructions which one to use. And now he wants to read every word and look at every photo since You're. Not. Here."

I grind my teeth at the taunting singsong. *Because this is where I want to be? I chose to come here?*

My boss, Bruce Patchett, had tried to overrule my time off, claiming my father would still be dead a week from now but the corporate brochures needed to be printed in time for the big trade show in Las Vegas the following month. I was inclined to agree. But the HR director had insisted.

So here I am.

I pinch the bridge of my nose and listen to the neurotically soothing melody of e-mails pouring in. At least this mess I know how to untangle.

I send a few e-mails and answer others. A surprising number of responses pop back almost immediately. It may be Saturday morning, but I'm in good workaholics' company.

Three hours later, I stand and stretch. The smell of breakfast from downstairs has evaporated. The coffee shop by Adler Law wafts through my memory. Or a Starbucks. At least there I can pretend I'm on a quick break from work. Caffeine and comfort.

I wonder if my nameless barista at the Starbucks a block from my office has noticed my absence. Every morning he waves a hello when I step through the doors. By the time I reach the front of the line, he's handing me a paper cup, "2 shot hazel" written in black Sharpie on the side.

I'll find a Starbucks on my way to my father's condo.

In the car, I key in the address. Four turns later I growl a "shut up" at the invisible lady giving me directions and turn off the navigation system. I know my way. It may not have been home to me, but I know exactly where it is.

The faster I clean it out, the sooner I can get it sold. And the faster it sells, the sooner I can return to my life.

I hit the blinker for a left turn and ease to the Stop sign. When it's my turn, I turn right instead and tap the gas. The rental picks up speed and coasts over the undulating roads, around curves that open into rolling acres of horse country. These roads have barely changed in the sixteen years since I was last here, and yet nothing is the same. I lift my right foot as I reach a four-way stop at the corner of Meadowbrook and Larks Lane. To the right is the property that was once our home. He sold it after he sent me away to boarding school.

The acres that led to the massive house on the hill are now

dotted with cookie-cutter houses, each one huge, generic, naked. The trees that separated our house from the road are gone, the rolling hills flattened.

There are no kids playing in front of the houses, no dogs chasing squirrels across the yards, no cats sunning on front porches. Garage doors are closed tight and curtains in the lower-level windows are drawn, like women clutching their sweaters closed. A shudder ripples through my body and I can't escape the thought that this property is jinxed.

In all the years we lived here, there was never a dog running loose in the yard. Never a cat terrorizing squirrels. Curtains were never opened. And I never played in the vast expanse of lawn. Instead, I wore a path through the woods and into the back paddock of the neighboring property—Jumping Frog Farm. I wonder if any of the kids who live in these houses use that path? If any of them escape to the other side of the creek and find comfort in the sound of hoofbeats?

There are two cars in the parking lot of Jumping Frog Farm this morning: my rental and a black BMW. For the second time in three days, I've arrived here without intent. Or at least conscious intent.

I'm greeted by the nonsilence of a morning at the barn. A lazy nicker, the scrape of a shovel, the stomp of a hoof. I slip into a happier time.

As long as there was a horse nearby and Jillian by my side, I was happy. Jilli was my first real friend. We had so much in common and yet we were totally different. She became the big sister I fantasized about. For the first time in my life, I was part of a family. Well, a family that actually acted like a family. More than mine at least.

I walk to the large doors of the barn and chase away the disappointment when Jack doesn't pop his head out in greeting.

From inside I hear classical music. And the soft three-beat thump of a horse cantering in the indoor arena. My toes flex and curl inside my sneakers in time to the tempo drummed out by the horse's hooves. My body moves, pulled by the equine magnet. Sixteen years away from horses and the desire still pounds through my veins like white-water rapids.

I stop at the edge of the indoor arena. The big gray horse and dark-haired man from yesterday canter by. I lose myself in the rhythm of the gait, the power of the horse, the perfect line between the rider's elbow and the horse's mouth, the slight swing of his leg as he asks the horse to bend into the turn. They take the diagonal across the ring and the horse executes perfect one tempis, skipping like a carefree child as he changes canter leads with each step.

"Beautiful, isn't he?" Simon's gravelly voice disrupts my trance.

"He is."

Simon bumps my shoulder with his. "I meant the horse."

I feel a flash of heat zip up my neck. "So did I."

The horse breaks into a walk with a satisfied snort. His rider leans to pat the muscular shoulder and, catching sight of us, waves.

"Ben, come meet Toad."

Horse and rider halt in front of us. "Toad?" Bushy dark eyebrows pull up and his face opens like a kid about to crack a secret.

"Emma Metz, this is Ben Barrett. Ben is our lead trainer. And this," Simon holds out a hand to the big gray, "is Wally."

Ben studies me while his horse frisks me. "You look familiar. Have I seen you at one of the shows?"

I shake my head, keeping my eyes on Wally and fingering his forelock. The horse senses a scratch opportunity and leans into my hand.

Ben tugs on the reins. "Damn, buddy, don't throw yourself at the ladies so quickly."

Simon barks a laugh and slaps the gelding on the neck. "He has good taste."

Wally turns his attention to Simon, nuzzling pockets that

still seem to hatch horse treats. Ben, on the other hand, zeros in on me.

"Wait, I do know you. Well, seen you. You're the girl riding Jack in all those photos, aren't you?"

I turn to Simon. I'd assumed all reminders of me would have been burned.

"Yup, that's Toad and Jack, winning every bloody show they entered. Best student I ever had." Simon wraps an arm around my shoulder.

"That was a lifetime ago." I tap the ground with the toe of my right sneaker, like a horse anxious to break away.

Ben swings his right leg over Wally's back and lands gracefully in the soft footing of the arena. He pats the horse's neck, then turns to run the stirrups up and loosen the girth. He looks over his shoulder at us, the shock of dark hair partially obscuring his face. "Are you still riding, Emma?"

"No." The word drops from my mouth before I can stop it; then, seeing his expression, I add, "I haven't been on a horse in years."

Simon gives me a gentle slap on the back. "It's like riding a bike. You never forget."

There are a lot of things your body—and your mind—doesn't forget. Like seeing the perfect distance to a jump and becoming one with the horse as he sails over it. Like the first kiss. Like the stab of betrayal.

Wally nudges my midsection and I stumble back a step. Ben jiggles the reins and the horse stands at attention. "I think he's had enough chitchat. Time for a shower, isn't it, big guy?" The horse shakes his head, the momentum rippling through his sculpted neck. "It was a pleasure meeting you, Emma."

Simon and I watch the pair walk down the barn aisle. The reins are looped in Ben's left hand while his right hand rests on the crest of his horse's neck. A stab of emotion catches in my throat. Trust between horse and human. A trust built on mutual respect and kindness. There are no hidden agendas with horses.

If only humans were that straightforward.

"Fun's over. Let's go into the office and talk."

"I didn't come to take up your time."

"You're not. We have a couple of years to catch up on. So quit stalling." Simon strides off, then stops when it's clear I'm stuck in place. "Twice in three days, Emma. I'm not buying the possessed-car excuse this time. Don't you think it's time we aired out the past?"

I take in one last look at the handsome gray horse and his not-so-bad-on-the-eyes rider, then close the distance to Simon.

He pushes open the door to the office and steps aside for me to enter. One step up and I've walked into the past. The same tweed couch under the large window looking into the indoor arena. The same wood coffee table with a stack of equestrian magazines on top, although I suspect those at least have kept up with the times. The same green rug covering the beige tile floor. And the same wood desk taking up half the space.

On the desk sits a sleek new computer, Rena hidden behind it. I see her hand lift, one finger up, before it dive-bombs a key on the unsuspecting keyboard.

"Damn machine won't do anything I tell it to," she grumbles without looking at who has entered. "Why did I ever let you guys talk me into putting all our records on this evil thing?"

"Stop bitching, will ya?" Simon walks to the couch and releases his body into its embrace.

"There's nothing about this that saves me time. Not. One. Damn. Thing. I ran this business long enough without a computer. Why did we have to break the process?" It's not a question, it's an accusation.

Simon rolls his eyes. "Why are you messing with that thing anyway? You know Jilli hates when you do that. She has barn schedules under control. Stop mucking about in there."

"Well she's not here, is she? Brian is coming in soon and I don't know who to keep in."

Simon rolls his eyes deeper into his head, then rolls them back. He releases a deep exhale. I stifle a giggle.

"You're back." It's suddenly quiet in the office.

"Don't be contrary, Rena."

Rena and I both turn to look at Simon. He stomps a foot, then bends to pick at his boot, ignoring her virtual daggers.

"I didn't mean to interrupt." I feel like the intimidated child. Worse, I sound like an intimidated child.

"Sit down." Rena tilts her head toward the sofa, then eases back in her chair, but not before giving the keyboard one last poke.

"Did you meet with the lawyers?" Simon asks after I've settled into the other corner of the couch.

"Yes. Lots of paperwork to go through. He's dealing with most of the practice issues, so hopefully I can get through the personal items quickly."

"How long are you staying?" Rena's voice still holds the bark of suspicion.

"I took a week off. My assistant is holding down deadlines."

"Assistant? Fancy. Shouldn't take that long to sort through your father's condo, should it? You could pay the lawyer to dispose of the personal items if you don't want them."

Dispose of the personal items. My shoulders twitch as a shudder takes possession of that thought.

"You're being crass. Leave her alone," Simon growls at her.

"When was the last time you saw him?" Rena looks at me but not *at* me, and it's so much worse than if her eyes were tunneling straight into my guilt. It was always her secret weapon. Age obviously hasn't softened that.

My mind trips back to Dad's last visit. A psychiatric conference where he was presenting and receiving an award. We'd met for dinner the night he arrived. I wasn't invited to the awards dinner. He never included me in any work function. Not even as a successful adult.

"Did you talk to him before the accident?"

"A few days before. I don't know, maybe a week before. Why?"

Rena's jaw moves as though she's chewing on the words. "Why are you back here, Emma? Once, fine. You said hello. You satisfied your curiosity. What are you hoping to find here now?"

I feel Simon deflate into the couch as my body goes rigid.

The door to the office opens, letting in a gush of musty air. With his long legs, Ben covers the distance in three easy strides, pulls out one of the guest chairs in front of Rena's desk, and flops down.

"Tony is on a rampage out there. I'm hiding in here with you guys."

Rena locks onto Ben and I say a silent thanks that he's taken the focus off me.

"What's got him worked up this time?"

Ben stretches, the movement releasing a deep laugh. "Your granddaughter. What else?"

"What now?" She slams a fist down on the table, making a mug sitting precariously along the edge wobble. Ben reaches out and steadies it before it tumbles to an untimely death.

Ben smirks and shoots an under-the-eyebrow look at Simon, who shakes his head in exasperation.

"She instructed him to prepare an extra stall. Found another horse she absolutely can't live without."

"And the problem is?" The tone behind Simon's question is one I'd heard many times growing up in Jillian's shadow. He indulged most of Jilli's whims. Rena was the enforcer. And it had been the kindling for many arguments between them.

Jillian twisted the situation to her advantage. Always. I didn't see it until later. By then it was too late for me—I was under her spell.

"There wouldn't be a problem if the new horse could go in one of the open stalls. She insists he be put in Oreo's stall, and everyone else gets moved down. That's a lot of shuffling. And a lot of shuffling that will keep Tony from finishing what he's supposed to be doing."

"He's supposed to be cleaning the stalls and taking care of the horses."

"Right." Ben drawls out the word.

I notice the corner of Rena's eye twitch. I wonder what Ben's relationship is to Jillian.

"When is she due back?" Hopefully long after I'm gone. Gone where? Back to the Mountain Inn or back to Chicago?

"Later tonight, I think." Curiosity arches one of Ben's eyebrows.

"I should go. I've taken enough of your time." I scooch to the edge of the cushion, the old bones of the couch complaining.

"You'll be back though, right?" Ben's eyebrows are still lopsided.

"No, I don't think so." I push up and march to the door, hoping to sidestep any additional questions. And hoping to make my escape before Jillian returns. That's one reunion I know I'm not ready for.

"She'll be back," Rena says.

4

August 1991

The house is big and empty. Every sound echoes and bounces and reminds Emma that nothing will ever be the same. The three burly moving guys shout directions to one another. She sits on the fourth step and winces at every yell. Or what feels like yelling.

"Scuze me. Coming through."

She presses her flat eight-year-old chest into her thighs, and scoots closer to the railing. The first moving guy either huffs at her or is breathing hard, but eases past without saying another word. The shadow of something solid passes overhead and she squeezes her eyes shut.

"I specifically ordered individual armchairs. Two. Black. Armchairs. I don't want a couch. I don't want a loveseat. I want two armchairs." Her father paces the length of the foyer, cordless phone pressed to his ear. He stops at the base of the stairs. "Emma, please find someplace else to sit." Tap, tap go the heels of his dress shoes.

Without looking up, she uncurls her body and peels her fingers from the balustrade. The front door is propped open, but she turns and walks through the kitchen and out the back door.

The house is perched on a hill; a long carpet of browning grass stretches to a strip of woods where she can just make out what appears to be a path. She looks back at the house. It doesn't welcome her back inside. Her father will still be pacing, broadcasting into the phone, ordering around invisible people. Her mom is most likely sitting under a shade tree someplace. Emma's eyes dart to the large tree by the side of the house. Not there. Oh well. She turns back to the woods.

It can't be any worse down there.

A rabbit scampers out of a tall patch of grass as she walks by, startling a gasp out of her. There aren't many rabbits running around in their Baltimore neighborhood. In what *was* their neighborhood. She's pretty sure she'll never see it again now that her father has moved them all the way out here.

At the edge of the woods, she turns back one more time. Is she hoping someone will be there waving her back? There isn't. Christelle, the nanny her father had hired a year ago, was let go before the move.

The path snakes into the woods, a clear invitation to escape from the harsh summer heat and the echoing stillness of the new house. She can't bring herself to call it home. She doesn't want to be here. The hour and a half between Emmitsville and Baltimore feels like light-years traveled between planets. None of her friends will come visit. They hadn't even come over to say goodbye. Kathy only stood in the window of her bedroom and waved at Emma as their car pulled away.

Without the blasting sun, the day doesn't feel nearly as suffocating. She picks up a stick and, pretending it's a crop, taps her thigh and clucks. She picks up her pace to a pretend canter and jumps a fallen log. That's another thing she'll miss about Baltimore, going to watch Kathy at her weekly riding lessons.

Her parents wouldn't let her ride, but they didn't know Kathy's instructor let Emma get on and walk around once in a while. She'd even taught her how to post the trot last time. Six awesome, butt-bouncing strides.

She jumps the log several times, clucking and tapping at her pretend horse with the pretend crop just as she's seen the bigger girls do in the class before Kathy's. Out of breath, she slows to a walk and continues down the path.

The woods come to an abrupt, blindingly bright end. Emma shields her eyes and scans the sprawling field in front of her. A wood-rail fence blocks her path. Peering between the bottom and top rails, all she can see is more grass. By pulling herself up onto the bottom rail, she's tall enough for a better view.

A building glimmers at the other end of the field, volleying sharp rays of light over the field. From somewhere in the distance, a horse whinnies. Emma catches her breath and waits. There it is again. Her new neighbor has a pony. Maybe living out here won't be so bad after all.

She jumps down and squeezes through the slats of the fence, then runs up the hill toward the silvery building. The neighbor doesn't just have a pony, the neighbor has an entire fancy stable.

Emma walks to the side of the barn and stops short. A girl about her age on a light brown pony is trotting around an out-door ring. She sits perfectly straight, posting in time to the pony's quick steps. In the middle of the ring an older woman stands, arms crossed over her chest, weight pushed into her right hip, a large floppy hat shading her face.

"Do you intend to ride that pony or just be an ornament?" the woman yells.

Emma cringes in sympathy for the girl.

The girl doesn't seem disturbed at all. "I am riding. This is boring." She slouches and bounces a few times until the pony slows to a walk. She flips a long blond braid over her shoulder and smooths at an escaped strand. They continue around the ring, the pony's head hanging low, the girl's shoulders slouching in a pout.

"Who are you?"

Emma looks up into piercing eyes. "Emma." Her voice squeaks under the scrutiny of the girl on the pony. "We just moved into that house." She jolts her hand up and in the direction she came from.

The girl follows the line, her mouth twitching. "Do you have a horse?"

"No."

"Then why are you here?"

"I was out exploring and heard a horse. I didn't think this place would be so big."

The girl is quiet, long enough to make Emma squirm. "If you live in that house you must be rich. Why don't you have a horse?"

"Jillian," the woman under the large hat yells. "That pony needs to be walked out. He's not a couch. Stop slouching."

With a final disgusted but somewhat curious look at Emma, the girl turns the pony and walks away.

The yeller takes a few steps in Emma's direction, her eyes commanding eye contact. She gives a quick nod and says, "You can look around if you're interested."

Emma hesitates for a fraction of a breath. She knows she shouldn't be here. Dad will be mad that she snuck out of the house. But she really doesn't want to go back yet. This place is like the stable in a movie she saw with Kathy and Kathy's mom. Oh man, Kathy will be jealous when she hears about this.

Big, cold house or big, amazing stable? Emma chews on the fatty part at the base of her nail on the left ring finger. Another thing her dad will yell at her about.

Big, amazing stable where no one will yell at her. Hopefully.

Keeping her distance, Emma follows the pony and his rider to the barn. She can feel the older lady watching her but can't look back. What if she asks to talk to her parents?

The girl stops her pony at the entrance to the stable and jumps off. She flicks a look at Emma but doesn't say anything.

A man comes out of the barn and stops, blocking their path. "What did you forget to do?" His tone is soft but Emma can tell he expects action.

The girl huffs, turns back to the pony, and loosens the girth. "I don't understand why you can't just have one of the stable hands do this."

"Because you need to take care of your own pony."

"That's boring. I just want to ride."

"You don't ride if you don't know how to care for the pony. Now get him inside and hose him off."

The man turns to where Emma stands. "Hello. Are you a friend of Jillian's from school?"

"I've never seen her before." Jillian shoots her a look before yanking at the lazing pony and pulling him into the barn.

"Um, I'm new. We just moved here." Once again, she lifts her hand and points at the megahouse on the other side of the woods.

A large, calloused hand reaches out to shake hers. "I'm Simon."

"Hi." Her voice squeaks again. "I'm Emma."

"Do you ride, Emma?"

"Um, no. I've been on a horse a couple of times. But I don't ride."

"With those long arms and legs, you should."

"Um, I don't think so."

She feels her face heat under Simon's gaze. Adults usually looked past her, talked over her. This man is looking *at* her, talking *to* her. She feels a smile break through her nerves. She likes this man. He reminds her of Kathy's grandfather. Emma doesn't have grandparents anymore.

She looks up, her smile widening. "My friend's riding teacher told me I look like a frog on a horse."

Simon tips his head back and laughs, a warm, welcoming sound. "I'm going to call you Toad."

"Toad." Emma tries the word out but it doesn't sound as nice coming from her mouth. Simon has a soft, gruff voice and an accent that reminds her of Zoe, the nanny before Christelle. She'd been from England.

The yeller with the big, floppy hat is watching her. Emma tries to smile but her lips are too scared to do more than pucker in the corners.

"Come on, I'll show you around," Simon says.

She follows him into the barn and listens carefully as he introduces her to all the horses.

"How old are you, Emma?" he asks when they're halfway down the second aisle.

"Um, eight." She keeps her eyes on the muzzle of the horse she's petting.

"Just a year between you and my granddaughter. You'll need to come around more. I think you two could be great friends."

Emma can't see how since Jillian made it clear she doesn't want her around. She watches a tall, dark brown horse being led out of the barn and blushes when she realizes her mouth is open. "He's beautiful."

"Yes, he is," Simon agrees. "Come on, Jilli should be giving Pogo a shower out back. He's quite a clown with the water."

Her mouth feels stuck in a silly grin but for once, she doesn't care. She follows him out a side door.

The chestnut pony stands quietly at the outdoor wash area, the hose clamped between his lips, his head bobbing side-to-side and spraying anyone who attempts to come close. Jillian stands to the side, left hand on left hip, a bored look on her face.

"Oh my gosh, he's so funny." Emma claps with joy.

Pogo turns to look at them, the stream of the hose arcing, spraying Jillian in the process. She shrieks and jumps, the sudden movement making the pony toss his head and spray Emma and Simon. Laughing, Simon grabs the unruly rubber snake but not before all three humans are wet. Even tight-lipped Jillian can't suppress the giggles. Not that it softens her for long, but for a few precious moments, Emma feels welcome.

With Pogo washed and turned out, Emma makes a final round to say good-bye to her new equine friends. At the barn door she looks back and, with a skip in her heart, heads home.

Like a magnet, the sign at the top of the parking lot pulls her closer. She runs her fingers inside the letters engraved in the wood, the dark green paint smooth to the touch. JUMPING FROG FARM. A place with a name like that has to be magical. And she needs a bit of magic in her life right now.

"Hey, Toad," Simon's voice booms from the entrance to the barn. "Come back soon. I want to see you on a pony."

She returns the wave, then canters into the woods. She'll be back. From someplace deep down in her eight-year-old gut, she knows she'll be back. This place is special. This place is meant for her.

5

I pull into the circular drive in front of my father's apartment building and flip on the hazards. The concierge will need to let me into the parking garage since the tenant swipe card had been in Dad's wallet and, as a result, burned to a crisp.

The building is on the border of Maryland and Washington, DC. Friendship Heights. Ironic. It's an old brick high-rise, walking distance to the Metro station, with more restaurants and coffee shops within skipping distance than you could visit in a week. *Maybe I should stay here instead of the out-of-the-way Mountain Inn.*

The glass door reflects my approach and suddenly self-conscious, I tug at the hem of my T-shirt and stomp off the stable dirt. Jeans feel entirely too casual for vising my father. Even if he's not here for my visit.

A man wearing running shorts and a bright yellow T-shirt blocks the entry while he fiddles with the earbuds connected to his iPhone.

I reach for the door and clear my throat. He steps sideways at the same time I do and we shift in a brief stranger-shuffle dance until he stops with a chuckle and pivots to let me pass. There's a prickle on the back of my neck. He's watching. I wonder who he is and if he knew my father.

Armed with a new tenant swipe card and an earful of sympathy from the concierge, I re-park my car in the slot marked

RESERVED 907. The elevator speeds past beeping floors at warp speed. The doors whoosh open at the ninth floor. My hands tighten around the rail behind me. A woman reaches out to hold the elevator door while a fluffy white dog darts in. The dog stops when he sees me and lets out a cross between a bark and a growl, then backs out of the elevator. I stay Velcroed to the back wall.

"Is this your floor?" The woman and the dog, snarling from behind her ankle, give me a suspicious once-over.

The idea of riding back down under their beady eyes seems worse than the alternative. I push off the wall and step over the fluffy beast.

My father's condo is at the end of the hall. The plush carpet muffles my progress, not that there's anyone here to notice. If I close my eyes I could be walking to my own apartment.

But I'm not.

I'm about to step into the unknown world of Edward Metz. He's lived here for almost fifteen years and I've been through those doors exactly twice. The last time, for one hour. One glass of wine before we went to dinner and he had the cab drop me at my hotel after. That was at least five years ago. The time before that? An hour. A month after he moved in. Long enough for him to make two phone calls before whisking me to the airport on the way back to boarding school after our winter "vacation" to California, where he worked four of the five days we were there.

I try to think how many times he visited my apartment. Twice maybe? No, three times. No, twice.

How utterly fucked up is that?

I suck in a long breath and clamp my lips together to keep air from leaking out, just like I did as a little girl before jumping into the deep end of the pool, then turn the key in the lock.

In front of me is a glossy magazine spread. Light bamboo floors, beige walls, two white leather couches parallel to each other, two black armchairs closing the not-so-cozy sitting arrangement around a glass coffee table. To the left, a black marble counter separates the living room from the kitchen. Spotless stainless appliances glint in the afternoon light, while the glass doors on the cabinets reflect the tall windows surrounding the living room.

The door clicks shut behind me, the minimal sound making me jump more than if it had banged shut. The deafening silence competes with the blinding starkness.

Next to the kitchen are two doors. One is open and I catch a glimpse of bookshelves and a black leather desk chair. Dad's home office. The closed door must be a bathroom. A shudder ripples up my spine at the thought of seeing Dad's toiletries. It's the personal side of a man who was far from personal. To my right is the closed door of the coat closet and rays of light coming from windows down a hallway.

I follow the path of light, turning a sharp left when I reach the end. A short corridor opens directly into a vast bedroom. Without kids or houseguests, I suppose he didn't need the privacy afforded by a door to his bedroom.

And yet his home office has a door. An open door.

He never left the door open when I lived under the same roof with him.

I resist the pull of the open office door and walk into the bedroom. Another room that had been largely off-limits, especially after Mom got sick.

The bedroom holds a king-size platform bed, low to the ground and sleek in light wood that almost matches the floor. A white comforter is pulled tight over the mattress. A silvery-gray squiggle shimmies up the left side, from the foot of the comforter to end someplace under the pile of white pillows. Out of six pillows, one is set slightly off, the only hint of imperfection. A dresser hugs the far wall, low and long with nothing on top except one framed picture and a dark brown leather tray to hold keys and coins at the end of the day. A quarter, two dimes, and a penny were left behind.

Black-and-white photographs traverse the walls of the bedroom, perfectly level, perfectly spaced, the only interruption caused by the door to the closet and the windows. I squint at the photograph closest to me. A dramatic shot of a building. The next one, another building. Each photograph, another architectural shot from a different angle in different lighting. Not one human to be found in any of them. I guess he preferred them in drawings, captured the way he wanted them to be.

I walk to the lone frame on the dresser. My hand stops mid-reach. It's also black-and-white but there are no fancy buildings in this one. A woman sits on a step, leaning against the column of a porch railing. A young girl stands on the lawn in front, her body turned as though in a last-minute decision to wave good-bye. I stare at my five-year-old self, trying to remember where I'd been going. My mom's right hand is up, mid-wave. The photographer has caught her in profile; the corners of her mouth are turned up but the smile looks wistful. Maybe it's the light in the photograph. Maybe it's the light in the room. Maybe it's the memory of the woman I never really knew.

I pull my hand back and hug my stomach, fisting the soft fabric of my T-shirt in each hand. I don't remember ever seeing this photograph. *Why this one, Dad?*

A phone rings on the other side of the condo, startlingly muffled, as though it doesn't dare disturb. I walk back through the living room and into the kitchen. No morning coffee mug in the sink, no ring on the granite from a sweating glass. I wonder if the cleaners were here recently or if this is how my father left it that last morning when he walked out the door and never returned.

The ringing cuts off, magnifying the silence. A tick-tick-tick from the office pulls me away from the kitchen. There are a handful of papers on the desk, perfectly squared on top of one another and set to the side. There are no piles of books or papers or envelopes on the floor. No messy piles for my father.

"Clutter, Emma, shows inattention. Inattention will not lead to success."

On his desk chair is a sweater, folded with the arms crossed in front and the neck just at the top slope of the chair back, as though its invisible occupant is leaning back in thought. I finger the sweater. Gray cashmere with burgundy trim along the neck and wristbands. Did he buy it for himself or was it a gift from someone? Someone who didn't send a generic box of chocolates.

I perch on the edge of the chair and swivel to face the desk. A leather pen box sits open, missing its pen. It's not like him not to put the pen back.

The first desk drawer opens easily, revealing a stack of notepads. The top one has indentations where someone wrote on a now-missing page. I run a finger over the lines. "Dictating patient notes, Dad?"

The bottom drawer contains a handful of hanging file folders, each labeled in Dad's crisp print. *Tax receipts. Bills. Emma. Barbara.*

I flick at the plastic label holder with my name on it, then push the folder open to peer inside. Envelopes of various sizes and colors. Some with my handwriting on the front, some with his address typed. Each envelope containing a quick, halfhearted wish for a happy birthday or holiday celebration. Why would he keep them? It's not like they revealed anything personal.

The thought jabs at my gut. Was there more I should have done? More I could have done?

"Why wasn't I ever good enough, Dad?"

I push past to the folder with my mom's name.

Inside the green hanging folder are several sealed manila envelopes and one unsealed envelope.

I pluck out the unsealed one and shake the contents onto the desk. A photograph of my parents on their wedding day. Their marriage license. Two simple gold wedding bands.

Sweat trickles down the back of my neck, sending a shiver of goose bumps up my arms.

The items on the desk look exposed and I feel a stab of guilt for uncovering them. I position the now-empty envelope at the base of the table and scoop its contents back in, fingers trembling at each touch.

I push the envelope back into the folder, my fingers spreading the two sealed envelopes apart. The one in the back has a return address label in the top left corner: Jumping Frog Farm.

"What's this about?"

I yank out the envelope and slit it open. Invoices.

Jumping Frog Therapeutic Program. Client: Barbara Metz.

"What the hell?" I yank the rest of the papers out and flip through. Twice a week for almost two years, Client Barbara Metz attended the therapeutic riding program.

Except, she was afraid of horses. She never wanted to come out there with me. And yet staring at me are two years worth of lies.

The tick-tick-tick of the office clock tickles my nerves.

I have to get out of here.

I grab the other envelopes from Mom's folder and stuff them into my bag.

The condo releases a sigh of relief when I open the front door to leave.

I release a sigh of regret as the door shuts behind me on a past I barely knew.

6

I call Jumping Frog Farm from the car, hoping to catch Rena. She probably wouldn't be very forthcoming on the phone but, then again, she hadn't been very open to me in person, either. She's not at the barn or the house.

I pull into the gas station at the decision-time intersection. A left turn and I'm going to the farm to talk to Rena. A right turn will take me back to the inn. I'll try calling one more time.

"Jumping Frog Farm, this is Jillian."

My breath freezes in my throat and my fingers fumble for the End button. "Shit." I grip the steering wheel tighter. "Shit, shit." No way I'm going back there now.

The parking lot at the Mountain Inn is almost full. The restaurant is booked, I'm told, but since I'm a guest at the inn they can get me a table.

The only open table is tucked into a nook. It's cozy and secure and I don't feel like the lonely-woman-eating-alone sideshow.

I order a cream of asparagus soup, a beet and goat cheese salad, and a local pinot noir, then pull the envelope containing the invoices out of my bag.

None of this makes sense. When we first moved to that house and I discovered the path to the stable, Mom had been adamant that horses were big and dangerous. Dad had grumbled that they were expensive and a waste of hard-earned money.

For the first few weeks in that house, I'd come from school to find Mom curled up on the couch, reading or sleeping. Always in the same clothes she'd been wearing in the morning. She seemed never to leave the house. She even paid the housekeeper to go to the grocery.

Those first weeks, I'd begged for permission to take riding lessons. Mom had said it wasn't safe for a girl my age to walk through the woods alone. My father wasn't around to lend his opinion.

But since my father wasn't around and my mom didn't pay much attention, it had been easy enough to slip out of the house and race through the woods to the stable.

Simon and Rena welcomed me immediately. Jillian not so much. At least not at first.

I'd sit for hours watching lessons. Even back then I was drawn to the therapeutic sessions.

I take a sip of wine and leaf through the invoices. How did I never see her there?

Because you weren't supposed to.

But why? Mom had a heart problem; the clients in the therapeutic program had emotional or physical handicaps. That wasn't my mom.

And yet, two years' worth of evidence say it *was* my mom.

I try to picture her in the ring with some of the clients I'd seen. A group of military veterans, some learning to live with missing limbs, some adjusting to life with emotional scars that made the Grand Canyon look like a crack in the sidewalk. A group of inner-city kids, hostile and suspicious.

Jilli used to complain that the therapeutic clients were creepy. I'd argue that they just needed someone to give them a second chance. That's why they came to Jumping Frog Farm. Horses are the perfect therapists. They don't judge.

It still doesn't add up.

The waitress returns with my dinner and for a few minutes I allow the past and present to slip away.

I give in to temptation and order a cappuccino bread pudding, then make a mental note to check with Drew about a spot in his spin class the day I get home.

There's one more envelope from the folder labeled "Barbara" that I haven't yet looked at. Inside are more envelopes, smaller, white ones, the kind you'd use for personal letters. All are addressed to my father at his office.

The writing has a familiar slant, the curves of the dropped letters, the haphazard location of the dots above the *is*. Mom's handwriting?

It's not.

The paper shimmies in my shaking hand.

October 1991

Dear Edward,

I too am glad you made the move to Emmitsville. It's a nice place, quiet, and people are friendly but far enough apart that you'll have your privacy.

If I may be so bold, consider giving your daughter the opportunity. I know you're not thrilled with the idea of her riding. Or perhaps it's her mother's involvement with the program? Regardless, it might be just what she needs to settle in. It's not easy for her.

I don't mean to overstep. Please just give it some thought.

Yours,

R.

That was two months after we moved here. It was also when he agreed to pay for one lesson a week.

R? Rena? Can't be. Why would they have been writing letters to each other?

I slide another letter out of its envelope.

July 1991

Dear Edward,
My thoughts are with you and your family. Please know I'm here if you need to talk.

Yours,
R.

July 1991. That was when Mom had been rushed to the hospital. Before we moved here. Before Emmitsville existed in my world.

I try to rewind my memory. The sirens from the ambulance are still clear in my head. But from that first time or the second I'm not entirely sure. I pinch the bridge of my nose and squeeze my eyes shut, hoping to locate the right memory. She'd spent a week in the hospital the first time the ambulance took her away. Dad had visited every day but said I was too young. Mrs. Tate, the old lady who lived in the house next door, stayed with me after school until my father returned home. She baked casseroles and cookies. Awful things. Totally turned me off tuna. And raisins.

I dump the rest of the envelopes on the table.

August 1991

Dear Edward,
This is in response to your last two letters. I'm sorry to have worried you by not responding sooner.

It's a hard call and I'm not sure I'm qualified to give advice. I don't seem to have done a great job with my own daughter. But from my experience, kids know more than we give them credit for.

Consider the truth.

Yours,
R.

"What truth?"
Thankfully there's only one couple left in the restaurant and they didn't hear—or at least are not acknowledging—my outburst.

It was her heart. My mother had a heart condition. My mother died of a heart attack.

Jilli's words push their way past sixteen years of repression: *"Your mom offed herself. She was crazy, total woo-woo crazy."*

7

The computer whirs to life and I stare as the number of unopened e-mails grows. I tilt my head to the left and close my left eye, waiting for the number to stop multiplying. The pinging finally stops at 1,612. It's only been two days.

Time for e-mail triage. I click on "sort by sender," then scroll through the list. First, I delete the newsletters I can't seem to bring myself to unsubscribe from yet never read. That brings me to 1,582. There's an update on the Friday-afternoon happy hour. Delete. A reminder that the window cleaners will be there on Wednesday. Delete. John, the handsome lawyer from the fifteenth floor, inviting me for dinner. Delete. Then undelete and send him a response that I'm out of town for a couple of days. Then delete again.

After almost an hour, I'm down to under a thousand. I read and reread five e-mails between Howard and the printer, each escalating in frustration and confusion. There's a sixth e-mail from the printer directly to me, begging for an intervention.

Typical Howard. He excels at getting things done. Where he falls short is in the tact department.

The trade-show-booth company almost fired us as a client two years ago after Howard had a hissy fit the week before the largest boating trade show of the year. And all because of the brand of espresso they'd purchased in bulk for our booth. Kathy, the account executive who'd been working with us for four years, had told Howard exactly where he could put the beans. Then, to me, she'd suggested rewiring the demo equipment for our communications service and zapping some sense into Howard.

The contracts guy bought me a referee whistle for Christmas that year.

That was the last time Howard was allowed near a vendor, especially during the tense final push before a big deadline. He'd assured me he could handle it this time. Bruce had been less convinced. There will, no doubt, be an I-told-you-this-was-a-bad-idea lecture from Bruce.

Like I had any control over my father's crashing into the concrete pillars of an overpass on the Washington, DC, Beltway at 2 P.M. What the hell was he even doing on the Beltway at that time of day?

I push the chair away from the table and reach into the box I'd brought back after my visit to Thomas Adler's office. I move a few things around until I find the most recent agenda and flip to "D" day.

"You need help, Emma."

Each hour has a first name and a number. Nine A.M., Tina 43. Ten A.M., Bruce 128. The numbers are for the file numbers he assigns each patient. He'd never put a first and last name in the agenda book on the outside chance that someone got hold of the agenda.

One P.M., Shannon 296. Two P.M., Liat 55. Three P.M., Stu 201. The patients at one, two, and three have lines through them. I dial the number for my father's office and groan when it goes to the answering service. Has his assistant already left for the day? I glance at the clock and palm my forehead. "It's Saturday night, you idiot. Not everyone works on Saturday nights."

If I'd been home I probably wouldn't have been working either. John and I would be having that rescheduled dinner. Oh who am I kidding, I would have been working, that rescheduled dinner would have been rescheduled again.

I push the unhelpful agenda back into the box. I'll call the office first thing Monday morning.

I turn back to the computer and click on an e-mail from Howard. A few colorful words jump from my mouth before I get past his first sentence. The next e-mail from him elicits the same involuntary reaction. As do the next five. All complaints. All increasing levels of Howard drama.

How have I survived with him for almost four years? Was he like this at the beginning? Nothing I can do about it now. Except hope he doesn't whip up a mass exodus of vendors.

There are at least 250 e-mails from Bruce. Short, sweet, and stinging. *"Why don't I have the confirmation for the suite in Vegas?"* Because your assistant sent it to me instead, knowing you'll delete the damn thing and ask me for it. *"I don't see press appointments on my calendar for Vegas."* Because we're a month out and no one will confirm that far from the event. *"Why is the PowerPoint template empty?"* Because it's a template and not the presentation I sent you four times last week. *"You're not answering e-mails . . . I need you to answer your e-mails."* I have no snappy comeback for this.

According to Bruce, I'm to be on call around the clock. When he has a question, I should be there with an answer. When he has an idea, I should be there to jump into action. It's an exhausting game we play. And after seven years, I've gotten pretty darn good at anticipating his questions and ideas. And pretty addicted to caffeine to keep up.

My fingers hover over the keyboard, waiting for instructions from my brain on answering his latest rant. I type a few words, then delete them. Type them again, and once again, delete. A slow, leaking breath whistles from between my lips.

When Bruce took over the company seven years ago, he took a chance on me. He liked that I was hungry to prove myself and appreciated that I was willing to put in so many extra hours. In two years I went from being an invisible assistant to being the director of communications. A year later, I became the youngest

VP in the company. During those seven years, we went from fifty employees to over two hundred, and from start-up to industry leader.

I was too busy and entirely too worn down from the unstable winds gusting in and out of Bruce's office to question why my personal life consisted of spin classes and one-off dinner dates, rescheduled multiple times.

Truth is, I thrive on the craziness. I've become a master at catching the balls Bruce hurls out of his corner office. Work is the perfect escape.

A subject line catches my eye, SOS. Anita Kincaid, the vice president of business development. *Surrender or Suffer! Dammit, Emma, you leave and hell breaks out in the place. What did you say to Bruce before you left? I haven't seen him this worked up since . . . I don't know, last week??? And someone needs to neuter that little terrier of yours. How do you put up with him? You must return. Now! Or suffer the consequences. Love you. Mwah!*

I laugh and send Anita my sympathies and a reminder that the emergency chocolate-covered pomegranate stash is in the bottom right drawer of my desk.

While I've been cleaning out e-mails, four new ones have popped in from Bruce. I stare at the bolded subject lines. I know what I'm expected to do and yet, for the first time, I don't have the energy or desire to jump to attention.

I've always been able to rely on work for a distraction. But today, there's no comfort in the chaos, no escape in the details. I exit out of Mail and snap the laptop shut.

I slip into shoes and leave the room, making my way to the main level of the inn. There's a great room to the right of the stairs and I hear the hushed tones of a discussion. I walk past and peek in. A woman stands by a bookshelf, her fingers brushing the spines as she rocks from side to side. She reads the titles to a long pair of legs stretching out of a tall wingback chair.

I hesitate for a fraction of a heartbeat, long enough for the woman to catch a glimpse of the eavesdropper at the door. She smiles and waves me to enter. I smile and wave "no thanks." Across the hall I discover a small library. I slip into the thick darkness and flip on the overhead light.

Pulled by the great-book magnet, I cross the room. Maybe the distraction I need is waiting for me in a good book and a comfortable chair on the inn's patio. When was the last time I sat down with a novel?

Three years ago on my beach vacation with my friend Julia. We'd spent ten days at a resort, baking in the sun, ordering umbrella drinks from cute young cabana boys, and talking. She'd insisted that a beach vacation wasn't complete without a great book.

She'd also insisted that a beach vacation wasn't complete without a horseback ride on the beach. Riding was easy, she'd said. Riding would be fun, she'd said. She didn't know about my horsey past.

Who knew food poisoning would be a welcome distraction? After a night cursing the shellfish from the dinner buffet, I was in no shape to go anywhere, much less a sunrise horseback ride on the beach. I'd persuaded Julia to go without me. She'd fallen twice. Two days later, we were on a plane heading back to Chicago. I swore off shellfish and Julia swore off horses.

Whether it's being back in Emmitsville or my visit to Jumping Frog Farm or just a reemergence of the horse-crazy little girl, I go straight for a book with "spur" in the title. The cover shows riders in fox-hunting attire and a quick flip to the back reveals the author with her horse.

I take the book and head to the patio. It's late enough that the sun has dipped behind the house, leaving the flagstones comfortably warm and the air with a slight chill. I crack the book open and read the first paragraph.

After reading it for the fourth time, I let the book drop to my chest and wrap my arms around it.

The fields behind the Mountain Inn stretch beyond imagination, dipping and then rising and then dipping again, naked grass flowing into clumps of woods and hugging muddy ponds. Fences separate neighboring properties, and if you look closely along the fence line, you can find the occasional jump, used by foxhunters as they canter from one property to another.

I'd been on one hunt during my short stint in Pony Club. The galloping and jumping had been fun until my pony decided the big red horse ahead of us was cramping his style. Turns out there's a strict rule in foxhunting that you're not to pass the hunt master. That was the end of my foxhunting career. And Pony Club.

A deer bounds across the nearest field. Three more follow, their delicate legs skimming the earth as they disappear into the twilight. I turn to look where they emerged, but the parade is over. My eyes trail back to the woods at the opposite end of the field, my upper body pitches forward, and the muscles of my legs tighten as the imaginary me gallops across the field and finds the perfect distance to the wood coop jump. The memory of hoof-beats pounding the ground echoes in my head. My heart.

8

October 1991

Emma tugs at the seat belt. It feels like it's going to choke her. Why is her father driving so slowly? She could have walked faster. She'd wanted to walk. She'd wanted to go alone. But no, he'd insisted on driving her.

She pulls at the strap again and moves her right arm over it so that it won't cut into her neck.

"Emma, the seat belt won't be much help in the event of an accident if you're not buckled in properly."

"We won't get in an accident. We're just going around the corner. We could have walked faster." She mumbles the last few words, keeping her head down as she repositions the seat belt across her chest.

"Emma."

She raises her head and meets her father's eyes in the rearview mirror. "Yes, sir."

They finally pull into the Jumping Frog Farm driveway and Emma unclasps the seat belt, then twists in the seat so she has a full view out the side window. She feels her father's eyes on her but he doesn't say anything.

"Look, look, that's Pogo. That's the funny pony I told you about." She taps the window as though that will help her father see the pony in the field. Her father doesn't turn to look, and Emma flattens her palm on the window in silent greeting to Pogo.

She's first out, barely waiting for the car to come to a complete stop. Her father reminds her to slow down as she skip-walks just ahead of him. This will be her first official riding lesson. She's so excited she feels like she's going to burst. Bang, like a popped balloon.

"Hey, hey, young lady, slow down or you'll be exhausted before you ever get on the pony." Simon greets them from the door to the stable. He reaches out to shake hands with Emma's father. "It's a pleasure to meet you, Dr. Metz. I've heard a lot about you."

Emma's cheeks blaze under the scrutiny of her father. She bites her lip and clenches her left hand into a tight fist to keep from chewing on her finger. She's pretty sure a lecture is coming about what personal information she should be sharing with strangers and she doesn't want to give him a reason to yell at her about chewing on her nails as well. It's not as though she's said anything about him or her mom. Whatever Simon has heard, it's not been from her. She peeks up at Simon, curious suddenly if what he said is one of those things adults say to be friendly or if he really has heard a lot about her father, her family, and from who. *Whom, Emma, whom.*

Simon winks at her. It's an adult thing. She releases the bottled-up breath.

"Yes, well, nice to meet you. Emma hasn't stopped badgering us about riding since we moved in. I appreciate you fitting her in."

"She's a pleasure to have around." Simon places a large, calloused hand on her shoulder and she immediately feels safe, grounded. She smiles up at him. He turns back to her father. "You're welcome to stay and watch."

Emma's father shifts his weight to the heels of his dress shoes, shiny and unscratched, so different from the scuffed boots Simon is wearing. She has the urge to grab his hand and beg him to stay. But the tightness of his body, hands pushed into pant pockets, stops her. He won't stay. He never stays.

"She's in good hands, I'm sure, and I have work to catch up on." He pivots forty-five degrees so he's angled away from Simon and toward her. "Be respectful, do as you're instructed. And don't overstay."

The urge to ask him to stay has been stamped into the gravel. She wants him to go, now. She studies the stones around her feet. Simon's fingers close gently around her left shoulder. She waits for the sound of the car door closing before she releases her breath.

"Are you ready?" Another gentle squeeze, this one with a twist of the wrist that turns her away from the parking lot.

"Yes, sir."

"No 'sir,' please. That was my father. He was a stuffy old fart. Hate to think I'm anything like that." Simon chuckles.

She skips to match his strides. "Oh, no, not at all."

He laughs. "Jillian may disagree with you on that."

Emma wants to disagree but she thinks that would be disrespectful even though she's not actually disagreeing. She likes the sound of "stuffed fart." It suits her father way more than it suits Simon. *There are times, Emma, when saying nothing is your best decision.*

"First thing's first, we need to get a proper pair of boots on you."

She follows him into a tack room. She hasn't been in this one before. Tack trunks line the wall under hanging bridles. Emma remembers watching one of the ladies wipe down her bridle after a ride, then twist the throat latch, as she'd explained it to a wide-eyed Emma, into a figure eight that secured the reins and bridle into a neat package. Emma's fingers trace the movements the woman had made. She hopes she can remember how to do that when it's her turn. The wall next to the bridles contains two rows of saddle racks. Each saddle has a shiny silver nameplate on the back strip. She can't remember what it's called. She gives herself a mental reminder to get a book and study the parts of the tack. And the horse.

Along the third wall is a brown leather couch and more

trunks. There are hooks on the wall with jackets, dark green with the barn logo on the back. She catches embroidery on the left chest of the jacket closest to her. She wonders whom it belongs to. How neat would it be to have one like that? Above the couch are a handful of framed photographs of people in fancy riding clothes and gleaming horses jumping big jumps. Maybe one day there will be a picture of her up there as well.

She closes her eyes and takes in a deep inhale of leather and horse. She's pretty sure this is the most perfect place she's ever been in.

"Sit," Simon commands. "Try these on."

He hands her a pair or short brown boots with a zipper along the top. They're a perfect fit. She grins at him, not trusting her voice.

"Brilliant. Take them. They don't fit Jillian anymore and there's no reason for them to sit here unused, collecting mouse poop. Now, let's get you on a pony, what do you say?"

She grins wider and nods. Her insides are full of happy and she wants to keep that bottled inside as long as possible.

Simon shows her how to enter a stall, how to put a halter on, and how to get an uncooperative pony into a tack stall. She giggles when Rusty shakes his head and stamps his left front hoof in protest.

She takes her time brushing Rusty, reciting the instructions Simon gave her. *Brush with the direction of the hair, stay angled so you can see his head (don't give him the opportunity to bite your bum), body close to his so he can't kick you.*

Simon helps her lift the saddle onto the pony's back and talks her through tightening the girth. He stays between her and Rusty's head, for which she's grateful because even though she's not making the girth tight, the pony is making mean faces and snapping his teeth.

"I don't think he likes me." She steps away from the pony until her back is against the wall. She's having second thoughts about this riding bit.

"He just wants you to think he's mean. He is a bit of a pisser though with his girth. You'll get used to him and learn when to call his bluff."

Simon hands her a black hard hat and helps her adjust the straps so they fit properly around her ears and under her chin. She wonders if she looks as professional as Jillian or if it's clear to everyone what a beginner she really is. She leads the pony to the indoor arena, mimicking how she's seen Jillian do it. She catches a glimpse of herself in the glass door to the lounge. She looks like a total beginner. She's glad her father didn't stay to watch.

It may not be her first time on a pony, but it is her first official lesson and it's the first time she's expected to control the pony herself. Her nerves threaten a toilet emergency. She takes in a long, slow breath.

Simon helps her mount and adjusts her stirrups. He tightens the girth and slaps at Rusty's muzzle when the pony snaps at his rear end. Emma grips the reins and squeezes her knees into the saddle.

"Relax." Simon jiggles her right knee. "You can't grip with your knees. Let your legs get long and soft. They have to curve around his sides. Do you feel that? That's where they go."

She tells her body to memorize the position Simon has molded her legs into.

"Now, nudge him into a walk and make sure he stays along the rail. He's a crafty cracker and will try to cut his corners. Don't let him. Use your inside leg to push him out and your outside rein to keep him on track. Got it?"

She nods. She can do this. She's doing it. Rusty is walking quietly along the wall of the arena. She's really, really riding.

They get to the small end of the ring but instead of staying on the track like he's supposed to, Rusty executes a sharp turn and cuts across to the other long wall, picking up his pace to an uncomfortable walk-trot the closer they get to the gate.

She pulls both hands back until they bump into her stomach, but instead of slowing down, he drops his head, yanking her out of the saddle. She barely catches herself on his neck before he shoots his stubby neck back up. She grabs a handful of mane, dropping the reins in the process.

They reach the gate with Emma clinging sideways, determined not to fall. Rusty stops and she wriggles herself back into the saddle.

Okay, she wasn't really riding. And she's not sure she can ride. It looks so much easier. She wants to slide off, she wants to disappear. She doesn't want Simon to be disappointed with her.

"You stayed on him. Good job, Toad. Not many first-time riders would have been able to do that. He's got a mean bounce when he wants. Now, bring him to the middle and let's chat for a couple of minutes."

Simon talks to her about hand position and how her hands talk to Rusty's mouth. How her legs tell him where to go and how to get there. How the movement of her body softens his gaits or makes him get tense and bouncy.

For the next few laps she mumbles Simon's instructions to herself, barely hearing what he's actually saying. They do small circles, big circles, diagonal lines that are only slightly zigzaggy, and figure eights that are exactly how she writes them—smaller on top and not completely round. Suddenly she realizes her body is working with Rusty.

Her mind has stilled and it's no longer Simon's voice in her head. She really is riding.

This may be the first time and they may have only been walking, but Emma knows that she'll never forget the moment she lost her heart to horses.

9

I kick the blanket to the foot of the bed and flop onto my back. There's a sliver of light peeking between the curtains and a noisy discussion going on among the bird population of Emmitsville, which have all apparently congregated on my balcony. The alarm hasn't gone off on my iPhone yet, so it must still be early. The ceiling fan thwacks the air above and I yank the blanket back up to my chin.

Sleep has slipped away, though. Even under the safety of the comforter, the doubts find me. It's Sunday. Normally I'd go to the gym, then pop into the office or work at my dining-room table for a few hours. But there's nothing normal about the last few days. I have nothing to do and nowhere to be.

I turn my head until the table comes into focus. My laptop sits, waiting, next to the box with my father's papers.

The alarm chimes and I slide my finger along the screen to silence it.

"You're not planning on being lazy all day, are you, Emma?"

No, Dad, I'm not. When was the last time I stayed in bed on a Sunday?

"Maybe I will stay in bed." I fluff the pillow and let my head drop back.

Or not. The smell of coffee pulls me out of bed.

I could take the day off.

And do what?

I don't take off days. I don't take sick days. Days away from work are days when the brain clicks over the things I don't have. *The things you never allowed yourself to have.*

Dressed in jeans and a T-shirt, I follow the aroma of a sharp, dark roast and fresh bread downstairs. A woman in her mid-fifties, wearing khakis, a blue Polo shirt, and light blue Keds, is fussing with baskets on a long buffet table in the dining room. Her bobbed blond hair swishes around her shoulders as her body sways to soft music. She turns and envelopes me in a smile that heats the room.

"Good morning." She stops in mid-arrange. "You're just in time. These are fresh out of the oven." She jiggles the basket, releasing an intoxicating scent.

"They smell wonderful. But I'm not much of a breakfast person. Just coffee will be fine." I walk to the buffet, where a coffeepot sits on a warmer. But it's the espresso machine next to it that has my attention.

"Nonsense. Everyone needs a good breakfast. Sit, sit. I'll prepare a latte for you and you really must try one of these." She plucks a perfectly round and still steaming roll from the basket, places it on a plate, and slides it in front of me along with a ramekin of whipped butter. "That's herb butter. Made fresh on the dairy up the road. And these are from an orchard just past the dairy. All local." She places a plate filled with sliced peaches, a small mound of yogurt, and a drizzle of honey next to the other plate.

The espresso machine hisses and grinds, spitting away any arguments of turning these goodies down.

"We haven't officially met. I'm Lucy Corcoran. I own this place. Gina mentioned you've been keeping yourself busy since you checked in. Do you already have fun plans for today? You're friends with Tommy Adler, right? Are you going out with him and his husband today? They're such fun, aren't they? If not and you need suggestions I can point you in any number of directions. It's going to be a perfect day. Warm but not as hot as the last few days. Perfect fall day to go exploring."

She turns and smiles and I suddenly realize I'm the one who's breathless. How can anyone talk so much and so fast?

I stall, sipping the latte, which is one of the best I've had. I make a mental note to ask what brand of coffee she uses.

"No plans with Thomas, um, Tommy. I have work to catch up on. Maybe I'll explore a bit if there's time after." I twist the mug, hoping to dislodge the foam clinging to the side.

"Work will wait. We won't have that many more glorious days like this. Give me that mug, and eat."

A happy sigh accompanies the hiss and burp of the espresso machine. Lucy places a fresh mug in front of me and taps the plates closer, then disappears out a side door. Maybe she's right about a good breakfast. I cut open the bread and breathe in. Why don't I ever get fresh bread back home? *Because you never make the time.*

When Lucy returns, I'm on my last bite of peaches, the bread long finished and the mug all but licked clean. She pulls out a chair next to me and places a piece of paper between us. It's a hand-drawn map of the region with a few places highlighted, including the dairy and orchard, a farm that raises sheep and dyes their own wool, and an up-and-coming winery. All within an hour or two's drive from the inn. There's a yellow trail complete with arrows pointing me from stop to stop and a scenic drive back.

With a satisfied nod and a gentle pat to my upper arm, Lucy takes my plate and bids me a fun, relaxing day. And not to worry about dinner, she'll save something for me.

A fun, relaxing day. This should be interesting.

My first stop, according to Lucy's itinerary, is The Spinning Ewe. Although why I'm going is beyond me. I've never held a crochet hook or knitting needle in my life. Never had the desire to. Yes, I know it's trendy to knit, I've seen friends gather for Stitch and Bitch or Wine and Hook parties. I always had a ready excuse—mainly, work.

What do you have to lose?

The rental purrs to life and I anchor the map on the passenger seat with my purse. Fifteen miles down the road, I realize exactly why Thomas booked me at the Mountain Inn.

We came every year on my birthday. I hated it at first. What kid wants to visit the cemetery on her birthday? But as I got older and could ride my bike here, I started to actually enjoy the visits with my mom.

I navigate the narrow lanes of the cemetery, trying to picture myself riding these roads. What I remembered as the first right turns out to be a new road that leads in the opposite direction. After several wrong turns and six-point attempts at turning the car around, I find my mom's grave.

I pull over and wait for a row of cars to snake past, a black hearse leading the procession. When the last car has disappeared from sight, I step out of the rental and walk to the grave.

"Hi, Mom." I sink until I'm eye-to-name with the marble stone, and wait, although god knows for what.

"I guess you know why I'm back?"

A crow caws from a nearby tree and I look around self-consciously.

"I don't understand, Mom." I drop my voice in response to another caw. He doesn't need to hear my discussion with my dead mother. "Why did you go to the therapeutic program? And why would you guys hide that from me?"

Jilli's accusation roars in my head. My mom wasn't crazy. Or had I just been too young to recognize what was in front of me?

I look at the marble headstone to the right of her. *Beloved Mother, Wife, Daughter. Forever in our hearts.* My mom's stone is strikingly absent of sentiment. Her name and the dates. No flower, no Star of David, no hints to the outside world about whom she left behind.

"Did you understand him? I wish I could remember how you

were together. Have you been up there watching us tiptoe around each other all these years?"

No, she couldn't have been. She would have found a way to fix us. Not that I fully believe in spirits. And the proof is, if she had been watching, she wouldn't have let him send me away.

"It's been sixteen years, Mom. I light a candle every year on your birthday. And mine. Did you know that?" *Oh my god, I have to stop doing this.* I rake my hands through my hair. Of course she doesn't know, she's dead, she's been dead for over twenty years.

Why would my father mandate my return to Emmitsville and a visit to the cemetery? He wasn't sentimental, and by the naked base of the headstone, I'm pretty sure he hasn't been here since the last time he came with me. There are no stones announcing recent visitors like on the other Jewish graves. That means he had a plan. *Of course he did.* I'm here to learn something. *Of course I am.*

Except this one I'll have to sort out on my own.

The black bird flies off without so much as a parting caw. I shiver despite the unseasonably warm weather.

"Did you know about his drawings? He was really good. He hid those, too. Jesus, what didn't he hide from me? There's one woman he seemed to draw a lot. There's something familiar about her but I can't place her."

So many unanswered questions. There has to be someone who can help me piece together my family puzzle. I pull the phone out of my back pocket and dial the number for the stable. I'm told Rena is sick and won't be there today. Rena is never sick. Even the few times she should have stayed home, she was at the stable ordering everyone around. So it won't be Rena, at least not today.

I glance at my watch and am surprised to see that I've been at the cemetery for an hour. I stand and brush the seat of my pants. "I need to go, Mom. I'll be back, though."

The rental crawls through the deserted roads of the cemetery until I reach the main exit. The map on the passenger seat ruffles in a sudden breeze. "Okay, I'll bite." Relaxing is unlikely and I'm not sure a day that starts with a visit to the cemetery can be classified as fun, but it's a beautiful day and Lucy may just have had a point, maybe a bit of exploring is what I need.

The roads are narrow and windy, rolling up and down through wooded areas and stretches of farmland. These aren't roads for speed or noise and I turn off the radio, content to listen to the squelch of tires on asphalt, cows mooing, birds calling. I breathe in air thick from the cows. Funny how a smell that makes your nose twitch and throat close can also bring back a wave of nostalgia.

The deeper into the unknown countryside I drive, the quieter my brain gets. The corner of my mouth crinkles when I realize I haven't thought about Howard or Bruce in the last forty-five minutes. I haven't thought about the mounting e-mails or barreling deadlines. I haven't even thought about my father or what family secrets are waiting in ambush.

"Well what do you know, Lucy just might be the smartest person I've ever met."

According to the map, I should be coming close to my first official stop. The road takes a gentle turn and the trees give way. Spreading before me is what could be a snapshot for a postcard. A white post-and-rail fence gleams against the lush green grass; a weeping willow tickles the top of a large white wood sign that says THE SPINNING EWE, the words painted like colorful yarn letters. I turn onto the gravel drive, smiling at the rainbow of flowers waving me forward. Fluffy sheeps' heads pop up from their grazing, only mildly curious about the trespasser.

In the small parking lot is a classic Chevy pickup, its ocean-green paint in bold contrast to the canary-yellow house in front of it. A sign in the same smile-inducing font welcomes me.

I stand at the open door and peer inside. Obviously someone is here, or has been, since the door is wide open, but a bleat from the pasture and chirping birds are the only sounds. I tap my knuckles against the yellow wood door. "Hello?"

"Oh hey, perfect timing. Can you help me?"

The voice sounds friendly enough and I step inside. In the middle of the room is a display unit that, had it been standing upright, would probably reach chest height but is leaning at a precarious angle. A hand reaches through an open slot and waves at me.

"I obviously didn't think this through very well. Can you help me right this stupid thing?"

"Oh my god, are you okay?" I grab at a shelf and pull the unit upright. "Ouuf, that's heavier than I expected."

"Right? Damn thing is solid. Which is great except when I'm trapped underneath." The silver-haired lady chuckles and extends a hand for me to help her stand. "Probably better if you help me." Her puff-do of short curls bounces around her head as she leans into my assist and hoists herself up.

"Do you need these?" I grab for a pair of crutches propped against a nearby table.

She waves them away and hops to a chair, heaving her left leg onto another chair. Her toes wiggle at the opening of a purple cast. We both stare at the fluffy sea of colors on the floor next to the now-upright shelf.

"What happened?"

She releases air that sends several curls straight up. "I decided to move what's left of the summer colors down so I can show off my new fall balls." Her hazel eyes sparkle, the gold flecks adding an extra measure of playfulness to the concept of fall balls.

"Fall balls?" I hear the skepticism in my voice. She laughs and points at a small mountain of yarn, twined into rounded shapes that resemble dinner rolls. *What's Lucy done to me? I'm fantasizing about bread and visiting a yarn farm.*

"Beautiful colors." I finger one twisted roll in shades of green from dark to light and back to dark.

"Thank you. Are you looking for something special?"

I reach for another roll, this one a mishmash of greens, oranges, browns, and gray. "Nothing special. I don't even knit. Or crochet."

"Gift for someone then?"

I want to say yes, to have a reason for being here. But there's no one to buy for and I'm here because of a map.

I shake my head and offer a sheepish shrug.

"So what brings you to me? I don't usually get a lot of drive-ins, except for open-farm dates. I'm not complaining. I'd be sitting under that damn shelf until Pete decided to come check on me. Which, knowing him, wouldn't be until dinnertime. By the way, I'm Ceila."

"Emma. I'm staying at the Mountain Inn for a few days." I swallow. A few too many days.

"Ahhh, Lucy sent you then." Ceila pushes up from the chair. I reach forward as she totters precariously on one leg but she shoos me away and pulls the crutches under her arms.

While Ceila clops her way to the pool of wool and begins stacking the balls into cubbies, I wander to the back wall where a window overlooks the fields. Hanging from the curtain rod are two clothes hangers, one with a knit sweater in shades of purple and another with a scarf in shades of turquoise. I pull the scarf down and wrap it around my neck, turtling into its softness.

"How much is this scarf? It's fabulous."

"I could sell it to you or I could teach you how to make one just like it." Ceila's dark eyebrows arch like playful caterpillars.

I snort and slap my hand across my mouth, then fuss with unwrapping the scarf. "I'm hopeless with my hands. And I have zero patience. Your beautiful yarn doesn't deserve what I'd do to it."

"Nonsense. I bet thirty minutes with me and you'll be crocheting like a pro. Come on, pick a color." She lifts a crutch and sweeps it in an arc. I wince as it narrowly misses a mug filled with an assortment of crochet and knitting needles in the center of the table.

"No, really, I don't want to waste your time." I refold the scarf as I walk to the front and place it on the counter, then reach for my wallet.

Ceila narrows her gaze at me. "What's your 'me time'?"

"Excuse me?"

"Your 'me time.' You know, what you do just for you. How you relax, unwind, forget about your day. Erase your anxiety."

"Does the gym count?" Aidan's kickboxing classes are a great way to shed anxiety. But somehow I don't think that's what she means. Her expression confirms my suspicion.

She drops the crutches and eases onto a chair. "Grab that one. With the blues, yellows, and greens. That's a good combination for you."

I do as I'm told then perch on the edge of an uncomfortable-looking wood chair across from Ceila. Her hands move at a speed that rivals her mouth. I watch, fascinated by the way she wraps the yarn around the index finger of her right hand, the way her left secures the yarn and allows her short pulls to get through, the way the needle twists and ducks and pokes and pulls.

"Just like that," she says and places a perfect rectangle of stitches in front of me.

That doesn't look so hard.

I imitate Ceila's hold on the yarn, clutch the needle in a death grip, then twist and duck and poke and pull. Except, the row of stitches I manage look nothing like the elegant knots she's created with no effort at all.

Ceila takes the tangle from my hands and pulls it apart. I watch as she repeats the previous movements in slower motion.

With a ta-da flourish, she hands over the reballed yarn and crochet needle and talks me through the steps. After I've almost successfully made it through two rows, Ceila excuses herself, picks up the crutches, and stumps away.

"Well look at you." A bottle of water waves in my peripheral vision. Ceila is leaning over my shoulder, pulling at the scarf my fingers have succeeded in crocheting.

I shift, suddenly realizing my butt is numb.

"Wow. Look at me." I smile up at her. "I'm actually doing it."

"More than doing it. Honey, you've done it. However, unless you're planning this for an NBA player, you might want to stop now."

She leans over and pulls the end of the scarf so I can see the length.

"Oops." I laugh. "I didn't realize how long it was getting or how quickly it grows."

Ceila gives me a funny look and laughs. "Quick? Sweetie, you've been at it for over two hours."

"No way." I twist to look at the clock ticking steadily above the door. "Holy shit. How did that happen?"

The funny look transforms into a strange mix of confusion and disbelief. "You were relaxed. I thought you were joking about the gym being your only downtime? Guess not."

"Not really."

"You, dear girl, need to find your way to inner peace."

I can only imagine my face looks as surprised as Ceila's. Inner peace. Not words I would use to describe myself. When was the last time I so completely lost myself in an activity? And no, working past midnight because I didn't realize how late it had become doesn't count.

"Everyone needs an escape once in a while. My sister, she meditates. The girl can sit on a pillow, pretzel-style with her fingers together, and breathe for half an hour. Thirty chirping minutes. I timed her once. Didn't believe anyone could listen to koi-pond sounds from an iPhone app and just sit for that long. But damned if she doesn't do it every day. Me? Five minutes and I'm peeking from under half-closed eyelids, hoping for a natural disaster to free me. But give me needles and yarn, and I lose all sense of time. It's fabulously therapeutic."

She makes a little sound, something between a sigh and a purr. "The shawl hanging over there." Ceila points to a yellow-and-orange shawl draped over a mannequin. "Lucy made that. She's part of our Monday Hookers group."

"The what group?"

She coughs a laugh. "Monday Hookers. There's five, sometimes six of us who meet here every Monday morning to crochet and knit. I make a big ol' pot of coffee and someone brings bagels and we lose ourselves for a couple of hours. It's a great way to start the week."

"Really? Every Monday?"

"Really. Every Monday. You should try it."

I look around the room and try to picture myself sitting in this same spot with a handful of women, crocheting and talking. Not likely. Even if I were here long term, which I won't be.

When I don't respond, Ceila pats me on the shoulder, repositions her crutches, and clanks away. "Try that pile over there. I think you'll find some colors that are perfect for you."

My eyes follow the direction in which she's pointing. Red bleeding into orange melting into yellow before pooling into purple. Like a woman possessed, I walk to the shelf and plunge my fingers into the soft yarn. By the time I make my way to the front counter again, I have my starter scarf and three skeins of the sunset-colored wool, generously donated by Margo, one of Ceila's ewes.

Half an hour later, I'm back in the car, inching down the driveway and craning to see the sheep grazing in the field, wondering which one is Margo. Next to me is a larger bag than I expected to leave with. In addition to the wool, I ended up buying a how-to book titled *The Happy Hooker*, the shawl Lucy crocheted, and two bamboo needles in different sizes.

At the end of the drive, I consult Lucy's map and decide to bypass the next two stops. I have a scarf to finish and inner peace to channel.

10

Inner peace lasts until I find my left hand bound in a colorful but unruly mass of wool. The more I tug to free the strand, the more convoluted the mass becomes. One hour on the Mountain Inn patio and I've undone the relaxed state I'd left The Spinning Ewe with.

"What about this is fun?" I shove the offending wool into the bag at my feet, grab the shawl—thankful for the last-minute decision to buy it—then, wrapped in its warmth, melt into the lounge chair.

The patio is deserted except for me and a tiger-striped cat. He's strolled by several times, careful to ignore me and careful to make sure I notice he's ignoring me. We've been sitting in comfortable ignoring. Except that now, without the busy hand activity, I'm restless. My companion opens an eye, stretches a paw, and releases a large yawn.

"Easy for you. You're used to being lazy. This isn't me. I never do this." My knee bounces. Tiger cat curls his paw underneath but his slitted eyes stay fixed on me. I glare back. "Oh don't be so smug."

He's right, though. I'm in a lovely setting, quiet, peaceful even. And my insides are churning like a blender on frappe. As if to make a point, my phone vibrates along the ceramic-topped table

next to me, a text from Bruce glows against the black screen, deafening in the soft country evening.

I breathe in, slow and controlled, then release to the imagined
rolling tempo of a cantering horse.

My father moved us here for the more relaxed pace and nurturing environment. At least that was the party line. And yet, my
childhood was anything but relaxed or nurtured.

That's not exactly true. I had a nurturing environment. It just
wasn't in my own home.

I close my eyes and let my head drop back. The final ray of
sun strokes my cheek before disappearing for the night.

A sharp, high-pitched whinny sounds somewhere in the distance and is quickly answered by a less urgent one. I wonder if
it's dinnertime or someone has been turned out into the field and
can't find his buddy.

Jack used to do that. Every time I'd release him in the paddock, he'd stand by the gate and whinny three times, short, quick,
get-over-here whinnies, and Soldier would come trotting from
whatever corner of the field he'd been grazing in. They'd touch
noses in an equine hello, then wander off side by side, big black
fancy show horse next to his hairy, miniature, brown-and-white
best friend. Soldier could almost walk under Jack's belly, but he
was the fiercest of companions.

I wonder who protects Jack from the hay and best-grass-spot
muggers these days. I didn't see Soldier when I was at the barn.
Then again, I hadn't really looked. I hadn't even given Jack a
proper hello.

Guilt can be one hell of a paralyzer. Or is it regret? Either way,
I let it keep me from reaching out to touch the horse who'd
stolen my heart and filled my emptiness.

Maybe Soldier was in the stall after all. He was pretty short
and I wouldn't have seen him from where I was standing. I hope
he was in there with Jack. No one should have to lose their best
friend.

I bend my legs and wrap my arms around my knees, curling
the ends of the shawl into my fists, creating a protective cocoon.

I'd always marveled at the loyalty between Jack and Soldier. Jack would snatch bites of hay from the wall-mounted hay cage and drop them on the ground for his short friend. They were never far apart.

People aren't as straightforward. I'd so wanted to believe that Jilli and I had been meant to find each other. Maybe it was even true when we first met. But by the time the raging-teen years kicked in, there were cracks in our friendship. Cracks I tried to ignore, cracks I tried to patch.

"Meow." Tiger cat is sitting on his haunches watching me, head cocked to the right.

"Meow." He deepens the angle of the tilt.

"It's really not that interesting of a story." I look around to make sure there are no humans on the patio.

I push up from the lounge chair and grab the bag of yarn. With a final look at my feline companion, I walk into the inn. On the sideboard in the hall is a bag with my name on it. True to her word, Lucy has packed a light dinner for me. I take it and climb the stairs to my room.

Ping. Ping. Ping.

I moan and pull the pillow over my face, mumbling a wish-you'd-sprain-your-thumbs curse at Bruce.

There's a hint of morning tickling the hills outside my window. That would make it still espresso-dark in Chicago. And Bruce is probably on his third cup by now.

Last year for April Fools' Day, the human resources director changed the office coffee to decaf. It had turned out to be a mildly mellow morning and a wildly frantic afternoon when Bruce caught on.

Ping.

I push the pillow away and grab my phone.

Are you sick? Did you get run over by a tractor? Why aren't you answering?

Because it's six o'clock in the morning. Except, if I were at home, I would have already answered his questions. But I'm not at home. I'm stuck in godforsaken-land, here to close out my father's affairs. And yet what have I been doing? Sitting for hours on a sheep farm and rekindling my childhood love of horses.

The box of my father's papers taunts me from the table on the other side of the room.

"Fine."

But first, coffee.

The weekday breakfast spread is less extravagant than the one I'd been tempted by yesterday. I snag a roll, pour a cup of coffee, and make my way to the deserted patio. From my bag I fish out a notebook and pen.

The fields surrounding the inn are quiet this morning. A spray of mist appears to hover over the grass, making the trees in the distance shimmer. There's a nip in the air, the promise of sweater weather, the perfect morning for a ride.

"Focus, Emma." I click the top of the pen, then study the tip as though I've never seen a ballpoint pen before.

Where do I start?

1. Rena re: Mom's involvement in the program
2. Thomas Adler re: timing on closing out the practice
3. Schedule appointment with realtor
4. Schedule appointment with bank manager
5. Howard re: corporate-brochure edits
6. Bruce re: press appointments in Vegas

I take a long sip from the now less-than-steaming coffee and squint at the to-do list.

"This won't do." I cross out numbers five and six with a tsk. I'm not supposed to be working. But I've never ignored Bruce's messages before. Instinctively I glance at my watch. Almost eight his time. I need to answer. He must be having rabid kittens by now.

"I asked you a question, Emma. Professionalism dictates that you answer in a timely fashion."

I was twelve. What did I know—or care—about *professionalism*? The only thing I knew was that my father wanted an answer about my report card. I'd waited to open the envelope until I was away from school. It was one of the rare days I chose not to go to the stable immediately. I'd gotten off the bus at the end of our drive and run down the path in the woods, stopping halfway to the stable. There, on a fallen tree that had played the part of a jump many times while I pretend cantered back and forth over that path, I slit the envelope open and collapsed in tears.

B+ in science.

The only other time I'd gotten a B+ was in PE after we first moved to Emmitsville. Like most kids, I'd done round-offs on the playground. But I'd never mastered straightening my legs or controlling the speed. Gymnastics had turned out to be a colossal failure for me. No matter how much I stretched or how hard I tried, I just couldn't do the splits or jump on the balance beam or do a proper cartwheel. But I pushed my eight-year-old muscles into trying. And for that, she'd given me the B+. I'd thought it was fair. My father grounded me for two weeks.

I didn't do B+'s after that. One A–, the semester after my mother died. He'd pursed his lips, opened the bottom desk drawer, put the report card in the folder with my other report cards, closed the drawer, and bidden me good night.

But a B+ in science was inexcusable in his eyes. This time, I couldn't even hide behind someone's death.

"How did this happen, Emma?" His voice had that practiced paternal calm that sent a shiver of dread down a kid's spine.

I had no answer. I'd studied. I'd turned in all assignments. But the A's had eluded my best efforts.

"I asked you a question, Emma. Professionalism dictates that you answer in a timely fashion."

I'd thought to point out the frayed edge of the area rug in his office. I'd wanted to point out that science just wasn't my strength. In the end, I'd apologized and accepted my punishment with a nod.

One month. No playdates after school. No riding until he was satisfied that I was taking my studies seriously. That I was being professional.

"Fine, Dad."

I refocus on the to-do list.

1. Howard re: corporate-brochure edits
2. Bruce re: press appointments in Vegas

Professionalism wins.

But curiosity trumps professionalism. I return the mug to the sideboard in the dining room and head for the front door.

The drive to Jumping Frog Farm is a blender of emotions. Guilt for not responding to Bruce, anxiety at confronting Rena, dread over a potential run-in with Jillian.

Plus a smidgen of anticipation at being around the horses. All these years later, my insides are right back to happy jiggles at the mere thought of being close to a horse.

"You're in trouble." I pull into the drive to the stable and inhale, then catch my reflection in the rearview mirror. "Big trouble."

There are several cars in the parking lot this morning and I hear Rena bellowing from the outdoor arena.

My feet carry me in the opposite direction, into the safety of the barn. I stop at the door to let my eyes adjust. There's the bristling scratch of a broom to my left. A man wearing baggy jeans and a T-shirt in the stable's hunter green, with STAFF across his back, sings to a song crackling from a radio. Reception had never been strong here, except for a country music station none of us wanted to listen to. I guess some things haven't changed.

The peacefulness of the barn is shattered by metal hitting wood. A horse stomps and there's a clang-thump as a crosstie bangs into the wall.

"Knock it off," a male voice grumbles, and is answered by another stomp and clang-thump. "Dammit, horse. Rena will turn you into a wall ornament if you don't stop denting her walls."

I take a few strides toward the commotion but stop when the wash stall comes into sight.

A blonde is leaning against the corner of the stall, her back turned to me, a long braid running down the middle of her back. "Why do you insist on pulling his mane? You know he hates it. Use the clippers. It's faster. And less dangerous for the walls." She shrugs and shifts, the movement revealing her profile.

Ben steps down from the step stool and retrieves a metal mane comb from the ground. "That's what you do, Jill. It's the lazy way out and I hate the way it looks."

My heartbeat and breath catch, like kids caught in a freeze dance. I want to move, turn, disappear, but the music hasn't started and I'm frozen in place.

"Hey. Emma's back." Ben flashes a grin at me and waves me over.

"Who?" The blonde pivots.

Sixteen years. Gone in the blink of an eye.

She still wears her hair the same. Still stands with the same defiant dare-you attitude.

"Jilli." The word barely registers in my ears. But it must have been loud enough because I see—or think I see—her wince.

"Emma."

Ben looks from me to Jillian, back to me, his grin sagging in the heavy air between us. "Huh." It sounds more like a hiccup and Jilli and I both turn to look at him. "Not the hello I would have expected from two old friends."

"That was a long time ago." She bounces the braid over her shoulder.

"It was." I agree.

At least we're agreeing on something. That's a start, right?

Ben studies us a heartbeat longer, then turns back to Wally with another "huh" hiccup.

"What do you think, Emma, pull the mane or trim with clippers?"

It's a test. One I don't have a prayer to get even a B+ on.

"I always liked the look of a pulled mane."

Jillian releases a derisive snort. She pushes off from the wall, startling Wally, who steps sideways and plants his right front hoof on Ben's foot.

"Move, you moose." Ben shoves at the horse's shoulder, then glares at Jillian. "What is your problem?"

She glares back. "You."

Before Ben can form a comeback, Jillian turns on me. "Why are you here?"

I feel a flush of heat spreading up my chest to coat my neck and face with what must be an ugly shade of incredulity. "Tying up my father's estate."

"No. I meant here." She nods her head, indicating the stable.

My shoulders start to rise in a shrug I haven't approved. No. I am not that eight-year-old girl afraid of her own shadow. I will not be meek. "I'm here to talk to Rena."

Jillian takes in my almost-new Converses, pressed capris, and clearly-not-made-for-horse-slobber silk shirt. "That's why they invented phones."

"It's personal."

"Your point?"

"I'm not here to take your time so why does this concern you?" I catch a glimpse of Ben ducking his head to cover a spreading smirk.

Jillian inhales deeply and bites the corner of her lip. "She's busy with classes. As the manager of the barn, her schedule does concern me."

"I won't be staying long."

The heat deepens when I hear the apologetic tone of my voice. And then scorches with the realization that after all these years I do still care.

11

March 1992

Th birds woke her up. She'd promised her mom to stay in bed later since it was Sunday but the birds obviously had other plans for the day.

The whole week had been warm and sunny. Perfect spring weather. Flowers were popping up everywhere and the trees were showing signs of life. Emma loved spring. Especially out here.

During her lesson on Friday, Simon said that if the weather held, he'd take her and Jillian on a trail ride Sunday.

Emma had spent Saturday staring at the sky and bargaining with the forces of nature. *If you make it a perfect day, I'll take the trash out without being asked for a full week. If you make Sunday warm and sunny, I'll come home immediately after the ride and do my book report without being reminded.*

Maybe she had some pull after all, because the sun was finally out. She's never been on the trail. In the five months since she started riding, all of her lessons have been in the indoor arena. Friday was her first time in the outdoor arena.

She couldn't imagine riding being any more perfect, but with the breeze tickling her face and the sunbeams warming her arms, riding was just that much more amazing.

Even Jillian was less crabby. She wouldn't go so far as to say they were becoming friends but at least they weren't enemies anymore.

There was a girl, Kimmie, in art class who was friendly enough although she usually hung out with other girls during recess and lunch. Jo, who was in her media group, rode at Jumping Frog Farm. She played with Emma during recess. They'd make up courses around the playground or pretend they were in a flat class walking, trotting, cantering in circles, and changing direction. On indoor recess days, they'd devour the horse books in the class library.

Jo had even invited Emma for a sleepover once. Emma's mom hadn't been feeling well enough to take her and her father hadn't gotten home until too late. There haven't been invitations since. And since then, she spends recess alone, reading.

She's been careful around Jillian. She tries to be friendly but aloof—that's what Rena calls how Tootsie the barn cat behaves. You know he'll purr if you rub his chin and scratch his back, but he walks past with his tail up high, looking in the opposite direction, and makes you come to him. He'll never let on that he really does want you to pet him. She always pets him and so do most people at the barn. If it works for him, maybe it'll work for her.

It does a bit. Jillian has watched a couple of her classes. And last week she stayed by the tack stall while Emma was getting Rusty ready. They didn't talk but Jilli handed her the curry comb at the exact moment Emma thought it was time to switch brushes. That was positive, right?

She won't let herself hope too much. She hasn't been very lucky with friends.

Emma looks at the stack of envelopes on her desk, tied together with a blue ribbon. Kathy's letters have been getting shorter and shorter while Emma's have been getting longer and longer.

"Emma, are you up, sweetie?" There's a gentle knock on her bedroom door. The door creaks open and Emma's mom looks in. "Come, I've made breakfast."

They match strides walking down the hall and down the stairs. Right foot, left foot, right, left. Emma skips when her shorter strides shift their parallel pattern and now they're back to rights and lefts together.

Her mom laughs and Emma beams. She's glad they moved here. Her mom is healthier and Emma loves this happier mom. Yesterday they planted herbs in a pot. Her mom said it was finally warm enough outside. Emma loved the smell of the basil and dirt.

Plus, if they hadn't moved, Emma wouldn't be riding. She can't even think what life would be like without the horses. They've become part of her already.

Emma canters across the kitchen and sits in her usual chair. Her mom puts a plate of french toast in front her. Emma cuts the bread into long, thin strips and spaces them on her plate like ground poles. Her index and middle fingers trot across the plate and over the toast poles in perfect strides.

"Look, Mom." She finger-trots around the circle of poles again. She eats two and spreads the others out. "Now it's a canter exercise."

Her mom smiles and slides a glass of orange juice toward her. "Are you going to help at the stable again today?"

"Yes," Emma says and swallows two big gulps of juice. "Is that okay?" She wipes her mouth, eyes big, heart skipping with dread that she won't be allowed to go.

"Sure, but not all day. You have a book report due tomorrow, right?"

Emma nods and chews on another pole of french toast. She needs to finish breakfast and get out before her father comes downstairs and questions her about the book report. She knows he won't allow her to go until it's completed and she's nowhere near being done.

"I'm almost done." It's a small lie. She's almost done reading. She hasn't actually started writing the report, but at least she's almost done with reading. She picked *Black Beauty*, again. She could write the report without rereading the book, she knows it by heart, but she loves the story too much not to read it cover to cover.

"Simon said he'll take us on a trail ride today because it's been so nice and we've worked hard. I promise I'll be home immediately after. Please, please?" She hears her father coming down the stairs. She jumps from the table and puts her plate in the sink. "Please, Mommy? Jillian will be going."

She knows her mom wants her to make friends.

"Are you and Jillian become friendlier?"

"Um-hm." She finishes the last swallow of orange juice and stacks the glass on top of the plate in the sink.

"I hope so. You could use a good friend your age, Emma. Just be your lovely self."

She really doesn't want to explain to her mom that she's playing cat with Jillian. She knows Mom will say it's always better to be yourself. But so far, being friendly and being herself haven't worked with Jillian.

"I better go, Mom. I'll be back around lunchtime. I love you." She gives her mom a hug from behind and kisses her cheek, then darts for the door.

"I love you, too," follows her out. She turns to make sure the door is closed and catches a glimpse of her mom, still sitting at the table, looking at the empty spot where Emma had been sitting. She doesn't recognize the look on her mom's face and she doesn't want to stop to figure it out. Not now at least.

She wants to get to the barn. She wants to ride on the trail. And, she realizes as she canters down the path into the woods, she wants to ride with Jillian.

12

'S cuze me." A voice from behind startles me. The man in the green stable shirt and baggy jeans is looking up, the broom poised to push a pile of discarded hay and horse hair past the spot I'm blocking.

Jillian stares through me. "Tony, when you're done with the aisle, RJ needs to be tacked up. He rolled in the field so make sure to give him a thorough currying first. I'll be in the jump ring setting up. Bring him out when he's ready." She gives me the disgusted yet somewhat curious look I'd seen so many times from her during our childhood, then marches off.

Wally stretches his neck, trying to reach me. My feet respond and the horse head-butts my torso. I slide my hands up his ears while he pushes deeper into my chest. The pressure, the presence, the power of this horse slows my heart pounding in my ears.

This is what I've been missing.

My hands travel along the angles of his jaw until they find the velvet warmth of his muzzle. I release the bottled-up air in my lungs and let the stress slither away. Or at least as much as it can.

Ben shakes his head, a smile spreading across his tanned face.

We both turn at a fake cough and watch Jillian stride out the back door. Gravel crunches under her boots as she makes her way down the path to the jump arena.

"Okaaay." Ben's gaze stays on the door a few gravel crunches after Jilli's departure.

"Well. Not exactly how I expected that to go." Wally nudges my stomach and I finger-comb his forelock.

"Yeah, she's bitchier than usual today." Ben climbs back on the step stool and resumes combing out his horse's mane.

"Guess I shouldn't be surprised."

"I am. Every picture of the two of you shows you with your arms around each other, smiling like you just won Olympic gold." I can feel him watching me.

"That was a long time ago."

Ben bobs his head, then stops. "Simon told me that you and Jack used to traumatize the kids in your division. He said you were the most talented student he ever had."

"Don't let Jillian hear you say that."

"Ha. Good point." He pulls a serious face that crumbles into a grin when he catches my eye.

Tony walks by with a saddle on his forearm and a bridle looped over his shoulder. He's still singing quietly.

"I never understood the people who came for lessons and arrived just in time to get on the horse, then bolted immediately after the lesson. Tacking and untacking were always my favorite parts."

"Mine too."

"Not that I'm complaining. Because of them I had summer and after-school jobs. And I got to enjoy that special time with the horses. But I always felt a bit sorry for those people. They never realized what they were missing out on."

I realize he's staring at me. "What?"

"Why did you stop riding?"

There it is, the question no one in my other life knew to ask. And that suited me just fine. But here, it was only a matter of time before someone asked.

"Long, ugly story." The truth of that muddies my voice.

Ben steps down and moves the step stool out of the wash stall, positioning it next to an overturned bucket. "Pick your throne, m'lady."

I pick the bucket. Not that it's cleaner than the step stool, or sturdier. For old times' sake I guess. Ben folds his lanky body onto the step stool, our shoulders almost touching as we watch Wally grab at the crossties with the side of his mouth.

Before he can poke at my history, I ask, "How long have you worked here?"

"Four years, give or take. Simon lured me here when he stopped teaching."

I twist to look at Ben, almost tipping off the bucket. "He's not teaching anymore?"

There's an odd crease between Ben's eyebrows and I can't tell if it's surprise, confusion, or concern.

"He'll do the occasional clinic but no, he stopped teaching. He's not running the stable either. Gave it over to Jill two years ago."

I swat at a fly that's been buzzing around my head since we sat down. "She goes by 'Jill' now? She hated that name when we were young."

"She still does. But it's fun egging her on."

The image of the two of them as a couple flickers through my mind, surprising me with a sudden jolt of something suspiciously close to envy. Envy at a life that wasn't mine. She'd stayed, continued riding, made this her career, and had a nice guy in her life.

"Are you two . . ." The rest of the question fizzles on my tongue.

Ben tosses his head, his shaggy hair flopping into his eyes. The human, dark-haired movement I'd seen his horse make. They say married couples start to look and act alike after years together. I always believed the union between rider and horse was similar.

"Oh hell no. I like my balls right where they are. Jillian would hang them over the rearview mirror of that ridiculous car she drives."

Tony walks by leading a chestnut gelding. Both horse and

groom have their heads down, the reins loose in Tony's right hand. Neither seems overly enthusiastic.

Ben nods as the twosome passes. "Even her horse knows she's a pill."

A snorting laugh escapes and I slap my hand across my mouth.

Ben laughs. "That I didn't expect coming from you. Don't." He pulls my hand from my mouth. "Don't be embarrassed by an unguarded response."

My insides tighten. An unguarded response. Not something valued in my corporate world. Not even in my private world.

"I'll try to remember that."

"You shouldn't have to try. It should be natural."

"I guess."

Rena's voice echoes down the aisle. Ben and I watch as she walks beside a black-and-white pinto being led by a man wearing breeches and boots, the hard hat still on his head but the chin strap flapping with each stride.

They pass, the man smiles, but the only acknowledgment from Rena is a fly swat of her right hand.

I twist on the bucket to watch them. There's an electric presence to the man, a weary restlessness. And yet the horse beside him is relaxed.

"That's Michael." Ben answers my unasked question. "He's one of the therapeutic riding clients. Hell of a guy. Rena has worked a small miracle with him. And with so many of the others."

"I'm glad she's still running the program. She was such a different person when working with the therapeutic clients. She was patient and caring. Not that she didn't care about her other clients, but there was something soft about her with the program folks."

"Don't let her hear you say she's soft." He laughs.

"She certainly isn't that any other time, is she? Anyway," I add after a too-long pause, "I always loved helping with those lessons."

"How were you and Jillian ever friends?"

"We had the horses."

"Still not buying it." He shakes his head, hair flopping onto his forehead. Wally mimics the move.

We're silent for a few minutes, watching Michael untack his horse and chat with Rena. Their voices are too low for us to hear, but by Rena's expression, it's serious. Michael mostly nods in response, one hand on the pinto the entire time.

"How long has he been in the program?"

Ben twists his mouth in thought. "Maybe a year."

"Do you know what brought him here?"

Ben shakes his head. "I help when needed but I don't ask questions. Some of the clients are open about what brings them here. Most don't talk much. Although Rena somehow gets them all to open up."

"There's something about her that makes people trust."

"As opposed to her granddaughter."

"What do you mean?" I shift to get a better look at Ben.

"She's managed to piss off a few boarders. One moved her two horses out and told Simon he'd lose more clients if he didn't muzzle Jill. Another client switched from jumping to dressage because of her. She's pretty good, actually. I should probably thank Jill. Another boarder refuses to talk to her, just leaves notes pinned to the bulletin board about what needs to be done for his horse. Even Rena almost throttled her after a very public and nasty tirade about the therapeutic riding program. In front of a couple of clients."

Jilli never had much of a filter between her thoughts and her mouth. "Guess time hasn't mellowed her mouth."

"Nothing can mellow her mouth." There's a heaviness to his tone, a there's-more-to-this that he attempts to hide with a stiff grin.

"Then why are they having her manage the stable?"

"Because she's the heir apparent. She may not be a people person, but she does have a decent head for numbers. And she's no pushover. She'll bust anyone who tries to overcharge or under-deliver."

That doesn't surprise me. She was always a sharp negotiator.

She's the only one who could talk a teacher out of giving home-work on a Friday afternoon or because the weather was too per-fect to be cooped up inside. She was always working out "deals" with the school kitchen staff for extra helpings. And she got the fancy show horse when she decided that was her next must-have.

"Why isn't Simon teaching anymore?"

"You need to have that discussion with him. Him and Rena." Something about Ben's expression prickles up my neck.

I shake my head. "I don't think that's a good idea. Anyway, I'm only here for a few more days."

"Then what?"

I hesitate for a fraction of a breath. "Go home."

Ben catches the hesitation. I can tell by the lift of one eyebrow. I hold my breath waiting for him to ask but he doesn't. I allow the air to slide out the corner of my mouth.

"Okay." He unfolds from the step stool and extends a hand to help me up. "I need to get this old boy exercised but I'm not done with you, Miss Emma. Before you 'go home,' I'm getting you on a horse." He winks and walks over to where Wally is play-ing with the crossties.

With a final rub for Wally and a good-bye to Ben, I walk down the aisle in the direction of the office. I came to talk to Rena. It's time to saddle up and ride in.

She's not in the office or the indoor arena. I wander to the end of the aisle and squint through the bright light to the jump ring. A figure on a chestnut horse is cantering around the arena. Rena could be out there, and if she is, our talk will have to wait. As much as I want to hear about my mom's involvement with the therapeutic program, it'll have to wait until Jilli moves to the moon. Or at least leaves the stable for a few hours.

I take my time walking up the aisle, reading the nameplate on each stall. Some stalls are occupied, the tenants munching their hay. Others are open, blankets neatly folded on the chain across the front, a neat flake of hay waiting for the occupant to return. Why am I surprised that none of these names are familiar? After all these years, did I really expect the same horses to be occupy-ing the same stalls?

Jack Flash.

Different stall but still here.

Jack takes the couple of strides from the hay pile to the door. His warm eyes watch me, head straight, waiting for me to make the first move this time.

"Hello, handsome." The fingers on my left hand drum a silent beat on my thigh. I didn't hesitate walking up to Wally. Yet I can't bring my legs to take the final couple of steps to Jack. Jack, the horse that was my life for so many years.

He tilts his head to the right, stretches his neck over the half door, and flaps his lips hello. He'd started doing that as a foal, his I'm-so-cute-give-me-a-treat signature move. And it still melts my insides.

Before I make the conscious decision to move, my arms are locked around Jack's neck, hands buried in his mane, face pressed into the soft indent between his head and neck.

"Not a day has gone by that I haven't thought of you." I in-hale the perfume of my childhood—horse, hay, sawdust. We've both aged, yet in this moment, nothing has changed. "Will you forgive me?" I whisper into his neck. Jack wraps his head around me in an equine hug.

I slide the latch up and slip into the stall, securing the door behind me. I take a hesitant step toward the huge horse, so much larger than in the memories I'd tucked away, so much smaller than the legend I'd built him up to be.

My hands move from his neck to his shoulder, his back, stomach, flank. Around to the other side and I reverse the search. What am I looking for? Scars? Evidence of the damage I caused? Or confirmation that he's perfect?

I find both.

A scar runs down his chest, disappearing between his front legs, like a river disappearing over a waterfall.

"Oh, Jack." The words scratch my heart and tears burn my eyes.

I squat to get a better look and trace the line, a gray reminder of a lapse in judgment that can never be erased.

My hands travel back to his neck and he nudges my shoulder.

"You are still magnificent."

"He's always been a stunner."

I start at Rena's voice. I'd been so engrossed in Jack that I hadn't noticed her leaning against the half-door of the stall.

"Perfect. Aren't you?" I kiss his velvety muzzle and laugh when he flaps his lips at me. "And still a flirt."

"You know I don't spare my thoughts, Emma."

I tense, waiting for her to tell me to get out. Her hands are grasping the top of the half door, her knuckles and joints gnarled like misshapen tree branches. She never had beautiful hands. It was one of the first things I'd noticed. They were calloused and bent from numerous breaks, the nails chewed and cracked. So unlike my mom's hands. Even when she was sick, Mom had taken care of her hands. She'd always said you can tell a lot about a woman by her hands. I shove mine into the pockets of my jeans.

Rena doesn't open the stall door. She wants to keep me trapped until she gives me a healthy dose of those thoughts.

My eyes flicker from her hands to her face. She looks far more relaxed than I feel.

"Why did you wait until now to come back?"

Because my father waited until now to die.

"Would you have come back if your father hadn't died?"

My head snaps up. I hadn't said that out loud, had I?

"Don't look so shocked. I knew your father wanted to keep you away."

"How did you know?"

"Because we argued about it."

"When? Were there more letters? Recent ones?"

"Only a few months before his accident."

I want to call her out on the letters I'd found, the letters she just avoided in my question. But it's the invoices that brought me here. They're connected, but which line of questioning has a higher probability of not seeing me slapped with a trespassing arrest?

"Why did my mom come here? Why was she in the therapeutic program? The people who come to the program have mental or emotional or physical issues. She had a heart condition."

"Your mom needed an outlet."

"That doesn't answer my question. Why was it a secret?"

"Your father insisted."

I grind my back teeth. This is worse than pulling answers from Bruce. "Why?"

A flicker of unease crosses her face and the left corner of her mouth pulls in. I brace for her response, for the confirmation. "Your father didn't care much for horses. Or horse people by association."

"Then why bring her—us—here? I know you were in contact before we moved here."

She avoids my eyes. "Your father was not my concern. Your mom was. And then you were."

"Why get in touch with him again after all those years?"

"Age gives you new insight. And loosens the censor in your brain. It was time to put the past behind us, before it was too late."

"Does it have anything to do with Simon handing over lessons and management of the barn?" That prickle from my discussion with Ben returns, fast-forwarding up my spine.

Rena tilts her head and I can almost see the question scrolling through her mind like a news crawler. "It had more to do with lowering the drawbridge for you to return."

"What does that mean?"

Sensing tension, Jack gives me a gentle push, then shuffles through the disheveled hay pile to the opposite side of the stall and sticks his head over the half door to the outside.

"Your father thought he was protecting you."

"Protecting me from what? This place was the best thing that ever happened to me."

"Life isn't as straightforward as that, Emma. There were things you didn't know about. Things your dad wanted to spare you."

"You mean like the fact that my mom was a client of the therapeutic riding program?"

"Among other things."

"What other things?"

"People. Heartbreak."

"Because I didn't know about heartbreak? I lost my mom, remember?" My breath catches. "He was protecting me from you, wasn't he?"

Rena winces as though slapped.

"That's it, isn't it? You guys cut me out of your lives."

I'd been unconscious for two days after the accident. When I came to, there was a nurse checking my vitals. She'd smiled, said welcome back, and that she'd go get my father. When I asked for Jillian, her smile had widened and she told me to rest while she went for my father. I'd asked for Simon or Rena. Her smile had disappeared. She told me she'd be right back with my father. And a sedative.

The police had been there. My driver's license was being suspended. Drinking. Drugs. People were talking.

It wasn't me! I'd cried. The blood tests proved I was clean. But a horse had been killed, another badly injured, and two teenage girls were in the hospital. Accusations were flying. But worse than that, the whispering had begun—was I destined for the same end as my mother? Was it really an accident? He wasn't going to allow that. Why the whispering that I'd end up like my mom? Her heart condition wasn't hereditary.

My father had shut down all of my questions. He'd made arrangements at a boarding school and I was leaving as soon as the doctor cleared me. I would be taken care of at the school. I would be safe there.

It's what my mom would have wanted, he'd said.

"Why was she a client here?" I force the quiver out of my throat. It's the question I came here to ask, the question she clearly doesn't want to answer.

The fight with Jillian echoes in my brain.

I will find out at least one truth.

"Was my mom a client because of her heart condition?"

"No."

"Did my mom commit suicide?"

"Yes."

13

She was right." The words ooze from my mouth like blood from a freshly opened wound.

"Who was right?" Rena's brows reach for each other.

All those years of "give your mom space, Emma, she has a heart problem," and "your mom is feeling weak today, Emma, you need to be extra good and quiet." Even after Mom died the lies continued. Especially after Mom died.

I force eye contact. "Why did she commit suicide?"

Rena visibly deflates. "This isn't a discussion you and I should be having."

Heat builds in my chest and flames up my throat, threatening to trigger the fire sprinklers behind my eyes. "Then who should I be talking to? My mom? I tried that. If she answered my questions, I couldn't hear her through the six feet of dirt between us. My father? I'll go knock on the Johns Hopkins morgue door."

Her mouth pinches, the lips pull in, causing lines to spread like cracks from a pinpoint hole in glass. And just like the horror of watching glass crack, I watch the strongest person I've ever known fight for composure. "Rena?" I take a step forward but she puts up a hand in warning.

"I have a class to teach. Maybe I was wrong. Maybe your father was right about keeping you away from here, away from the truth."

Behind me, Jack snorts. Is he agreeing with Rena or support-ing me?

"Why did you want me back, Rena?"

She looks fragile gripping the top of the stall door. What could have changed to make her reach out to my father after all this time? And why the change of heart now that I'm here?

My phone chimes with a meeting reminder.

The lines around Rena's mouth release their tight hold. "You have someplace to be. Take care of the business you came here to address, Emma."

Voices from the other end of the barn roll through the empty aisle: "Man it stinks in here." "I don't wanna be here. Horses are dumb anyway." "Just give it a chance." "You can't make me."

"My next lesson is here. Good luck, Emma." She walks in the direction of the voices, her steps far less commanding than the Rena in my memories.

I give Jack a final hug and leave his stall.

Simon is standing two stalls away, arms crossed, his features drooping. "She doesn't really mean it, you know that."

"Mean what?"

"That you shouldn't be here."

"She sounded pretty convincing to me."

He exhales and closes the distance between us, then tilts his head for me to walk with him. "It hasn't been an easy time for her either. After the accident—after you left—aging—" His voice clips each aborted phrase.

"I need to go help her, Emma. Please come back. More needs to be said." He reaches for my hand and gives me a squeeze.

Since when has Rena needed help with her lessons?

I trail Simon to the indoor arena. In the center is a small clus-ter of people and ponies.

Rena is crouching next to a young boy who's clawing at his adult companion. "Come on, Tyrone, give it a chance. I put you on the sweetest horse in the barn. His name is Oreo because he kind of looks like an Oreo cookie. Do you like those?"

She takes his hand and gives him a gentle tug forward. Tyrone wails and flaps his arms, gyrating until neither Rena nor his chaperone can hold on without the risk of hurting him. The moment their hands release him, the boy crumples into the soft footing of the arena. He grabs a fistful and hurls it in the direction of the remaining group of people.

A black pony with a wide, white blaze tosses his head but doesn't move. A chestnut pony to his right, however, shies, knocking into the pony on her other side.

Rena bends to Tyrone's level. "It's okay to be a bit afraid, Tyrone. I won't push you to do anything you don't want to. But can I ask you to do something for me?" The boy shrugs and Rena takes that as enough encouragement to continue. "Next time, will you let me at least introduce you to the horse? I think once you see how soft and lovely he is, you'll feel better."

The boy appears to shrink into himself but doesn't cry or fight.

Rena touches his arm. "It's okay, really." She stands and addresses the woman who'd attempted to contain poor Tyrone earlier. "Mrs. Ellison, maybe you and Tyrone can wait in the lounge. I think you'll be more comfortable in there while the lesson is going on."

Mrs. Ellison nods although she seems far from pleased. With a hand under Tyrone's armpit, she lifts him out of the arena footing and guides him to the door.

The alarm on my phone chimes a second warning. I'll have to rush to get to my father's condo in time for the meeting with the realtor.

T.J., it turns out, is a feisty five-foot-two-inch platinum blonde with dark roots and dark streaks. She arrives at the apartment building a few minutes after I do. She has a surprisingly authoritative handshake for someone who looks like she should still be carrying a backpack, and rocking Uggs and college-logo sweatpants.

She leans in and whispers, "Don't worry, I'm old enough to go drink champagne with you after we sell this place." And by her choice of attire and accessories, she's quite capable of getting healthy commissions.

While she scrutinizes the condo, I perch on one of the barstools and check my messages. My fingers fly in response to Howard's six missed texts and Bruce's twelve e-mails. With each tap at the Send button, my pulse picks up speed.

T.J. click-clicks back to the kitchen and perches on the barstool next to me. "What's your time frame?"

I look up, thumbs at attention waiting to finish the e-mail. "Tomorrow?"

Her throaty chuckle reminds me of the old Hollywood starlets. The only thing missing is the cigarette and big hair.

I raise my hand, as if the phone explains everything, then add, "I have to get back to work."

She waves, giving me permission to continue typing. I'd meant go back to Chicago but she's already moving around the living room behind me. I take the opportunity to finish a response to Bruce.

"What about the furniture?"

"Sorry?" I frown at the phone and look at T.J. Multitasking is not working well for me at the moment. Out of the office for a few days and I'm losing my skills.

"Are you taking the furniture? Do you want to donate any of it? Sell any of it?" She sweeps long fingers to make her point in case I'm still confused.

"I'm not taking anything." I cringe at the sting in my tone. T.J. doesn't care about my personal attachments or lack of. She just cares about the commission. "Whatever you think is best for attracting buyers."

She assesses me the way she assessed the couch and floor-to-ceiling curtains. "He had very elegant taste. The apartment will sell better with the furniture. I'll offer it with or without. What doesn't sell can then be sold separately."

I mumble, "Fine." Did Thomas tell her whose condo she's selling? He must have. She'd said "he" and there's nothing feminine in this place to indicate it could be mine.

I compare my father's designer-inspired decorating with my anything-goes approach. Maybe I should keep a few of his pieces after all. Except that my apartment is too small to stuff one more thing in and nothing here is waving the pick-me flag.

An hour later, we have a plan. I leave T.J. in the lobby, phone glued to her ear. I have a fleeting thought to ask her if she'd like a job. She could give Howard a lesson or six in efficiency. Not to mention tact.

On the drive back to the Mountain Inn, I'm kept company by half of the Washington, DC, population. My father enjoyed complaining about the sardine rush hours in this area. It's why he bought a condo within walking distance to his practice and a Metro station.

I'm not one to poke. My apartment is a couple of blocks from the office. The only traffic jam I have to negotiate on the way to work is the Starbucks order and pickup line. People aren't always friendly waiting for their caffeine fix.

I look at my reflection in the rearview mirror and mutter, "Like you're any better?"

The cars inch forward. My neighbors look bored or annoyed, tired or frazzled. Some talk to hidden microphones in their cars, some sing along with lyrics audible only in their cocoons, some curse at fellow commuters and mistimed traffic lights.

By the time I pull off the main roads onto the country roads leading to my destination, I'm ready for a drink.

A sign for a winery points in the opposite direction of the Mountain Inn. I flick the blinker and follow the promise of wine from the pouring bottle on the sign.

I find it nestled in the Maryland hills, the neat rows of vines dipping and rolling with the terrain. A wood A-frame structure perches at the top of a hill, the late-afternoon sun bouncing off the wall of windows. A wraparound porch overlooks the rows of vines and an almost empty parking lot.

I pick a table in the corner of the deck and order a cheese plate and a glass of cabernet franc, one of the most ordered, I'm told by a young lady wearing an apron with a picture of smiley-faced grapes and the words "pick me, squeeze me, make me wine."

My father tried to educate me about the subtleties of wine. I'd failed him there, too. Gin and tonic has always been my favored drink.

I take another sip of wine and look at the picturesque view spreading to the corners of my imagination. *Did you ever come here, Dad?* It's beautiful though not nearly as fancy as that vineyard in France he took me to.

The fall of my senior year in college, he'd invited me to join him on a trip to France. We'd stayed at a chateau and toured several nearby wineries. It was hard to tell if he'd suggested the trip as an attempt to connect with his daughter or as an attempt to educate his daughter. Either way, the trip had been less than a success.

Was there ever a time we were a warm, happy family? The photograph in my father's condo blinks through the fractured memory of my childhood.

There's not the slightest hiccup of a memory for that lake house. Or Mom with long hair. No matter how hard I sift through my past, I simply cannot capture any hint of that life. The life I remember is Mom in a pixie cut, her brown hair limp and lifeless. Her face gaunt, her upper body folding in, sheltering the secrets she was protecting.

I pull the stack of letters from my bag and slide the off-white paper out of the top envelope.

November 1996

Dear Edward,
I have to agree, the holidays always come upon us with such force. I'm not sure what the trick is for being prepared.
    I'm not a fan of surprises either. But kids love them and I'm delighted that you're thinking ahead for Emma.

My suggestion—stick to something related to horses. You can't go wrong.

Yours,
R.

That was the year I got the new saddle.

That saddle was exactly the one I had been eyeing in the catalog. Right size with the stirrups and leathers I'd dog-eared.

Mom always had me write out a wish list, and every year I'd get a couple of things from it. One thing for Hanukkah, one or two for Christmas. Mom had been equal opportunity with the holidays.

The year after she died, I'd made a list. My father hadn't asked and I hadn't gotten anything that was on it. Granted, my top item was having my mom back. Second was a horse of my own. I'd gotten a sweater with a horse embroidered on it, a pink diary with puffy hearts on the cover and a small lock to keep those puffy thoughts secret, and a large stuffed horse.

The sweater and diary were shoved into the closet but the horse stayed on my bed. I guess in a way I did get my own horse.

The following year he'd asked in passing if there was anything special I wanted. I'd shrugged and answered, "Nothing special." The magic of the holiday wish list had been broken.

He'd turned to another holiday elf for help. Hanukkah was forgotten and Christmas had become a minitree already decorated by the florist. Gift ideas were obviously coming from Rena.

Because there's no question R is Rena. Using an initial is either familiar or coy. She'd played it off that they weren't on friendly terms. That I believe. I don't think my father was on friendly terms with many—any?—people.

So that leaves being mysterious as the other option. And that makes no sense.

January 1997

Dear Edward,

Thank you. Your letter couldn't have been better timed. I desperately needed a good laugh. I think you're right about that colleague of yours—the toupee won't solve his dating problems.

Remind me when your next trip is? I'll be looking forward to hearing how he fared.

Yours,

R.

I reread the letter, stopping at the word "laugh." I'd never thought of my father as someone with a sense of humor. He'd always been so dry.

I flip through a few envelopes looking for a postscript shortly after, hoping for the next clue to my father's sense of humor. A stab of hurt pierces my gut. It was supposed to have been me and him. But it never was.

And it never will be.

March 1997

Dear Edward,

For once, I have to disagree with you. Okay, it's not the first time and I'm sure it won't be the last. But I disagree.

March is absolutely the worst month. It's cold and rainy and muddy and gray. I dislike everything about it.

I know April is painful for you and Emma, but for me, it's the most cheerful of months. Even the rain and mud have a more optimistic feel. The world stops smelling moldy and starts smelling like rebirth.

You can disagree with me—although you know I'm always right—but I think you need to find a new, positive spring tradition for you and your daughter. It's time to look forward, my friend.

Yours,

R.

"*My friend.*" More pretense? It makes absolutely no sense that she would hide their friendship from me. Did they think it would upset me? Would it have? The stable was my escape. Would knowing my father had more of a connection have tainted it for me? Maybe not when I was younger, not in those first couple of years. But later, if I'm completely honest with myself, then yes, it probably would have.

June 1993

Dear Edward,

Your last letter broke me to bits. I wish I had the words to make sense of what's happening or the words to help the healing. I don't.

You, my friend, have the words for your patients. But you cannot expect to heal yourself with the same words.

I beg of you to reconsider talking to someone—a therapist maybe? Me?

Yours,
R.

A drop falls on the letter and I swipe at my cheek before any others follow the same trajectory.

That was two months before my mom died. No, before she committed suicide.

He'd known it was coming. He'd seen it coming and he'd shared his pain with someone else. He wouldn't have told me, I was too young, I suppose. It's not like I didn't know something bad was happening. I just didn't know what. I needed him to tell me something, anything. Instead, he chose to talk to someone he barely knew.

The silence in the house during those months had been deafening. She'd looked hollowed out, her body unable to produce more than a whisper, her eyeballs too heavy to see beyond her feet.

For Valentine's Day, I'd made her a ceramic heart paperweight. While other kids in art class made bowls and mugs, I'd molded and remolded my chunk of clay. My mom's heart may not have been perfect but I was determined to give her a perfect one.

She'd smiled and said it was the loveliest gift she'd ever received. When my father arrived home, I ran to show him the perfect new heart I'd made for my mom and now she'd have to get better.

He'd said it didn't work that way.

The words on the letter in front of me blur.

No, Dad, it didn't work that way. My perfect heart couldn't fix her any more than your perfect words did. I guess we both failed.

14

May 1992

Emma clutches her backpack over her head and sprints up the driveway, jumping the puddles and squinting through the rain pelting her face. She'd asked Mom where the umbrella was before leaving for school but Mom had waved her out of the house and said the rain wouldn't dare ruin her plans for the day.

Guess Mom doesn't have as much influence on Mother Nature as she thought.

The back door is unlocked. She keeps telling her mom to lock the door, but her mom keeps forgetting. Father always has the house locked tight when he's home and fusses at her mom, who then reminds him that they no longer live in the big, scary city.

Emma drops her backpack by the door and toes out of her wet tennis shoes, then speed-walks upstairs. Running isn't permitted in the house. Her riding clothes are folded on the desk chair, the bag containing her riding boots propped up next to it. She has the shirt over her head and jeans unbuttoned before she enters her bedroom. She has a riding lesson in an hour and knows Pogo well enough to expect him in a full-body mudpack.

It's been a couple of months since the trail ride with Jilli. They'd laughed and had fun together. They'd almost been friends.

Jillian is at least acknowledging her on the school bus now even though she pretends Emma is invisible at school. But she's been hanging around a bit more when Emma is at the stable. Not exactly friends. Not exactly unfriends.

Emma's dropped trying to be aloof. It wasn't working and she's tired of pretending.

She looks at her desk and the white stationery with the purple horse on it. The beginning of a letter to Kathy stares back at her. The only words she's been able to write are "Why aren't you writing back anymore?"

She crumples the paper. She isn't going to waste time—or precious stationery—on anyone who doesn't want to be her friend. Kathy. Jillian. Whatever. She doesn't need anyone.

Especially now that she has Pogo.

"Mom?"

She stands in the middle of her room, riding breeches pulled up over one leg, and listens. Nothing.

She really doesn't want to go through the woods today, not with the rain, and was counting on her mom to drive her.

"Mom?" Her voice drops to a loud whisper.

For the last few weeks, she's come home to find her mom either in the kitchen baking or in the sunroom reading. Maybe her father had been right about moving here after all. Mom has been spending less time in the bedroom, she's smiling more, engaging more. Even her father seems a bit less starched.

She grabs the brown paddock boots Simon gave her to wear. Jillian had kicked up a fuss, claiming the rich girl's parents should buy her new ones, but then shrugged, flipped her braid across her shoulder, and walked off with a parting, "Whatever."

Emma rubs the scuffed toes of the boots. She'd asked for a new pair as a birthday gift.

Dad had said absolutely not. He was already spending far too much money on this horse nonsense. Her mom had found her sitting on the steps to the backyard, cleaning the hand-me-down boots, her tears mixing with the brown shoe polish.

"Does it really mean that much to you, Em?" She'd sat on the top step, their shoulders and knees touching. Mom fingered the zipper on the boots.

Emma had nodded, the words stoppered under a cotton ball of emotion. Why didn't her parents understand? The horses were her only friends. They didn't judge her, didn't look down on her, didn't look through her.

She'd heard her parents talking that night. It was a week before her birthday. For her birthday she'd gotten a couple of books, a stylish pair of jeans her mom insisted would make her the envy of all the girls—jeans that never left the closet—and a white T-shirt with a pink horse head on it—Emma hated pink. No riding boots.

She glances at the clock and yanks the breeches on. She's going to be late if she doesn't hurry. She stops in front of her parents' bedroom and knocks. There's no answer. "Mom? I have to go. Are you in there?" Still no answer.

She darts down the stairs, sending out a few halfhearted "Moms" into the silent house. She opens the door to the garage. Empty. Had she missed a note? She scans the kitchen on her way out. No note. Now she's really going to be late.

The rain has stopped but the path through the woods is slippery. There's no time to take the longer path to avoid the mud. Emma's boots skate through a mud puddle and she slows to a fast walk. The passing time ticks in her head with each squishy step. With the edge of the woods in sight, she picks up a jog. Her right foot lands on a patch of soggy leaves and she sails forward, landing on her side, her left arm jammed under her body.

A few squirrels chatter their annoyance at her cry, but there's no one around to help. Emma pushes herself up but can't put weight on her left arm. She twists sideways, getting the right side of her breeches as muddy as the left, but finally manages to scramble up.

By the time she reaches the barn, it's fifteen minutes into her lesson time. Simon tells her to hurry. Cleaning and tacking up a pony one-handed turns out to be much harder than she'd imagined.

In true pony fashion, Pogo picks up that his rider isn't in control and takes every opportunity to tug the reins out of her hands.

Every bouncy pony step jars a spear of pain up her side. By the time Simon calls the end of her lesson, Emma can't hold the reins in her left hand. She lets Pogo walk himself to the middle of the ring.

"Hey, what's going on? You certainly aren't on top of your form today?" Simon takes hold of Pogo's bridle and studies her face.

Maybe it's the pain finally catching up or the concern in a grown-up's face, but Emma loses the battle to hold it in. She melts from the pony's back into a crying heap at Simon's feet.

The X-rays confirm a broken wrist.

It's only when the pain medication finally kicks in and the doctor is putting the cast on her arm that Emma notices her mom sitting in the corner of the hospital room, legs crossed in a tight pretzel with the top foot jiggling to a spastic beat. She's wearing a pair of jeans and boots. Emma can't remember ever seeing her mom in jeans. Boots sure, but always high-heeled, fancy boots. These are low heels and have mud on them. Maybe her mom had been gardening. Except, she hadn't been home.

Emma tries to force her brain to cooperate. If Mom hadn't been home, then who had brought her to the hospital? And why does it smell like horses in the hospital?

The only thing she knows for sure is that she really, really wants to sleep.

She hears voices from somewhere far away. Her mom. Now Dad. Mom again. Dad's voice louder, saying it's hardly surprising she got hurt and they should reconsider this riding nonsense. Her mom shushing him. The sound of the door clicking shut.

More voices and the sharp light as someone opens the curtains. Emma groans at the light and rolls away from it, then gasps at the pain from rolling onto her arm. She'd forgotten about that.

"Careful, honey. You're due for a pain pill. Can you sit up?" Her mom steps to the side of the bed, blocking the view of the door. Emma is sure she heard a man's voice. She says a silent plea that it isn't her father, coming to tell her she isn't allowed to ride again.

She takes the pill and water glass from her mom and swallows with a noisy gulp, then allows her mom to fluff the pillow behind her back.

That's when she sees them standing at the door.

"Hey, Toad. You gave me quite a scare yesterday." Simon walks to the side of the bed and sits on the desk chair. Emma giggles at how small and girly it looks under him.

"Your mom said it's a clean break. You'll be good as new and riding again in no time." He pats her shoulder gently. So they're not going to make her stop. She nods, not wanting to release the emotional frog in her throat.

She shoots a quick look at Jillian, hovering behind her grandfather and clearly uncomfortable. Emma scoots up in the bed and motions for Jillian to sit.

Jillian's eyes are locked on the cast as she perches on the edge of the bed. "I've never broken anything. Does it hurt a lot?"

"No." Emma shakes her head, the movement sending a sharp jab down her arm. "Yes." She nods.

"Guess that mud cast you were wearing during your lesson didn't do much." Jillian giggles, then slaps her hand across her mouth and looks from Emma to Simon to Emma's mom.

But the giggle is contagious and soon Emma and Jillian are in tears over the mud Emma had been coated in—more than even Pogo himself had managed—and the giggling only escalates when Simon mentions the wet-horse smell taking over the emergency room.

An hour later, Emma's mom ushers Simon and Jillian out of the room. Jillian bends to pick something up. "Almost forgot, I brought you these. They're my favorite books of all time."

Emma blinks at the book covers through a haze of tears. *Billy and Blaze.* Kathy had gotten one of those books for Christmas and Emma had started reading it during one of their sleepovers, but Kathy hadn't let her borrow it to finish.

"Thank you." Emma clutches the books to her chest with her one good arm.

Jillian lifts the end of her braid up to squint-distance and bounces on the balls of her feet. "Well, I'll stop in tomorrow. If that's okay?"

Emma nods, the tears making it look like Jillian is swaying and suspended in midair.

Alone again, Emma opens the first book. Inside, Jillian has scribbled a note. *Get better soon. Pogo misses you.* And next to "Pogo" she's inserted, as an afterthought, the letters small and angled, *and me.*

15

After coffee and a quick breakfast, I fire up the laptop. Today, I'll choose the lesser of the two evils—Bruce and work over my father and his secrets.

I open an e-mail from Howard with URGENT in all caps in the subject line. Three words in and I'm wishing I'd chosen family secrets.

In three days, Howard has rewritten a brochure that took me two months to write and get approvals on. Since Bruce dictated the changes, he's going with that as approval since it's now a tight print deadline. *No shit.* It wouldn't necessarily be a problem if he'd proofed and fact-checked the damn thing. I've caught four mistakes in a cursory glance at page 1.

My call to Howard lands in voice mail. I'm both annoyed and relieved. I call the printer and leave a message there, too. If it hasn't already gone to press then maybe we can fix the mistakes without a huge expense.

Five hours later, I've responded to the majority of really-truly-need-a-response-today e-mails and left half-a-dozen voice messages. Why isn't anyone calling back?

When I'm down to only a handful of unopened messages, I stand and stretch. From the balcony, I see a handful of people having lunch on the patio. My stomach growls in protest.

"Bruce." I wheel around on my heel and stab at the laptop

keyboard to wake it up. How had I not paid attention until now? In all the e-mails and voice mails, there was not one recent message from Bruce. Not one. This from a man who texts or e-mails or calls at least twenty times an hour.

My insides twist into a knot tight enough to keep a horse from bolting.

I type a quick "just checking in" e-mail and hit Send. And wait.

"Shit." I stare at the nail of my left ring finger, where a drop of blood has appeared. Dammit, I can't start that again.

"Your mother would be appalled, Emma," my father used to scold. But the more stressed or nervous I was, the harder I chewed. Only that finger.

My psych-major roommate in college was fascinated by me and convinced she'd be able to cure my crazy habit. She hadn't. Another friend insisted a manicure was the only way to break me. She'd been almost right. Weekly manicures for most of my professional life ensured that I didn't chew. Until now. *Another reason I need to get back to Chicago as quickly as possible.*

The computer pings with an incoming e-mail. A notice for 20-percent-off water bottles and limited-edition logo towels from the gym.

"Shit," I grumble and hit Delete. No point staring at the screen. Maybe lunch will help distract my nerves.

Two hours later, still nothing from Bruce.

Still nothing from Howard.

Still nothing from the printer.

But I've been invited to a happy hour and last call for getting in on the group baseball ticket purchase.

At 5:30 P.M., I get my answer.

From: Bruce Patchett
Subject: Follow-up to the All-hands Meeting

All—
Thank you for attending the impromptu all-hands meeting today. I appreciate that everyone is busy and taking so much

time from your day puts a strain on deadlines. In the coming days, HR will be meeting with the individuals affected by today's news.

As always, I have an open-door policy and welcome you to stop by if you have questions.

With thanks,
Bruce Patchett
President, NewComm

An all-hands meeting? I scan through my e-mails looking for clues. Nothing. The last time we had a surprise all-hands meeting was three years ago, when the company was sold. The new owners had corporate pinky-promised that they wouldn't be making big changes.

Nothing major. A more casual dress code followed by tighter restrictions on telecommuting. A fancy coffee machine in the kitchen but fewer paid holidays.

Management hadn't called meetings for any of those changes. This feels like a renege on that pinky promise.

My butt hits the chair and I blink at the computer screen.

"Dammit, Bruce, what is this about? And why the hell aren't you responding?"

HR will be meeting with the individuals affected by today's news.

I glare at the phone, willing it to ring, then I hit Bruce's smug face in the contact list and listen as his assistant's voice tells me to leave a message. Apparently Bruce's open-door policy doesn't translate to an open-call policy.

I send a text to Anita. We'd exchanged a couple of quick messages since her *surrender or suffer* e-mail but only about personal matters. She hadn't said a word about what was happening at the office.

Hey, cookie. Be thankful you're not here. Although I wish you were!

At least she answered.

What the heck is going on? Saw the all-hands e-mail. Bruce is AWOL with messages. Fill a girl in?
Give me a few.

I wait a few. Then a few more.

When my phone rings I pounce. But it's a Maryland number, not Anita's face staring at me from the ringing screen.

"Hello?" My voice breaks, an unfortunate combination of not having spoken for much of the day, nerves, and frustration.

"Is this Emma?" a deep male voice pokes my brain for placement.

"Yes."

A sigh of relief. "It's Ben." Then, "Ben Barrett? From the stable?" His voice ends in the uptick of a question mark.

"Yes. Ben." I pull in a deep breath. *Relax, Emma. Don't assume the worst. They're just busy getting ready for the trade show.*

HR will be meeting with the individuals affected by today's news. That's not trade-show prep. That's serious corporate crap that's about to ruin your life.

Ben's voice pulls me out of the panic spiral. "It's a beautiful afternoon and I have a couple of horses that need hacking. Can I tempt you with a ride?"

"Thanks, but I don't ride."

"There are a few pictures around this place that bunk that excuse. Not to mention an old man with quite a few stories."

"What stories?"

"Ah, gotcha. You'll just have to join me for a ride if you want to know."

"I don't ride."

"So you've said. Still not buying it."

"I don't have riding clothes."

He laughs. "Good try. We can find a pair of chaps and boots that will fit you. I know of at least one person in this stable who's your size."

Before I can counter, Ben adds, "Jillian is out of town for a couple of days. Any other excuses you want to try on me?"

"I have a lot of work to do?" We both laugh at the tentative question.

"I'll see you in thirty minutes."

Ben ends the call and I'm left staring at a black screen.

"This can't possibly end well."

I look from the now-silent phone to the all-hands e-mail. Neither "this" will end well.

"I thought you'd enjoy Wally since the two of you seem to have some little thing happening." Ben shakes his head and smiles when the gray horse shoves his forehead into my chest.

A large bay stands in the next tack stall, pawing the rubber matt underfoot. She snorts a reminder to Ben that it's her turn for attention.

"Do you remember how to tack or do you need help?" Ben's eyes twinkle and the right corner of his mouth twitches.

"I think I can figure it out."

"I'm right next door if you run into trouble." The twitch spreads into a full-out smirk and he ducks under the crosstie before my hand can make contact with his upper arm.

"Aren't you supposed to be encouraging your students instead of making fun of them?"

"You're not my student."

"So does that mean I can poke fun at you, too?"

Ben peeks at me from under his horse's neck. "You could. But I wouldn't recommend it."

"Oh really?"

"Really." He waggles his eyebrows at me, then ducks back as the bay snaps at his behind. "Damn horse."

I laugh. "Looks like she's on my side."

Our eyes meet for the fastest of beats before I scoot sideways to hide behind Wally's massive body.

My fingers fumble with the buckles of the bridle before reconnecting with the memories. This had been second nature once upon a life. The sudden insecurity of my fingers is an unwelcome reminder. I close my eyes and breathe in Wally's sweet smell until my fingers regain their composure, tightening the noseband, checking the throatlatch, tucking the ends of each leather strip into its loop.

When I'm finally done, I lean into Wally and bury my nose in his neck. This isn't new. This is the one place I belonged. This is the one place I never doubted myself.

"Here, put these on?" Ben hands me a pair of paddock boots and dark gray leather chaps.

His voice from behind startles me and I step back, heat spreading up my chest. First the flirting, now I'm smelling his horse. What he must think of me.

Wally and I follow Ben and Lulu out the side door and across the back parking lot to the path leading to the jumping ring. Ben motions me to the mounting block, then holds Wally's bridle while I climb the three steps. I'm painfully conscious of the tight leather chaps binding my thighs and calves. Even from the top step, I have to bend my left leg higher than it's been lifted in quite some time. I curse my lack of stretching and the tight chaps and hope Ben doesn't notice how awkward I look. Or what the chaps must be revealing of my behind, which, despite hours on the spin bike and in kickboxing, is no longer the size and shape it was the last time it poked out of chaps.

Lulu bites at the crop in Ben's hand, distracting him long enough for me to hoist myself into the saddle. I say a silent thank-you to the grumpy bay mare.

I get into half-seat, lifting my butt slightly out of the saddle and letting my weight drop into my heels. My thighs and calves mold to the shape of the horse. A quiver of energy radiates through Wally into my legs.

Oh my god, it feels good to be on a horse. A small moan of pleasure rumbles up my vocal cords and I muffle the sound with a cough.

Ben mounts with a few choice words for his mount, who has spread her hind legs and is rocking side to side.

"What the hell is she doing?" I laugh.

"The flaming bitch has learned all sorts of tricks for intimidating her owner. Which is why I'm being paid a small fortune to ride this beast. She does this stunt to freak Dawn out, who is convinced the mare will collapse and they'll both have to be shot for broken limbs. Tempting."

He grins. "Last time she was out for a lesson, Lulu dumped her, ass-up, at the end of the diagonal."

He looks up from adjusting the girth and moves his foot before the mare can bite the toe of his boot. "The drill was to canter the diagonal and switch leads at the end. She does her flying changes but likes to play dumb. I wanted Dawn to use the wall to ask for it. She asked. Lulu here skidded to a stop, nose in the wall. Ugly pony stunt plus unbalanced rider equals face-plant in the dirt."

"Ouch."

"Only her ego. It was a slow-motion dive."

"Still."

"Yeah. Well. She's actually a stunning mover under the right rider. She just doesn't get along with her owner."

We nudge our horses forward, side by side down the path until we enter the large jump ring.

"I thought you'd want to warm up a bit in the ring, get the feel for a horse under you again, and then we can head into the woods."

"Good plan." I swallow a large knot of anxiety.

For the next twenty minutes we walk, trot, and canter around the ring. Even after all the years away, my mind clicks into autopilot and I urge Wally through a typical warm-up. Sadly, my body doesn't have the same sharp memory and I fight my hands and legs into what I hope looks like semi-proper position. My inner thighs are starting to burn and I feel a raw patch beginning to rub where the seam of my jeans is trapped between the chaps and the saddle.

I give Wally a loose rein and pat his neck. Ben and Lulu fall into step beside us and the two horses snort their complaints.

"Not bad for someone who hasn't been on a horse in ten years."

"Sixteen," I mutter and resist adding that it feels like much longer.

"You haven't forgotten much."

"Tell that to my muscles. Nothing works the way it should."

Ben chuckles. "You can't expect to get on a horse after that long and have it be perfect."

I shrug.

"You don't know how to do something if it's not perfect, do you?"

Another shrug. He's right, of course. And that makes me more uncomfortable than the chaps biting into my thighs.

If I was perfect, I'd be in the office right now. I'd know what the all-hands meeting was about. I'd be making damn sure I wasn't on that list HR would be contacting.

If I was perfect, I would have had a closer relationship with my father.

Ben leads the way from the ring. "Come on, time to relax a bit."

I wonder if he means me or the horses. Both, most likely.

The horses stretch their necks and settle into a steady, comfortable walk. My body sways with the motion of Wally's long stride, the movement familiar, soothing.

The path winds away from the barn, across the field, around a pond, and into the woods. How many times had I ridden this very trail? I look to the right, where wood planks create a jump between the two properties.

We'd canter through the field, break into a trot through this patch of woods, then take the path to the right, over the jump and canter up the hill. Jack hated that coop. Every time we'd break into the woods, he'd arch his neck and snort a warning to the boogieman he was convinced resided in the woods. But he never spooked and never refused.

"That coop scares the crap out of me."

I look to my left, surprised to find Ben next to me.

"I always loved it. There's such a feeling of freedom coming out of the dark of the woods, pushing the horse forward for the last two strides, and flying into the open field."

"Simon said you lacked the fear gene."

"I wish that were true."

"What are you afraid of, Emma Metz?"

"Making the wrong decision." The words come out without my realizing they were there. They fall, heavy and out of place among the swishing of the leaves and the delicate trill of the birds around us.

"You don't seem the type to make bad decisions. Or doubt yourself."

"It's all an illusion. Years of perfecting the Edward Metz approach to success."

"That's your dad?"

"Was."

Ben nods but I'm not sure if it's in acknowledgment or an understanding of what I didn't say.

We arrive at a fork, and Ben turns Lulu to the left. I don't recognize the path but both horses continue quietly and I manage to relax under the playful light of the sun playing peek-a-boo through the leaves.

"Where does this trail go?"

"It's the long way back." Ben grins at me.

Instinctively I glance at my watch and Ben barks a laugh.

"Were you always this uptight? Or is that what being in the corporate world does to you?"

I bristle despite the easy lilt of his voice and wide smile. "I'm not uptight." His smile broadens and I add a grumbled, "Okay, maybe a little."

"Oh relax. You're stressing the Wall-man."

He's right. Wally's head has come up and his strides have gotten bouncier. I take three long, steady breaths and wiggle my fingers to release the tension. I focus on the dappled light and silently count the four beats of the walk, allowing my body to sync with the sway of Wally's body.

The horses scramble up a dry riverbank and I'm surprised when the barn appears ahead of us.

"I can't believe we're back already."

Ben pulls Lulu to a stop and hops off. I reach down to pat Wally's neck, delaying the moment I have to dismount.

"We were out for over two hours."

"Seriously?" I practically give myself whiplash looking at my watch. When was the last time that happened?

At the yarn barn a few days ago.

Maybe Emmitsville has something going for it after all.

Sure it does. Horses and heartbreak.

16

November 1992

"Hey Ems, you're coming for Thanksgiving dinner, right?"

"I don't know," she mumbles into Pogo's side, pushing her shoulder into him so he lifts his leg. Picking hooves is one job she hates.

"Why?" Jillian is now standing behind her.

"You know my father, he's not big on tradition. And Mom hasn't been feeling well."

"Even more reason to come, then she doesn't have to cook. I'll tell Grandma to talk to her."

"I don't know." She doesn't bother to tell Jilli that her mom doesn't cook anyway. Holiday meals come from the gourmet market in town.

Her mom has been more encouraging of her time at the barn since Simon and Jillian came after she broke her arm. She thinks it's sweet that Emma is making friends. Even her father has been less grumpy about her boots in the entry or the pages and pages of horse doodles on the legal notepads from his office. He's even complimented one of her drawings. She immediately tacked that one on the wall in her bedroom.

"Don't you two have homework?" Simon's voice carries down the barn aisle.

"Yes, Grandpa. We're almost done," Jilli hollers back and grins at Emma. "We should get going before he sends Grandma after us."

They get the winter blankets onto the horses and sneak an extra flake of hay into each stall. Huddled together under a fleece cooler that had been hanging on Pogo's stall door, they trudge through the slush left over from the previous night's surprise snow.

"Do you want hot cocoa?" Jilli asks the moment they're inside the house. She pulls two mugs from the cabinet without waiting for Emma to respond.

"Okay, thanks." Emma pulls school books and homework from her backpack and arranges them on the kitchen table. She feels the prickle of being watched. She turns, self-conscious. "What?"

"Nothing. Why?" Jillian hands her a mug of cocoa with tiny marshmallows bobbing in it.

"You were staring."

"I was not. Okay, I was."

"So? What?"

"Why don't you ever want your parents here?"

Emma pokes at a marshmallow, then sticks her finger in her mouth. It's not that she doesn't want them here. She does. Except she kinda likes that this place is hers without their interfering. "I don't know."

"Yes you do."

Emma blows on her mug, sending the mini white lumps scattering. "I did, do, want them to come. Sometimes. But now, I don't know. It's just that my family isn't like yours. They don't fit here. And I like fitting in here. I guess I sorta feel like I wouldn't anymore if they were around."

"That's stupid. Your parents aren't you, you know. Jeez, if that was the case, I'd be a goner." She rolls her eyes dramatically and launches into a chair at the kitchen table.

"Your family is perfect." Emma sits in front of her stacks and repositions a couple of books that Jilli bumped during her descent.

Jilli laughs. But to Emma, it sounds fake. She's heard that laugh before but usually from adults who want you to think they find something funny but really don't.

Emma takes a verbal tiptoe into a topic that's been mostly off-limits with Jilli. She feels bolder since Jilli started the discussion. "Will your mom be here for Thanksgiving?"

Jilli gulps her cocoa with loud swallows and fishes out a last stubborn marshmallow. "Nah, not after the fight she had with Grandma last time she was home."

Jilli takes both mugs and puts them in the sink. She returns to the table and grabs her school bag. Out come books, pencils, composition notebooks, and random loose-leaf pages. From inside one of the black-and-white composition notebooks she removes an orange envelope and hands it to Emma. "Read."

Emma slips out a card with a puppy wearing heart-shaped sunglasses on the front and, barely holding on to the edges, lets it fall open. She's pretty sure she doesn't want to read it but she's dying to know what's inside. She's only seen Jillian's mom a couple of times and no one talks about her when she's not here.

My dear Jilli,
Isn't that puppy adorable? I wish I could send you a real one in-stead. I wish I could be with you for the holidays but I've got a great new gig that's going to make enough cash that I'll be able to send for you. Think about it—winter break on the beach. Just you and me, kiddo. Won't that be awesome?
Be good for your grandparents and don't believe everything you hear about me.
You're my babydoll!!!

Love,
Mom

Emma chews the inside of her lip as she tries to make sense of the note. She's not much closer to really understanding the inner workings of Jilli's family but she's oddly comforted to know she doesn't have the only screwed-up family. She slips the card back into the envelope and hands it to Jillian. She tries to think of what to say, what to ask, but all she can come up with is, "The beach would be so amazing. You're lucky."

It takes a couple of long minutes before Jilli answers. Emma is sure she's messed everything up and they won't be invited to Thanksgiving now.

"There won't be a beach trip. There never is. She always has some brilliant plan but none ever work out. More likely, Grandpa will end up flying to wherever she is to bail her out."

"Does that happen a lot?"

"Yup." Jilli stiffens and shoves the card into her backpack. "We have homework. Grandma will be PO'ed if she comes home and we're not done."

"At least she cares, Jilli. My parents only pay attention when report cards come home."

They're quiet for a while, except for papers rustling and pencils tapping the table. They both look up when Simon walks into the kitchen, bringing with him a gust of cold air through the back door.

"It's bloody cold out there. I'll drive you home when you're ready, Toad. Too cold for you to walk." He stamps his feet on the inside mat, sending mud and snow spattering across the floor.

The muddy pattern mesmerizes Emma. Simon takes a large step to avoid a newly formed puddle, then with one foot he pushes a towel that's been sitting on the floor by the door. Emma pictures herself walking into her own house and doing that. Nope. Boots would be removed before entering. And there would never be a towel left like that on the floor.

She closes her writing notebook and files it under Math and Spelling, then takes her social-science notebook and slips it into place ahead of Spelling.

Jilli laughs, a real one this time. "You're such a goon."

"Hey." Emma laughs and flicks Jilli's notebook shut. "You could learn a few things from me about being organized."

"And you could learn a few things from me about being

spontaneous." They toss a discarded assignment-turned-ball at each other.

"Spontaneous." The word sounds exotic in Simon's accent. "Big word, Skinny Breeches." A large hand reaches between them and plucks the crumpled paper ball in midflight.

"It's the word of the day on my calendar. Give me a break." Jilli pulls a pout that sends both girls into giggles.

Simon shakes his head, his smile growing with each sideways pass. "I'm going to warm up the truck. Don't be long."

"I'll talk to my parents about Thanksgiving. It would be nice to spend it here with you." Emma tucks her head into the scarf she's been wrapping and rewrapping around her neck. She hopes Jilli doesn't notice the flush of her cheeks. Even though they've been friends for seven months, since Emma's broken arm, she still feels shy.

Their friendship is different from the one she had with Kathy, who hasn't written since the get-better-soon card that she'd only signed, not one additional word of encouragement or friendship in her flowery handwriting. Her friendship with Jilli feels more grown-up.

"Come on, I'm going with." Jilli hops to her side, shoving her arms into one of Rena's coats at the same time. She looks like a kangaroo. "Hey, Ems, I'm glad you moved next door. You're the sister I always wished I had."

Emma feels warm inside her winter coat and scarf. Warm and happy. "I'm glad we moved next door, too."

Jilli sticks her pinky out and wraps it around Emma's. "Horse-and-heart sisters. Way better than blood relatives. We'll never hurt each other."

17

I wake to the cheerful chirping outside my window. Damn birds are up too early. They don't get up this early in Chicago.

I hug a pillow to my chest and will the dream to return. Five more minutes of fantasizing about Wally and Ben. No, Wally. I'm not fantasizing about Ben. Well, maybe a little. But only about riding with him.

Last night after cooling the horses off, Ben invited me to stay and eat with him. Nothing fancy, he'd said. Not a date, he'd insisted.

The "nothing fancy" had turned out to be chips, a bowl of homemade guacamole, and a couple of cold Dos Equis.

The "not a date" turned into a fun evening discussing horses. I've been telling myself I didn't miss that world, that I didn't need it. It's all been a lie. I did miss it. It felt so easy being there. Not to mention being around someone who wasn't expecting anything from me. I didn't have to be perfect. Didn't have to measure every word. Didn't even have to wonder if we'd end up in bed.

Not that ending up in bed with him would be a bad thing under different circumstances.

I stretch and wince. No, no need to worry about the awkward morning after. Only a sore one.

For someone who tackles spin classes like a rabid hamster,

I'm amazed at how cranky my muscles are this morning. Then again, a spin bike isn't shaped like a barrel.

Maybe Ben's right: I do need to start riding again. I'm sure I can find a good stable back home.

In the meantime, I have a few more days here. I could probably fit in another ride or two. Maybe even a lesson. I squeeze my eyes shut while my toes flex and curl in an imaginary canter. It would be pretty amazing to jump again.

Except that's not why I'm here. I groan and flop back into the softness of the bed.

T.J. hasn't contacted me yet about the condo. Radio silence from Thomas about signing the rest of the legal papers. Those are the reasons I'm in Emmitsville.

At the office I'm the deadline queen. When there's a project to complete, I'm the one who pushes all the boulders to the finish line. I even followed our corporate lawyer into the men's room once to get his sign-off on a press release.

I don't sit around and wait. So why am I waiting now?

I sit up and reach for my phone. I call Thomas Adler and get his voice mail. Same result with T.J. The clock on the bedside table reminds me that it's not even 8 A.M. yet. That's no excuse. Okay, maybe a small one.

I fire up the laptop and scan through my inbox. After the diarrhea of urgent messages the first couple of days, we've gone to hard-core e-mail constipation.

Nothing from Bruce or Howard. Even Anita has disappeared into the black hole of in-the-know.

And I am clearly out-of-the-know.

How the hell did I let that happen?

I grab the notepad with the to-do list I'd started. Underneath it is my father's drawing pad. Like a suicidal moth, I open the notebook and turn the pages, my fingers barely grazing the paper. Though most of the faces he drew are strangers', there's something familiar in each one.

I scribble a note to call his office at a more worker-friendly hour. His office manager may be able to shed some light on whether these people were clients.

The intricacy of his sketches makes the faces come alive. Some look at me, others past me. Some have a secret they can't wait to share, others implore me to turn the page and leave them alone.

"Why didn't you draw me? Or Mom?" I hover at one drawing, the face more familiar than the others.

The computer beeps with a meeting reminder. The weekly senior-leadership staff meeting. I dial the standing conference-call number. An automated voice tells me that the number has been changed. I text Bruce and fight down a growing sense of unease as the seconds tick by without a response. When I can't hold my breath any longer, I call Sue, Bruce's assistant.

"Hi, Emma," she greets me after the second ring.

"Hey, Sue. I can't dial in to the staff call. Can you please transfer me in?"

Through the distance of several states, I hear her muffled response to someone in the office. I should be there. Not here. I should be the one standing in front of her desk. Not breathing into a cell phone waiting for a response.

"I'm sorry, Emma. It's a closed meeting this time. You're back next week though, right?"

"Yes. But come on, Sue, you know this is torture for me."

She mumbles a thank-you to someone.

"Sue?"

"Yes, sorry. It's just really busy right now."

I pinch the bridge of my nose. I should be in that blender of activity. "I gathered that. What was with the all-hands meeting?"

"I really can't get into that right now. I need to go, Emma. We'll see you on Monday."

"I can't wait until Monday. I'll lose my mind by then."

She chuckles but it's tight and humorless. "Put that angst toward that lawyer of your dad's."

"Can you just tell me if it's bad news?"

The hesitation sends the caterpillars in my stomach on a

stampede and I slap my hand over my mouth to stop the sudden urge to wretch.

"It's going to work out, Emma. Right now, you need to focus on yourself. You've had a huge loss and you need this time to heal. We'll see you on Monday."

She doesn't give me the chance to argue that I need to focus on work, not healing. The line goes silent and I'm left with the echo of her words: *It's going to work out.*

The barn appears deserted when I arrive. But there are a few cars in the parking lot and at least one wash stall has evidence of recent use.

I walk down the aisle and peek into the stalls standing open. Sawdust bedding evenly spread, fluffy and inviting. A single flake of hay, loosened just enough for easy munching. Brass nameplates nailed on the sliding doors gleam in the soft light of the barn.

At the end of the aisle is the indoor arena. A course of jumps is set up and sprays of light filter through the high windows, creating spotlights on a few of the obstacles. I step off the padded aisle and sink into the soft footing. My eyes trace a line from jump to jump, around the end of the ring, back across the diagonal line, along the left edge of the arena, to the opposite diagonal.

"You're counting strides." Simon comes to stand next to me. His accent thicker, the timbre of his voice older. The left side of his mouth pulls into a lopsided smile. "I know you. You're counting."

I turn back to look at the course again, hoping the unreliable light will mask my flush of embarrassment. I was counting.

"You used to do that all the time. Visualize a line and count the strides. Just little puffs of noise. Used to drive Jilli nuts." He chuckles at a memory that's lost to me.

"She'd just wing it. But not you. Always careful, always precise. You have a gift for seeing the perfect distance. Do you remember the time she convinced you to go look at the litter of puppies instead of studying the course?"

When I don't respond, he continues. "You met the Swedish oxer coming off the right bend at an awkward distance and jumped it long. Jack caught the back rail. It wasn't the prettiest of efforts. You came out of the ring stoic."

"I remember."

I push a clump of dirt with the toe of my sneaker.

With Simon's arm around my shoulder, I'd stayed for the ribbons. A rare fourth-place finish for us. I accepted the ribbon and congratulated the others.

I'd smiled the best I knew how and silently thanked the gods that my father hadn't decided to make one of his rare appearances. By the time I got back to Jack's stall, the tears were leaking and my breath was catching. I hugged Jack, blubbering my apologies. I'd let him down and still he'd taken care of me. Any other horse would have dumped my ass. But not Jack Flash.

Simon had threatened to pull me from the rest of the classes if I didn't give myself a break. I promised.

And while Jilli played with puppies, I studied the courses. We came in first in every class the rest of the day.

"Ben accused me of needing to be perfect last night, too."

I can feel Simon shifting next to me and feel his eyes on me.

I turn and stare him down. "I'm not twelve. That look doesn't work on me anymore."

"I don't have the foggiest idea what you're referring to." His accent deepens and the smile broadens.

I scrunch my forehead trying to match *the look*.

The lines around Simon's mouth tug down and there's the smirk that used to send Jillian into fits. "You don't have the spit for that look, little girl. I spoke to Ben this morning. He said you did brilliantly."

A raspy laugh vibrates up my throat. "'Brilliant' isn't the word I would use for how I rode."

"You never did. Even when you were."

"Yeah, well, there's always room for improvement."

"True."

A thick quiet settles between us. I toe a half circle in the arena footing. A horse nickers in the distance and is answered by the bleating of a goat.

"You have goats?"

"Only one. That would be Jukebox. He's Jack's buddy. They're out in paddock two if you want to say hi."

"What happened to Soldier?"

"We lost him a few years ago. Jack was beside himself."

"Poor Jack."

"Yeah, not easy losing your best friend."

I sweep my foot in the opposite direction, erasing the half circle.

"We adopted Jukebox and an off-the-track Thoroughbred several weeks before and had them in the paddock with Jack and Soldier. Juke took it upon himself to console the big guy and they've been inseparable ever since. When Rena uses Jack in the therapeutic program, Juke insists on being there."

"Aww."

"Not so 'aww' when he head-butts you. He's very protective of Jack. Doesn't like strangers coming around him."

"I'm glad Jack has another friend. Not everyone is lucky to find that kind of friendship once, much less twice."

"Who's your Jukebox, Emma?"

I shake my head. "No one."

"It's important to have someone you can count on."

"I thought so, once."

Boots clomp behind us, scattering the discussion.

"Scuze me, boss? You want I water the ring?"

"Yes, please. Tony, have you met Emma? She's an old friend. Used to ride here when she was younger."

"Hello, Ms. Emma." Tony ducks his head in an abbreviated bow.

"Hi, Tony." I smile at his attempt at formality.

"We'll get out of your way." Simon turns and puts a hand on my back, guiding me forward.

We walk through the barn, the sound of sprinklers kicking

on with a hiss and whine of pipes behind us. I squint as we step into the light and adjust my stride to match Simon's. The morning sun darts behind a dark cloud.

"Ben said you turned over management of the stable to Jillian. Why?"

Simon pulls in a wheeze of air, his step faltering. "She needed the responsibility."

I chance a sideways look to gauge his expression. It doesn't reveal much.

"And I needed to get rid of some responsibility."

"Why?"

"You may not have noticed, but I'm not as young as I used to be." He winks but there's no humor in his eyes.

"This stable has always been your love."

"It still is. But I love my human family more."

Did I imagine the catch in his voice? He nods in the direction of the paddock, deflecting attention away from him. Jack and Jukebox walk to the fence. Jack's large head hangs over the top rail while Juke angles his pointy chin through the middle and flaps his lips at me.

"Are you still teaching at least?" I know the answer from my conversation with Ben but I want to hear it from Simon.

He pats the black horse's neck and receives a friendly nudge in response. "Not much."

"That's a shame. You were the best riding teacher I ever had."

"Considering the only other person who taught you was Rena, that's not a tough contest."

"Good point." I laugh, then look around to make sure Rena hasn't magically appeared.

Juke's busy lips make contact with the hem of my shirt and he tugs, yanking me into the fence.

"Hey." I tap his muzzle, which only makes him pull harder. Jack snorts and nips at his buddy's rump. That works. Horse and goat bump muzzles. "Is that the four-hoofed equivalent of a fist bump? 'Well done, dude. Another notch in the ripped-shirt contest for you.'" I smooth out the hem of my shirt.

"He's the best friend that would get you tossed out of school." Simon shakes his head but can't disguise the note of tenderness in his voice.

Now that my shirt is no longer a buffet item, I turn back to prodding Simon. "How's business?"

"It's pretty steady. Boarders come and go. Some old-time clients left when I handed over the reins to Jillian. She runs things differently than I did. Ben has brought in new clients. He's also taking on some of my lessons, although he grumbles about the beginning flat ones." Simon releases a long sigh. "I've retired from managing the barn but I still seem to be in charge when it comes to people. Jillian hasn't mastered that yet."

"Don't think she ever will."

"No."

Surprised by the weight of that one word, I turn to look at Simon. "What did you mean about her needing the responsibility?"

"Jilli made a lot of bad decisions. Her mom wasn't a great role model, you know. Rena and I tried, but she wouldn't hear anything we had to say. She was convinced that we'd turned against her. Somewhere along the way, she'd gotten it into her head that we were favoring you, overcompensating for your family situation. Rena blamed herself for that, too."

He looks at the line of trees at the edge of the far pasture as though the past is hiding in there. "After the accident she got worse." He falters, rubs the back of his neck. "She barely finished high school. She'd cut school at least once a week. Stopped riding entirely. She even ran away a couple of times. Bloody hell, she put us through the ringer. And she'd be spitting furious that I'm telling you this."

My hand cups Jack's muzzle and he leans in. The weight of his head straightens my arms and I lean forward until my chest is resting on his forehead.

"She came back about eight years ago."

"Back?" He'd said she ran off a couple of times but the idea that Jillian had actually left Jumping Frog Farm catches me off-center. I never pictured her away from here.

He nods, undeterred by the surprise in my voice. "She left right after graduation. Not that she went to the ceremony. It wasn't obvious she would even graduate until the last minute. The day her diploma arrived in the mail, she stuffed a few items into a duffel bag and left. For the first years we barely heard from her. An occasional phone call when she needed money. It nearly killed Rena.

"Then she started sending postcards. She'd gotten herself to Wyoming and was working on a dude ranch, taking care of horses and guiding trail rides. That was the longest she lasted in a job. I think she was there almost two years before she messed it up as well. It was her boss who called us. Said he wouldn't press charges if she got help. He had a soft spot for her because of the work she'd done with his horses. I flew there and dragged her home. Rena had her hands full keeping that girl straight. But I think that second close call scared her enough that she started making an effort to get better. Taking on the responsibility of the farm seems to be helping."

Second close call? I try to read his face. It's not the open invitation that I remember and the question tickling my tongue gets shy and retreats.

"It was always our dream to run Jumping Frog Farm."

"You were the dreamer, Toad. You had plans for the future. You were the one with the heart for this place." He looks at the paddocks and the horses, then turns to the barn. "Rena and I didn't do a bang-up job raising her. I was too soft on her, wanting to ease the sting of her screw-up mum. I felt guilty about having failed her, having failed them both. And Rena, she dealt with her guilt by riding Jillian even harder. She was determined to make Jilli a success. The last thing Jilli wanted was success based on how we defined it."

I draw in a long breath of horse mixed with earth and grass and the promise of rain. I rewind long-archived memories of dreams and daydreams shared. There was never a doubt in my mind about the future. "*I'm going to be an Olympic show jumper and run the stable with my best friend.*"

Jilli had parroted my declaration. Memories blur over the years, becoming what we want them to be. Maybe Simon is right, maybe that had only been my dream.

Sure, she flipped through fashion magazines and swooned over the pictures of models in fancy couture clothes. When I'd pointed out how impractical those clothes were for someone running a stable, she'd huffed about designing a line of riding clothes so I'd shut up.

"I'd trade with her in a heartbeat." The words rush out, unbidden, unwelcome.

"Why? You've made a life for yourself in the corporate world. Oh don't look so surprised. I know you talked to Rena and she admitted to being in touch with your father."

"He told you?"

"He said you settled into a successful career."

"I guess."

"You guess?" It's his turn to sound surprised.

"Depends on what you consider successful."

"I always defined it as fulfillment. You?"

"Status. Title. Money."

Simon studies me and I wait for the lecture that there's more to life than status, title, and money. He nods instead.

Jack blows a warm horsey breath onto my neck, his muzzle tickling the exposed skin where my shirt has stretched.

Simon smiles. "You don't get that kind of love in the corporate world."

"If you do, chances are you'll end up in court over it."

Simon lets out a deep, growling laugh. "I've missed you, Toad. It's nice to have you back."

I open my mouth to say I'm not really back, not for good at least, but instead I say I missed him, too. That's the heartbreaking truth I've refused to voice.

With a last loud pat on Jack's neck, Simon steps away from the fence. "I need to get back. Stay out here for a bit. I think you guys have some catching up to do. When you're done, can you bring him in?"

"Sure."

"Be careful when you open the gate. That thing," Simon points a finger at the goat, "will shoot out like a hairy cannonball."

Jukebox lets out an offended bleat. Or maybe it's a proud one. I never was well versed in goat speak.

I watch Simon walk away. His steps are slower than they were sixteen years ago, his body less commanding.

I turn back to Jack, standing quietly by the fence while Jukebox bounds around him. The hollow spots above his eyes seem deeper and the hairs around his eyes show the telltale gray of age.

The air catches in my lungs.

For sixteen years, the horses, the people, the physical property of Jumping Frog Farm have stayed protected in the cocoon of my memories. Now here, those years pass by my eyes like time-lapse photography.

The barn has aged, faded, boards on paddock fencing have warped next to crisp replacement boards.

The time has imposed changes on Simon, Rena, and Jillian. I have the sinking feeling Jillian is the least changed. And not for the better.

18

The condo seems to suck in a breath when I open the door, as though unsure of the intruder. It's only been a couple of days since I was here with T.J., but, true to her word, she already has several potential buyers lined up.

I scan the condo, then look down at the detailed task list she e-mailed this morning and back at the magazine-spread layout in front of me. Obviously, T.J. saw room for improvement.

I glance at my watch. Two hours before she comes to inspect. I should have come sooner. My father's place is so perfect that I didn't imagine there would be more than a few pillows to fluff. But nooooo, I had to frolic with sheep and horses and an uptight goat.

Now that I'm here, the list looks daunting. The living room has the fewest to-do tasks and personal items, which makes it the perfect place to start. I shake my head at items one and two but do them anyway. She may be petite and young but T.J. scares me. I won't risk crossing her.

I straighten the cushions and rearrange the throw pillows, the white ones on either side of the cushion line and the teal one angled in the center. On the coffee table, I reorder the three glossy photography books, *Wonders of the Sea* at the bottom, *Frank Lloyd Wright's Fallingwater* second, and *The Splendor of DC* on top.

Yes, T.J.'s notes are that specific.

There are no family photographs, no knickknacks, zero personal effects in this room. No afghan to tuck under your feet while reading or watching TV. There isn't even a TV.

We had one TV when I was growing up. Mom spent a lot of time curled up on the couch staring at images as they blurred from show to show. I'm not sure she really watched anything though.

After Mom died, he donated it along with her clothes.

When I got my apartment after college, my first purchase was a TV.

I move to the kitchen and open the refrigerator, careful not to leave finger smudges on the gleaming stainless door. It is completely empty.

I open drawer after drawer and neaten the contents. The junk drawer holds two extension cords, a pair of scissors, and four take-out menus. So different from my drawer at home where I stuff anything I don't know what to do with or think I may need tomorrow or in the next decade.

T.J.'s list instructs me to domino the silverware, turn all mug handles to the left, and reorder the pots and pans by size.

I'd love a peek at her house. Do people actually do that in real life or is this just a staging trick? You certainly won't find an organized silverware drawer in my place.

I pull open the silverware drawer. The condo gasps as the air-conditioning kicks in. I yank my hand back. The intimacy of eating jolts through my limbs, paralyzing me. It's something we all do, something we don't think about when we do it. We use silverware touched by others in restaurants, when eating at a friend's house, even in our own homes. And yet looking at a dead man's forks and spoons seems like an invasion.

Not just any dead man. My father.

I spin around and walk out of the kitchen. Three rooms remain: bedroom, bathroom, and office. The three most uncomfortable rooms.

T.J.'s instructions yell from the paper. Toss everything out of the medicine cabinet. Toss all bottles from the shower. Toss any personal-hygiene items from the linen closet. Replace the soap by the sink with an unused bar. Refold all towels in the linen closet and hang the large green-and-blue-striped towel on the rack. Not just any towel.

I open the medicine cabinet and position the trash bag underneath. Three sweeps and the shelves are empty. The bag sags with the weight. I don't look. I reach into the shower and sweep the bottles into the trash bag. The bag stretches and I grab it lower, desperate to avoid a tear.

The linen closet is mercifully generic. Three towels, precisely folded; one salon special bottle of shampoo and its partner conditioner; one sealed toothbrush. I breathe in the fresh smell of the handmade mint-oatmeal soap.

Mom used to buy lavender soap. She'd said it reminded her of their honeymoon in France. Every few months a shipment would arrive, carefully packed, personally addressed by a shop owner that Mom had befriended during that trip.

After she died, the shipments stopped. Every lavender soap disappeared, replaced with mint-oatmeal bars.

I replace the used soap in the clear-crystal dish, then remove the striped towel from the top shelf and center it on the hanging rack.

How had T.J. caught so many nuances during one quick sweep?

A meeting-reminder chimes in my pocket. I silence the alarm on my phone. I have forty-five minutes. How did three rooms with almost nothing personal in them take me over an hour? On the bright side, that doesn't leave much time to overthink the last two rooms.

I ignore the ghost standing in the entrance to the office and walk across the condo to the bedroom.

There's no hesitation about where to start. I go straight for the photograph on the dresser.

The photographer had been standing behind Mom but enough to the side to catch her profile. Her hair cascades over her right shoulder, a ripple that could have been caused by movement or a breeze or my imagination.

I move my head, a slight toss to the right, conscious of the feeling of hair falling over my shoulder. *Is that what it felt like, Mom?*

I mimic the expression on her face. *Were you smiling or saying something?*

I raise my hand, a mirror of the wave from the young me. *How far would I have gone before you'd come after me?*

I pick up the frame and tilt it into the light coming from the window. A ray skids across the grass, hiding my mom from prying eyes. A slight movement of my wrist, and she's back. If only.

I stare at the picture, my vision blurring with focus. But unlike those images that reveal a hidden picture the longer you study them, this one only reveals more questions.

"Where were you taken? Why don't I remember?"

We didn't take vacations.

My father went on business trips. Mom and I stayed home.

My father traveled all over the world. Mom and I went to Upstate New York. Once.

I slip the photograph out of the frame and flip it over, half hoping to find a note, half hoping to find nothing more than shiny white paper.

No date, no location, no clue.

"Helloooooo," a sharp soprano vibrates through the condo. "Emma? The concierge said you were here. Hellooooo?"

"In here."

It takes sixteen stiletto clicks for T.J. to arrive in the bedroom.

"I saw the trash bag by the door. You're making progress. That's fabulous. How's it going in here?"

I replace the photograph in the frame and slip it into my bag.

She doesn't wait for an answer but pulls open the top drawer of the dresser. My father's socks, underwear, and belts are neatly placed, each grouping taking up exactly a third of the drawer. I wince and turn away.

"I'm sorry, Emma. I'm sure this must be very hard on you. I'll take care of this if you'd like."

I nod, not trusting my voice.

With T.J. in charge of the bedroom, I retrace my steps to my father's home office.

Bookcase by bookcase, I follow the directions on the piece of paper. On the last shelf is a brown leather box wedged between medical textbooks. I pull it out and flip the lid, expecting his collection of fountain pens. It's not pens.

For a moment I'm paralyzed. Inside the box are more letters. Years of letters. Who was this man who was sentimental about letters with a virtual stranger? A bubble of rage floats in my vision. He cared this much about his correspondence with Rena and she all but lied about it.

A phone chirps on the other side of the condo.

I empty the contents into my bag and replace the box between the books.

The desk chair swivels when I bump into it and an arm of the folded sweater flops loose. I lift it to refold. My fingers close around the soft fabric, bunching it in my fist. Like a crushed mint leaf, the sweater releases a hint of my father's cologne.

I pull the sleeve to my nose and inhale. He could have just pulled it off and left the room to make a cup of coffee.

Dammit, it wasn't supposed to happen this way.

We may not have been close, we may not have even liked each other, but you were all I had left.

I wanted you to be proud of me.

I wanted you to love me.

Because I loved you.

I take one last inhale of my father. It's time to say good-bye.

The first potential buyer is due to arrive any minute. I survey the room one last time. This room is my father. This is where his passion was. Most of my memories of him are of him in his home office. I wish I could have seen him in this one.

Were you happy in here, Dad? Were you able to be yourself in this room?

I swallow the emotion. He'd expect that from me.

"Emma, do you need help with the boxes?" T.J.'s sharp clicks are a harsh reminder that I'll never know.

As an afterthought, I grab the sweater from the back of his chair and stuff it into the bag with the letters.

That's when I notice a charcoal-gray linen spine tucked between two medical reference books on his desk. Another sketch pad. I slide it into my bag, one more thing to discover about my father.

After leaving the condo, I spend two hours at the bank going over paperwork to close out my father's accounts. By the time I pull into the Mountain Inn parking lot, all emotional energy has been syphoned out of me.

Lucy takes one look and sends me to the porch with a glass of wine and a plate of cheese and fruit.

The sun sinks, its orange glow melting into the hills. Evening sounds take over the woods in the distance.

Tiger cat saunters along the edge of the patio. The tip of his tail twitching, the only acknowledgment of my presence.

I reach into my bag and remove the newly discovered sketch pad, the stack of letters, and the photograph I'd found in my father's bedroom.

I flip open the sketch pad, but where the previous ones were filled with people, this one doesn't include a single human. This one is dedicated to horses. One horse actually. There are a few drawings of others, even the goat, but the majority of the pages are of Jack. My breath catches on a drawing of his head, the muzzle jutting out in a hello-whatchya-got-for-me, the knowing eyes that seem to see straight into my heart.

My father had captured the wistfulness, the fear, the longing in his human subjects. He captured the gentleness, sincerity, loyalty in Jack.

Who was this man who could see into people and horses with such clarity? This wasn't the same man I grew up with.

I close the sketch pad and reach for the letters. They are all addressed to my father's office, all in Rena's slanted handwriting.

July 1994

Dear Edward,

You cannot continue to torture yourself with "what ifs." Should you have guessed she wanted to return to the lake cabin because of her state of mind? Maybe. I won't blow air and tell you there was nothing you could have done.

Maybe the signs were there. Maybe you could have gotten her help again.

Maybe. There are always maybes.

But, Edward, I cannot indulge this spiral into self-flagellation. You would never allow that from your patients.

Be strong, my friend. For yourself. For your daughter.

Yours,

R.

I slide the photo closer and trace my mom's profile, the angle of her arm, the waving hand.

"You were saying good-bye to me, weren't you?"

19

August 1993

Someone has propped open the front door of the house. Emma sits at the top of the stairs, the skirt tucked around her legs and anchored under her butt, arms circling her knees. There's been a surprising number of people coming and going today. All of them wearing serious clothes and serious expressions, all of them shaking her dad's hand and looking at her with pity.

She overhears one lady wonder what will become of "that poor child now that her mother is dead." Another volunteers that Edward should consider an au pair or boarding school. Yet another whispers, "Did you hear what *really* happened?" at which point the gaggle of gossips works their way to the front porch.

The grinding of her teeth sounds louder than the hushed discussions around her. She wants these strangers to leave, she wants to push each one out the door and slam the door behind them. She bites the edge of her left ring finger. No one will tell her not to. At least not today.

"Why are you sitting here?" Jillian takes the stairs two at a time, then nudges Emma's shoulder with her butt until she scoots over.

"Because I'm out of the way here. I'm going to scream if one more person pats my back and tells me it's going to be okay."

"But it will be okay." Jilli sounds so sure.

"Maybe. Someday. Today it's not. Anyway, they're just saying the words. None of them believe it."

"Want to go to the stable and see Jack? He always makes us feel better."

"Yeah."

Jilli stands and clomps down the stairs before Emma's answer has a chance to settle on the stairs between them.

She eases up and follows, hugging the wall so as not to be seen. Not that anyone would notice. Besides, they prefer talking about her in the abstract. *Poor motherless Emma.* It makes the adults uncomfortable having her in the room.

Does it matter that having them around makes her uncomfortable? That the more people stuff into their house, the more alone she feels? None of these people can bring her mom back.

She stops at the kitchen door when she hears her father's voice. But he's not talking to her. His back is to the door. Emma wants to run to him and pull him away, out of the house, far from these people who don't mean what they say and don't really care. But he'd just tell her to be polite and smooth the jacket where she'd grabbed it. Then he'd wave his hand, dismissing her. Like always.

Once outside, she breaks into a run and easily catches Jillian just in time to be swallowed by the woods.

They hustle to the tack room and tug on breeches and boots, discarding their skirts and fancy shoes in a heap.

Pogo shuffles to the door of his stall and Emma slips him a mint and a kiss on the muzzle before following her friend to the large stall at the end of the aisle. Inside, Cassie munches hay while three-month-old Jack Flash sprawls in the middle of her snack. Cassie nudges his front legs and snatches a mouthful before he moves again.

Emma and Jillian lean over the door to admire their foal. Because he is *their* foal. They'd been there when he was born, they'd named him Jack Flash, and they play with him every day.

Whenever the girls are nearby, Jack trots after them, the little brother wanting to play.

"Isn't he gorgeous?" Emma asks, her voice more awed prayer than question.

"The most."

"I could watch him forever."

"Me too. But at some point we'd have to go the bathroom. And sleep. And eat." Jilli grins and leans into her friend.

They're silent for a few minutes, the only noise from Cassie chewing hay and the occasional stomp or bucket bump from another occupant somewhere in the barn.

"Who do you think will get to ride him first?" Emma asks.

"I bet Grandpa will have Kate train him. She's good."

"When do you think we'll get to ride him?"

Jillian shrugs.

"I can't wait to ride him. I bet he'll be amazing." Emma sighs, leaning her chin on her arms on top of the open half-door. When Jillian doesn't respond immediately, she rolls her head. "What?"

"Are you moving in with us?"

"No. Why?" She snaps upright, startling the two horses.

Jillian gives an all-knowing eleven-year-old's shrug. "Just wondering."

"Of course not." Except, she's not nearly as confident as she wants to be. "Do you think?"

"I don't know. It's just that my room seems to be as much yours these days. And now with your mom dead and all . . ." Jilli lets the final words roll down the aisle into the silence.

The last few months, she'd been spending more and more nights with Jillian. Simon had moved a second twin bed into Jilli's bedroom and the girls arranged them head-to-head. It made whispering late into the night without getting caught much easier.

"My dad will need me. I bet he'll be around a lot more now." She squares her shoulders and imitates the nod she saw those ladies in the house use as they declared what her future would, no doubt, look like.

"Probably. Although, I kinda hope you do actually."

"You do? Why?"

"Think how much fun it would be. One big sleepover."

"Except we'd still have homework and school and chores."

"Yeah, but we'd be doing them together. I like it better when we're together. I don't feel like I'm the big bull's-eye center of their universe, you know. When you're here, I feel like a normal kid and like, for that time, they're not worried I'm going to turn into my mom."

Emma takes a half step sideways until their shoulders are touching again. "I like it better when we're together, too. I don't feel like I'm invisible."

Jack wobbles to his legs and comes to nuzzle them. Thoughts of missing parents almost disappear.

Until that evening, when Emma's father arrives at Jumping Frog Farm, looking tired and uncomfortable. He thanks Simon and Rena, then closes the door to the backseat after Emma gets in. He doesn't say a word on the way home and the drive seems to take three times as long. She stares out the window, wishing she could jump out and canter along the path in the woods instead.

Her father pulls the car into the garage and turns the ignition off, but doesn't make a move to get out. The garage feels empty. She suddenly realizes why. "What happened to Mommy's car?"

"We don't need a second car anymore."

She stares at the back of her father's head. She wants to ask him when he sold the car, whom he sold it to, and if they would take good care of it, but by then he's getting out. The dome light makes her squint and the sound of the car door closing makes her wince.

They walk into the house, two almost strangers. The kitchen counter is covered with casserole dishes and plates of food. Emma's stomach growls.

"Are you hungry?" Her dad moves a glass dish, squaring it with the one next to it. Emma wonders why he looks even more out of place here than he had at the stable.

"No." She pushes a fist into her stomach to keep it from arguing.

"Are you tired?"

"No."

"Okay. How about a bath then?"

"Okay."

She takes her boots off and clutches them to her chest. She knows she should leave them by the front door, but she also knows she has to keep them with her. She needs something that hasn't changed, that won't—can't—be taken away. She needs the smell of horses, the comfort that she can only find at the stable.

She sits in the lukewarm tub, thighs pushing into her chest, chin digging into her knees, arms squeezing her shins tight. She hears sirens outside.

They sound the same.

Except then, they'd been loud, then louder. The noise had stopped when the ambulance stopped in their driveway. The lights had kept flashing though, around and around. It had been raining and Emma remembered the raindrops, clear, red, clear, red, pinging off the window.

A sob shudders through her body. She pushes the lever for the hot water and lets the burn of the water release her tears.

"I miss you, Mommy," she whispers after the receding ambulance. "I will always miss you."

20

I glance at my watch. The woman who answered the phone at Adler Law assured me Thomas would be in by noon. He had meetings all morning and was not reachable but she'd have him call me the moment he returned. I remind her to remind him to call and stress that I'll probably be returning to Chicago sooner because of "office things."

What those "office things" are, though, I have no idea. Only a pit at the bottom of my successful, corporate-executive gut.

I close my eyes, take in an imaginary breath of sweet horse smell, then call Howard. When the voice mail beeps for the message, I hang up and redial. My mind went into auto-listen mode the moment his nasally voice recited the various reasons he wasn't able to answer my call. But something was off in the message. I wait for the five rings, mumbling "come on, come on" into the phone. There it is. That's what was bothering me.

"Hi. You've reached Howard Kelly, communications manager. I'm in the office, but . . ."

I stab at the phone to end the call. I don't care why he can't come to the phone. I want to know when he became communications manager. A few days ago his title had been communications associate. Since I'm the communications VP and his manager, shouldn't I have known about a promotion before it happened?

I stare out at the hills while the laptop whirs to life, imagining the feel of a horse cantering up a hill, the sound of hoofbeats pounding against the ground, the wind pricking my face as we pick up speed down the other side, seeing that perfect distance to the takeoff.

My imaginary horse gallops to the edge of the ravine and skids to a stop. I'm thrown back into the corporate world.

The first e-mail I read is from Bruce to Howard. I'm on copy along with the human resources director and Bruce's assistant. He's congratulating Howard on his promotion and "in Emma's absence, you will be reporting directly to me."

"Absence? What the hell? One lousy week." And I'm due back in a couple of days.

I scroll through the rest of my in-box looking for a response from Howard.

Nothing.

At least the printer copied me. The revised brochures are being delivered today. There's an invoice attached to the e-mail for the change, the reprint, the reprint of the reprint, and the rush. That will be a hit to the budget.

I pinch the bridge of my nose, trying to slow my streaming thoughts. I need to change my flight. I'm going back today. Whatever needs to be done here can be accomplished long distance. There's a flight in the early afternoon and with the one-hour time difference, I can be in the office before the end of the day. Yet I can't make my fingers click the buttons to confirm the change.

"You got back on a horse yesterday and survived. You can do this." The pep talk does little to settle the galloping butterflies.

I tap at Bruce's number, then swallow hard as a particularly excitable butterfly threatens to send me running to the bathroom.

"Hello, Emma."

The butterfly flops to the pit of my stomach at the sound of his voice. No happy-to-hear-from-you lilt in those two words. Not that I expected it. But still.

"Hi, Bruce."

"I hope you've had a nice visit."

My mouth opens to respond, then snaps shut. "A nice visit"?

I'm here because my father just died. I'm here because I have a person's life to close out. I'm not here to have a nice visit.

"I'm not exactly here on vacation."

"No."

Bruce's usual clipped responses spark at my nerves. "I saw your e-mail to Howard."

"Yes. Corporate changes. We needed someone to take charge."

I am in charge. I was in charge.

"I'm away for one week, Bruce. And reachable by phone and e-mail."

"Yes. But you're busy with your personal life. We need projects to move forward."

I push my fingers into the festering headache. *We.* He'd emphasized that word twice. "What other changes do I need to know about?"

"We announced a corporate restructure. Didn't want to bother you while you were on vacation. It can wait until you're back in the office."

The butterflies morph into giant angry moths. "I'm not on vacation."

"No. Of course."

"Do I need to come back today? I've checked and I can be in the office by five P.M." I swallow a lump, equal parts dread, fear, frustration, defeat.

The acidic burn of realization flames through me. I've put my heart and soul into this job. Allowed it to consume me. For what? For the pleasure of an ulcer?

For the pleasure of success.

Simon had asked what I thought defined success.

Status. Title. Money.

I have the status and the title and even the money. But none of that equals security. Or, I suddenly realize, happiness. That burning desire that once drove me has turned to embers.

"That's not necessary. You're back on Monday, right?"

"Monday," I confirm.

We say good-bye and I close the computer on the unconfirmed flight.

Simon defined success as "fulfillment."

"Were you fulfilled by your success, Dad? Because it's sure as hell not doing it for me." I release a breath and add, "At least not anymore."

The familiar smell of cut grass greets me as I turn into the driveway. Tony waves as the tractor bounces along the strip of grass between the road and the fence. My feet become lead as I enter the barn and see the small cluster of people.

I may not have been excited about calling Bruce, but there's one thing trending higher on the don't-want-to-deal-with-this meter—dealing with Jillian.

But there she is, leaning against the open door to the barn office, arms tight across her chest, eyes anchoring me in the middle of the aisle.

"You're back." She doesn't sound any friendlier than she looks. The two people she's talking to scatter and I wish I could go with them.

"I'm back."

"I thought you weren't staying long."

"Leaving in a couple of days."

"Shouldn't you be busy meeting with lawyers and stuff?" She waves a hand as though that clarifies the stuff I'm supposed to be dealing with instead of invading her world.

I don't feel like defending myself. Not now. Not today. Not about being here.

"You can pretend I'm not here."

"I'd prefer if you really weren't here." She tightens the pretzel of her arms, her ice-blue eyes drilling a hole through sixteen years of emotional fortitude.

Sixteen years during which time I replayed that damn day over and over. Show days were my favorite and this one was extra special. Jillian and I were going alone for the first time. Simon still wasn't feeling well and said we were perfectly capable to school each other before the morning classes. Plus, Drew Ellison was going to be there. We'd been competing against each other for years and had become show friends. He went to a different school so I didn't really know him outside of the show world. But like most of the girls, I'd had a crush on him. After a party at his house that Jilli had reluctantly agreed to let me tag along to, Drew and I went from show friends to show sweethearts.

It was the last jumper class of the day and of the three of us, I was the only one who'd qualified for the jump-off. Jilli had taken Tolstoy to the trailer where she could sulk in private. Drew stayed at the gate with me, talking about the jump-off course. He was tucking a stray wisp of hair from my face and giving me a good-luck kiss when Jillian returned.

When Jack and I trotted out of the ring with the winner's sash around his neck, neither Jillian nor Drew was there to cheer for us.

Marlene said she'd seen Jilli return to the trailer. Sure enough, Tolstoy was tied to the trailer, so Jilli would be there as well. Probably in the tack stall, changing clothes. There was a pyramid of empty beer cans on the cooler by the door to the tack stall.

I opened the side door to the trailer, arms full with my saddle and bridle, excitement bubbling. "Hey, Jilli, guess what?"

There was Jillian, on her knees, back to the door, one hand under Drew's shirt. Drew's hands were pressed against the wall on either side of his body, his legs slightly apart, eyes closed, mouth open.

He groaned and I gasped.

I'd dropped my load and slapped my hand over my mouth to smother the sob, then turned and ran. I heard Drew cursing: "Shit, Jillian. Emma, wait . . ."

Over the years, I'd fumbled through the puzzle pieces that had led us there. Why would my best friend hurt me? And not just stealing my new boyfriend. That had been just the beginning.

Maybe I'll finally get an answer sixteen years later. I return her stare. "Why were you threatened by me? Why are you still threatened?"

"I'm not threatened by you. I never was." The icy blue of her eyes grays.

"So what then? You went from being my best friend to hating me? Because of a couple of placements at a horse show? Because of a guy? What?"

Nothing in the way she's standing changes, yet the change in her catches my breath. There's no hate in her eyes. What I see reflected back is vulnerability.

The discussion with Simon replays in my head. The defiant person standing in front of me seems far less intimidating than she did a couple of days ago.

She shakes her head, shaking the ice back into place. "It was more than that, Emma." She turns and walks away.

Maybe it was a mistake coming here looking for answers. But it's the only place where I have a chance at getting any answers. I make my way to where Jack and his sidekick are mowing through a patch of grass in their paddock. They both look up but neither seems disturbed by the intrusion.

Unwilling to interrupt their peaceful companionship, I stay by the fence and watch. Jack bends his left front leg while his teeth grab at a patch of grass. His tail swishes at unseen flies and his ears twitch at unheard sounds. Jukebox hops to another grassy patch, keeping his beady eyes on me.

I let the lazy sounds take me over, losing track of time and movement until Jack ambles over and rests his muzzle on my shoulder, steady and soothing. Long, warm breaths melt into the fabric of my shirt. My head tips to the side until we're touching, and we stand, taking comfort from a friendship that doesn't require words or excuses or apologies.

Jukebox bleats and trots to the fence, keeping a safe distance from me. He stuffs his head between the wooden slats, sending another high-pitched greeting into the universe. It's then that I notice a man leading a pinto toward the adjoining paddock.

"Sorry for interrupting. I'll let Taco loose in his field and get out of your space."

"You're not interrupting."

The commas at the corner of his mouth punctuate an expression that's neither smile nor frown. The pinto named Taco yanks gently at the lead and moves a step closer to a tuft of grass. There's the same prickly restlessness that I'd noticed in him the other day. He both unnerves and intrigues me.

The pendulum swings closer to unnerved and I break eye contact. "I'm Emma."

"Michael. And you probably know Taco." He gives the horse's neck an affectionate slap.

"We haven't had the pleasure of meeting. Taco?" I raise an eyebrow in question.

"Hard to explain. You'll see in a minute. He likes to show off."

Michael tugs the lead rope and Taco shuffles a few steps, keeping his head close to the ground, cropping as he walks. Michael unlatches the gate, leads the horse through, removes the halter, and steps back as the horse bolts and bucks, then with tail high he struts the perimeter of the paddock until he's made a full lap. Back at the starting point, he stretches his neck and twists to the right, tongue sticking out the side.

"Wait for it," Michael says, pointing at the horse without taking his eyes off him. "This is how he got his name."

The horse folds his tongue in half, the shape oddly resembling a taco.

"How does he do that?"

"No idea." Michael laughs, a deep, full, confident sound.

Now I'm back to intrigued. I can't say why I was expecting someone sad or reserved. Ben hadn't given me any indication why Michael was in the therapeutic program. And yet I'm surprised by the shift from the weary, calculating way he first assessed me to the ease and affection in the way he looks at the horse. He's older than I originally pegged him to be. And that intrigues me even more.

I'd always somehow imagined that with age came a settling

into who you are. That the insecurities and doubts that fueled our youth are put to pasture. Yet maturity has succeeded only in changing my insecurities and doubts. So why does it surprise me that a man ten or fifteen years older would have need of a therapeutic program? Who knows what his background is. And anyway, isn't that need for comfort why I'm out here snuggling with Jack?

"Is he yours?" I nod at the pinto, who is now shoving his folded tongue in Michael's face.

"No. I wish he was, though. I come a couple times a week." He hesitates a breath. "I've been part of the therapeutic riding program for about a year. Taco and Rena saved my life."

I certainly wasn't expecting him to be so forthright.

He turns from the horse and assesses me before asking, "Are you a new client here? Lessons? Boarder?"

"None of the above actually." Under the lock of his gaze, my nerves lose their hold on my mouth. "I rode here when I was a girl but haven't been back in sixteen years. I had to return on personal business and, well, here I am." I lean into Jack, needing reassurance that it's okay for me to be here.

"You're the girl in all those pictures with Jack."

I nod.

"Nice."

"That was a long time ago."

"You don't ride anymore?"

I pull my mouth into a line and shake my head.

"You should."

"If only it were that easy."

"It is. You love horses. You ride."

"That easy?" Jack's breath tickles the side of my neck.

"He doesn't do that, you know."

I turn to look at Michael, bumping Jack off my shoulder in the process. He snorts and repositions, sending a warm breeze down the front of my shirt.

"Jack. He's not a touchy-feely horse. With Simon somewhat, but he tends to keep to himself with other humans. He's good with the therapeutic clients although he seems to prefer that fool's company." I follow Michael's outstretched finger to where Jukebox is attempting to sit on a large yellow rubber ball.

I laugh at the crazy goat, then turn back to the warm brown eyes inches from mine. "He's always been like this. When he was a foal he'd sleep with his head in my lap. Just a big lovable puppy dog, aren't you?" I hug Jack's muzzle.

"Then why did you leave?"

"It's complicated."

"That," Michael waves a hand wrapping an invisible bow around Jack and me, "that's not complicated. Me? I'm complicated. The bond you have with that horse, not so much."

"You don't know anything about me." Jack's head whips up and I wince at the sharpness of my tone. I hadn't meant it.

"True. So tell me why you left."

"History. Anyway, I'm only here for a couple more days."

"He'll miss you." Michael nods at the horse but his eyes stay on me.

"I'll miss him but my life is in Chicago. Not here. I have a job to get back to."

"Your aura tells me otherwise."

"My aura?"

He doesn't react to my disbelief. That was the last thing I expected from a man who looks like he's just walked off a marines recruiting poster.

"Before you noticed me, your aura was clear. You were at peace. It" —he circles his hand, palm out, fingers splayed— "got murkier as we talked. At the mention of your life in Chicago, it darkened to a storm cloud."

"Is this where you try to recruit me into your cult?"

He laughs. A larger-than-can-be-contained presence fills the space between us. I shift my weight, pushing my back into the wood fence.

"I'm not in a cult. Well, not really. I know it sounds crazy. I'm sorry if I wigged you out. I spent six months living with a holistic healer in a hut in Tibet after getting out of the marines. It wasn't one of my better decisions. But I wasn't making many good decisions back then."

Ex-marine. I was right about one thing at least. Despite the unease, I find myself relaxing. He's not dangerous.

"Anyway, you should rethink going back. This place may have uncomfortable memories for you, but it's pretty clear that this place is also your homecoming."

Jack pushes down on my shoulder, apparently agreeing.

"How did you go from a holistic hut in Tibet to Jumping Frog Farm in Maryland?"

"I had to do something to save my life." Our eyes meet and I see a mirror of myself. Someone grasping for a why and a how, someone searching for a way home.

Jack gives me a nudge, breaking the contact between Michael and me.

"When I got out of the marines, I wanted to die, I deserved to die, for what I'd done and what I hadn't done. My wife threatened to leave me if I didn't get help. Said I'd never see my child again. So I left her. Them. I followed a marine buddy to Tibet. Five months later he killed himself. A month after that, I came home but Angie refused to take me back. Said I was as fucked up as when I'd left. Maybe more. She's a psychologist at one of the area hospitals. She said to try this program, that Rena had a reputation for helping people who weren't helpable."

"You thought you weren't helpable?"

"I knew it. I came those first few times because I couldn't die with the disappointment in Angie's eyes being my last memory of her. Her last memory of me. I wanted my daughter to know I'd at least made an effort to be the kind of father she deserved. One week led to two, led to a month, and here I am a year later."

"Have you and Angie gotten back together?"

"No." He gives his head a sad shake.

"Do you see your daughter?"

"Not as much as I'd like. She's fifteen and every bit the moody teen. She'd rather be with her friends than her parents. Especially her fucked-up dad. I scare her friends."

"Do you still want to die?"

"Sometimes."

"What do you do then?"

"Come here." Michael's upper body turns so slightly that I almost think it was the wind ruffling his shirt. He watches Taco slurping water from the metal trough in the corner of the paddock.

"I wonder if that's what my mom did."

I hadn't realized I'd said that aloud until Michael asks, "Your mom?"

I nod, the cotton ball in my throat stopping any attempt at speaking.

Michael lets me off the hook. "I rode a few times when I was young. Vacations mostly. It was fun but I never imagined it becoming part of my life. Until I had no life. A horse doesn't judge what you've done wrong. They give you the opportunity to do right. Here, it doesn't matter who I was. Michael the marine doesn't exist. I can't think about those days. If I do, Taco reminds me to stop. Through him I can feel my tension and I can find my peace."

"I wish my mom had had a Taco."

"Maybe she was more of a sushi girl." He winks.

Despite the weight of the tears, I feel the corners of my mouth lift.

"Maybe. I'm glad you have Taco. And Rena."

"Me too. You have Jack and Rena. And Simon."

I nod.

"That's your reason to stay."

21

March 1995

A re you done with that magazine?" Jilli points a pair of scissors at the *Practical Horseman* magazine Emma has been
leafing through, looking for the perfect picture for her collage.

It's been pouring outside and is still winter cold. The kind of
early-spring day that makes you doubt Mother Nature remembers how to make warm and sunny. Emma is ready for spring.
She loves spring.

She listens to the rain pounding on the metal roof. She wishes
it would ease up. Usually riding in the indoor arena with rain
pinging on the metal roof feels cozy, the sounds almost hypnotic.
But the downpour this morning had made it hard to hear Rena
and had unsettled the horses. It hadn't been one of her better lessons. And that always leaves her feeling out of sorts.

Emma slides the magazine to Jilli and reaches for another
one. Her collage isn't moving nearly as fast as Jilli's. Then again,
Emma's collage has a theme and each picture is neatly trimmed
and glued in place. Jilli is taking an everything-goes approach
to hers.

The phone rings and Rena answers on the second ring. After
abbreviated pleasantries, Rena's voice jumps with alarm, making

both girls stop in mid-cut or paste. "But you're okay? Well that's more important. Of course, of course. We'll manage. Don't give it another thought."

She hangs up and drops her head into her hands. "Oh this is not good."

"Grandma? What's wrong?"

"Carolyn was in an accident. The roads are slick and people don't know how to pay attention. She's okay but her car isn't. She's not going to make it today. And that means I'm shorthanded for the afternoon therapeutic lessons." She flips through the class list and groans.

"We'll help." Emma ignores the glare from Jilli.

She's been watching the lessons since she started coming to Jumping Frog Farm. She likes the slow, steady pace, the focus on connecting with the horse. She's enchanted by the Rena who leads those groups. She loves watching any and all lessons—especially the advanced riders. But there's a pull to the therapeutic ones that she can't explain.

"Are you nuts?" Jilli hisses at her.

Rena's mouth pulls into a lopsided thought expression.

"Way to go, Emma," Jilli mutters. "I have homework," she volunteers before Rena can rope her in.

"This morning you said you didn't." Rena's thought face turns to suspicion face.

"Just remembered a book report due on Tuesday. And I'm only halfway through the book."

Rena raises a questioning eyebrow at Emma.

"I can still help." Emma sits taller.

"Okay then. I have two lessons I could use the extra hands with."

"I can do that." She hears the giddiness in her own voice and doesn't care. So what if Jilli doesn't want to help. Until now, the only thing she'd been allowed to do was lead ponies in and out of the arena, tighten girths, cool out horses after. But never full-out helping. Like in the ring, leading-a-pony helping.

"Good. The first lesson will be here in less than thirty minutes.

Can you please help Daniel with the horses? We need Jasper, Timmy, and Star. Halters over the bridles."

"Yes, ma'am." Emma shoots up and out of the office, ignoring the mimicking *yes ma'am* from Jilli.

She still doesn't understand what Jilli has against the therapeutic program. Granted, Jilli isn't much of a watcher even with regular lessons but there are a few that she hangs with Emma to watch. Never the therapeutic lessons, though. The only explanation she's given Emma is that the clients creep her out. Emma doesn't see anything creepy about the people who participate in the program but she's never been able to convince Jilli otherwise.

Emma retrieves Star's tack. He's her favorite of the three that will be used in the lesson. She kisses his muzzle and slips him a mint.

They're ready by the time the lesson group arrives. Three adults, three kids. A boy about her age is walking with the assistance of short metal crutches. A band wraps around each arm just below the elbow and he's gripping rubber handles. He's followed down the aisle by a girl in a wheelchair. Emma pegs her to be nine, maybe ten. The woman pushing the wheelchair seems to be out of breath already and Emma wonders how she'll manage in the indoor arena. The third kid is tall and skinny and bald and walks slowly behind the others, his hands buried in the pockets of a coat that looks three sizes too big. She thinks he may be about her age but he looks and walks older.

Rena greets them all by name and asks questions about what each has been up to since their last lesson.

The tall, skinny boy named Nathan says he's glad to be back after two months away.

She realizes she's staring when he turns and stares back. She also realizes that he's raised an eyebrow except he doesn't have eyebrows. She tries a smile and hopes it looks less shocked than she feels.

"Emma," Rena refocuses the group, "can you help Nathan mount, please? You'll stay with him throughout the class but let him control Star as much as he feels comfortable."

She nods and busies herself tightening the girth and checking the bridle. Why did Rena give her this guy? Maybe he isn't as uncomfortable with her staring as she is. She feels her cheeks heat up.

Don't be a child, she scolds herself. *Otherwise, Rena won't let you help again.*

She leads Star to the mounting block and holds him while Nathan gets on. She fixes the length of the stirrup leathers, her eyes trained on the boy's brown paddock boots.

"It's okay, you know." His voice still has the higher pitch of the boys in her class. A few of the boys in Jilli's class have started cracking and croaking when they talk. It's weird. She's glad girls don't have to deal with that. Although from what she hears from friends and what they learned in health class, she'll have worse things to deal with.

"How old are you?" She feels less awkward now.

"Eleven. I'll be twelve next month."

"Almost like me. My birthday is in two months."

They smile at each other, another chunk of unease dropping into the footing of the arena.

"What's wrong with you?" She knows it's rude to ask, her father would be appalled. He'd pull her aside and say, *Emma, I'm appalled at your behavior.* She secretly loves the idea that she's done something her father would hate. She's also embarrassed that she feels that way. "I'm sorry, I shouldn't have asked." The apology is as much to Nathan as to her father.

"I have cancer."

"How long have you had it?"

"Two years. I'm doing okay though."

She's never known anyone with cancer. Actually, that's not true. Kathy's mom's sister had cancer. She'd met her a couple of times when she was over at Kathy's house. That was before they moved here, when they'd still been friends.

She can't think of anyone else although she's sure there must be someone.

"Doctors say I should be A-OK soon." He makes the okay sign with his left hand.

"How long have you been riding?" She gives Star's bridle a gentle jerk to keep him from getting too fast.

"A year?"

He doesn't sound completely sure and Emma can't remember seeing him before. Not that that means anything. She's not here when many of the therapeutic lessons happen. But those are usually adults who come during the day while she's in school.

"Do you like it?"

She turns a bit to look at him when he doesn't answer and catches the tail end of a nod.

"It's the only time I'm not a cancer patient. At school, kids are weirded out by me. They treat me like I'm contagious. At home, my parents are terrified of me. They treat me like I'm going to break. I can't play soccer anymore because I'm too weak. I can't even walk my dog alone because he's big and he pulls when he sees a squirrel or bunny. I broke my elbow last year when he jumped after a rabbit and yanked me down onto the pavement."

"I can't imagine."

"Yeah, it stinks. But here I'm just a kid on a horse. Yeah, I'm in a special program and all, but the horses don't know that. They don't treat me any different than they do Caitlin or you. Well, maybe you because you're an awesome rider."

Emma stops abruptly, her mouth open. Star tosses his head, annoyed at the loss of forward momentum.

Nathan grins at her. "Busted. I've watched you ride."

"Emma, keep that horse moving," Rena bellows from the center of the ring.

They continue the slow walk around the outside of the arena. She stays by Star's shoulder as Nathan steers him in a figure eight, then in a circle, across the diagonal, another circle, another figure eight.

At the end of the hour, Emma helps Nathan dismount with a hand on his back to keep him steady.

"That goes by faster than any other hour," he says.

"I know, right?" She's always amazed at how slowly time moves when she's at school or at home. But it zooms when she's here.

They walk together back to the tack stall, Emma on the horse's left, Nathan on his right.

"I hope you'll be helping more often." He peeks under Star's neck and grins at her again. She likes his smile.

"Me too."

She watches as Nathan and the others leave, then goes back to Star. He doesn't need to be cooled off, he didn't work up a sweat, but she gives him a good brushing anyway. He may not have worked hard but he performed like a champion.

She's always felt more herself here than anywhere else, so she's not surprised that Nathan feels the same. But she is surprised at the emotion in his voice when he talked to Star. For her, riding is confidence. For Nathan, riding is living.

22

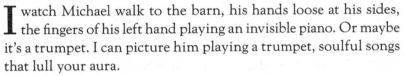

I watch Michael walk to the barn, his hands loose at his sides, the fingers of his left hand playing an invisible piano. Or maybe it's a trumpet. I can picture him playing a trumpet, soulful songs that lull your aura.

He's an interesting character.

In the distance a siren rushes the quiet of a country afternoon. The sound gets closer until the flashing lights turn into the driveway to the stable. The horses and goat, agitated by the disruption, gallop to the far end of the field and hide under the sweeping branches of the big willow tree.

I sprint toward the barn, heart hammering even before the exertion kicks in. By the time I skid around the side of the barn, I see paramedics removing a medical bag and a stretcher from the back of the ambulance. I kick up my speed and arrive at the outdoor arena as one of the paramedics kneels next to Rena.

I stop next to Ben and Michael and a couple of people in breeches. "Oh my god, Rena. What happened?"

Ben stretches his arm in front of me, barricading the entrance to the arena. "I'm not sure."

A girl standing on the other side of the fence sniffles into a Kleenex. "We were in the middle of my lesson. She was sitting on the jump in the middle of the ring and got up to raise the outside line for me. I came around the corner and she was crumpled on the ground with the standard on top of her."

Simon and Jillian hover, moving a step left, two steps right as the paramedics attend to Rena.

Rena moves and I release the stranglehold on the top rail of the arena fence. The paramedics lift her onto the gurney. She gets a few halfhearted swats in, telling them to leave her alone, that she's fine. She may be alive, but she most certainly doesn't look fine.

"You have to let them do their job." Simon grabs at one of her arms, only to end up with a swat to his chest. "You'll be back terrorizing everyone in no time. Stop being such an ornery old mare."

While one of the paramedics straps Rena onto the stretcher, the other tells Jillian to follow them to the hospital in Rockledge.

"I'm not going to the hospital. I have lessons to teach." There's little of the patented Rena spit in those words. She closes her eyes and appears to melt into the gurney. "I'm just a bit dizzy."

"We'll get an IV in her as soon as we're in the ambulance," the first medic tells Simon, who's walking next to them, one hand resting on Rena's shoulder. "We need to get her to the hospital."

"I'm right here, dammit. I hear you. Just give me the damn fluids. I don't need to go to the hospital."

"Ma'am, you're going to be fine."

Rena grabs Simon's arm and yanks him closer. "You tell that pipsqueak to stop talking to me like I'm a senile old goat."

Simon pats her shoulder and eases out of her grasp, mumbling "good luck" to the medic as they lift the stretcher into the back of the ambulance.

Before the doors close Rena locks eyes with me, then turns to Simon. "Emma is to take over the therapeutic lessons until I'm back."

Slam. Slam.

I'm trapped in Jillian's glare.

"Jilli, we need to go." Simon's voice is overshadowed by the crunch of gravel as the ambulance rolls away.

Jillian turns to Ben but her attention stays firmly on me. "Cancel the lessons for the rest of the day and tomorrow. We'll see how to divide the rest of Grandma's schedule when I get back from the hospital."

"Rena made that decision. Emma will teach instead." Ben crosses his arms, challenging Jillian to contradict her grandmother in front of the group assembled around the arena.

I watch as anger and anxiety prickle Jillian's resolve.

"She," Jillian spits the word in my direction, "will not be taking over anything. I manage the barn. And the lessons." In the flip of a braid she turns and strides to her car, spastically clicking the Unlock button. The car beeps spastically in return.

Simon draws in a long breath, releasing it in short puffs. "Ben, can you and Emma look at Rena's calendar? She's right, Emma, you're the person to lead the therapeutic lessons. Will you?"

Jillian honks, backing the car out of its parking spot faster than is safe, then honks again for good measure.

"Jillian was adamant about not having me involved."

Simon lifts a hand. "I still own this barn. I still have final say."

"I'm only here two more days."

"We'll take it." Ben grabs me at the elbow and pulls me aside as Jillian backs to a stop inches away.

"Thank you," Simon mouths and gets in the passenger seat. Jillian guns the engine, sending gravel hurtling at innocent bystanders.

The small crowd watches the ambulance, followed by Jillian's silver sports car, disappear around the bend in the road. No one speaks, no one moves.

Finally, Ben breaks the trance. "Okay, folks, we need to keep this place running. Arianna, please go check on your horse. He was pretty hot when Tony took him in. Hose him down and walk him. Emma, you and I have a schedule to split."

I follow Ben into the office. He flips on the computer and prints a couple of calendar pages, then starts highlighting and circling and crossing names out. A shudder travels up my spine. This morning I was looking at flights to Chicago.

"Ben, I don't know about this. I'm not a teacher and I'm certainly not qualified to work with the therapeutic clients."

"You helped with the program before."

"Helped, yes. But that was years ago."

He leans back in the chair. "The boss believes you're the right choice."

"Why though? I don't get it. She's been friendlier than Jillian, but far from pleased to have me here. Why the drastic change?"

Ben doodles a bubble font question mark on one of the calendar pages. Finally he looks up. "She has her reasons."

"Has this happened to her before?" A cold prickle slithers down my spine at the image of Rena on that gurney.

"Once."

"What's wrong with her, Ben?" I lean forward, willing him to tell me it's nothing, that she just pushes herself too hard.

He releases a heavy sigh. "God, Emma, you need to talk to them about this, not me."

"But you're the one left to deal with me. And I'm not agreeing to anything until I know the truth. Dammit, Ben, haven't I had to deal with enough lies and surprises lately? Why can't anyone just give me a straight answer?"

None of this is his fault, but between my father, Rena, work, and Jillian, I can't contain my frustration any longer. Ben looks up from his doodle. The question mark has morphed into a fat exclamation point.

"She had a heart attack four years ago. That's why Simon stopped teaching. She refused to stop, so he became her right hand."

I slam back into the chair, knocking the breath and words out of me.

"Will you stay and help?"

"I have a lot to do before I return." There's the sale of the condo, plus transferring the money in the bank accounts and finalizing the sale of the medical practice. All excuses.

I look at the calendar printout in my hands. My heart overrules my brain.

Two days. Then I'm going back to Chicago.

I hold up two fingers and Ben's face spreads into a relieved grin.

Half an hour later, I have three lessons to teach—a "regular" lesson, as Ben calls it, and two therapeutic classes. Ben has added one more lesson to his already full schedule, and pushed two privates to next week. I leave Ben sorting through the schedule for the following day.

The barn is eerily quiet. I walk the aisles looking at empty stalls. Most of the horses are outside enjoying the cooler weather. There's an hour before my first lesson, a talented young rider, according to Ben. She'd started with Rena when she was six and at thirteen is now spending most weekends at horse shows, a "mini-Emma," Ben teased. I didn't believe for a hairy minute it was coincidence that she was the only "regular" lesson I ended up with.

Libby, it turns out, is indeed a mini-me in many ways and the hour lesson flies by. At the end she asks if I'm going to be her permanent teacher and mumbles "bummer" when I explain that I'm just subbing for Rena.

I'd been so absorbed by the girl and her horse that I'm surprised to see Michael sitting in the spectator pavilion.

"You're still here."

"I wasn't ready to leave after what happened with Rena."

I nod. I don't think I would have been able to leave either.

He tilts his head, indicating Libby. "You're a natural."

"She's easy to teach." I walk to the fence, the excitement of the lesson pulsating through me. Together we watch as Libby rides her chestnut pony around the ring, letting him catch his breath.

"When she has a good teacher." He chuckles. "She does great with Rena. Not so much the times Jillian teaches."

"I'm sensing a recurring theme here."

He grins, and a mischievous spark flashes before he blinks it away. "I better hit the road. It was nice meeting you, Emma. I hope to see you around here again."

He exchanges heys and see-yas with Tony, who's coming out

of the barn leading two horses. Trailing behind are two boys probably not much older than Libby, but clearly out of sorts with their misfortune at being in a stinky barn. One boy tugs at the strap of his helmet and scowls at the back end of the horse. The other has his hands shoved so far into his jeans that the waistband has slipped down his hips. My first therapeutic session will not be as easy as my first regular lesson.

The next hour is spent coaxing two reluctant and uncooperative boys and their mounts. The counselor who came with them keeps her eyes glued to her phone the entire time, uttering an unhelpful "pay attention" each time one of the boys rides past her.

By the end of the lesson I'm not sure whom I'll be happier to see the back of—the boys or their counselor.

After the lessons are done and the horses are tucked into their stalls for the night, I collapse into an Adirondack chair in front of the lounge, too tired to make my way back to the Mountain Inn just yet.

"Well that was one hell of a day," Ben says, handing me a beer and sinking into the chair next to mine.

"Cheers to that." I tap the mouth of my bottle to the one he's holding.

"Have you heard from Simon or Jillian?"

With the daylight fading, the pastures have taken on a droopy melancholy.

"Spoke to Simon about an hour ago. They're keeping Rena in the hospital a few more days. It wasn't a heart attack this time, but she's not in great shape. Simon asked how you were doing."

"Well, I didn't break Libby and hopefully I didn't traumatize the therapeutic kids beyond repair."

Ben smiles. "That's pretty much what I told him."

"Nice. Thanks."

"Seriously though, you were great today. Thank you."

"Can I trust you to keep a secret?" I take a long swig, stretching the quiet into the deepening evening.

"Depends if it's in my best interest." The shadows conceal the expression on his face.

"I had fun teaching and helping out in the barn. I didn't realize how much I missed being around horses."

"That's not a secret."

I pull the corners of my mouth into a frown but can't keep them down.

Ben laughs, then hands me a piece of paper. "Here's your schedule for tomorrow. I'll juggle the rest after I get some sleep."

"You have me for two more days, Ben." My stomach clenches and I imagine the darkening aura cloud swirling around me.

"Are you done with your dad's affairs?" He ignores my timing comment.

"No. But enough that I can finish the rest from Chicago."

"Can't you take more time off? It would mean a lot to Rena and Simon knowing you were here. And that would give you more time to finish whatever is left to be done."

"I have a job."

"Is that the only thing pulling you back there?"

"Isn't it enough?" I study the bottle in my hand, squint at the warning label as though I've never read it before.

I don't need a spotlight on Ben to know he's giving me a don't-bullshit-me look.

"Simon also told me to have you check out of the inn and move your stuff into the second apartment. It's not being used, and it doesn't make sense for you to be shuttling back and forth."

"I can't."

"Can't stay in the apartment or can't stay to help?"

"Both?" It's more question than statement and Ben laughs at my indecision.

"He said that would be your answer. Why can't you stay in the apartment?"

"The state of Maryland won't survive the explosion when Jillian learns I've moved in. It's safer for all of us if I stay at the inn."

Ben repositions and the wood chair groans in protest. "So, you're staying to help?"

"What?"

"You said 'It's safer if I stay at the inn.' That means you haven't ruled out staying and helping."

"Yes. No. No, it doesn't mean that. It means I don't want to deal with Jillian's temper tantrum over me being here."

Even in the gloaming light I can tell Ben is smirking.

"Jillian will get over it. She'll have to. She can't take on all the lessons and I certainly can't absorb much more than I already have. We need you. Rena knew that."

He stands abruptly and asks if I want another beer.

We need you. Rena knew that.

"Sit." I point at the chair and Ben refolds into it. "What did you mean by 'Rena knew that'?"

He drops his head into his hands. "Oh crap. Rena will geld me for this."

I lean back and cross my arms. "Talk."

He shoots me an under-the-flop-of-hair assessment, probably trying to decide whom he's more intimidated by or feels more sympathetic to. "Shit. Fine." He pushes into the back of the chair and straightens his arms as though preparing for liftoff.

"Talk."

"Damn you're bossy. Is that what they teach you in the corporate world?"

I glare, or at least try to glare.

"Your dad used to come here. He'd sit away from others mostly, close enough to watch but just removed enough so no one would get the idea he was here to socialize. He always had a dark gray notebook with him. Writing, drawing. I don't know what he was doing."

A million questions zip through my brain but none finds the exit through my mouth.

"Rena would sit and talk to him. They never seemed to agree, though. At least they never laughed or looked relaxed around each other. She was always moodier after his visits. Anyway, she wanted him to call you back. She was hoping that if you came, you would decide on your own that you belonged here. But I think she was also ready to make a case for it."

"How do you know all of this?"

"Rena and Simon have been very good to me. They're more than my employers. They're also friends. She tried to take on more after Simon was forced to slow down. But her health is worse than his. She's just way more stubborn. When her health took a dive, the helping reversed. But Simon can't keep up or take more on."

"My father sent me an e-mail a few weeks before his accident. Something about needing to talk." My brain cells scroll through the vast number of e-mails, trying to recall the exact words of my father's last e-mail to me.

"He didn't say what about?"

"Nope. Trying to manipulate as always."

"Wow."

I can't tell if that's a judgment on me or my father. "Did you ever talk to him?"

"No. But I didn't get the sense from what Rena said that he had horns and a pitchfork."

"Designer ones."

"Funny."

Our conversation is replaced by the chatter of evening—noisy bugs and restless horses.

I try to picture my father here, sitting on the bleachers with his notebook. I try to imagine what he looked like sketching. Did he think about me while he was drawing Jack? Did he think about Mom when he was drawing the scene from a therapy lesson?

"So?" Ben's voice pulls me back. "Will you stay and help?"

"I can't. There's a lot going down at the office and they're expecting me back."

"There's a lot going down for you here, too. Maybe it's time to put yourself first."

"Now that's a unique idea."

"But a good one, right?" I hear the smirk in his voice.

My stomach flops, from nerves or excitement or a combination of both?

"My boss will have a nervous breakdown."

"Is that a bad thing?"

We both laugh, and just like that, the flopping in my stomach stops. I pull out my phone and send an e-mail to Bruce, copying human resources and Howard.

There's a giddiness at the idea of spending four more days with the horses and a sudden freedom at the idea of following my heart.

But there's also a swirling of dread that, once again, I've been manipulated by my father.

23

My phone vibrates in the back pocket of my jeans. "And walk," I tell the horse cantering circles around me at the end of the lunge line, then with my free hand I reach for the phone. The horse comes to an abrupt halt. In the time it takes to flick my finger across the screen and accept the call, the horse has turned and is breathing into my face. "Stop that." I push him away.

"What did I do?" A man's voice asks, the tone somewhere between affronted and amused.

"Jeez, I'm sorry. Not you."

"Oh good." I hear what could be a chuckle or a throat clearing. "I have some good news. At least I hope it's good news."

My brain whirs, trying to place the voice. Maybe it's the prolonged quiet, but the voice adds, "This is Tom."

Tom?

"Thomas Adler?"

"Of course. I'm sorry. Good news?" I shove at the dark brown horse who clearly has an issue with personal space.

"I have papers for you to sign to close out your father's practice."

"Already?" Feeling suddenly unmoored, I grab at the large shape in front of me.

There's a hesitation on the other end of the line. "You seemed anxious to have this resolved as quickly as possible."

"Yes, I was. Am."

You're still leaving the moment Rena is back on her feet.

Except that the conviction from those first few days, that absolute certainty that I don't belong here, is softening like ripe cheese.

I didn't belong here. Until I started belonging again.

"I can bring the papers to you if that'll be easier?"

"Actually that would be great. I'm working all day and probably won't be done until long after you close tonight."

"Work?" The surprise in his voice leaps out of the phone.

"I'm helping a friend for a few days."

I give Thomas the address of Jumping Frog Farm and return my attention to the beast trying to stomp on my foot.

"Dude, manners. We've got some work ahead of us. Personal space. Listening. Patience." I pull my foot out from under his hoof again. "Now get back out there. We're not done lunging yet."

After another ten minutes of trotting and cantering in circles, Charlie settles down. Or at least he's not bucking every third step. And he's not trying to pancake my feet. I look at my watch. Another ten minutes before his owner, Scott, arrives for their lesson.

The rest of the morning is a whirlwind of dust and horses. I'm surprised when Thomas walks into the barn looking freshly pressed and surprisingly casual. He's holding an envelope in one hand and a white paper bag in the other.

"I brought sandwiches." He swings the paper bag from side to side.

My stomach snaps to attention at the mention of food. "You're brilliant. Thanks. Can we start with those?"

He grins and pulls the bag closer to his body. "Maybe I should hold it as collateral. Get your signature on those legal documents first."

"Don't worry, I'll sign."

"Sure you're not having second thoughts?" He takes in my

less-than-couture-ish attire, my hair pulled into a sloppy bun, and smiles.

I'm supposed to say "no second thoughts." About the medical practice there are no second thoughts. Not even a hiccup about selling the condo. And yet, there's a significant drop in urgency over leaving.

"Hand over that bag." I won't let the stomach stutters over returning to Chicago color what needs to be done.

We sit on the patio, the fields dotted with horses enjoying the fall day. Carlisle, Simon's black Lab, flops at my feet. Poor dog has been cooped up inside the last few days with Simon spending most of his time at the hospital.

I take my time with the sandwich, sharing a piece of turkey with Carlisle.

Thomas is watching, the left corner of his mouth inching higher.

"What?"

"You look completely different."

I wipe my hand along my pant leg, then self-consciously pick at a slobber spot courtesy of Jack and a grass stain courtesy of Jukebox. "Aren't you glad I didn't show up in your office looking like this?"

He winks. "The look suits you. The smell not as much. No offense."

I narrow my eyes. "Is there a right way to take being told I look better wearing horse and goat slobber than the fancy clothes I spent a small fortune on?"

"You've smiled more in the half hour we've been sitting here than the entirety of our previous meeting."

"You didn't feed me last time."

He laughs. "Touché. But somehow I don't think my sandwich choice is the magic ingredient."

I shrug. "I've enjoyed being back."

He hesitates, as though wanting to say more, then picks up the envelope and turns it over several times like a magician waving a magic handkerchief.

"You're returning to Chicago tomorrow?"

I reach down to pat Carlisle. "No. I extended my stay by a couple of days." *Four, not a couple, that's a couple plus a couple more. Although technically only a couple since two of those days are weekend.*

"Hopefully it's not because of this?" He taps the envelope against his thigh. "I assure you, Emma, that we can finish the final paperwork via mail."

I nod. "It's not."

"Any progress on the condo?"

"Actually yes. T.J. left a message earlier. She's had a request for a second visit and expects to have an offer by the end of today."

"She's fabulous, isn't she? I knew she was perfect. She went to college with my partner. Found our townhouse for us and negotiated a killer deal. Aaron is her biggest fan and pimps her to everyone he can. She may be petite but she's a bulldog."

"Your partner?"

Thomas sighs, then chuckles. "Don't get me started. He hates when I call him that."

Lucy had said "husband." "You're married?" I indicate the wide band on his finger.

"We are. But I can't bring myself to call him husband. That would make me the wife? Nope, thank you. No offense." He wiggles his eyebrows at me.

"This time, none taken." I like this guy. I can imagine us being friends if I stay. Which I'm not. "Thanks again for recommending T.J."

My attention falters as Ben leads Wally to the outdoor arena.

"Ah," Thomas says, a smile pulling across his face.

"Meaning?" I tighten the leash on my attention span.

"Staying to help out a friend."

My eyes follow where he's looking.

"Not that friend. The owners of this stable."

"Ah."

"Are you going to give me those papers or not?"

"Absolutely," he says, handing over the envelope and attempting to smother the smile.

Two red dots blink through the swirl of dust as Thomas Adler taps the breaks at the end of the driveway.

"It's gone, Dad. I signed the papers." *Was it worth it? Was that medical practice so much more important than your own family? For someone who knew so much about reading people, you were completely blind to your own family.*

Ben comes to stand next to me at the edge of the patio. "What's wrong? You look upset. Bad news?" His eyes dart to the road in time to watch the car pop over the hill and disappear around the bend.

"Nothing's wrong. I guess you could say that things are moving along perfectly."

"So why the scowl?"

"An unplanned trip down memory lane."

"Courtesy of the guy in the fancy clothes?"

"He just loaded the baggage. I'm solely responsible for the destination."

"Wanna talk?"

"No."

"Okay." He hands me two halters and untangles their lead ropes from the others he's holding. "Then walk with me. We need to bring in a few horses for the afternoon lessons."

We cross the parking lot and ease through the crowd of horses crowding the gate. Of course the horses we need are in the back pasture. We walk, side by side, stepping over mounds of horse poop, both fresh and petrified.

"Did you have a good relationship with your parents?"

"I thought you didn't want to talk."

"I changed my mind. Did you?"

"Mostly. My dad didn't get why I wanted to squander my talent on this profession." He sweeps his hands, indicating the property around us. "Careful." He points at a still fresh poop pile in my trajectory.

"What did he think you should be doing instead?"

"Physics. My specialization was high energy theory. I was all set to go work at Brown University with *the* expert on black hole physics."

"Why didn't you?"

"I fell in love."

I twist to get a look at his face and trip on a large rock.

"Hmm, maybe I shouldn't have brought you out here. You have done this before, right?"

"Give me a break." I swat at him with the end of a lead rope. "So what happened, she didn't support your decision to go there?"

I can't tell if my incredulous reaction is because someone wouldn't support her significant other or that he'd dropped a career path for the sake of a relationship. What if I'd accepted Stephen's proposal and moved to Seattle? I look at Ben's face, searching for a clue to what I gave up. Maybe I should try to find Stephen. No. Some things really are better left in the past.

Ben looks at me in surprise, then smiles. "I fell in love with a horse."

"Seriously?"

"Seriously. I started riding in college. Don't look so surprised. Not everyone starts riding before they can walk. Anyway, my college girlfriend had a horse and spent most of her free time at the barn. If I wanted to see her, I needed to either turn into a horse or learn to ride one. The first option wasn't very appealing. So I started taking lessons. Junior year we both competed in a show and somehow our riding instructor entered us in the same class. Guess what happened?"

I snort a laugh. "You beat her, didn't you?"

"Beat the custom boots right off of her. She withheld sex for a month after that."

"You're kidding?"

"Like you've never used that punishment before?"

"Why punish myself in the process?" I duck under a low tree branch and chance a look at Ben.

His left eyebrow disappears under the shock of hair, leaving no question about the twinkle in his eye.

Shit, back up, back up. No flirting.

"So what happened?"

"Nothing. She broke up with me shortly after. And I continued to ride. When I needed a part-time job to pay for grad school, one of the professionals at the stable hired me to hack some of his horses. He taught me everything I know about dressage.

"He let me show one of his mares, Izzy. She was a stunner. Seventeen-hand dapple gray Selle Français. Perfect in every way. When he decided it was time to sell her, I was crushed. He offered her to me at a hell of a price, she would have easily sold for sixty or seventy K. But I was a poor grad student, there was no way I could afford even half that. Not to mention board, and vet, and you know the sob story. So he offered me a full-time job. Board and everything else would be part of the salary."

"Wow. Nice."

"Right? Except now I had a dilemma. A highly competitive job in astrophysics or a highly competitive life in the equestrian world. When it came time to pack, I realized I couldn't stomach the idea of spending my days in a lab staring at computer screens. I turned down the position at Brown and signed my life over to Izzy."

"Where is she now?" I catch my breath, afraid I've opened a sad can of nostalgia.

Ben grins. "She's retired. Enjoying life as a granddam at a friend's farm. He's bred her a few times. Wally is her baby." He beams like a proud papa.

"And your dad never approved?"

Ben tosses his head from side to side. "Dad's a space buff. He wanted to brag that his son was doing breakthrough research. He didn't approve but he didn't disapprove. Does that make sense?"

I nod.

Ben unlatches the clasp holding the metal gate closed, then

lifts the gate enough to swing it past a mound of dirt. I step through and wait for him to close it behind us. The horses we're after are at the far end of the field and clearly unimpressed with our effort to get them.

I fall back into step next to Ben.

"My parents schlepped all over the U.S. to watch me show. They even went to Germany to cheer me on. Although between us, I think Dad was more drawn to Germany by the beer than the horse show."

"My father came to three horse shows. My mom didn't come to any."

He tries not to look surprised but I can tell he is. The in-gates are always crowded with horse-show moms holding ponies, a towel over their shoulder for that last boot wipe before their babies trot into the ring. Simon and Rena had been there for me. And Jilli, at least at the beginning.

"All three of the shows were within driving distance. Well, within an hour drive. And he brought colleagues. Once it was the dean of the GW medical school whose daughter wanted to ride. Another time it was an editor of one psychology journal or another whose wife was an avid rider. I don't remember who he brought the third time. I just remember that he'd been sitting in the stands talking to someone when I walked the course. By the time I finished my ride they were gone."

"Why didn't your mom ever go? Was she afraid of horses?"

I bite the inside of my lip. "She was sick. She died when I was ten."

"I'm sorry."

I nod. It's the least, and the most, I can do.

The truth is a secret I'm not sure I have the right to uncork.

24

July 1995

It was another hair-melting-hot day. Emma and Jillian spent the day at the stable as usual, helping with the horses and "little kid" lessons. Emma even managed to wiggle herself into helping with a therapeutic session.

"I'm starving. Are you ready to get out of here?" Jillian shifts from one leg to the other and fans herself with a piece of cardboard. "I can't stand it in here one more minute."

"We're not done yet." Emma scans the chore list Rena had written on the whiteboard earlier. This was their summer "camp"— barn chores for extra riding lessons. And once a week, a long trail ride. They still have to check that the fans in the occupied stalls are turned on and that each horse has fresh water and a salt block. "You do the left side, I'll do the right. It'll be faster that way."

Jillian huffs but moves to the first stall. Soon they're giggling and trying to outpace each other in and out of stalls. By the time they finish, both are out of breath, dripping with sweat, and laughing.

"Race you to the house." Jilli bounds out of the barn.

From somewhere behind they hear Simon's "no running in the barn," but they're already halfway across the parking lot to the Winn house. They reach the house and bend over to catch their breath.

Jillian links arms with her as they skip over the paving stones leading to the mudroom. "You know what we should do? Fix sandwiches and eat them in the baby pools. Seriously, I'm so hot. I think I could just sit in cold water all night."

Emma grins. "I call the seahorse one."

Jillian pretend glares but can't hold the look for long. "Oh fine. You're spending the night, right?"

"I have to ask."

While Jillian bustles around the kitchen, Emma calls her dad. "Hey, Dad, can I . . ." She bites her lip and listens, then starts over, "Hello, Dad. May I stay with Jilli tonight?" She scrunches her face at Jillian, who's pretending to have a conversation with a head of lettuce.

"Yes, sir. Yes, sir. But . . . Of course. Yes. Thank you." She unravels the phone cord from around her finger and replaces the receiver on its base. She feels the question before she turns and looks at Jilli's arched eyebrows. "He said yes. But I have to go home after morning barn chores."

Jillian's brows and mouth drop. "But tomorrow we're trail riding."

"I'll be back in time."

"Promise?"

"Promise."

"What if he doesn't let you?"

"He will. I just have to work on the essay. Believe me, he doesn't want me in the house all day. If I'm here, he's free to go to his office."

"Okay, good."

They change into swimsuits and take their dinner outside, balancing sandwiches and chips on plates on top of soda cans. The two baby pools don't take long to fill and it takes even less time for them to splash in.

Jillian squirms in the shallow water, then sends a spray of water with her foot onto Emma. "I wish we had a pool. A real pool. One you can swim in, not just soak your butt in."

"Hey, my sandwich." Emma shifts to protect her dinner. "What did you put in this anyway?"

Jillian beams. "Great, isn't it? It's a lasagna sandwich. I added lettuce so that Grandma won't complain we're not getting our greens."

Emma chews slowly. She wouldn't call this great but it's not bad. Different. Interesting. Unique. She takes another bite, then licks a glob of cold pasta sauce from her finger. Okay, it's kinda great. But she's not sure how much of the great is the actual sandwich and how much of it is eating in the baby pool as the stars fill up the sky above them.

Rena steps out of the house an hour later. "Girls, it's time to come in." The screen door slaps shut behind her, startling Romeo, the Winns' mastiff, who's finally settled down after splashing through the baby pools and helping himself to sandwich and chip leftovers. He's wedged between the two baby pools, one paw on the edge of Emma's pool so that with each move, more water drains out. The smell of wet dog overpowers the potted night jasmine at the edge of the patio.

"Do we have to?" they chorus.

"It's not like we have to get up early for school tomorrow," Jilli adds for good measure.

"Yes, you have to. Now up. And drain the water out of those pools. I don't want to find any animals bobbing around in there tomorrow morning."

Emma gets up and Romeo takes the opportunity to army crawl into the baby pool.

Rena scrunches her nose. "Dry him off before you let him in the house, please. Bad enough he drools on my pillow, I don't need wet-dog smell next to me all night."

"He could sleep with us." Emma hugs Romeo and he smiles at her, the twisted jowls and exposed canines giving him a goofy, and not entirely friendly, expression.

"No way." Jillian pushes at his backend. "He snores. And he farts."

"Because you don't?" Emma curls her lips and squints, mimicking Romeo's smile.

"I hate you." Jilli kicks a stream of water at her and mock growls in a poodle-ish rather than a mastiff-ish way.

"Okay, okay. Bring it inside." Rena wraps a towel around each of them, then picks up the plates and empty soda cans.

Jilli takes the first turn in the shower. By the time Emma gets in there, the room is steamed and the hot water is mostly gone. But the water pressure feels good on the top of her head and her shoulders and she ends up standing there, leaning forward and to each side until the water gets cold.

She opens the door of the bathroom, clutching the towel around her. Checking that the coast is clear, she darts for Jillian's bedroom, pushing the door shut behind her with a relieved whoosh.

Jilli is sitting cross-legged on her bed, her hair freshly braided, her pink boxers and tank horse-print pajamas a striking contrast to the sophisticated *Vogue* in her lap. She looks up and frowns. "What's your problem?"

"I thought I heard Simon."

"So?"

"I'm in a towel?" She grabs tighter as one end slips.

"So?" Jilli repeats with a "duh" shrug-and-head-shake combo.

"He doesn't need to see me like this." She bites her lip. Simon has seen her in towels before, in a swimsuit, even a hospital gown. But lately she's started noticing small changes in her body.

Jilli is a year older but probably three ahead in development. Emma still marvels at the bumps and curves that are taking over her friend. She's both anxious and terrified to see what nature has in store for her. She wants to ask Jilli about it but she wishes Jilli would start the conversation. This is one of those times she really, really misses her mom.

"Can I borrow a big T-shirt to sleep in?" She moves to the dresser and waits for permission to open the drawer.

Jilli shrugs and flips another page in the magazine. "You never ask. Why are you being so weird?"

"I'm not." She slips a large shirt over her head, tightening her grip on the towel with her free hand, then letting it slide as the T-shirt drops over her butt. She feels Jilli's eyes on her, then the heat of a flush.

"Jeez you're a spaz. Sit, I want to show you something." She scoots over to make room for Emma, shoves the open magazine in her lap, and taps at a picture. "Look at that. Isn't it perfect? Someday I'm going to wear a dress like that."

Emma looks at the picture and murmurs that it is beautiful but it's not barn attire. Jilli huffs at her lack of fashion sense.

"Look at how it shows off her boobs. And that slit up her leg." Jillian stretches her left leg and points her toes, making the muscles in her calf and thigh stand out.

"You don't have boobs like that."

"I will." She cups the small mounds and pushes them together. "I will, you'll see."

Emma rounds her back to create more space between her mini-bumps and the fabric of the shirt.

Footsteps announce Simon's arrival. "Bedtime, girls. Lights out and Chat buttons to the Off position."

They crawl under the summer blankets. The beds are at a right angle to each other, Jilli's is under the window with the big tree in front of the house, and what everyone refers to as Emma's bed is under the window that faces the barn. She likes sitting up in the morning and looking at the barn first thing. Sometimes at night when she can't sleep but Jilli can, she takes comfort in the nearness of the barn.

The house settles around them. They hear a muffled discussion across the hall, then footsteps as someone—Rena by the sound of it—goes downstairs, then comes back up. More discussion and Rena's laughter.

"What's wrong?" Jilli's voice is a whisper, barely louder than the hiss of the air-conditioning.

"Nothing." She pulls in a sniffle, hoping to mask it under a loud, fake yawn.

"Don't BS me, Toad." Jilli only calls her that when she's trying to channel Simon's authority.

Emma releases air through clenched teeth. "It's just hearing your grandparents. There's never muffled talking in my house. Or laughing. You get used to the silence. Most of the time it doesn't bother me." She nibbles on the fatty part of the ring finger on her left hand to stop the rest of the thought from pouring out.

A hand reaches from the dark and tugs at Emma's. "Don't do that."

"Sorry."

"Why do you do it?"

"I don't know. I don't mean to."

"Doesn't it hurt?"

"No. Yes. Sometimes."

"Is that why you do it?"

"No." The answer is quick and sharp and stings Emma's mouth coming out. She never really thinks about it. It's just something she started doing at some point.

It wasn't really "at some point." She knows exactly when she started. It was the night her mom had been taken to the hospital that first time, when they still lived in Baltimore. She'd been so scared. She'd wanted to cry, scream, but she couldn't. Her father had told her to be strong. So every time the urge to cry or scream built inside, she chewed the skin at the edge of her nail. Just that one finger, just that little fatty part, just enough to distract her.

The fact that it drove her dad crazy became a bonus.

"Do you think you could stop?"

She'd intended to stop. Even thought she had stopped. But then she'd get upset or nervous or scared and snip, rip, there went the skin.

"Probably. Not."

"You're such a spaz."

They dissolve into laughter that gets louder when a loud

"Girls!" barrels down the hallway. They change the subject, talking about horses and school and plans for the rest of the summer. They talk about the essay Emma has to write, her father's idea to keep her mind engaged during the summer break.

The quiet time between topics gets longer and longer. Her eyes are heavy and she's tired from the effort of talking.

"Hey, Em."

"Mmm . . ."

"You know you're not alone, right? You have me now. All of us actually. Maybe that'll be enough to help you stop?"

"Mmm . . ." She releases herself to the comfort of the family she adopted. And sleep.

25

Tiger cat escorts me down the front path of the Mountain Inn. I set the suitcase down and kneel to pet him. He arches his back and rubs on my leg, tail high in the air.

"So today you decide I'm okay? Or are you here just to make sure I'm really leaving?"

He turns and gives a small hop, rubbing against my other leg.

"Silly cat. I'm actually going to miss you." I rub behind his ears. "You behave. Keep Lucy in line, will ya?" He bumps me, then, tail twitching, saunters off. I've been dismissed.

I load up the rental car and mumble a good-bye to the inn. Thomas had been right about booking me here after all. But I have to admit that I'm rather excited about spending a few nights in the apartment above the barn. It always seemed so romantic to live up there and be close to the horses. Of course, I was younger then and a bit more horse crazy than I am now. At least younger.

On the drive to the hospital, I rehearse my questions. How long had she been in touch with my father? If they'd made peace, why not be up-front with me? Why dodge the truth about the letters?

A pleasant volunteer at the information desk points me to the cardiac wing. The closer I get to Rena's room number, the slower my steps become. What if she gets upset and has a heart attack?

I have to ask the questions. She's the only person who can help me piece together what I don't know about my own family. *Please don't let her get upset and have a heart attack.*

I stop at Rena's room and gently knock. The door is open just enough that I can see the foot of the bed. Simon's voice tells me to come in and I give the door a nudge. His eyes dart from me to Rena and back to me. He smiles, a tight, tired smile, and motions for me to enter. I release a lungful of anxiety and step into the hospital room.

In my mind, I'd pictured Rena sitting in bed, bossing everyone around. That was the Rena I was going to confront for answers. The woman in the hospital bed is old and frail, sick. She watches me take a couple of tentative steps into the room. She doesn't encourage me forward or scowl me away, just watches.

Simon gets up and drags a second chair closer to the bed. "Come sit. Ben says you're doing great with the lessons."

"It's going okay."

"You've extended your stay." Rena's voice wobbles and I'm not sure if it's a question or a statement. "And staying in the vacant apartment." It wasn't a question.

I take a step back, wanting to undo the decision to come here, but Simon puts a hand on my back and nudges me to the chair.

"It makes sense for her to stay in that apartment, Rena." He waits for me to sit before grunting into the chair next to mine.

Rena gives one slow nod.

A card on the side table catches my eye. There's a horse on the front, the saddle on the horse's belly, and the rider sitting on the ground with the words, "Hope you're back in the saddle soon."

"Did you know my father used to draw horses?" It's not the question I'd planned to ask or even the question I most need an answer to. But the fact that she knows more about my father pushes it to the firing line.

Rena squints as though trying to bring something into focus. "Yes."

I'm not surprised and yet I'm utterly shocked.

I pull the gray linen notebook from my purse. She stares at the unassuming book, the creases in her face becoming more pronounced. I open the book and place it on her lap.

"He was quite talented."

"Yes, he was. Mom was the one who drew pictures for me when I was little. He never would. Said he didn't draw. There are other sketch pads but those are of people."

She nods.

The flap of the thick paper as I turn the pages fills the gaps between the beeping of machines.

I stop at one image about two-thirds of the way through the notebook. "This is my favorite."

"He spent more time staring at Jack than anyone else in the barn."

The resolve I'd been working into a lather dries in the current of her words.

I thought coming back here would be a quick in-and-out. Gallop in as the confident adult me, deal with my father's things the way I deal with all business, then gallop out leaving nothing but a dust cloud behind me. *And how's that plan working for ya?*

"I keep looking through his sketch pads, looking for an answer."

"What do you think old drawings will tell you?"

"That there's more to him than I knew."

"Isn't that a given? There's always more to people than we truly know. Everyone has their secrets."

"He was the master of secrets." I don't try to mask the anger.

"You should give him the benefit of the doubt."

"Why?"

She slides down in the bed like a child hoping to disappear under the covers. I snatch a glimpse at Simon to see if I've stepped out of line with my tone. A glance passes between them.

The conversation I had with Rena replays in my mind. I've gotten some insight from Ben, but I want to hear it from her. "Why were you guys in contact again?"

She flinches and the sensors on the monitor by the bed beep louder. Simon leans forward and grabs her hand. "Rena?"

She pulls in a raspy breath, the effort registering in the faster tags moving across the screen.

We fall silent, listening to the beep and hiss of the machines monitoring Rena's vitals. Her life beeping and hissing for everyone to hear. This isn't the woman who scares little kids and big horses.

Simon's eyes are glassy as he looks at his wife. His oversize hands protect her fragile hand as his thumb sweeps a semicircle around the bump of the IV.

I'm hypnotized by his thumb. "This is why you stopped teaching."

A lone tear trickles down his cheek and he looks down at their hands. "Not entirely. Knee-replacement surgery slowed me down too much. And yes." He raises his eyes and the rest of the explanation floats away in his tears.

I close my eyes, not wanting the reality in front of me to be real.

"Where do I fit in whatever you and my father were hatching this time?"

"This time?"

I can't tell if she's hedging or really can't remember. "The letters. Now the meetings."

"I hoped you would come back. I needed you to come back. I was afraid you wouldn't come back."

"Why though?" I swallow impatience, frustration, dread. *Please don't say for good-byes.* But what else could it be?

"I hoped you would visit and the past would be forgotten. I wanted to rewind the years. When he didn't agree, I pushed harder. I tried forcing his hand, I thought I could appeal to him on a personal level. He came to me when your mom needed help. Now I needed help." Another tear escapes. She swipes at it and winces when the movement tugs at the IV line.

I slap my hand to my mouth. "Oh my god, he was coming to see you when he had the accident."

Her chin touches her chest. "Yes."

Beside me, Simon stiffens. "I think we need to let her rest now."

"No, I need to finish." She grabs at my arm. "Then you were there, in front of me, and you weren't the girl I remembered. You're not a girl anymore. You're a woman with your own life. One that doesn't include us."

"But if you wanted me back, why were you so . . ." I search for a softer word, then give up and finish, "hostile."

"Because looking at you, I realized that maybe your father had been right. Maybe it was wrong to drag you back into our lives."

I want to counter that my father hadn't been right, that he hadn't known what was best for me. Her eyes droop. I'm running out of time to ask my question. "Why did you want me to take your lessons?"

"Because your father wasn't right after all. You may be grown-up but you're still the same person inside. It's time to come back home and follow your dream. And I need you to show Jilli how to move forward."

26

The doctor had pulled rank and I'd been shooed out of Rena's room. The drive to the farm was noisy, my brain refusing to settle on one thought.

What did Rena mean about teaching Jillian to move forward? How the hell am I supposed to teach her anything when she clearly hates the air I breathe?

I pull into the parking lot at the farm, ready for my dose of Jack.

The trailer is parked in front of the barn next to Jilli's sports car. I've never been a big believer in bad omens, but the trailer-Jilli combination sparks a riot with my nerves. The day didn't start well and it looks as though it won't be getting better in the near future. Unless the trailer means she's leaving for a few days.

My wound-up nerves explode the minute I walk into the barn office where Jillian and Ben are in the midst of an over-heated discussion.

"Fabulous. Look what walked in."

"Deal with it, Jillian."

I take a step back, hoping for a black hole that will spit me out after Jilli drives off.

"No you don't." Ben traps me mid-flee. "This isn't my call, ladies."

"What's happening?" I look from Ben to Jillian.

"This is bullshit," she mutters, throwing herself onto the couch.

Ben motions me to the chair in front of the desk. I feel like a kid being called into the principal's office. He waits for both of us to settle, then draws a deep breath before stepping into the middle of the lion's cage.

"The two of you are going to pick up a horse for Rena."

Nope, this day isn't getting better.

Jillian sulks deeper into the cushions. "I can go alone."

"No you can't."

"Then you go with me."

"Can't. I have a full lesson roster. Emma isn't teaching until later." He turns to me with what could be sympathy or a plea for forgiveness.

"Plus, Rena specifically said Emma should be the one to go."

"Whuuu . . ." I sputter. "I was just there. She didn't say anything about this."

"You were at the hospital?" Jillian is ramrod straight on the couch. "Why would you do that?"

I match her stare. "I wanted to see her. It's something people do when someone they care about is in the hospital."

She looks as shocked at my words as I feel at having uttered them.

"Ladies." Ben taps at the desk with a pen, the lion tamer with a very short whip.

"What about the horses that need exercising?" I grasp for an out.

"It's nice enough today. I'll let them out for a couple of hours. They'll be fine."

"Where is this horse and why does it need two people?"

I expect Jilli to jump on that wagon but she stays oddly focused on a tear in the upholstery.

"Jillian," Ben swivels to look at her, "would you like to fill your friend in?"

"No." The tip of her finger disappears into the stuffing.

Ben assumes the measured tone of a teacher dealing with uncooperative kids. "Jillian, you'll drive but you're to stay in the
truck. Do. Not. Get. Out. Emma, you'll retrieve the horse. Ask
for Mark. Rena talked to him this morning. He's expecting us.
You're to get the one horse. Chestnut gelding, comma-shaped
star. He's the one you're to come back with. Don't let Mark convince you to take a different horse. Understood?"

"Understood. Come on, Ben, why the secret-agent tactics?"

He pinches the bridge of his nose. It's the first time I've seen
him look stressed.

"These guys have a bad reputation. They don't treat their
horses well. Rena has been trying to close them down. Looks like
she's succeeded. But the horses that are left are earmarked for the
slaughterhouse. That chestnut gelding was one of ours before his
owners sold him. Rena wants him back. The owner of the place
is trying to stick it to her, which is why he may try to switch
horses on us."

My pulse picks up speed. "How many horses are left there?"

"Not many, from what I've heard. This guy is a class-A asshole." Though he's talking to me, Ben is studying Jillian, who is
studying a lump of couch stuffing.

"This smells worse than Jukebox. Would someone like to tell
me what the hell is really going on?"

Ben and Jilli lock gazes, a clear standoff of wills.

"Let's get this over with." She pushes up from the couch and
walks past me, not waiting to see if I follow.

The idea of getting in the truck with her makes my palms
sweaty. It's making my brain sweaty, too. Is this part of the
moving-forward lesson? I feel like I'm being tested and failure
looks like a heap of mangled steel.

I take three deep breaths to slow the pounding in my chest.
"Ben?"

"Ask her."

"She won't tell me. She doesn't want me around. She'd eject
me out of the damn truck if she could."

His mouth twitches, a smile that doesn't mature.

I tilt my head toward the door. "Why only the two-horse trailer?"

His jaw ticks left then right. "We can't save the whole world."

"We run a therapeutic program. How can we turn away those who need help—human or equine?"

"If only it was that easy. The humans bring in money, the equines eat it."

"It's not right."

"It's not, I agree."

I hear the rumble of the diesel engine and picture Jillian losing what little patience she has to begin with. "I guess that's my cue."

I stand and walk to the door. If I'd stuck to the original plan, I'd be on my way to Chicago right now, not facing the most terrifying drive of my life.

There's an uncomfortable chill in the cab of the truck. I pull my hands into the sleeves of my jacket and stuff them between my thighs. Jillian pulls a sleeve over her knuckles and smirks. She's decided to take revenge by freezing me—literally and figuratively. Not one word has passed between us during the hour's drive.

Despite the cold, I've been sweating the entire time. My body is rigid from the crushing combination of fear and freezing.

I should have told Ben I couldn't ride in the truck with her. I should have said I'd follow in my car. I should have told Rena the truth and then maybe she wouldn't have insisted I be the one to go.

The truck jolts over a pothole and I grab the armrest, my heart pounding.

She chuckles but the sound is hollow. "Relax, we won't be crashing today."

She allows the rig to idle at a Stop sign, keeping her eyes on the side mirror in case someone comes up behind us.

"It's just down that road." She nods to the left. "I'm not supposed to be on their property. They are the lowest form of humans and deserve worse than being shut down."

I turn to get a better look at her. Her profile doesn't reveal much.

She sighs and I catch a flick of a look in my direction. "They have a restraining order on me. As long as I don't get out of the truck and as long as the owners don't get a whiff of me, I'm okay."

"What happened?"

"Let's just say not one of my finer moments."

"Did it involve alcohol?" My breath makes tiny white clouds.

The diesel engine rumbles and moans. Jillian's profile stiffens. I resist the urge to apologize for poking at an old wound.

I think I knew in the back of my mind that accusing her of being a drunk would blow our friendship to bits. I never imagined it would be the seal of death. I'd wanted to shock her into realizing there was a problem and admitting she needed help.

"No." It's little more than an exhale that fogs a pattern on the side window.

"I shouldn't have said that."

Her shoulders twitch. "I guess I can't really blame you." I twist against the seat belt but she holds up a hand. "Don't." Her left pinky moves away from the steering wheel and flicks the turn signal. The blink-ping ricochets through the truck.

She navigates the sharp turn into a driveway.

The truck heaves left as the front tire slips into a deep rut. Wood planks in the perimeter fence create awkward angles where they've popped away from the post. A walk-in shed in the pasture to our right is missing half of its roof.

Inside, a chestnut pony stands between the wall and a hanging aluminum sheet from the defunct roof.

"Stop." One hand grabs for the door handle while my other fumbles to release the seat belt. "That's him."

Jillian slams on the breaks and grabs my arm. "Wait."

The chestnut's head hangs, nose almost touching the ground. His back curves up, accentuating the sharp lines of his rib cage.

He moves, and in the impossibly narrow space between him and the wall is a black pony, skinnier than any other animal I've ever seen, with eyes devoid of the will to continue.

I recognize the absence of hope in those eyes. I'd been too young to recognize the pain back then. But I'd seen it. In my mom. In Jilli.

"We have to find Mark. We're taking them both."

Jillian releases my arm and grips the steering wheel. "We can't."

"The hell if I'm leaving that poor pony behind."

"It's not your call."

My heartbeat pounds in my ears, muffling her words and the rumbling engine. Heat burns through my chest, anger at the cruelty, desperation to make a difference. "I'll use my own money. And find another stable if I have to."

Jillian shakes her head but doesn't say anything. The truck inches forward until we're even with the iron paddock gate.

"This is as close as I'm getting." She slams the gearshift into Park and crosses her arms in a final exclamation mark.

A man emerges from a garage at the end of the driveway.

"Get out before he gets to the truck." She stares out the driver window, leaving me with a view of the back of her head. There isn't even a reflection in the window to catch her expression.

I slip out and take in a gulp of air. It's colder here. Or maybe it's the scene in front of me that's left me shivering.

"Are you Mark?" I meet him midway between the cluster of buildings and the truck.

"You're Emma?" he answers without answering. "Horse you want is in there. Good luck loading him." He shoves his hands into the pockets of his jeans and shifts his weight to his heels, in case I had the slightest thought of asking him to help.

"I'm taking both horses in that field."

"Not the arrangement I have with Rena."

"What do you care? It's one less horse you have to worry about."

He studies me with dark, rat eyes. "Five hundred dollars."

"I'll be back tomorrow with your money."

"Cash. And if you're not, I'll come for it."

I refuse to flinch under his beady stare.

He releases something that sounds like a cackle. "Crazy fuckers, the lot of you. Take those horses and get off my property. And be sure you have the money here before tomorrow ends."

He stares past me, squinting into the light, then turns and walks off. I drain my lungs and pull in air untainted by his presence. A ray of sun sparks off the truck and I realize why Jilli stopped where she did. Mark couldn't see who was behind the wheel.

It doesn't take much effort to load both horses. Neither puts up a struggle. Jillian drives around the half-circle by the barn, lowering the sun visor as she pulls past and turns her head away from the buildings.

A precarious peace settles between us. She's even turned up the heat in the truck.

She waits until we're halfway to Jumping Frog Farm before speaking. "I tried to run over that fuckhead."

I must have looked like a cartoon character when her mouth drops, literally, to the ground, because Jillian lets out a laugh. A real laugh.

"Seriously. He was terrorizing a pony who didn't want to load into the trailer. I was in my car getting ready to leave the show grounds and the next thing I know, my car's hood is crumpled, there's an airbag in my lap, the trailer has a massive dent, and that asshole has a broken leg. I guess I'm lucky his body moves faster than his brain or it would have been worse than a restraining order."

"What happened to the pony?"

"Grandma found him a good home." She jiggles the car keys with her right knee and flicks at the windshield-wiper control with her index finger. A long minute later, she asks, "How much did you pay?"

"Five hundred."

Her head whips around. "What?"

"My money, my business." I cross my arms and stare out the passenger side window.

"Why the hell would you do that? Shit, he would have gotten rid of that thing for fifty bucks."

A tidal wave of emotions crashes over me.

"That *thing* is a living, breathing animal being left to die. She deserves more."

Jillian opens her mouth, then snaps it shut. Her right hand taps at the temperature dial.

I rest my forehead on the window and shiver at the sting from the frigid glass. The rolling farmland and patches of woods blur.

I know it's not what she meant. She would have saved that pony as well.

How am I supposed to help Jillian move forward when I also seem to be holding fistfuls of resentment.

27

February 1996

Emma blows on her fingers. It's too cold not to have gloves on but she can't braid Taylor's mane with them on. She's already had to redo a couple that came out crooked and they're scheduled to leave for the horse show in an hour. Rena will be blasting in at any moment. She gives a last blow, wiggles her fingers, and parts another patch of mane.

"The spacing is off between those last couple." Jillian leans against the corner of the wash stall where Emma has the mare in crossties. The light is better here and right now, Emma needs all the help she can get.

"They're fine." She blows a puffy white cloud into the air. "I don't see your horse ready."

"Didn't feel like braiding. It's too cold." Jillian sips at her hot chocolate, steam twisting out in taunting spirals. Emma has the urge to dunk her frozen fingers into the mug.

"How can you show an unbraided horse? It's so unprofessional."

Jillian shrugs. "I'm not showing him in the hunter classes. It doesn't matter."

"Rena will be furious."

"So? What's the worst thing she can do? Tell me I'm not going?"

"Why are you being like this?" Emma stuffs her numb hands into her armpits, anything to find a bit of warmth.

Jillian lifts her braid and studies the ends, fanning the strands between her thumb and index finger. A petulant stubbornness washes over her face, a look Emma is seeing more and more these days. And liking less and less.

"Ladies." The word thunders through the sleeping barn. "Why aren't the tack trunks loaded? Tolstoy's legs aren't bandaged and his mane hasn't been braided. And, Jillian, those boots are not show-clean."

Jillian seems to shrink but teenage stubbornness roots her to the spot. "We're only going down the road. They don't need bandages for such a short trip. Takes longer to wrap than the damn drive there."

Rena stops dragging the trunks out of the tack room, the sudden silence too loud in the sleeping barn.

"Don't you ever use that language in front of me, and I don't care if you're trailering a horse to the end of the driveway or across the country, he should always have shipping wraps."

Jillian shrugs, a move that makes Emma cringe, anticipating the lightning zap from Rena.

"Emma, finish up. I'll get the tack loaded. Jillian, I'm scratching you from the show."

"You can't do that," Jillian shrieks, startling Taylor, who tosses her head up, unbalancing Emma.

"I can. And I am." Holding Emma's saddle and Taylor's bridle over her left arm, Rena turns on the heels of her spit-shined paddock boots and walks to where the back of the trailer blocks the exit to the stable.

Jilli stomps to regain the attention. "Wait until my mom hears about this. She's going to be livid."

"Livid? She has no right to be livid about anything." Rena turns for a stare-down with her granddaughter. "Your mom's mom owns this place. And if your mom was here, I'd tell her the same thing I'm telling you. Until you fix that attitude, you're not riding for me. Now go home."

Jillian huffs, pushes herself off the wall, and shoots lasers from her grandmother to her best friend. Emma shrinks behind the protective barrier of her horse. Rena responds with an I-dare-you line of her eyebrows.

Emma whispers, "Come on, Jilli. I'll help you get Tolstoy ready. Come on. Please?" She hears the plea in her own voice and hopes her friend will soften to it.

"No. I don't need this shit. She doesn't give a crap if I'm there. *You're* her golden child." The resentment in Jillian's eyes knocks the air out of Emma's lungs.

Tears sting her eyes. "That's not true. We're H and H sisters, Jilli. I need you there."

"You don't need me. You have my horse and my grandmother."

"That's not fair."

Emma melts under the blaze of Jillian's teenage fury. "Not fair? Is it fair that they gave you the perfect horse who wins every class she's entered in? Is it fair that you always get what you want because everyone is afraid to upset you? 'Poor little Emma, her mom is dead and her dad is an ass,'" Jillian singsongs.

She wants to rail back at Jillian. She wants to yell that it was Jilli who'd suggested she start showing Taylor. She wants to argue that she doesn't *have* Rena, she doesn't have any grandparents. And she wants to scream that she's not poor little Emma.

But while Jilli is free with her emotions and outbursts, Emma can't release that part of herself.

"Enough." The stamp of Rena's boot scatters the arguments from both girls. "Jillian, you are to leave this minute and not return to the barn until we've spoken about your behavior."

Jillian gives her grandmother one last defiant glare, then turns to Emma. "Good luck today. For your sake, I hope you win. It would be such a shame for you to land in the losers' pit with me."

Emma never fully warms up that day. Even when the temperature bumps up enough that the horses no longer look like smoke-breathing dragons, she keeps shivering despite the horse blanket draped around her shoulders. She places first in three of her four classes and second in the fourth. But the day's success feels hollow.

The drive home is worse than the drive there. Rena tries for an enthusiastic discussion, which fizzles faster than an open bottle of soda.

Jillian isn't at the stable when they arrive. She doesn't answer the doorbell when Emma goes to the house. The house phone rings and rings even though Emma knows she's there.

Emma spends the rest of the weekend hiding at home. The pull of the barn holds an unfamiliar current of anxiety. She wants to see Jillian and clear the air. And she really, really needs the comfort of the horses. But what if the resentment she'd seen in Jillian's face is still there? Is it possible that Jilli honestly feels she's pushed her out of the spotlight? Emma doesn't want to be in the spotlight, she just wants to ride, to be good at something. No, she wants to be great at something. She wants to win her dad's attention. But not at the expense of her best friend. She's never tried to one-up Jillian. Never.

Emma had been perfectly happy riding Stormy. They'd been at a show and Jilli set her determination on buying Tolstoy. It was time for her to have a true jumper, a horse who would win, and Tolstoy was the one. She said Taylor would be the perfect next step for Emma.

She was right. At least about Taylor and Emma.

While Emma and her hand-me-down horse win most of the classes they enter, Jillian and her fancy mount struggle to connect with each other.

And somehow it's Emma's fault.

She tries talking to her dad about it but he just brushes it off as a teenage-girl mood swing and turns back to his newspaper.

By late afternoon, she can't stand the deafening volume of her own doubts. She bundles up and trudges through the thick mud until she reaches the property line.

She leans against the fence, watching the horses graze. She

can't bring herself to walk up the hill to the barn but she also can't bring herself to leave. The sun disappears behind the hills and she shudders deeper into her winter coat.

She twists to look at the path back to her house. She should probably be getting home to make dinner. Her father has been in his home office all day. She'd asked in a roundabout way if they were going out to eat. They never did, but a part of her still hopes that one day he'll surprise her, that a perfect report card or top ribbons at a show will be rewarded with a father-daughter date.

"What are you doing down here, Toad?"

Emma looks up into the shadow. "Just hanging and watching the horses."

"Why here though? It's freezing." Simon zips his coat all the way, then pushes his hand back into the glove. He tucks his chin inside the coat and his wool hat covers his ears, like a knight hiding behind a rampart of a fortified wall. Emma doubts he'll be able to save her this time.

"Dunno. Didn't really feel like coming to the barn."

"Ah yes. I spoke to Rena yesterday after the show. I know what happened. Want to talk about it?"

She feels his eyes on her and wishes she'd worn a hat and scarf to hide in.

"Hey, Simon." She has to ask, knowing he'll give her an honest answer. "Do you think my father is a, an . . . a bad guy?"

She tried to say "ass," wants to taste the word on her tongue, see how it feels to call her dad that, feel the power that Jillian commanded. But she can't, not to Simon at least.

"I don't think he's bad," he answers too quickly.

"But you don't think he's a good father." It's not a question and the look on Simon's face tells her she's right.

"Do people tiptoe around me because they're afraid to upset me?"

He takes longer to answer this time. "Sometimes. Not as much now."

She wishes she could un-ask that last question. "I need to get back." She turns, keeping her head high until the woods swallow her from sight. Only then does she allow the tears to come, but she won't look back. She doesn't want to see sympathy in his eyes. She doesn't want people feeling sorry for her. She doesn't need people feeling sorry for her.

What she does need, wants actually, is to yell, scream, throw a hissy fit. She wants to let out the years of hurt and anger and fear.

She wants understanding, not sympathy.

28

Great lesson, Alex." I smile at the kid on the bay pony. "Keep it up, bud."

The nine-year-old grins, then turns to where his mom leans against the entrance to the indoor arena.

"Do you really have to leave tomorrow?" he asks, and I feel the weight of the request in the expectant quiet.

"Rena should be back to teaching soon." *I hope.* "I think Jillian will be teaching you until then." I force the corners of my mouth up.

"Why can't you stay, Emma? Don't you love it here?" The nine-year-old emphasis on *love* tugs at my heart.

I'd tucked my return to Chicago in the back of my mind where it couldn't interfere with the almost-peace I've lulled my nerves into.

Over the last three days, a new Emma has emerged. The fancy clothes I came in are folded in the suitcase, replaced by breeches and boots. My laptop and iPhone are mostly idle, my fingers busier with reins and crochet needles than a computer keyboard.

I'd taken the five hundred dollars to Mark, and the black pony is now officially mine. Jilli had fussed at me about the money, said I should take far less to him and he'd never counter, but I couldn't. That pony's life is worth more than five hundred dollars. Despite the public stink over the rescue pony, I've caught glimpses of Jilli sneaking extra food to both of them. Whatever crusty shell she wants others to see, inside, horses are still her weak spot.

While the anxiety of career turmoil has hummed in the background, its presence has become more white noise than burning pressure.

I adjust my wool hat, pulling it down over my ears. Ceila will be happy to know that I made the pattern she'd given me. Although it wasn't as piece-of-cake as she'd promised. It took four false starts before I got the magic ring to work its magic, and my counting skills failed somewhere around row twenty-six. The end result isn't exactly what the picture shows and my head isn't quite large enough, but I'm proud of my accomplishment nonetheless. It's part of the mellower Emma, the Jumping Frog Farm Emma.

Every morning here starts the same. Coffee on the front porch with Ben and Tony, watching the fog release the hills and the shadows of the night make way for the brilliance of October days.

Few words are exchanged. Not the awkward avoidance of discussion of my Chicago life.

And when did I begin compartmentalizing—Chicago life versus Emmitsville life?

Tomorrow I return to that other life.

I watch Alex hop off, loosen the girth, then lead the pony to the stable.

You have a job to return to.

A job I've thought about very little in the last few days. I've checked messages, even responded to a couple, but the deluge of calls and e-mails from those first days has eased to a pinging trickle. And my need to check has eased to an afterthought. So why shouldn't I stay?

Because your life is in Chicago.

What life? My we're-here-for-you-anytime friends haven't called to find out why I haven't returned, and not even a "hey, how are you, how about our date" from John.

Out of sight, out of mind.

Yet, Lucy called yesterday with an invite to join today's Hookers' meeting. She said Ceila had been asking after me and tsk-tsking that I hadn't been back to The Spinning Ewe. I'd turned her down. I had lessons to teach. They offered an evening Hookers' meeting instead, but my last night in Emmitsville belongs to Jumping Frog Farm.

I give Alex a hug and get a pinky promise from him that he'll continue to work hard. *Don't you love it here?* The question echoes in my heart as I watch the taillights of his mother's SUV blink good-bye.

Tucked into a sweatshirt, I curl up in my favorite Adirondack chair, the bag of yarn next to me. I've unraveled the scarf so many times that the wool has started rebelling. An owl hoots in the distance and I close my eyes as though that simple act will trap the memory forever.

Someone settles into the chair next to me.

"Hey."

"Hey yourself. I thought you were sleeping." Ben's voice is muddy, like the thickening sky.

"Listening."

"To what?"

"The evening." The horses quieting down, the air settling, the night coming alive. "Did you hear the owl? My father loved them."

The owl answers with another mellow hoot.

"I used to find my father sitting on the back patio, a tumbler of scotch in one hand, his glasses in the other. Around this hour, sometimes later. Most of the time he didn't even know I was there. I guess that's the thing about living in a house weighed down by depression, you learn to disappear into the background. I was good at being invisible."

"Depression? Your father?"

"Mother. Although they always said she had heart problems." I open my eyes, a memory clicking into place. "That's not true. It was only him. He was the one who insisted she had a bad heart."

Ben doesn't answer. But the owl does.

"I asked my father once what he was listening to. He said the owls. He said they were the best part of living out here. I wonder if he missed them when he moved to the condo."

"Do you miss her?"

"Mom? No."

Ben doesn't hide his surprise.

"Yes but no. I know that doesn't make sense. I miss the idea of her. I miss little things like the way she used to rake her fingers through her hair from the base up then let it drop like a fan. Or the way she'd curl up in the corner of the couch and raise the end of the throw for me to crawl under with her. Or the way she'd make circles with her thumb against the tip of her middle finger when she was thinking about something.

"But no, I don't miss the sobbing coming from her room or having to tiptoe around so god-forbid I disturb her during one of her episodes. And I don't miss the guilt that somehow I was responsible."

"How could you have been responsible? Depression is a disease, not a cold she would have caught from a sniffling kid."

"Tell that to a kid. But it was the way my father wouldn't—couldn't—look at me that convinced me I was to blame."

"Tell me about your father."

"What about him?" I pull myself higher in the chair and square my shoulders for another bumpy trip down memory lane.

He shrugs, an open invitation for me to answer whatever question I can.

"Done deal."

"What is?"

"Everything. His patients have been handed off to other psychiatrists. His condo is under contract. Some lucky schmuck will find a whole lotta fancy suits at Goodwill. There was nothing left of the car. Or of him."

"You."

"Me what?"

"You're left of him."

"How ironic. The one thing he never really cared about is the one thing that will survive from him."

"You don't really believe he didn't care?"

"Moot point. I did everything possible to matter to him, to please him. Guess I'm now free to do whatever I please." That freeing thought paralyzes me. I've been making my own choices, doing what I want. Except that every move and every decision was made with the calculated anticipation of how my father would react.

Now the daddy-boulder has been lifted from my self-doubt and I don't trust my legs to know the right direction.

"What do you want to do?"

I shrug. It's the most honest answer I can come up with.

"Does that mean you're considering staying?"

A rumbling laugh ricochets up my throat. "Rena is home from the hospital tomorrow. That means Jillian will be taking over. And that means it's time for me to return to Chicago."

"Interesting." Ben smirks.

"What's interesting?"

"You said go back to Chicago."

"I live there."

"You didn't say go back home."

"Word choice, Ben, just word choice."

"Sure it is." His smirk broadens and he slouches deeper into the chair.

"Hey, boss, can you come take a look at Jack?" Tony calls from behind us, the urgency in his voice freezing the already cold evening air.

Ben shoots up as though scalded by the chair and disappears into the barn.

I'm a split second behind but by the time I get there, Ben is already in Jack's stall and running his hands over the horse's belly.

"What's wrong?" The words are sticky in my mouth.

"Colic. Tony, get Doc Marshall over here. Now. And if he's not available, call Dr. Buchman."

The black horse groans, nips at his belly, and then folds his front legs to lie down.

"Oh no you don't. Up, up. You are not going to die on me." Ben taps the horse's legs to keep him standing.

Heat courses through my insides. I'd helped with a couple of the horses who had colic when I was young. I remember the hours walking them, making sure they don't roll and their intestines don't twist. I remember being on poop watch, making sure things start working properly on the inside. We'd lost one mare to colic. We'd been lucky with the others.

I don't believe in God and I don't believe in praying. But I pray—to the protector of horses, to God, to whoever is up there and listening.

Please don't let Jack die.

"Shit, I'm tired." Ben stretches his neck left, then right. "It's late, Emma, you should go to bed. I've got this."

We've been alternating walking Jack since the vet left almost three hours ago. Even though Doc Marshall had arrived quickly and assured us it was a mild case, I can't quiet the fear.

"I'm not leaving him." I lace my fingers into the black mane.

"Won't be the first time." Jilli's sharp voice pierces the darkness.

My fingers curl into a fist around a hunk of mane and Jack leans into me with the pull.

"It wasn't my choice to leave back then."

"Of course not, what was I thinking. Everyone made decisions for you, didn't they? What happens now, Emma? Who's going to tell you how to live your life with Daddy gone?"

My mouth opens and I can feel it forming shapes that might have turned into words had I not been so stunned.

"What the hell is wrong with you, Jillian?" Ben lashes out.

Her body turns to confront him but the laser beam of her focus stays pinpointed on me. "She doesn't belong here and I want her away from my horse."

"Your horse? Are you fucking kidding me? I don't think I've ever seen you give this horse a second look. Emma has been taking care of him every day; talking to him, brushing him, walking him when he can't be outside. Your horse." He spits the last words in disgust.

I feel the scorch of heat under her glare.

"You're wrong, Jillian. I love this place as much as any of you." My eyes sweep over the small group huddled around Jack's stall. Tony polishes the brass nameplate with his thumb. Jillian glares at me, no doubt wishing she had magic powers to make me disappear. Only Ben nods encouragement.

"I have no doubt." She crosses her arms and rocks back on her heels.

The slight sway of her upper body unsettles my equilibrium and I grab tighter to Jack.

"What did I do to make you hate me?"

"I didn't hate you. I felt sorry for you."

I felt sorry for you.

"Why?"

"God, Emma, really? Haven't you let it go yet?"

"I let it go. I moved on." I match her glare, the discussion with Rena swirling inside me. Dammit, I'm *not* that betrayed sixteen-year-old girl.

"And yet you're here."

"Why?" I'm not backing down, not this time.

"Because you lived in a sheltered little bubble. Poor Emma. Be nice to Emma. Emma lost her mom. We need to be there for Emma. Emma doesn't need to be burdened with that. Be supportive of Emma. Emma needs us." Jillian's singsong tone hardens with each mention of my name.

She pulls her green fleece jacket closed and tucks her left hand deep inside, against her body. She shivers and gives another tug, maybe wishing she could vanish inside it. She tucks her chin down, muffling her response. "Because of you, I lost everything."

"Because of *me*?" I blink the past into focus. "I didn't take anything from you that you didn't push away. How was what happened that day my fault? Look around you. What did you lose? You had and still have the perfect life."

Jack groans and begins to fold his legs, heaving his aching body to the ground.

"Dammit." Ben pushes past Jillian and tugs the horse back to his feet. "I'm not losing him because the two of you are stuck in some teenage drama. Get the hell out of my way."

We watch Ben lead the black horse down the aisle and into the indoor arena.

Jillian moves first. A tug to her braid, a move as familiar as if it were mine.

A horse snorts in a nearby stall. Another stomps his foot. The horse in the stall next to Jack's pushes the lever in his automatic water bowl, releasing a whine from the pipes.

"You wanted the life you thought I had." Her words barely match the sounds of the waking barn. "I wanted that life, too."

29

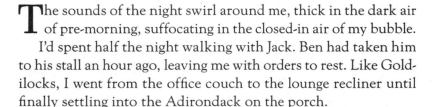

The sounds of the night swirl around me, thick in the dark air of pre-morning, suffocating in the closed-in air of my bubble.

I'd spent half the night walking with Jack. Ben had taken him to his stall an hour ago, leaving me with orders to rest. Like Goldilocks, I went from the office couch to the lounge recliner until finally settling into the Adirondack on the porch.

Jillian's wrong, I didn't *want* her life, I wanted to be part of her life.

No, she's right, and that insight fuels the defeat inside me.

I did live in a bubble back then, but I've always imagined I was the one who had inflated that protective cocoon around myself. I had to find a happy place, a place where families ate together and talked about their days. A place where parents were supportive and engaged.

I was good at pretending my life was like everyone else's. I listened to what other kids said during Monday-morning share time, and from their weekend excursions, I created my own stories. My family went on picnics. We planted flowers. We went on bike rides. Our excursions were always ones I could make up details about without having to stretch the truth too much. Once when I found a mailer for a new art exhibit, I studied the glossy paintings and read every word in the description. Three Mondays later, I happily reported that my family had been to see the exhibit. Timmy Hart had been there the week before but he'd been more impressed with the edible fruit sculptures on the tables than the actual paintings on the walls.

Even as an adult I pretend, although now I have the experience to weave much more interesting stories. But mostly, I keep those stories to myself. I no longer feel the need to share my "family time" with anyone.

Family time. That's a joke.

None of my friends questions why I always stay in Chicago over holidays, or if they do, it's not directly to me. There's a sudden burn in my chest. Do they feel sorry for me, too?

No, my bubble was mine to mold and I've modeled it like an exquisite pair of leather boots.

Tony jogs by, his mouth tight in concentration.

"Tony?"

"Jack isn't good. Mr. Ben wants the vet back," he says without stopping. The door to the office slams shut behind him.

Jack.

I break the no-running rule and sprint after him. Ben is tugging Jack into the arena.

"Get Jillian. The two of you need to keep him moving."

I turn and run to the tack room at the end of the aisle. Jillian looks up from the couch when I burst in, out of breath.

"I need your help with Jack."

She tilts her head, a look of annoyance wrinkling her brow, and for a split second I think she's going to tell me to get out.

"For Jack," she says, moving far slower than I have the patience to witness.

She catches up to me halfway back to the arena. "Ben may think you belong here, but you don't."

"Don't worry, I'm not staying." Despite Rena's request, I'm going home in a few hours.

"I wasn't worried." Her words bounce lifelessly between us as she overtakes me and disappears into the arena.

For the next few hours, the only words exchanged are about Jack. We alternate who leads and who nudges him forward. The unfinished argument follows us like a dark cloud in a cartoon. I have the laughable urge to take the long whip in my hand and poke that cloud, let the ugliness dump where it will.

But I don't.

Instead, I chew the inside of my cheek and run through the argument in my head, rehearse my retort. Somewhere into the second hour, I realize the words jumbling in my head aren't directed at Jillian; I'm rehearsing my argument for staying in Emmitsville.

Which is crazy. I'm not quitting my job. I have a plane to catch today.

I look at my watch.

I had a plane to catch today.

"You missed your flight." She's not asking, not even accusing.

"I couldn't leave with Jack in trouble."

"He seems to be out of immediate danger. You could reschedule." The hostility that's punctuated everything she's directed at me since I arrived is gone.

I stop walking and Jack bumps into me. Jillian shuffles to a stop and gives me a what-gives eyebrow raise. "I'd like to stay a few more days. Until we know for sure he's okay. And until Rena is back on her feet." *And until I figure out how I'm supposed to help you move forward, whatever that means.*

Jillian pulls her lips tight, creating unhappy creases at the corners of her mouth. I brace against what will come next. "I'm not surprised."

That's not the answer I'd expected but I'm not looking a gift horse in the mouth.

"I'll take over for a while," Ben says, reaching for the lead rope. I hand it to him as my feet transform to lead bricks, rooting me to the middle of the arena. Jillian stands next to me. "Go shower or get something to eat or coffee. Or shower, really." He shoos us away.

An uneasy ease settles between us as we leave the arena.

I hesitate at the bottom of the stairs to the barn apartments. I want to ask her about Rena. I want to ask why she's clinging to the past. Deep down, I know the answer to both.

She pushes her hands into the pockets of her jeans, roaching her back. The Jillian I remember always pushed her shoulders back.

"Okay, well, thanks for helping with Jack." She looks at my shoulder, my hands loose at my sides, my boots.

"Jillian, you were right, I did want the life you had. But I wanted to live it with you, not as you."

Her eyes track a line of sawdust marking the path of a wheelbarrow. "There wasn't room in it for both of us."

My cell phone rings, a Chicago number I don't recognize. I freeze for two rings before swiping Accept and uttering a hesitant "hello."

"Is this Emma Metz?" The man's voice is deep and warm but not friendly.

"Yes, it is."

"I'm glad you answered. I was hoping to meet you tomorrow in the office but it appears that we'll have our first discussion by phone. Do you have a few minutes now?"

I scan the apartment, suddenly uncomfortable, and clutch the towel tighter around my chest. *No, not really. I was just going to shower. And I have a sick horse downstairs.* But the little something-is-amiss alarm is getting louder in my sleep-deprived brain.

He takes my silence as the go-ahead. "I understand you're dealing with some personal affairs. Bruce has filled me in as best he can. I'm sorry to hear about your father's passing."

I hear him take a breath. This is where I'm expected to say something. "Thank you. I'm sorry, I didn't catch your name."

"Oh." I'm surprised by the surprise in his voice. A butterfly in my stomach performs a kamikaze drop at the realization that I haven't checked my work e-mail in two days. How much can change in two days?

"Pierce Frank. The new chief executive officer at NewComm."

And there go the rest of the butterflies. Splat.

"What happened to Bruce?"

"You really haven't been keeping up with the e-mails, have you?" I can't tell if that's amusement or annoyance in his tone. Either way, it seems like I may just be royally screwed.

"Sorry, I've had a lot to take care of here." I squeeze my eyes shut not to see the details of the cozy apartment and evidence of what I haven't been doing in the last few days.

"The board of directors have brought me on to take the company in a slightly different direction. Bruce will be assisting me in an advisory capacity."

My assistant was promoted and my boss was fired. I'm not screwed, I'm fucked.

"Do I still have a job?"

"Yes. I do, however, need a firm date when you'll be back at work. I see from the HR files you've pushed the date back a couple of times. You are planning on returning?"

My legs turn to rubber and I sink to the floor.

Am I?

Of course I am.

So why haven't I?

The truth blazes past like a blowtorch. Because I've been finding excuses not to.

"Emma?"

"Yes."

"Yes, you *are* returning?"

"I am returning. There was an emergency last night. I can be back in the office on Monday." My voice sounds puny, a little kid anticipating a reprimand.

"Monday. I'll have my assistant set up a meeting for us. I'll look forward to speaking in person."

Monday. That gives me five more days.

Five days for what, though?

I fist the ends of the towel around my chest and stretch my legs, the wood floor cold on the back of my exposed thighs. I let my head drop back against the edge of the bed. Next to me is the sweatshirt I'd been wearing. I reach for it and bury my face in it. Sawdust, hay, horses.

"This isn't your life. It's not what you've been working for all these years."

I close my eyes, searching for the smells of my Chicago life. Expensive coffee, exhaust fumes, sweaty people. That's the life I've been living and it's the life I have absolutely no desire to return to.

30

June 1996

Emma looks at the clock above the door for the hundredth time in the past twenty minutes. This day will never end. She can't keep her leg from jiggling and it's making the metal chair squeak. Her teacher has already given her a couple of stern looks.

Nine more minutes to go.

Eight minutes to go.

Someone pokes her from behind. "Pay attention," the poker whispers loud enough for pretty much everyone in the room to hear.

"As I was saying," Ms. Monroe catches Emma's eyes, "your reports will be due tomorrow. Five pages."

A collective groan rumbles through the room.

Report on what? Before Emma can raise her hand to ask for clarification, the bell rings. Secure in the din of scraping chairs and the eruption of voices, Emma turns to her neighbor. "What's due tomorrow?"

Jason stuffs his notebooks into his backpack. "Man, you're a space cadet today. What's up with that? Ms. Monroe was talking right at you. Now, thanks to you, we have a five-page report to do. It's the last stinking week of school. Way to go, Emma."

He hoists the backpack over one shoulder and walks off to

join his friends. Laughter, probably at her expense, follows them into the hallway.

"Emma." Ms. Monroe is waving a piece of paper. "The assignment. Whatever has you so distracted, I suggest you deal with it before tomorrow."

"Yes, Ma'am." She takes the paper and hurries out. She has a bus to catch and a riding lesson to get to. Today will be her first time riding Jack and there's no way she's missing that. The assignment will just have to wait. Anyway, writing a five-page report is easy.

She finds Jillian in the cool-kid section of the bus, scrunched down with her knees wedged against the back of the seat in front. Two boys are facing backward in their chairs talking to her, and a girl leans across the aisle to join in the discussion.

"Hey." Emma squeezes past Talia and collapses onto what's left of the seat next to Jilli. "I thought today would drag forever."

Jillian's eyebrows lift but she doesn't break the conversation with her fan club.

"Whatcha guys talking about?"

"Nothing important."

Talia snickers and one of the boys tosses a wadded piece of paper at her. The boys turn to face the front as the bus lurches forward.

Emma sighs. It's been much like this since the weekend of the horse show a few months ago. She hates when Jillian gets into these funks but lately, no matter what she does, Jilli finds something to get upset over.

"Come on, Jilli, talk to me. Who are you riding in the lesson today?"

"I'm not."

"What do you mean you're not?"

"I mean I'm not. I'm not taking the lesson with you today. I've decided to start training with Kate instead."

"What? Why?" The bus takes a sharp right onto the main road and Emma grabs at the seat in front to keep from falling.

"I just think it's time for me to move on. Grandma and

Grandpa are fine and all, but I need someone who can focus on me and help me win the big shows."

"Oh." Emma wants to protest that Rena and Simon can take them both to the next level, that they're supposed to be doing this together, but Jillian has turned to look out the window, an invisible DO NOT DISTURB sign.

Emma's stop is first. Jillian mumbles "see ya" in response to her good-bye. The moment she's out of the seat, Talia leans over and the boys turn in their seats.

She swallows the lump in her throat. Message received.

After the initial letdown at not having Jillian in the lesson, Emma gives in to the excitement. She's been watching Kate work with Jack. She knows how he moves, what aids he responds to. She's fantasized about this day since he was born.

She takes her time brushing him, letting the motion soothe the sting of Jillian's brush-off.

Here, with Jack, it doesn't matter. Here, she doesn't doubt herself. Here, she's never alone.

Riding Jack is exactly the way Emma has imagined all these years. His walk is long and free. Her body sways with each step, an extension of his legs. His trot is confident and balanced. Each step moves her body in perfect posting tempo, the movement born of instinct rather than learned. His canter is smooth and measured. Her body rocks in perfect time to his strides, as though she's one with him. She feels like she's floating.

She closes her fingers on the reins and tightens her lower legs around his girth, then sits deeper in the saddle. Jack collects himself into a perfect transition from canter to walk. She gives him a pat on the neck and, glowing, turns to Simon. "He's perfect."

By the time the lesson is over, she's forgotten about Jillian.

"Nice riding, Toad." Simon lowers himself onto the step stool by the wash stall with a loud "ouuffff."

"Thanks." She hopes the flush blazing over her cheeks isn't obvious. But she has to admit that she hasn't felt this great in a long time. Ever.

"You know, I think you two will be ready for your first show next month."

She stops brushing, hand frozen in mid-sweep. "Next month. Already?"

"Yes, already. We can take Taylor as well. You can show her in the equitation classes and Jack in the jumper classes."

"Against Jilli? We haven't competed against each other in so long." Emma chews the fatty part on her left ring finger. When they were both showing in the children's division they'd regularly come home with first- and second-place ribbons. It never mattered who was first or who was second. Most of the time the ribbons went into one display jar that sat on the mantel in the barn lounge.

She's not sure when the change started, but at some point Jilli began to resent sharing the stage with her. Tolstoy was Jilli's ticket back to the spotlight. Emma didn't have a mount who could compete at that level. Until now.

"I don't know if that's a good idea." The excited flutters give way to worried jitters. She bites harder, the metallic taste of blood making her wince.

"Come sit. Tell me what's going on."

Emma flips a bucket and sits next to him. "I just feel like everything I'm doing lately is wrong and she's starting to hate me. I'm afraid that if I show Jack in the same division, she'll hate me even more."

"She doesn't hate you, love. You're part of the family, and sometimes family members get the explosive end of the dynamite stick. Jilli is having a hard time adjusting to being a teenager. Her mother isn't strong enough to handle her mood swings. God knows she has enough of her own. And Rena and I can only do so much."

"It's more than that. I don't think she wants me around anymore." She closes her eyes, wishing she'd been able to mask the hurt in her voice.

"How could you possibly think that?"

"She doesn't include me in anything. She's been sitting with other friends during lunch and, like today on the bus, they stopped talking the moment I sat down, then started again when I got off. She's always in a pack of people. People who I don't fit in with. She's not even riding with me anymore."

She swallows, determined not to let the tears loose. "I don't mind it as much here, but the way she treats me at school kinda hurts. She's becoming a different person. And not always a nice one. I just really miss my H and H sister."

She stops, suddenly afraid she's said too much. Jillian is, after all, his granddaughter and Emma is the outsider.

Before she can form the words to an apology, Simon pats her leg.

"You and Jilli are so much alike and so very different at the same time. Give her time, I know she'll come around. She loves you and needs you."

Emma isn't sure time will do more than widen the gap between them. If this is what being a teenager is like, she's not positive she's looking forward to it.

"My next lesson is here." With a creaking of knees, Simon gets up. "Don't give up on her, Emma. She'll need your strength."

She's not sure about Jillian needing her but she is sure Simon's wrong about one thing, she's not the strong one.

With Jack cooled off and back in his stall, it's time to head home before it gets dark. She hates walking through the woods in the dark and tonight there's no one to walk her even partway.

The light is on in Jilli's room but she resists the urge to ring the doorbell. She can see the silhouette of her friend, the curly cord of the phone anchoring her to the window seat.

A pang of hurt lodges in Emma's throat and she picks up the pace, disappearing into the darkening woods. An owl hoots, sending her heart and feet into fast-forward.

"Seventy-two, seventy-three . . ." The words collide with the gulps of air she's forcing into her lungs. With the longer strides, she should be out of the woods before she gets to two hundred.

"Hundred eighty-four, hundred eighty-five . . ." The light in her bedroom shines like a lighthouse beacon. Thank god she forgot to turn it off this morning because the rest of the house is dark.

She unlocks the back door and walks into the kitchen, flipping on all the lights. Dad will be annoyed about wasting energy but he's not here. She looks at the phone, black and silent on the strip of counter her mom had called "the cooking office."

It won't ring tonight. Jilli is the only friend who ever calls her. And she's busy talking to her new friends. Emma turns to the backpack hanging on the back of a chair. She has a report to write.

She won't long for something she can't have and she sure won't mourn something that was never hers to begin with.

So what if Jillian doesn't want her around anymore? And so what if the kids at school don't accept her?

She has Jack. He's all she needs. He's all she'll let herself need.

31

The morning air has a bite that sends me deeper into the collar of my fleece jacket. Jack is on the mend, Rena is home, and the barn seems to release a collective sigh.

After checking on the patient, I pour another mug of coffee and walk to the front porch. I have only three mornings left. I've pushed my return to Chicago to the very back of my brain. It's there, I can't completely forget it, but I don't want to think about it. I've found a rhythm at the barn. It's hectic and peaceful, frustrating and fulfilling. With each passing day, I'm less sure that I don't belong here.

The October air smells musty, an earthy combination of leaves and damp ground. It rained during the night but the day ahead promises to be crisp. A perfect day for a ride. Maybe I can persuade Ben to go on a trail ride if he has time between classes.

Sandwiched between two horses, Tony walks past me to the field. There is an unspoken agreement between them as they walk, heads down, strides matched, the lead ropes draped over the horses necks.

When the crunch of gravel under their hooves has quieted, I hear the hum of a muffled conversation. Two people are sitting on a pile of jumps tucked along the side of the barn by the door to the indoor arena. Rena is shaking her head, her hands clasped tightly in her lap, her upper body curled inward as though protecting her hands. Michael is staring ahead, his mouth pulling into a defeated line.

I take a quick step back, not wanting to invade their privacy. But I can't bring myself to walk away. Has Michael had a relapse? Is Rena telling him she can't work with him anymore? Has Michael decided to quit the program? Is she suggesting he needs different help?

The swing of a lead rope in my peripheral vision startles me. I've been so engrossed in eye-dropping the conversation, I didn't notice Tony walk back up from the fields.

"They've been talking for over an hour. I don't like it." He shakes his head and continues into the barn.

Rena takes Michael's hand in hers. She says something, then stands and releases his hand. He lets if fall onto his lap, like an unwanted gift. She turns and walks away, her gait slow, awkward over the uneven parking lot. She seems to have aged in the last couple of weeks. I'd been dumbstruck at the change in her and Simon when I first returned but time seems to have sped up since.

And stayed still for me. I'm still here when I should be back in Chicago.

I turn at the sound of a stone pinging off metal.

"Hey." Michael stops in front of me. "I hear you're leaving soon. Pity."

"Thanks." I look into his sad eyes. Asking what he was discussing with Rena feels like an intrusion. Instead, I track Rena's slow path to her house.

"I'm going to miss this place. It's become my salvation. I came without much hope, and found my home. It's magical." The corner of his mouth twitches up but it doesn't catch into a full-blown smile.

"You're leaving?"

He turns and I'm acutely aware of the lack of personal space between us. He's tall, muscular, commanding. Intimidating, although maybe I'm projecting since I know his background.

"I'm leaving."

"Why?"

"Because I don't have a choice. What's your excuse?"

I take a step back. No, he is intimidating.

"I don't have a choice either. I have to get back to work. Why don't you have a choice, Michael?"

He studies me from above and I feel my spine curl under his intensity.

"She's shuttering the program."

"No." It's as much a gasp as a word. She can't be. This program is Rena's passion. Even if she's not healthy enough to keep running it, she'd never close it down. She'd find someone to help.

He moves back a step, his expression registering as much surprise as mine must have at that moment.

"You don't know?"

"No." This time the word limps out.

"She's been struggling to keep the program funded for years. There was an anonymous donor but she just learned that the funding was pulled. Sucks if you ask me. But nobody asked me."

He shrugs and turns, there's nothing more to be done.

This can't be happening. She can't shut the program down. It means too much to so many people.

"Hey, Ben, do you have a minute? I need to talk to you."

"Sure, my next lesson canceled. We can talk while we ride." He nods, sending his thick wave of hair airborne. The action, so like the one his horse makes, brings a smile to my face.

"You read my mind."

Twenty minutes later we leave the open space of the field and slip into the shadows of the woods, me on Wally and Ben on Picasso, an off-the-track dressage horse whose owner broke her ankle a few days ago in an unfortunate encounter with a lopsided curb.

"Hey, Ben."

He laughs. "Hey, Emma."

"You're making fun." But I laugh anyway.

"No, I'm having fun. We need a bit of that after the last few days."

"True." I sober, reluctant to spoil the moment. But I have to. Time is running out. "What do you know about Rena closing the therapeutic program?"

"Probably not more than you do. Only heard that her largest donor pulled out. She can't afford to keep it running."

"Why would someone just pull funding without an explanation?"

"Good question."

"Do you know who it was?"

"Nope. I keep my nose out of the therapeutic program. Rena keeps a tight lid on anything to do with it. She won't even let Jillian get involved."

"Can you imagine? Like those poor folks don't have enough problems in their life?"

Ben laughs. "See? You're a natural fit here."

We allow the rhythm of the horses to lull us into companionable quiet. Ben points to the left, where a doe is chewing slowly and watching our progress.

We arrive at a fallen log and Wally steps over while Ben's mount jackrabbits, careful not to let the scary wood touch him.

The sun reaches a tentative ray through the branches, only to yank it back. A squirrel scurries down a tree, stopping at eye level with me, his tail swishing through the air. A bird hops along a branch, head tilting from side to side.

The smell of wet leaves and dirt mixes with the pine and wood and a far-off fireplace. I breathe in. It's the smell of the holidays.

My eyes sting under the realization that the holidays are coming and I'm alone. Completely alone. I don't have memories of large family dinners, lounging by the fireplace together and watching the snow fall, or the flutter of wrapping paper and oohs of delight. That wasn't my childhood.

But even when we weren't together, my father was still part of my life.

Wally comes to a stop and I pull myself back to present-day

Maryland. Ben has dismounted and is leaning over something in the middle of the trail.

"What is it? Please not a dead animal."

"Come look." He remains bent at the waist but waves me over.

I dismount and bring Wally side by side with Picasso, who lays his ears back and shakes his head in pretend annoyance. Wally ignores him and Picasso pushes at Ben's behind as though saying "let's go, this is boring."

Ben squats to get a closer look and points at the shed antler.

"Wow. I've never seen antlers in the woods before." I lean over Ben's shoulder to get a better look and run a finger along the velvety hardness.

"Impressive, isn't it?" He turns his head to look at me, a mischievous smile lighting his face. "Do you feel lucky?"

I straighten. "Excuse me?"

"The antlers. According to folklore, deer represent instinctual energy, independence, and regeneration. That energy tells us to trust our gut reactions because those instincts will guide us when to fight and when to flee. If you find one and feel like you're supposed to take it, it's considered a gift from the spirits of the forest. That's good luck."

"You're shitting me."

"I shit you not. Way to break a perfect spirit moment." He stands, groans, and rubs his right knee. Picasso nudges him forward.

For a minute we both stare at the discarded antlers. A gift from the spirits of the forest? For me? Doubtful. I don't feel lucky. I haven't felt lucky in years.

And yet, I'm out here, riding an amazing horse, with a wonderful guy, and I've loved every moment of the last few days. Despite what brought me here.

"What does your gut tell you, Emma?"

He's close, close enough that I can see the flecks of brown in his green eyes and the lines fanning from the corners. I breathe in the warmth of his body, as an unfamiliar tingle shimmies up my spine.

And just when I feel the air between us compress, something wedges us apart.

"Damn you, you big, jealous moose." Ben pushes Wally's head out of the way, the words a cross between a sigh and moan.

Would he have really kissed me? What would my gut have said about that? "What do you think the spirits of the forest are saying?"

"They're not talking to me. They're talking to you." He taps my nose with his index finger.

"Independence and regeneration, eh? I'm not sure they're talking to me if that's what they're saying."

"You don't think you're independent?"

"Oh I am. Always have been. Had to be."

"That sounds lonely."

"There's a big difference between being alone and being lonely. I'm alone because I choose to be. Because it's easier. This way, I don't get disappointed and I don't get hurt. I can focus on making the right business decisions and not about saving my sorry heart."

"And you think that makes you independent?"

"Of course." I don't rely on anyone. I make my own decisions. I've created a careful, controlled life. One that, it turns out, mirrors my father's. *Very independent, Emma.*

"Are you making those decisions because you really truly believe they are the best for you, or because they are the safe decisions?"

The earlier defiance behind my "of course" puddles at my feet.

Did I make choices because they were safe? No. I didn't take the easy way out. I worked my ass off to get to where I am.

That's not what he meant and you know it.

"Give me one 'best for Emma' decision for why you're returning to Chicago."

The answer is automatic: "I have a job to return to."

Ben shakes his head. "That's a safe decision. You're hiding from what your gut is telling you."

He mounts Picasso and, while I stare at the antler, looking for an answer to come to me, adds, "Look around you, Emma, then look inside. Every time you talk about Chicago, there's a hardness that takes over. It's not there when you work with the kids, or when you're riding. Your gut might have something important to tell you if you're willing to listen."

He motions for me to mount, and without another word we follow the path until it dumps us into an open field, Jumping Frog Farm barely visible at the other end.

"Come on," Ben says, urging his horse into a canter.

Wally chomps on his bit and jerks his head after his equine friend, asking permission to follow.

What does my gut say?

My gut says the right decision is to allow my horse to gallop. And with the crisp October air pinpricking my face and the rolling of the horse's power between my legs, I can almost hear the spirits cheering.

32

April 1999

"Hey, Jilli, what do you want to do for our birthdays next month?" Emma dunks the sponge in the murky bucket, then squeezes, watching the dark water splash home. She takes a deep breath, the smell of saddle soap and leather filling her nostrils. It's the smell of everything she loves.

"Don't know."

"We could go to a movie."

A shrug from Jillian.

"Sleepover?"

"We're too old for that."

Emma huffs and tosses the sponge into the bucket, secretly pleased when the splashing water reaches Jilli's bare legs. In what world is fifteen and sixteen too old for sleepovers? "I slept at your house last week. It was okay then."

"That wasn't a 'sleepover.' You stay over all the time."

"So why not for our birthdays?"

"Because I want to go out."

"We can go to a movie."

Jillian uses her fingernail to scratch at a spot on the noseband she's cleaning.

"Is your mom going to be here?" Emma detours the topic.

"She's busy." Jilli's mom has missed more birthdays than she's been around for. Her absence is one of the subjects no one talks about. Kind of like her own mom. Except that her mom is dead and Jilli's isn't.

"My dad won't be around either."

"Nothing new there." Jilli shrugs.

Emma bites at the inside of her cheek, the urge to chew her nail having been dampened by the film of saddle soap on her hands. It won't help to get in a fight so she doesn't point out—again—that her dad is busy with medical conferences while Jilli's mom is busy in rehab programs.

"But we always celebrate together." Emma can't hide the pout in her voice. She doesn't want to be alone and she doesn't like the changes between them.

"Yeah, but, I dunno. I was thinking maybe I'd go to a party. You know, with a few other friends. Mostly juniors and seniors. People you don't really know."

"Oh."

Emma dunks the sponge in the water, then swipes it across the saddle soap bar. She scrubs at a spot of dried sweat on the brow-band. She knows what goes on at those parties. Not that she's ever been to one, but she's heard stories. Jilli herself had bragged after the last one about how hungover she was.

That's not Emma's idea of fun. Then again, neither is being left behind. She has enough of that in her life. "Hey, how about taking me with? It would be fun. We've never done that together."

Jillian turns in an are-you-crazy slow motion. "I dunno. I don't think you'll fit in. You'll hate it."

"Come on. It won't be the same celebrating our birthdays apart. At least this way we can still be together. We don't always have to do the same things. I'm happy doing whatever you want." She hates the begging sound but the thought of spending her birthday alone is even worse.

"I dunno. You don't know these guys."

"So introduce me."

Jillian snaps her gum. "Okay, I guess. Tomorrow night. There's a party at Drew's house. He's hot. And I think he's into me. Jory is driving. You can come."

Emma isn't sure if the rolling in her stomach is excitement or dread. She isn't worried about getting permission or negotiating a curfew. Her father isn't due to return from his trip to Seattle until Sunday.

What she is worried about is fitting in. She knows Jory from school, not that he ever speaks to her or anything. Of course she knows Drew and she'll admit that he's super cute.

But more than fitting in, she's worried about how strained her relationship with Jilli is becoming.

Last week when she'd stayed over, it had been like old times. They'd practiced different ways of braiding their hair, looking for the perfect fit under their hunt caps. And they'd talked until 1 A.M.

Deep down, Emma knew they wouldn't stay the naïve H&H sisters forever. Horses wouldn't always be the center of their world. Boys were inching up the interest tree. Even with the changes, though, she'd sort of assumed they'd still be H&H sisters. Older, more mature, but together.

Emma watches Jilli put the bridle back together and wonders if joining Jilli at these parties will help re-cement their friendship or be the final nail that splits them apart.

She's been jittery most of the day, rehearsing her excuse to get out of tonight's party, but she knows she'll still go. If she backs out, Jilli will never include her in anything again. This is her one chance to show she's as grown up as Jillian.

She sneaks a look at Jilli, who's posing in front of the full-length mirror in her bedroom. Her T-shirt is snugger than any Emma has seen her wear so far, with a deep V that exposes the edges of a purple polka-dot bra. Her cutoff shorts have recently undergone renovation and are showing as much leg as a modest swimsuit. It isn't that she's surprised at Jilli's choice, but she can't deny the prickle of unease at what that choice means for the evening.

Emma pulls the rounded neck of her T-shirt up to her collarbone.

Jillian flicks her a look. "At least put some makeup on."

"I'm not allowed. You know that."

Jillian makes a show of searching the room. "Is he here? Is he invisible?"

When Emma doesn't take the bait, she adds, "He's not going to know and I'm not taking my grandmother to a party. Loosen up."

Someone honks and Jillian lobs a tube of gloss at Emma with a sharp directive to move faster. Emma swipes on a coat of gloss, then wipes most of it off.

She follows Jillian down the stairs and out the door, ears tuned for a "stop right there." But no one stops them and before she can quadruple-guess her decision, she's mashed into the backseat between two boys who acknowledge her by making an extra two inches for her to fit in.

They sway into one another for the next thirty minutes as Jory negotiates the turns and stops. Music blares, making it hard to hear the discussion, although no one seems to be directing anything at Emma anyway.

She's the last out of the car and the last into the house. Whatever delusions she had about "hanging" with Jilli are scattered faster than bowling pins in the path of a barreling marble ball. She follows the general path Jilli took, weaving through groups of people who don't move to let her pass. By the time she reaches the kitchen, the prickle of unease is drowning in sweat.

"Looking for a drink?" Someone pushes a blue plastic cup into her hands.

"Thanks," she mumbles and takes a gulp. Her eyes and throat burn as the liquid flames a path to her stomach.

Whoever handed her the drink has already melted into the crowd. The laughter surrounding her could be at her expense or just part of the party. She's not sure, although she suspects at least some of it is at her expense. She pours the clear liquid into the sink and fills the cup with water.

An hour later, the noise hits a level that she's pretty confident will have police arriving any minute.

From her perch on the kitchen counter she has a decent view of the couples and tribes forming and splitting. A few people chat with her but only for the time it takes to grab a drink from one of the coolers on the counter next to her.

There's absolutely no question that she's a square peg. Jilli was right, she doesn't fit in and she never will. She looks around, hoping to find Jory and beg a ride home.

"You look like you're planning an escape." Drew steps into her line of sight.

She feels the heat prick her cheeks. He's even better-looking in jeans and a dark gray T-shirt that hugs muscles she hadn't noticed before. "It's a fun party."

He laughs and she feels the heat slither down her spine. In one graceful move he's sitting on the counter, close enough that their knees knock hello. She squeezes her thighs together, then silently scolds herself for being uptight. How many times will she have the opportunity to knock knees with Drew? She releases the cramp-inducing hold on her thighs.

"I'm glad you're here. It was a nice surprise finding you in my kitchen."

Two girls saunter over under the pretense of getting beers, interrupting him. A redhead Emma doesn't recognize leans against Drew's leg and flips her long hair. He introduces them to Emma, not that either notices she's there.

"Anyway, as I was saying," Drew turns back to Emma, earning her a glare from the redhead, who model-walks away with a last look to make sure Drew noticed. He shakes his head. "Don't pay attention to her. I think this is the first time we've seen each other outside of horse shows. I like it."

Emma likes his smile and the sound of his voice, the accent on *like*.

"Me too." She pulls her shoulders back, wishing she'd listened to Jilli and worn a more flattering T-shirt.

Drew, it turns out, is as funny as he is cute and as sweet as he is talented and she sends a thanks that Jory was nowhere to be found.

While the noise escalates around them, they talk horses and English Lit, the favorite subject for both of them. It's not until the crowd starts to thin and her butt tingles that she realizes how late it is.

"Oh crap, I need to find Jilli. Hopefully Jory hasn't left without us."

"Jory's right there." Drew points at a cluster of guys in the family room. One of them speaks and Jory laughs, tipping sideways and sloshing beer on himself. "Looks like he's had a couple too many. You're not going home with him."

"But he's my ride."

"Not anymore. I'll drive you." He puts his arm around her shoulder.

"Hey, what's happening here?" Jillian's voice slices through the private moment. She wobbles toward them and nudges Drew's knees to the side, just enough to squeeze between his legs and provide a scenic overlook to her cleavage.

"We were just talking about you."

Emma can't help noticing that his eyes drop to the cleavage.

"I felt it." Jillian gives a little shimmy that makes her boobs jiggle and causes Drew's left knee to bump into Emma's right knee. He puts his hand on her knee and squeezes, then winks when she looks up. Jillian catches the exchange and bumps Drew's knee until he refocuses on her. "What were you talking about?" She puckers her lips around the mouth of the bottle.

Emma forces her eyes away, like when she'd seen the dying fox on the side of the road.

"I was telling Emma that I'll drive her home since Jory seems to be a crap choice for a designated driver."

"What about me?" The pout deepens.

"You too if you need a ride. But I assumed Chris had you covered, considering what I saw in the bathroom earlier."

Emma catches a flash of uncertainty in Jillian's expression before her friend lets out a throaty pretend laugh and chugs the rest of the beer.

"Jealous are we?" The words slur together and she tips forward, her boobs brushing Drew's arm. "Oops." She giggles but doesn't move.

"Jilli, you're drunk." Emma's surprised at her revulsion.

"Oh, hi, Grandma. I didn't know you were coming. Well, duh, it's a party."

Emma swallows the bitter bile clawing up her throat. The girl in front of her, wedged between a guy's knees and blatantly offering herself, is a stranger. No wonder she hasn't been welcome at these parties. She should never have come.

She hops off the counter and grasps Jilli's upper arm. "Come on, we're going home."

Jillian yanks her arm away, the force knocking her off-balance and into Drew. Emma sees the hesitation on his face, his Adam's apple scooting up, then falling, his eyes locking on Jilli's gyrating mounds. Jillian sees the hesitation as well. "There's still beer and I'm not done." She wraps her lips around the opening of the bottle, eyes locked on Drew.

Emma turns away, suddenly feeling sick and all she's had to drink is water. She has to get out of here.

"Emma, wait . . ." Drew calls.

"Let her go. Wanna do ta-fuck-ya-shots with me? I have the yummiest spot for the salt."

Emma lurches for the front door. She'll walk if she has to. She'll call a taxi from the first gas station. Anything is better than being here.

"Emma, wait. I'm taking you both home." Drew grabs her hand and leads the way to his car. Jillian does a jog-walk to catch up to them, yelling "Slow down," which only makes Drew stride faster.

He unlocks the passenger side and opens the door. She can

hear Jilli wheezing a few steps behind. A wave of annoyance propels her forward until she's in the front seat, where she knows Jillian wants to be. Not this time.

"Hey, that's my . . ." Jilli doubles over, vomit arcing to an inch from Drew's feet.

"Damn, Jillian." He jumps to the side and closes the car door, securing Emma in the coveted passenger seat.

Jillian attempts a glare at her but the alcohol makes her wobble, reducing the effectiveness of the threat. If it had been anyone other than Jilli, Emma would have found it comical.

It wasn't that long ago that they'd watched Jilli's mom stumble out of a car, too drunk to walk the straight path to the front door. Jilli had apologized to Emma for having to witness that and swore she'd never end up like her mom. Emma watches Jilli in the side mirror as Drew pulls the car out of the driveway.

Except for a few moans that turn to snores in the backseat, the only sound during the rest of the drive is the rumble of the engine.

Maybe it's not a choice. Maybe we become what our parents are. It's not a thought that comforts Emma. Who would she become? Her sickly mom, who died young, or her cold, ambitious dad, who prefers his work to his family?

Neither one. She'll make sure of that.

Drew squeezes her left hand. A tingle races up her arm. She's glad she came to the party but she also knows she'll never go again.

33

Thanks for seeing me on such short notice." I shake Thomas Adler's hand. I'd called him from the car on my way to his office, an impulsive act fueled by forest spirits and the need to prove my independence.

"I'm always happy to fit you in. Although I admit, I was surprised to hear you were still in town."

"Something came up."

"Not about the condo I hope?"

"No, the sale is going through. The buyer is anxious to get in."

"So what brings you to my door with singed hair?"

"I want to hire you."

"But I'm already working for you."

"Separate from my father's things. This is for me, personally."

He eases back in his chair and studies me, the fingers of his right hand rolling a pen along a yellow legal pad, then grins. "The reason for the singed hair. Let's hear it."

"I want to invest the money from the sale of the condo and practice in the therapeutic riding program at Jumping Frog Farm. The main donor has backed out and without that money, Rena will have to shut it down. I can't let that happen." My foot jitters faster with each word.

His hand flattens, quieting the gentle rolling sound of the pen.

His expression fades like a slide show from friendly to curious to reserved. "May I ask why?"

I channel the Chicago Emma, the one who sits in executive board meetings and doesn't take no for an answer. "A lot of people rely on that program. I've always loved it, even before . . ." I complete the thought in my head.

Thomas nods, his mouth pulling into a contemplative line.

Under his gaze, new Emma begins to waver. "I don't need the money from the condo or practice. I don't want that money. It needs to go to something positive. My father may have paid for lessons but he never supported my passion. That was really all I ever wanted. He can finally give me that."

Thomas leans forward as though to say something, but instead he takes a deep breath and closes his fingers around the pen.

"Can you draw up the papers for me to sign before I leave? I'm on a flight Saturday afternoon. Please. I realize it's a rush job, I'll pay whatever fees you want." The words trip over one another.

Just when I'm ready to reach across the desk and shake an answer out of him, he nods. "Of course."

Air whooshes through me. "Thank you."

But there's something in his expression that dams the release of adrenaline.

"There's a 'but'?"

"No." He shakes his head. "Well, yes. It's not a 'but,' I can pull those documents together. But there is something you need to know."

I'm not going to like this. My stomach clenches tighter.

"The funding for the therapeutic program has been coming from an anonymous account that your father established after your mom died."

I stare through the distance between us, through the years of arguments over my expensive hobby, through the years of silence.

"That's ridiculous."

His eyebrows raise in a maybe-but-it's-the-truth.

"Why would he do that? And why anonymous?"

"I'm not sure it's my place to say more."

"Then whose place is it? My father sure as hell can't. He never gave a shit about the horses. Or what was important to me. Now I'm supposed to take your word that he had a soft spot after all?" Anger slams into realization. The dark gray linen notebook. The hours he'd spent at the stable drawing the horses and the people of the therapeutic riding program.

"Thomas, did you know that my father used to draw?"

Thomas tilts his head, pointing with his chin at a framed picture to my left. It's a graphite drawing of a young lady standing by the beach, hair and dress billowing in the breeze.

"He did that?" My mouth locks in an awed O.

"Yes. That's my sister. Well, inspired by my sister. She never went to the beach. Although it was always her dream."

I turn to look at him but he's far away, on that beach with his sister. "Is she one of his patients?"

"Was. She died five years ago." He pulls himself away from the memory of a beach trip that never was.

"I'm so sorry."

"Thank you. She had cancer. It was a hard time but your father was a godsend during that period. He gave her that drawing a few months before she passed."

I turn back to the drawing. What an emotionally generous move. "I found sketch pads in his things. Most were of people, one of horses."

"He explained to me once that he drew what he saw in people, not what they actually looked like. Drawing horses was a more recent passion."

"Do you know if he gave other drawings away?" I make a mental note to look around the stable office again for any of his drawings.

Thomas shakes his head. "He was very private about his drawings. Said they were his personal therapy."

"Then why this one?" I turn back to the picture of Thomas's sister.

"Your father was a client here since before I became a

lawyer. He worked with my father. Then when Dad retired, I took over. Angela was first diagnosed when she was seventeen. Your father helped my parents through that initial blow. When the cancer came back, she started seeing your father as well. He knew her since she was a little girl. He was more of a family friend than the family psychiatrist."

The idea of my father being that close to another family sends my emotions to a rolling boil. I have to leave before I spill over. I push to my feet. "I need to go. Can you please prepare the documents?"

He startles at the abrupt change in my manner and the sharp move. "Of course. I'm sorry if I've upset you."

"You didn't. It's all his doing." I walk to the door and reach for the knob.

"Emma, do you want your participation to be anonymous?"

The word "yes" rolls out of my brain but detours before coming out of my mouth. "No," I hear myself say instead. I never hid my love for the stable. I'm not my father and I no longer need to hide in the shadow he created for me.

A vision of Rena in the hospital bed stops me from turning the doorknob. "Can you include a caveat that as the primary backer, changes won't be made to the program without my approval?"

If something happens to Rena, I can't allow Jillian to dissolve the program. She may not be a fan of it, but it's part of Jumping Frog Farm and I intend to keep it that way.

"Of course. I'll swing by tomorrow morning for you and Mrs. Winn to sign the paperwork."

"Thank you." I open the door and let in a beehive buzz of activity from the outer offices.

Thomas steps around the desk, holding a box. "I almost forgot. This is for you. I'd planned on sending it but since you're here . . ." He takes a few steps in my direction and holds out the box. "It was in a locked drawer in his office."

I take the beige cardboard box, and finger the fake metal label frame. There's no label giving away the contents.

"Thank you." I tuck the box into the crook of my elbow, the shape pushing my arm out at an awkward angle, making me bump into the doorframe on the way out.

Rena's SUV isn't parked in front of their house or at the stable when I return. Tony tells me that Simon stopped by while I was out, then left with Rena. He volunteers that Jillian hasn't been at the stable all day. Not that I'd asked about her or particularly wanted to see her.

I thank him and take the mysterious box to the porch, where I drag my favorite Adirondack chair to the side so I'm partially hidden behind the potted cypress tree.

My index finger traces the edge of the box, short side, long side, short side, back to the start. My thumb pushes at the corner of the lid, just enough to create a slope, not enough to show inside. One more little nudge and it pops off. Inside are two stacks of envelopes.

I take the top envelope from the left pile and pull out the letter.

August 1996

Edward,

It saddens me that you still feel the need to apologize. Your letters are never a burden.

I can only begin to imagine how difficult this period is for you. A teenage girl isn't easy in the best of circumstances much less during the anniversary of her mother's death.

She's a strong girl with a good head on her shoulders. You've done right by her and Barbara would be proud.

Yours,
R.

It's short and nice, and yet it ignites an anger that flares, threatening to consume everything in its path. *Done right by me? When did he ever do right by me?* He didn't raise me. I raised me. Rena and Simon raised me. And when I needed them most, he sent me away and cut off all ties.

I grab the letter from the top of the pile on the right.

February 1998

Edward,

I was happy to receive the postcard. The Swiss Alps are absolutely glorious.

I'm glad you were able to go with Emma. Maybe this will be the first step toward a new relationship between the two of you. I do hope so.

It's been five years, Edward. It's time to forgive yourself. If not for you, then for Emma. Both of you need to move forward. Time is not in your favor, my friend. Emma is becoming a young woman and soon the window for a connection between you will seal shut. You don't want that. I know how much it hurts you to see her withdraw deeper into herself.

Use this trip to crack that window open a bit more. Reach out to her. Connect with her. It won't happen overnight but it can happen.

Yours,

R.

I remember that trip. My father had "surprised" me with the news that we would be spending New Year's in Switzerland. He had a conference there in early January and "what a wonderful opportunity to make this a nice vacation. Just the two of us."

Like it would ever be anything other than just the two of us. Although "just the two of us" and "nice" weren't words I'd normally string together.

A pang of guilt pokes at my stomach. He had made an effort, booking an extra night in Austria so we could go to the famed Spanish Riding School. We'd sat in the darkened arena, the magnificent white stallions dancing in their spotlights. I'd been utterly mesmerized by their beauty, the precision of their movements, the relationship between human and horse. My father had spent the performance jotting notes in a tiny notebook. Maybe I'd just been conditioned to this behavior, or maybe I'd finally given up, but I remember the feeling, the heavy wool sweater of disappointment tightening around me, creating a barrier from the outside world.

After the performance I'd begged to go to the gift shop. My father bought the books I plucked from the shelves. The rest of the day was spent in the hotel room, my father working on a lecture, me losing myself in the books.

August 1993

Edward,

My heart goes to you and I so wish there was more I could do!

Separating the emotional from the logical may not be possible now. Don't expect too much from yourself. You are still a mere mortal—my apologies for having to remind you of that—and you are entitled to feel the pain that we mortals feel when a loved one dies.

And I do understand, believe me I do. When faced with such a deep wound, it's much easier to turn away, lose yourself in anything but. But please, Edward, please reach out. Emma needs you.

Know I am always nearby.

Yours,

R.

Two hours later I look up from the stack of letters. The world has settled in for the night. Someone has turned on the light in the lounge behind me, allowing me to read without interruption. I shiver but can't bring myself to get up and go in. There's one unread letter left.

October 1999

Edward,

Please don't shut us out!

The hospital wouldn't let us see Emma. Wouldn't even give

us her status. You don't answer at the house. Please! You should know by now that we consider Emma a member of our family. We love her and can't bear the thought of losing her.

We don't believe she was responsible. We would never hold her responsible. You must know that.

Simon and I are wrecked over this tragedy and the guilt. Oh, Edward, you of all people should understand the guilt. How could we not have known there was a problem? How did this happen under our noses? What could we have done to prevent this?

Please, Edward. That's all I can say . . . Please?

Yours,
Rena

34

October 1999

Emma pushes past the line of people waiting for the bathroom, ignoring their complaints. The show organizers brought in porta-potties but there's no way she's going into one of those. She elbows someone out of the way and pushes her hand to her mouth in a pathetic attempt to keep the retching under control. Secure behind the locked door, she vomits into the toilet, tears mixing with the lunch Drew had insisted she eat only a couple of hours ago.

Someone pounds on the door.

"Go away." She wheezes through the sobs and doubles over as another wave races through her stomach.

"Emma, it's Drew. Let me in."

She grabs for the knob to make sure it's locked, then slides down the door until her butt makes contact with the cold, dirty concrete floor.

"Let me in. I need to talk to you."

"No."

"Please, Emma. It's not . . ."

"Don't," she yells, then buries her face in her hands. "Don't say it's not what it looked like."

"Will you please let me in so we can talk?"

"Go. Away."

A muffled voice comes to her rescue. "Listen to her. If you leave, she'll come out. See this line? People want to get into this bathroom."

Emma says a silent thank-you to the person with the full bladder.

The knocking slows to a few halfhearted taps. Her butt's getting cold and sore from the concrete floor. She's not sure how much time has passed, but she needs to get up and check on Jack. She can't hide in here forever. How will she face Jillian and Drew? She'd left Jack tied to the trailer. He hates being tied to the trailer. She has to get up. It doesn't matter how she feels. Jack needs her.

She pulls herself up and looks in the mirror. Her eyes are puffy and red and her cheeks are blotchy and stained. She splashes water on her face and rinses her mouth, then flushes the toilet one last time for good measure. If only she could flush herself and not have to deal with the crap outside.

But deal she must. She opens the door and sucks in a greedy breath of horse smell. The air freshener in the bathroom was starting to give her a headache. She walks away from the arena and the final jumper classes. For the first time, she doesn't want to spend a minute longer than she has to at the show. She wants to get home and stand in the hottest shower she can tolerate until she's washed away the smell of vomit and the feel of Drew kissing her.

There are a few stragglers around the parked horse trailers. A few people smile at her, congratulating her on a successful day. She bites the inside of her lip and mumbles thanks. Applause and a whistle signal a clear round. Someone will be happy. She hopes that person's happiness lasts longer than hers.

Since they were the first to arrive, the Jumping Frog Farm trailer is the farthest in the field. Emma and Jillian had been so excited to come on their own for the first time. Rena had a couple of new therapeutic clients coming today and Simon was still under the weather from a stomach virus. He'd said he would try to come later in the day. Emma's now glad he hadn't.

Jilli is sitting in a beach chair, feet propped up on the cooler, when Emma reaches their parking spot. She's been watching her, Emma can feel it.

"Well lookee who dragged herself out of the loo." Jillian rolls the "u" sound, whether an exaggerated attempt at mimicking her grandfather's accent or a side effect of the beer cans she'd seen earlier, Emma isn't sure. "About damn time, too. I'm fed up of this place. I want to get home and changed."

Emma bites harder on the inside of her lip until the taste of blood makes her stomach heave. "I'll get Jack ready to go."

Jillian takes a long drink from the Coke can and wipes her mouth. Emma's eyes sting.

"Why did you do it?" The question bursts out of her like the lunch she'd just lost into the toilet, leaving the same aftertaste.

"Oh come on, you knew I liked him. You're the one who muscled in at that party."

"There was nothing between you and Drew. You were doing whatever you were doing with Chris. Drew chose me."

Jilli shrugs, less defiant than before. "Whatever. He's too old for you anyway."

"That's not your call. You're my best friend. Why would you be so mean? Because you're jealous that I placed higher in that jumper class today?"

Jillian's icy eyes flash. "I guess being Little Miss Perfect didn't get you the most important trophy, did it?" She grabs the folded chair and pirouettes, the metal and green fabric of the chair slicing a half circle around her.

Emma's mouth opens to respond but Jillian is already tossing the chair into the tack room at the front of the trailer with a noisy clang.

Jack paws the ground and snorts and Emma moves to his side. "I'm sorry, baby. Let's get those shipping wraps on you and get home."

"What the hell? It's just down the road. Seriously, Emma. Get him loaded already." Jilli leads Tolstoy around them and loads him into the left side of the trailer.

"It won't take me long." She's not trailering Jack without his shipping bandages. No way. Rena would kill her.

"You're such a damn goody-goody."

"I'm not." She is. "So what if I am? At least I'm not a slut." She cringes but squares her shoulders. She's done being the timid little shadow.

Jillian whips around. "If you knew how to keep your boyfriend happy, he wouldn't have been so desperate for me. It was only a matter of time anyway."

Emma feels her stomach roller coaster again but she's not backing down, not this time. "Why are you being such a bitch?"

For a long minute they stare at each other, contempt versus need, bitterness versus sadness.

"Like you would understand. You've never had to fight for anything." Jilli flips her braid over her shoulder and latches the bumper behind Tolstoy. She steps back but miscalculates and slips off the ramp, rolling her ankle and banging her elbow into the trailer as she tries to regain her balance. She turns and glares at Emma. "What are you staring at? Get him in the trailer so we can leave."

"How much did you drink?" Emma wants to believe that was a simple slip, it's not like she hasn't done that before herself, but the earlier smell of beer and the cans that disappeared while she was hurling in the bathroom are too fresh.

"Get over yourself. I tripped. Big stinking deal." Jillian takes careful strides until she reaches the lead rope they'd strung along the side of the trailer to display the ribbons. Seven ribbons flutter in the afternoon breeze, six of them Emma's. Jillian plucks them one by one. "Weren't you just the little star today. Grandma will be so proud of you."

"Hey, Jilli, you coming tonight?" a brunette Emma recognizes from school asks as she walk-skips to keep up with her three friends.

"Better believe it."

"Want one for the road?" The brunette holds out a beer can, then quickly pulls it down and into her stomach, looking around to make sure no one saw her.

Emma's intuition sounds the warning bell. Jillian may not be drunk like she'd been at Drew's party, but Emma is pretty sure she isn't completely sober either.

Jillian's eyes dart to Emma. "Nah. If my grandma smells that, she'll have a fit. And this one will snitch." She tosses a nod in Emma's direction.

The brunette turns a landscaped eyebrow on Emma before dismissing her with a shrug.

Jillian looks after the three retreating bodies. "Save some for me." The brunette waves as she catches up to the others.

"We should call Rena to drive the rig back."

"Are you fucking crazy? She'd kill me."

"Why, Jillian? Because you're drunk?"

"I'm not drunk."

"I don't believe you."

Jillian flinches. There's a stab of doubt in her eyes that's gone with a blink.

Is the doubt whether Emma will go through with the threat to call Rena? Or is it the sudden realization that maybe this time she's crossed the line?

"I don't care what you believe." The defiance is back but with more whimper than growl. "You can't call her. She'll be furious and ground me forever. She'll never trust us to go on our own again.

"Then I'll drive."

"You can't. You've never driven with a full trailer. Please, Emma? I'm sorry, okay? I swear I'm fine to drive." Emma's seen that look before. It's the look Jilli gets every time her mom shows up and then disappears again.

Those are the times she's needed Emma the most. Because Emma understands loss and disappointment, she knows the longing of wanting the love and attention of a parent. And Emma understands the crushing need to prove yourself.

"You swear you're okay to drive?" She bites her ring finger and waits for the giant moths in her stomach to settle.

Jillian nods and Emma feels the familiar tug of wanting to please her friend. Because despite what happened, they are best friends and they will get past it, Emma will make sure of that. Jilli's always worse right after an incident with her mom. And this time was one of the harder ones. This time she'd had to pick her mom up at the jail after her mom was arrested for a DUI. Rena had refused to go. Jilli had begged Emma to go with her instead.

"You swear you haven't had too much to drink?"

Jillian holds her left hand, middle and index fingers together, other fingers folded into a fist. It's their promise sign, a silent symbol of the bond between them.

Emma nods and ignores the moth of uncertainty flopping in her gut. She has to believe her H&H sister. What else can she do?

They finish loading the horses in silence.

Jillian maneuvers the truck and trailer down the long driveway and onto the blacktop. Emma's eyes flick to the speedometer as they pass a speed-limit sign. They're going one mile an hour over. Jilli's hands are at the perfect ten and two spots on the steering wheel. Emma allows her muscles to relax. They'll be at Jumping Frog Farm in less than thirty minutes.

A blue Nissan sedan honks and pulls into the oncoming lane next to the truck. Two girls hang out of the open windows, yelling to Jillian to hurry up. The brunette from the showground reaches into the car, then leans farther out the window, trying to hand Jillian a beer. It falls out of her grip and crunches under the wheels of the trailer. The driver guns the engine and pulls in front of them, saluting with a beer can out the driver's side window. Jillian laughs and presses the gas to keep up with the speeding car.

Emma grabs at the armrest and dashboard. "Slow down."

Jilli laughs harder and gives the gas pedal a push.

"The horses. Slow down."

"Oh get a grip. I'm just having fun."

"You're scaring me."

"You seriously need to loosen up. A few drinks wouldn't hurt you."

"Oh my god, Jilli. Please." She's hyperventilating. She can feel it. She can't stop it. She should never have gotten in the truck. She should have stayed with Jack. She can't undo this. "Slow. Down."

"I want to get to the party before those losers drink all the good shit. Oops." She taps at the brakes as their truck veers wide around a bend in the road and corrects back to the right lane.

"You're going to get us all killed."

"Would you relax? Jesus. No wonder Drew dumped you. Maybe they're all right about you after all."

"What's that supposed to mean?" An icy spear slices through her and Emma squeezes the door handle until it feels like her knuckles will break through the skin.

"I've always defended you but I'm starting to think they're right, you're just like your mom."

"What does this have to do with my mom? She's been dead six years."

"Everyone thought you were weird when you first moved here. I told them you were okay. Timothy said he'd heard your mom tried to off herself. I told him it wasn't true. They said crazy was contagious."

Emma's afraid to look away from the road, as though her focus is the only thing keeping them on the narrow, curving asphalt. "What is wrong with you?"

Jillian releases a sound between surprise and rage. She turns and stares at Emma, an ugly mix of disgust and pity twisting her face. "It's always about you. Always about poor Emma. I'm so sick of you and your weak little self."

"Eyes on the road. Oh my god, Jillian, slow down."

"If your crazy mom hadn't killed herself . . ."

"She died of a heart attack and you know it. Stop it, Jillian. You're being cruel and you're scaring me. Alcohol makes you mean." Her teeth begin to chatter and her body shakes, loosening the tears and the sobs.

A tree branch slaps the window and Emma ducks and shrieks. Jillian laughs, hollow and hard. "You're ridiculous."

"You're crazy. Slow down."

"Crazy?" Jillian shrieks. "You're calling me crazy. Look in the mirror. You're the one with the mental genes."

"Shut up."

"You're going to end up just like your mom."

"Shut up!"

"In the loony bin."

"SHUT UP."

A yellow right-angle Turn sign flashes past.

"Woo-woo crazy."

"Shut up. Oh my god." She grabs Jilli's arm. The truck needs to turn. She has to fix it. They're going too fast. The trees on her right side blur. They have to turn. NOW.

"Let go."

Oh my god. The ditch. They're going to end in the ditch. "TURN."

Her head slams into the side window, and her back arches as she tries to escape the stranglehold of the seat belt.

"STOP." She feels the burn of the word but all she can hear is the screeching of tires. The smell of burning rubber stings her nose.

Her forehead slaps the window. The seat belt yanks her back.

"EMMA." Jilli's head bounces off the steering wheel. Blood gushes from her mouth.

Someone screams. Her? Jilli? A horse?

"JACK."

Jilli's head twists and their eyes meet. Emma's breath echoes in her ears, competing with the pounding heartbeats. Time slows.

A tree moves. Too fast. Into their path.

The slam of metal into wood is like the explosion of fireworks.

She feels the scream as pain shatters her right side.

Jillian moans.

A horse screams.

She tries to move. She is moving. Her body flames with the effort.

"Emma. Please. Move. Please."

Move. Where?

Another searing lightning bolt and the world tilts with jerked motion.

"You. Have. To. Tell. Them."

"Whuuu . . ."

She's falling. Sliding. She opens her eyes, moves her arms, flexes her hands. She closes her fingers on the steering wheel to make the swaying stop.

"Please, Emma. You. Have. To. Say. You. Were. Driving."

She grips tighter and pain shoots into her lungs. Jilli leans closer. "Sorry." The snap of the seat belt splits through the noise in her brain.

"Why?" Her lips move but she's not sure her lungs released enough air to make the sound.

"Please."

Silence.

Sirens.

Darkness.

35

Someone takes the envelope from my hand, wraps a blanket around me, then settles into the second chair with a groan.

"I'm amazed he kept these." Rena picks up the box, her fingers walking through the stacks of envelopes.

I blink at her. They started writing to each other before we moved here, kept it up the entire time we lived a woods-distance away, then stopped when our lives broke apart.

Like so many other things in my life, I had only one side of the story. I'd seen only the reserved, for-public-eyes side of my father.

How is it that he confided in her? Why Rena of all people?

"You're angry."

"I'm angry."

She puts the box back down between the chairs.

"I'm hurt, too." I can't bring myself to match her gaze.

"Why, Emma?"

Why? Thirty-some years of trying to penetrate his cold bubble, doing everything to be worthy, and the only person he let in was someone he barely knew.

Apparently knew much better than you thought.

I squeeze my eyes shut, searching for a snapshot of my childhood. "He was so closed off. All he really cared about was his work. When Mom was healthy she was an asset, the beautiful wife on his arm at receptions. But a renowned psychiatrist can't have a sick wife. And me? I just got in his way."

"Oh, Emma, that's not true."

"How can you say that? You were there. You saw how uninterested he was. He never cared if I was at the house. He seemed much happier when I stayed with you. I'm surprised he didn't offer for you guys to adopt me. Give him the freedom to live his life without the baggage of a fucked-up family."

Rena sucks in a harsh breath and I wait for the reprimand. Cursing was never permitted in her presence. Not by her family, not by the stable help, not by her students. That never stopped Simon, although he generally reverted to the softer British terms that fell under Rena's censor radar.

She doesn't reprimand me. She doesn't say anything at all for a few inflated minutes. The stretch in time pokes at the raw wound of my self-worth.

"He loved you. It hurt him that you spent so much time away from home, but he thought it made you happier."

"If it wasn't so damn sad, it would be funny."

"There's nothing funny about this."

"No."

We listen to the night, horses pawing in their stalls, a TV from one of the apartments above, the beep of a microwave, an owl sending an all-clear.

I deflate into the chair, the anger gone. "How did it start?"

She looks at me before responding, maybe trying to decide what the "it" was. "He was looking for anything that might help your mom."

Nope, she knows.

"Why you? Why here?"

"It's not an accident that your father bought the property so close to ours, Emma. After your mom had the breakdown, her doctors recommended various treatment options. One of her doctors was an old acquaintance. In addition to his private practice, he worked with military vets. That's how we met. One of the patients he worked with was also a client in the therapeutic program. Leo was impressed with the progress this guy had made and started sending patients he thought would benefit. He ended up writing a number of papers that were published in the medical journals. Anyway, at Leo's suggestion, your father contacted me. He was worried about you and your mom."

"Why was he worried about me?"

"Depression affects more than the person suffering from it. He wanted to protect you from the gossip. He wanted you to have a fresh start. For all of you to have a fresh start."

"If we moved here because of the stable, why was he so against me riding at first?"

Rena restocks her air supply. "It wasn't so much that he was against you riding. I think he was more worried about how you'd feel if you knew your mom was part of the therapeutic program."

"That doesn't make sense."

"To him it did. He didn't want you to see your mom as damaged. And people in the therapeutic program are damaged."

I'd seen my mom as fragile and sad but not damaged. My father, on the other hand, I'd always thought of as damaged.

"For a while, your mom seemed to be improving. You were becoming quite the little rider, and you and Jilli were becoming close. Edward seemed to relax."

I laugh, one dry, weary laugh. "'Relaxed' is not a word that ever fit my father."

"He came to a couple of shows. And asked me to help pick out a new saddle for you."

"He didn't do it because it was the best thing for me. He did it because it assuaged his guilt. If I was at the stable, I was fine. If I was at home, I might need his attention. And that was something he couldn't spare. Money, easy. Give-a-shit? Not so much."

She picks the box up again and flips through the envelopes. "Did you read all of these?"

"And the ones I found in his home office."

"Then how can you still think he didn't care?"

The smart-ass response fizzles on my tongue like a bitter dissolvable pill. The person at the other end of those letters was hurting and confused, someone who was trapped and didn't know how to reach out. All those years of trying to earn his love and now I'm supposed to just flip thirty-two years based on a few letters?

"The person I knew didn't care." I hear the petulance in my voice.

"The Edward Metz I knew cared. A lot. For both of you."

"The Edward Metz you knew was a pen-and-paper person. Not the real man I lived with. You can put anything in a letter."

"Did you keep a journal?"

She knows I did. For Christmas one year she bought matching journals for me and Jillian. I'd written religiously in it. And every Christmas, Rena had bought me another one. Jilli wrote three entries, then chucked the journal into the bottom of her desk drawer and forgot about it. She'd scoff when she saw me writing in mine. It became my private outlet. Usually while I sat under a tree watching Jack graze or cross-legged on the mounting block while Simon taught a lesson or Rena worked with a therapy client. Often I wrote huddled in the secret cave I'd made in my bedroom closet.

"So? We're not talking about my father penning his deepest secrets in a journal. He wrote letters to someone he barely knew."

I'm embarrassed by the resentment I feel toward her, like a child hurt by someone else's knowing a secret you aren't privy to.

"Did you talk to Jilli or Simon about the things you wrote in those journals?"

"Of course not. Those things were private."

"Why do you think it was easier to write than to talk to the people who loved you?"

"Jilli would have judged me. She would have made fun of me."

"And Simon?"

"I didn't want to burden him."

"Exactly. It's much easier to write about your feelings, especially when you know it's between you and the paper."

"But it wasn't between him and the paper. I wrote knowing no one would read my ramblings. He was writing to someone."

"True."

My journals never responded with advice or pep talks. They didn't care in return. I think about the letters I wrote Karen. Granted, we'd been all of eight at the time. "Deep" consisted of the size of my new room or the horse I'd ridden the previous week or the new friends she was making. That's when our letters had stopped, when she found a new best friend.

That pen-pal experience had lasted a couple of months. My father and Rena kept it going for over eight years.

Sure, I'd confessed plenty of secret desires and heartbreaks in e-mails to friends and they'd had plenty of advice. But there's an intimacy in handwritten letters, an intimacy that he denied his own family.

"Is that the reason he never came to the stable when I was there?" My mind bounces from thought to thought.

"Is what the reason?"

"You were his journal. Okay, not exactly his journal since you wrote back but he confided in you the way I confided in my journal. Do you think he was afraid to see you in person because of the secrets you knew about him?"

"I think your dad was able to confide in me because he knew me but he didn't *know* me. He knew I would do anything to help you and your mom and because of that he was able to open a degree of trust between us. Knowing me personally—seeing me face-to-face at the stable—would have made that harder for him."

The anger seeps out of me, replaced with sadness.

"Why didn't he ever take your advice?"

"He did, in his own way."

I shiver and pull my legs up, curling into as small a ball as I can in the chair, and tuck the blanket around my legs. "His own way."

My entire childhood, my father's way was unyielding. What child doesn't crave a positive word, a wink, a secret exchanged with just a look? What child doesn't dream about sharing the pride over a stellar report card or seeing her parents cheering from the sidelines? What child doesn't need a steadying hand or the unspoken bond spoken through the simple act of a hug?

As an adult, "his way" had been inflexible. All those years of doing everything I could to make him proud. I followed the path he "suggested" would be best. And I excelled. At the end of that path was recognition. Even if I couldn't earn his love, I damn well could earn his respect. But did I?

When I finally speak again, my voice is thick. "I never expected to hear him say 'I love you.' I'm not sure he even knew those words. But 'good job' or 'well done' or, better yet, 'I'm proud of you.'"

"He was proud of you."

"Does a tree falling in the woods make a sound if no one is around to hear it?"

"I heard it."

I swallow, loud, painful. It doesn't help with keeping the sobs down.

"I wasn't here when the tree fell. Now I'll never know, will I?"

"Oh, Emma." She pushes up from the chair and kneels in front of me, pulling me into a hug. "I wish I'd kept his letters so you could see for yourself. He was proud of you and he did love you. He was a good man, sweetheart, he just didn't know how to open himself up."

In her arms, the tears flow, hot and draining.

"He was proud of you," she repeats. "He'd be even prouder if he knew you were doing what made you happy."

She gives one final squeeze, then unfolds and turns to leave. I listen to the shuffle of gravel under her boots, the sound fading into the symphony of the crickets.

Are you proud of me, Dad? Would you still be proud of me if I didn't have a fancy job? Did you really think keeping me away was the right thing to do? Why all the secrecy with the drawings and funding the program? Were you afraid I'd see the real you? Would that really have been so awful?

The answers aren't in the letters he kept all these years, or in the night, or even in the woods. I stay curled up in the hard Adirondack chair on the front porch of the place that always made me feel whole, listening to the crackles and the whispers coming from the woods surrounding the property.

No trees falling tonight.

36

W hat are you two gawking at?" I push my way between Ben and Tony, who are blocking the door from the lounge to the barn aisle.

Rena is standing in front of Taco's stall, talking to a tall, curvy redhead.

"What's going on?" I try again, since neither man has acknowledged my arrival.

"Potential buyer."

"For Taco?"

"Yeahhh." Ben draws out the word, his eyes widening, grin spreading. "She'll be a nice addition to the barn."

"Seriously?" I slap him gently across the chest.

"What?"

"But, boss, that don't mean she'll board him here." Tony shakes his head, and somehow I think he's sadder about the idea of losing her than seeing the horse go.

"She can't sell Taco. He's a star in the program. Michael would be lost without him."

"No more therapy program," Tony says.

"Did sleeping outside last night freeze your brain?" Ben stares down at me. "We talked about this yesterday, remember? No more funding. No more program."

"I need to talk to Rena." I elbow both men out of my way and

stride down the aisle to where Rena and the redhead are standing.

Taco sticks his head over the stall door, rolls his tongue, and
sticks his muzzle in my face.

"You're such a goofball." I rub his forehead.

Rena introduces me and explains that the intruder is interested in purchasing a couple of horses to build up her lesson
barn.

Not our horses. No, no, no. That's not happening.

"Sorry for interrupting, but, Rena, I need to speak with you
a minute."

Rena excuses herself, giving the unwanted poacher free rein
to look around.

Enjoy the view, lady, you're not getting anyone from this barn.

"You can't sell the horses," I blurt the moment we're inside
the office.

With a sigh, Rena eases into the chair behind her desk. She
looks tired, older. "I'm sure Ben has already told you, but the
donor who was keeping the program alive has pulled the funding. Without that money, I can't keep it going. It was great while
it lasted, and it lasted a long time. I'm thankful for that. And, Emma,
I can't keep going either. I'm done, honey. I've been pushing and
pushing because I couldn't let everyone down. Now, well, now
the decision has been made for me."

"But . . ."

"No buts. Done deal. I don't have it in me to fight."

"But it's not a done deal."

Rena raises a hand to stop me. "Emma, I talked to the lawyer
at length yesterday. There's nothing we can do. I don't know why
now, but the timing seems like a message."

"The donor died. That's why now."

She looks at me, confusion replacing the weariness.

"It was my father. He's the one who's been funding the program all these years."

"Edward? Even after . . ." She lets the obvious fade into
disbelief.

"Even after what happened."

"Why would he do that?"

"Maybe you were right. Maybe he wasn't such a bad guy after all." My shoulders and ears meet in a halfhearted shrug.

She gives me the of-course-I-was-right look.

I wave it away. "I went to see his lawyer yesterday afternoon. You'll be able to keep the program going."

"Not to dump salt on the wound, Emma, but Edward is still dead. And that means our funding is still dead."

"But that dead man's daughter inherited his money. And I want to put that money into the therapeutic program."

Rena pulls her mouth into a tight circle and I can almost hear her brain cells arguing over how to respond. *Jump on it. You can't let her do that. You need that money. She needs that money.*

"Before you say anything, I've asked the lawyer to draw up new papers. He's coming by this morning for us to sign them. Please, Rena. I want to do this. I need to do this."

We both startle as the door pushes open.

"Do what?" Jillian stands in the open frame, her left hand gripping the handle while the right fist pushes into her hip. The expression on her face tells me she's overheard more than I would have chosen for her to know at this point.

Can't very well do this without her knowing, though, so get it over with it.

"I've offered to keep funding the therapeutic program."

A flash I can't read passes over Jillian's face. The stride of her riding boots echoes on the tile floor as she walks to the open seat across from Rena, clearly leaving me outside the decision-making circle. "Of course you did. Golden Child Emma, here to save us all. Why not? We need a new outside donor if we're going to keep the program going. I'm not surprised that you wouldn't want his money."

Rena winces.

I don't. "I didn't mean as an outside donor." Not entirely at least.

Both women practically give themselves whiplash to get a better look at me.

"What the hell are you talking about?" Jillian growls at the same time Rena says, "What are you saying?"

I address Rena. "I spent all night thinking about what you said. I'll never know if he was proud of what I've accomplished or if he wanted something different for me. But I have to let it go. I think it's why he included the instructions for me to come back to deal with his affairs. He died before you guys had a chance to hash through it, so this was something he'd been thinking about. It was his way of releasing me."

"You're not thinking about staying?" Jillian wrinkles her nose and looks at me with the same disgust as if I'd farted in her presence.

I fight the urge to laugh. That won't further my shaky footing. Not that I need her approval but I'm stunned to realize that I want her to accept my offer.

"Can you stay and help run the program?" There's a set to Rena's mouth that tells me it's not really a question. It's what she'd planned on talking to my father about the day he died.

"No. This is *our* business, a family business, and She. Is. Not. Family." The words find their mark, the sharp point dulled only by the slight slur.

Rena squints at Jilli, who's suddenly intent on the photographs hanging on the back wall. She heard it, too. She turns back to me, waiting for an answer.

"I'm not staying. But I don't want to be a silent partner either."

Jillian flails her arms in a dismissive wave. "Sign the damn papers then and go back to your cushy life. We don't need your suggestions."

"I have no intention of running the program, much less the stable. But it's important to me that the program survives and I'll do whatever I can to make that happen. I'll help you hire someone to run it if needed. But the program cannot die." I shift my weight and cross my arms across my chest. It's a physical exclamation mark I learned from Bruce when he addressed the board or senior leadership.

It has less of an effect on Jilli, though. She raises one eyebrow and matches my crossed arms, although her tone is less belligerent than before. "Why is it so important to you? You stayed away for sixteen years. Now, suddenly, it's your life's mission?"

Rena stiffens. "Emma, will you please give us a minute?"

I'm rooted, the answer to Jilli's accusation burning a trail up my throat.

"Emma, now please."

I turn to the door but the misery in Jillian's sagging face stops forward motion. In the lines around her mouth, I see every day of the last sixteen years. The years I'd spent battling guilt and insecurity, forging past betrayal and disappointment, led me to a successful life. To the outside world, I have everything.

To Jillian, I have a life she couldn't have.

Because I did move on.

For the first time, I see the truth—that she didn't. She's living in the same house, doing the same thing. Every day, she sees Jack and the river-shaped scar. I scan the pictures on the wall above her head. Jilli and Tolstoy. Me and Jack. Every day she's reminded about what she lost, and can't escape.

Our eyes connect and it's my H&H sister looking back at me.

In the skip of a heartbeat, her face tightens, all emotion shuttered behind blinds of resentment.

I walk to Jack's stall and bury my face in his neck, but I still hear the yelling coming from the office.

"Wow," Ben says from the other side of the stall door. "That must have been some shit bomb you dropped in there."

"It was."

"Do tell." He pushes the half door open and steps inside.

I shake my head, each move digging my forehead deeper into Jack's silky neck.

From the depths of my denial I hear Tony giving directions

to Jack's stall, then the crisp click of dress shoes walking down the aisle. Now what?

"Emma? I have the papers for you to sign." With one ear pressed into the horse, Thomas's voice sounds slightly muffled.

"Good timing." This shit is going to short-circuit even an industrial-size fan. I force a smile that's more grimace at Thomas, then turn to Ben. "That was a smoke bomb. This is the grenade." I make an explosion motion with my hand.

Before I can explain, the office door slams open.

My body reacts, flinching into roly-poly safe mode. It's going to be okay. *Sure it is.*

"Never," Jillian yells and storms out the back door of the barn.

"Wow," Ben repeats. By the bemused look on his face, he's enjoying this show.

I pull in a long you-can-do-this breath and leave the safety of Jack's stall. "Let's get this over with."

An hour later, Thomas Adler drives away, signed papers in his briefcase.

Ben walks over, mirroring my crossed-arm stance. "So, wanna clue a guy in? Rena sent the bombshell away. Told her none of the horses are being sold, at least not yet. What do you know about that?" He bumps my shoulder with his. "Just a heads-up, Tony's crushed. You may want to make your own coffee for a few days until he gets over it."

"What did Rena tell you?" I push my hands into the pockets of my jeans and roll forward on the balls of my feet. My nerves are crackling and I feel as though they'll catch on fire at any moment. If Jillian walked up right now I'd probably disappear with a flaming bang.

"She didn't say anything. What is up with you? You look like you're about to explode right out of your skin."

"I have to get out of here. Can you leave?"

"Sure. I don't have lessons until the afternoon."

"Good. You're driving."

We get in his car and Ben waits for instructions.

"Back the car out. At the end of the driveway, stop, look both ways, then turn left."

He gives me a "seriously?" scowl. Ten minutes later I give him directions to The Spinning Ewe.

"Sheep? That's what will calm you down?" He raises his hands in surrender and pulls into a parking space.

"I discovered this place shortly after I arrived. The owner of the B and B I was staying in suggested it."

"You knit?"

I laugh at the disbelief on his face.

"Sort of. Not really. The owner taught me how to crochet and I've made a scarf and a hat. The beanie is better suited for an elephant than a human being. The scarf was for a giraffe. But I love wearing them anyway. Oh don't look at me like that." I mock glare at him. "You'd be surprised how soothing it can be."

"Well in that case, I'll buy out the entire store."

We walk down the path and I divert us to a bench under a tree. I wave at Ceila, who's fluffing yarn balls in a basket by the door.

After a few minutes, Ben leans forward, resting his elbows on his knees, and turns to look at me. I suck in air and release the words on the exhale. "The reason the donor pulled the funding from the therapeutic program is because he died. It was my father."

"Seriously?"

I nod.

"Wow."

I nod again. "Yesterday, after our ride, I went to see the lawyer. He told me. Can't say I expected that."

"I bet."

"That's not all. When I was cleaning out his home office, I

found a bunch of letters. He'd been corresponding with someone for years. Started before we moved here after Mom's first episode, and stopped after he sent me off to boarding school. Eight years. His pen pal for eight years was Rena."

"Whoa."

"Yup."

Ben leans back and our shoulders touch. "Why did he send you away?"

I wonder how much to tell him. I wonder how much of the truth I know myself.

"I always thought he did it because he was embarrassed about the accident and was afraid that the news would ruin his reputation. 'Renowned psychiatrist's unstable daughter involved in near-fatal crash that killed one horse, injured another, and left two teenagers in serious condition; drinking suspected as cause.'"

"Was it the cause?"

"No. Maybe. But I wasn't the one drinking. Or driving."

I squeeze my eyes shut as the sound of brakes locking, metal crunching, and horses' screaming fills my head. I should have listened to the warning sirens in my head. I should have known better than to get into a fight with her. I should have been stronger.

I should have done so many things differently. Maybe I could have salvaged our friendship and helped her. We were horse-and-heart sisters. I should have been there for her.

Lots of should-haves.

But she hadn't wanted my help.

"You've spent time with Jillian over the last few years. Has she been drinking the entire time?"

Ben releases a whoosh of air that sounds a lot like the word "fuck."

I nod. "Did others notice?"

"Maybe Rena and Simon but no one from the outside. Honestly, it's only become a problem again recently."

Since I've been back. The weight of that knowledge karate-kicks the air from my lungs.

We're both quiet for a moment. Then Ben releases another "fuck," this one loud and clear.

"Oh, Emma, I didn't mean . . ."

I shake my head to make him stop. Every word is another back-fist of guilt. Everyone felt sorry for poor Emma. They all thought I was scarred. But it was Jillian who'd been crying out for help.

"I did this to her."

"What?" He shifts to get a better look at me, probably trying to decide if I'm serious.

"I did this to her. All Jilli wanted was to be the center of someone's attention. Her mom was too selfish and screwed up. All she had were Simon and Rena. They were basically her parents. They adored her and gave her everything, but they—well, Rena mostly—were hard on her. That's where I came in. I was the perfect doll she could twist and turn. I was so hungry for anything resembling a normal relationship, that I became what she wanted me to be. And as long as I was in her shadow we were great." I pick at a rough piece of wood next to me on the bench and a large sliver comes loose.

"The day of the accident was the last straw for her, I guess. I made the jump-off, she didn't. The guy she wanted chose me. She had to turn the attention back on her. She couldn't do anything about the show results, but she definitely could about the guy. I shouldn't have let it go so easily, but I hated fighting with her. I needed her friendship."

I swallow. I hadn't been any better than Jillian back then. She'd needed people to idolize her. I'd needed people to care about me. And if I'm being honest with myself, I knew people gave me the dead-mom/harsh-dad concessions. I never thought of myself as meek but looking back, I can see it. I let people think that and I let myself be that. Because I needed to belong.

I take in a breath of calm country air. "She insisted that she wasn't drunk. She seemed okay and I took her word for it. It's what I did. I'd seen her falling-down drunk before, and she wasn't. We loaded the horses and when I suggested we call Rena to come drive us back, she freaked. I offered to drive and that just made it worse. The sun was going down and it was that weird light, you know that crazy in-between hour that's not dark and not light and nothing looks quite right?"

Ben nods but keeps his eyes on the sheep grazing a few feet from us.

"It went from fine to out-of-control so fast. One minute we were on the road and the next we were in the pasture, the truck in a tree and the trailer on its side. I remember her pulling my arm and yelling that I had to get in the driver's seat before anyone came. That I had to say I'd been driving. The next thing I know I'm in the hospital and it's a week later. Then he sent me away."

I push the sliver of wood back into the slot it escaped from. It doesn't fit. I twist it and turn it, but the gap seems to have changed shape. Or maybe it adjusted. Maybe once you leave, there's no fitting back in.

Jillian had told everyone I'd been driving. That she'd told me to slow down, but I'd been upset because my boyfriend had dumped me, and being an inexperienced driver I'd misjudged the turn.

I'd tried to tell my dad and the nurses what had really happened. No one believed me. I heard them when they thought I was asleep. "She's had a serious concussion. It's likely she'll never fully remember."

I remembered. I relived that accident in my dreams for years. But no one had wanted to hear. And my father made the decision to send me, and the truth, away.

"Why do you think he did that?" Ben squeezes my hand.

A sheep bleats from the other side of the fence and sticks his black head between the wood slats, blinking at us.

It suddenly makes sense. My father hadn't been protecting himself, he'd been protecting me and Rena.

He *had* believed me. But he knew that Jillian's involvement would shatter Rena. And that my connection to Jillian needed to be severed.

"Come on." I stand and pull on Ben's hand. "Let's go see what new colors Ceila has come up with."

Half an hour later Ben pushes me out the door of The Spinning Ewe, a large bag swinging from my hand. Instead of walking to the car, I lead him to the fence surrounding the pasture. We watch the tranquil scene, the sheep barely registering our presence.

"I had papers drawn up to fund the therapeutic program with the money from his condo and medical practice. And a large chunk of the money I was to inherit." My voice catches on that word. I was used to not having my father around. But he was always out there. There was always the hope that we'd find a way to connect.

The only thing out there now is an inheritance.

Ben turns to face me. "What about you?"

"Rena wants me to stay and help with the program. But you already know that."

He doesn't try to hide the smile. "Yup."

"Don't get all smug. I said no. I have a job to get back to. The last week has been fun, but it's like being on vacation. You can pretend to be someone else but at some point, it's back to reality."

He takes my hand and tugs me toward the car. "Reality is, I have a lesson to teach. And there's a black horse in that barn who can teach you a thing about reality. Listen to him."

We're quiet for the ride home, each lost in our respective worlds. Except the world that fit me only two weeks ago feels far away. Will I settle back in, like after a vacation? Or is Ben right and my reality has shifted?

We turn into the driveway of Jumping Frog Farm and Ben parks the car. He pats me on the knee, then points to the back paddocks. "The answer is out there. Good luck."

He gets out and walks into the barn, riding boots stamping an easy cadence.

Advice from a black horse and forest spirits. How can I go wrong?

37

The mid-October sun turned down the heat during the short drive back from The Spinning Ewe. I zip my fleece jacket and round the barn, heading for the back paddocks. Ben's laugh tumbles out the barn doors and I can't help but smile.

Jukebox bleats as I approach. Jack steps around him, leans into the fence, and nickers. "Hey, guys." I pull two mints from my pockets and distribute them, careful to arc my fingers back as much as possible when it's Jukebox's turn. He attempts to frisk me between the rails. He's figured me out, he knows the pocket where I keep the mint stash. I hop out of the way. "Think I don't know your tricks, mister?" He bleats again, then turns and flicks his mitten-shaped tail at me.

A deep gravelly chuckle from behind surprises me and I whip around. Simon is leaning against the rails of the paddock across the path. He'd been hidden behind the tractor shed as I walked up.

"Why are you hiding back there?" I cross to where he's wedged between the wood fence and the metal shed. It's warmer here and I weasel my way next to him.

"Who says I'm hiding?"

I point at the shiny metal wall behind us.

"Okay, I'm hiding. I needed some quiet. Rena and Jillian have been going at each other all day. They're making me crazy."

My stomach knots. "Because of me?"

He nods, the nod turns to a shake. "More than you."

That answer doesn't exactly ease the knot. "It's time for me to get back to Chicago. I don't think my being here is good for Jilli."

"You being here has caused a bit of upheaval. No question about that. But as painful as it can be, that kick in the ass may be just the ticket."

I suck in a shallow breath. It's not like Simon to be so blunt. That's Rena's specialty.

We watch the two rescue ponies grazing in the paddock. Every step the chestnut makes, the little black mare matches. She lifts her head and looks our way, then leans into her buddy for comfort.

"You did a good thing bringing her here. She's a sweet girl. I think she'll end up a nice addition to the therapeutic program."

"It wasn't a popular decision."

"The right ones rarely are."

"I couldn't leave her. She'd be dead by now."

We're silent, watching the ponies and lost in our own thoughts. I release myself to the hypnotic sound of horses cropping grass, their muzzles skimming the ground as they shift from spot to spot.

Jilli had been less than pleased with my decision, although I think the displeasure was more that I did it instead of her. But it was also the first time that she hadn't been furious with me, either. There'd been hints of the old friend Jilli the day we picked up the ponies, the slightest quiver that the past could be filed away.

But it can't be, not completely anyway. We may have once been best friends but it's easier to forgive when you're young, during those years when you wear your emotions openly. Or, in my case, not as closed off. Life was so much simpler back then. There were no hidden agendas. Jillian and I needed the same thing—love and acceptance. We just went about finding it in different ways.

If we met now, would we be friends? Probably not. That realization saddens me.

"How long was she sober?" I chance a look at Simon.

His head ticks in my direction but his expression doesn't change. I can't read this Simon. I wonder when he changed from the easygoing man who always wore his emotions for all to see. Just when I think I've overstepped, he responds. "Three years. It was a condition for her to take over management of the barn. She had to be sober a full year first. The year before was rough. This was the only way we could think to force a change. I had my doubts that she could do it."

He rubs a hand over the stubble on his cheeks and returns his attention to the horses.

"Had she been drinking all along or did she start again after Rena's heart attack?"

He snorts something between annoyance and amusement. "Ben told you?"

"Not all of it. She was drinking in high school." I feel him stiffen next to me and hear him release a breath, but he doesn't respond.

The chestnut pony wanders our way, close enough to check us out with just enough distance for safety. Simon pulls carrot pieces out of his jeans and reaches a hand forward, the orange treat in the middle of his palm, fingers squeezed together. The pony stretches his neck, his lips twitching and contorting, trying to suction the carrot.

"Come, come." Simon coaxes under his breath, staying as still as a post along the fence line. "Come, come."

The pony shifts his weight until his lips find the carrot piece. By the third treat, he's moved closer. The black pony watches us warily from behind her friend. Simon hands me a supply of treats and I repeat the process he went through, hand stretched, coaxing gently. The mare takes slow, careful steps until she can reach my offering. I slip another piece of carrot into my palm. She rests her muzzle in my hand. A warm tingle travels up my arm and down my spine.

"You need to stay."

Careful not to startle the pony, I turn to look at Simon. "Didn't we agree my being here wasn't a good thing for Jilli?"

"We did. But it's good for the rest of us, you included. And Jillian, well, she needs to deal with her demons. You being here forces her to do that."

I cup my hand around the velvety muzzle and look at the warm brown eyes, still wary but alive. The defeat that had broken my heart the day I made the snap decision to buy her is gone. I wish I could make time stand still, like this, exactly like this.

I close my eyes, wanting to trap this moment in my memory, like a camera snapping a picture. The mare steps away, leaving my hand suspended and cold.

The truth sparks a tumble of emotions in me. I don't want to leave. Despite the secrets and heartbreak, I've found the inner peace that has eluded me all these years.

The ponies continue their search for good grass spots. In the opposite paddock, Jack dunks his muzzle into the water trough and drips a slobbery waterfall onto Juke's back. The goat gives a little shake but doesn't move.

"I have a flight back tomorrow afternoon. And a meeting with my new boss Monday morning. I've accomplished what I came for and I think I've accomplished what my father set out for me."

"What about her?" Simon nods at the little black pony, now grazing at arm's reach from us.

"You'll take care of her. And she'll take care of Rena's clients in the program. I'm not disappearing for good. I'll be checking in on the program, making sure you guys are using my money properly." I shift until our shoulders bump gently.

The corners of his mouth tick up into a smile that betrays the truth. "I should get back now. Don't trust Rena unsupervised for long. Damn stubborn old mare."

"Simon." I have to tell him. No more secrets.

"Yes, love?" He straightens, stomps a clump of mud from his boot.

"The accident, it wasn't me driving." Like pulling off a Band-Aid, there's a momentary sting followed by a rush of relief.

The open-emotion Simon is back, looking at me with wet eyes.

With the Band-Aid gone, the words gush out of the wound. "I told her we needed to call Rena but she knew she'd be in trouble. I guess both of us had something to prove. To you, to each other, to ourselves. I've replayed that day in my head so many times. To the point that I'm not always sure if the memories are real or shaped by years of hurt. But I wasn't driving."

For a few long, loud heartbeats, he doesn't say anything. I hear my breathing, the horses eating, the goat pawing at the metal water trough, a car arriving—or leaving—on the gravel driveway of the farm.

"You told your dad?"

I nod.

"He knew you weren't driving. We all knew."

A burn of anger flashes through me. "You all knew and still let me take the fall?"

Simon's shoulders sag. "Your father knew we were in a custody battle over Jillian. We'd filed a petition to keep her away from her mum, away from our own daughter. Jilli didn't know. We had to do something or she was going to end up like her mum, a drunk, an addict, screwing up her life. If it became public that she'd caused the accident, we wouldn't have been able to stop the tornado of self-destruction. If the truth had come out, she would have ended up in a juvenile detention center or a foster program. We couldn't let that happen."

Like a gas burner, the flame inside me goes out and I shiver.

"Bloody hell. We—I—owe you an apology, Emma. Not that it'll fix this or make any of it less shitty, but you deserve an apology. We did what we thought was right. We were wrong. And then it was too late to reverse direction. Grown-ups aren't always as brilliant as we would like to think we are."

How many mistakes were made in the name of protecting the

ones we love? And how easy was it to latch on to those mistakes and use them as crutches?

Simon pulls me into a bear hug. "In the end, we lost both of you in that crash. I don't want to lose you both again."

"You won't," I mumble into his shoulder.

He releases me and crosses the gravel path to where Jack is leaning into the fence, demanding his share of the carrots from Simon's pockets.

I hear the crunch of carrots followed by a ping as a rock ricochets off another. I close my eyes and picture Simon walking, hands pushed deep into his pockets, the slight roll of his shoulders. From where I'm standing I can't see him, although I can still hear his progress in the crunch and ping of the gravel drive. The Simon walking away in my mind is the man in my dreams, sixteen years spunkier.

Next time I won't stay away for so long. There's no longer a reason to stay away. I can come back for vacations and holidays. I'll stay at the Mountain Inn with Lucy and visit Ceila and the sheep. I'll watch my pretty little black pony blossom. I'll have Rena and Simon and Jack. And Jillian.

We all deserve a second chance.

I distribute the last of the treats between the two ponies, Jack, and Jukebox, then walk the same gravel path Simon has just taken. The sun makes a momentary appearance, sending an arrow of light onto a smooth, round rock a few feet in front of me. I stoop and pick it up. It's dark gray with a white marbled line zigzagging through. It's warm in my palm and my thumb traces circles over the smooth surface. This one is going back with me. This one will be a reminder of the other life I had, even if for just a short time.

38

January 2000

Hey, Emma, we're going to the library to study for the history test. Want to join?"

Emma stops walking and turns to the three girls who've just parted paths from her. Stacy, her roommate, looks at her expectantly.

"Thanks. I think I'll pass, though. I have reading to do for English Lit." She raises a gloved hand in a halfhearted wave, then ducks her chin into the wool scarf and continues toward the dorm. Behind her she hears, *Why do you keep asking?* Indeed, why? Emma resists the urge to turn around and catch the response.

It's been almost three months since she came to Briarwood. It's been two months since she stopped using crutches. And about a month since she stopped walking with a limp.

She'd told everyone it was from a skiing accident. When they asked where and what, she'd thrown out a vague Switzerland and claimed not to remember more than the start of the run and waking up in the hospital. At least the last part was true.

It didn't take long for the questions to stop, although the speculation behind her back continued. It wasn't that different from those first months at Emmitsville Elementary. She's just gotten better at shutting out the noise.

Emma lets herself into the dorm and stops at the mailbox. She's been here almost three months and she's yet to get any mail but still checks every day.

She's sent a couple of cards to her father. All of the cards she's written to Rena and Simon and Jilli are in the bottom drawer of her desk; addressed, stamped, unsent. She's not sure why she keeps expecting something from them. They probably have no idea where she is. But here she is, checking anyway.

Emma nods at a few familiar faces walking down the hall but doesn't make eye contact. That encourages people to talk and she doesn't want to talk.

She flips on the overhead in the room and sighs at the mess. Stacy's half of the room is taking up two-thirds of the space. She's not used to seeing clothes multiply and books breed. Her father would never have tolerated that.

The food wrappers, however, are beyond what she can tolerate. The first month, she'd cleaned around Stacy's things, thrown out wrappers and empty food containers. She'd even folded a load of laundry that exploded out of the hamper. Stacy had seemed more amused than pleased at first. At least until the day Emma tossed a sandwich that had been on the desk overnight. Apparently Stacy had scribbled an assignment on the wrapper and now had no idea when it was due. Emma didn't touch her side after that. Now when Stacy's things cross to her side, she discreetly moves them back.

She turns on the desk lamp and shuts off the overhead. It's dark enough outside by now that without the overhead, she can pretend there's nothing beyond her circle of light.

She opens her backpack and pulls out her history notebook. She really does need to review her notes for the exam. And yes, she should have gone with the others.

It's only been three months, she justifies. She's not not friendly. And it's not that she doesn't want to make friends. But being friends means letting people in and letting people in means opening up. That's where it gets complicated.

She taps a rhythm with the end of the pen and watches the

fine green tip twitch up and down. When did she start doing that? It used to drive her crazy when she was studying with Jillian. That was Jilli's thinking assistance.

Emma rips out a piece of paper from the back of her history notebook.

Dear Jilli,
It's been over three months. I'm off crutches and walking almost normally again. No visible scars at least. I wonder about you.
Were you injured as bad? Worse? Do you remember more about the accident than I do? Why, Jilli? Why did you do it?

Light floods the room as the door is flung open. Emma's cozy cocoon is cracked open.

"Oh my god, Emma, you should have been there. Jeremy and Patrick were studying with us. We were taking turns quizzing each other. Jeremy got every single question wrong. We thought he was goofing on us but no, he really, really didn't know. He started making up answers and then started answering in French. We were laughing so hard, old lady Marshmallow told us to get out."

"You shouldn't call her that, you know. One day someone will say it to her face and she'll be hurt."

Never make fun of people, Emma. You don't know what their real story is, and how would you feel if you discovered someone was being mean about you? She'd been in fourth grade and amused by the nickname Mrs. Potato for the lunchroom aid Mrs. Porter. Mrs. Porter really did look like a potato. Then she'd heard a couple of kids call her Embryo Metz. She'd been in the bathroom and had lifted her feet and waited until she knew they were long gone. She'd been late returning to fourth-period math. She had to look up what "embryo" meant. Mrs. Porter stayed Mrs. Porter after that.

Emma catches June and Lyn exchange looks behind Stacy's back. Stacy rolls her eyes and performs a leap-and-twist to land cross-legged on her bed. The bed creaks and complains. Emma wonders if she does that in her own house or just at the school, where there are no parents telling you not to. It's not like the RAs enforce things like that.

"So? Did you finish the reading for Lit?"

Emma slides the letter she's writing under last week's geography test. "Nah. I'm not in the mood to read."

"Good. Then come with us to dinner. Patrick asked about you. He made me promise you'd come." Stacy scoots to the edge of the bed and grins at Emma, batting her eyes for added effect.

Emma's noticed the way Patrick looks at her. She's ignored it as much as possible. He's the only guy who offered to carry her bag when she was hobbling around campus on crutches. She declined whenever possible. The last thing she wants right now is to get mixed up with another boy. Especially since she hasn't been successful at censoring Drew out of her dreams, yet.

Lyn claps her hands twice and everyone turns to look at her. "I'm hungry. Can we please go now?"

Stacy pushes off the bed and grabs a sweatshirt from a pile by the bed. "Let's go. Emma?" she stops wrestling the sweatshirt long enough to ask.

The group dinner doesn't appeal to Emma. She's been going at the end of the mealtimes, when most kids have already finished and moved on. But today she's hungry. That's what she gets for skipping lunch. And she doesn't feel like eating alone.

"Yes, I'm coming. I need to make a quick call, though."

"We'll go to my room to dump our stuff and swing back by for you," Lyn says, taking charge of logistics.

Emma follows them partway down the hall until she reaches the closet-turned-phone-booth. She waits until the girls have disappeared around the corner and steps inside. Her fingers tap the numbers.

One ring. Two rings. She catches her breath.

"Hello?"

"Jilli?"

A long pull of air. "Who is this?"

She's pretty sure Jilli knows. "Emma."

Click.

She stays with the phone pressed to her ear, listening to the silence of a friendship severed.

Voices carry from down the hall. Emma replaces the receiver into the base and hurries back to the room. She yanks the paper with the beginning of the letter to Jillian from its hiding place and tears it into tiny, unrecognizable pieces.

Click.

Her heartbeat pounds in her eyes and her eyes burn.

Click.

No. Not this time. This time she's in control.

"You ready?" Stacy asks from the door.

"Yes." Emma releases the blizzard of shredded paper into the trash can.

She'll make new friends, she'll meet new guys, but she's done needing other people. Maybe her father was right after all.

She follows the girls into the hall and pulls the door shut behind her.

Click.

39

A questioning meow greets me at the foot of the stairs to the barn apartment.

"Whazup, Beast, buddy?" I lean down to pet the black barn cat who's taken up residence with me the last few nights, snuggling under the blankets and growling unhappily when it's time to get up in the morning.

Meow.

"Did Simon tell you to convince me to stay?"

Meow.

"It's not that easy."

Meow.

"Okay, so, easy for you maybe. You haven't spent years climbing the corporate ladder and putting work ahead of everything else in your life. I can't just walk away from everything I've built."

Meow. He twitches his tail at me and jumps onto the bed where my suitcase is waiting to be filled. He stretches with a lion yawn, then sprawls on top of the suitcase, blinking at me as though to say, "Yup, it's really that easy."

I flop onto the bed, making the suitcase jump. The cat glares at me.

I turn my head so I can see part of the bedroom. The queen-size bed fills most of the room. With the dresser along the foot-end wall, there's just enough space to open dresser drawers without having to sit on the bed and hike your legs up so you don't hit your shins. There's an armchair in the corner of the room that doubles as a laundry holder most days.

I turn my head in the other direction. The afternoon sun winks through the large window. I can't see them, but I know the trees at the edge of the pasture are changing colors. On the drive back from the The Spinning Ewe, I drank in the reds and oranges in the scenery.

There are quite a few trees between my apartment in Chicago and the office building. But they're city trees. They don't stretch their limbs, welcoming visitors to lounge under their brilliant umbrella, and they don't show off their colors. Like most city people, they stay in their space, tight and unobtrusive, and in the fall, they drop their leaves like a commuter dropping a crumpled receipt.

It's not the trees I'm going back for. It's my career, my life. The career I've barely thought about over the last few days and the life that's moved on without giving me a second thought.

Oh, because you've made an effort, right?

I haven't. I haven't called any of my friends, and their texts and e-mails have dried up. Who was the last to check in? Are they waiting for me to respond or am I waiting for someone to reach out to me first?

Why is it so complicated there? Ceila and Lucy have called several times to tell me about the Hooker get-togethers. A couple of days ago, Ceila texted a picture of a new yarn she'd just dyed that reminded her of me.

I bolt up, jolting the cat awake.

"You're right, Beast, it really should be that easy."

I march to the kitchen and grab my phone.

Bruce answers on the second ring. "Hey, Emma. I was wondering when I'd hear from you."

"Guess I was wondering the same."

"Touché. It's been a bit," he hesitates, "crazy around here."

"I spoke to Pierce. He gave me the CliffNotes version. We have a few things to catch up on when I get back, don't we?"

He hesitates again and I pull the phone away from my ear to check for connection. His voice is unfamiliar when he speaks again. "How's life in the country?"

Despite the caterpillars crawling around in my stomach, I smile. "Good. I've been spending a lot of time at the stable actually. Even started riding again. And you'll never believe it, but I bought a pony. A rescue, but she's mine."

One breath leads to two, then three. I shouldn't have said that. Now he's going to think I'm not committed to my job. He may not be CEO anymore but he is still advising, and with the current corporate upheaval, I can't afford for anyone to question my commitment.

"Listen, Bruce . . ."

"Listen, Emma . . ."

We both laugh, a short, uncomfortable chuckle, then Bruce takes charge. "Me first. Listen, Emma, I know I've been hard on you over the years. I told Pierce you're a huge asset to this company. Your position is safe and, based on my recommendation, you should be getting a promotion in the near future."

My mouth flaps with a silent "I don't know what to say" because I honestly don't know what to say. This isn't the Bruce I've worked for all these years.

"Pierce seems to have a good vision for the company. I think you'll do fine with him."

I mumble a thanks and silently curse when I can't think of what else to say.

"You are still coming back, right? There's an office pool on whether you really will return."

"Seriously?" Although I'm not really sure why I'm so surprised. "What side did you bet on?"

"Twenty that you're not coming back."

"Seriously?" That surprises me.

"I don't know what they've done to you there, but the Emma I know would never have stayed away this long. Or thrown money away on a pony."

I open my mouth to argue that I wasn't throwing money away

and that he didn't really know me if that's what he thinks. But it's who everyone in Chicago thinks I am. It's who I allowed myself to become.

I ask about his plans for the future, but I'm not really listening. After a polite and awkward few minutes, we say good-bye and hang up. All those years working together, spending more time together than with our significant others (those rare periods when I actually had a significant other), and just like that we're done and moving on.

From the open window I hear barking and yelping and yelling. Beast bolts from the bedroom and jumps onto the window ledge in the family room to see what the kerfuffle is about. I join him and together we watch as Tony holds Carlisle while a deer stands by the gate to the nearest pasture. The deer seems to look right at me, blinks, then bounds off into the woods.

Meow.

"Right you are." I rub Beast behind the ears and he leans into me, purring, the deer and dog forgotten.

"Hey, Emma," Ben yells up through the open window. "Can you come lend a hand? Jillian is, um, not feeling well."

"Coming." I quickly change and usher Beast out of the apartment. He grumbles and takes his time, stopping to rub on every object on the way to the door.

Ben and I stare at the lesson roster for the afternoon.

"Dammit, today of all days she pulls a no-show? Like we're not juggling enough crap around here lately." He runs his fingers through his hair, giving a slight tug at the ends, and releases a growl of frustration.

"I can take this one." He points at a class of four labeled Beginner Flat. "Can you take those two though?"

That leaves me with a therapeutic client that Jilli was subbing on for Rena, and one of Jilli's show clients. How hard can that be?

"Any idea what happened to Jilli?"

"Nope. She was at the house until an hour ago. She left me a voice message ten minutes ago, ten minutes before she's to teach, that she's running behind and won't make it back in time. For. Any. Of. Them. That's not running behind. That's running away."

"Has she done this before?"

"Nope."

The discussion at The Spinning Ewe swirls between us.

"I'm up first," he says and turns to go check on his lesson. Even angry, there's a casualness to his carriage. I'm going to miss him.

There's still an hour before my first lesson but the class list has Toby as the horse we're to use and yesterday he came back to the barn favoring his left front.

"Hey, Ben," I call after him. "What's the scoop on Toby?"

He turns and walks backward, his hands diving into his hair again. "Shit. Double shit. I forgot about that. Can't use him. I don't know who else to give you."

"What about Jack?"

"Can't. The kid is too small. He's intimidated by the large horses. And he's terrified of Jukebox. Maybe just have him brush Toby instead of riding this time."

I scrunch my face at the idea. That's not a horrible idea; I'd helped Rena with plenty of therapy sessions that didn't include riding.

"I have an idea."

"Oh god." He groans, only half joking.

"Hope. It'll be her debut into the program."

"Hell no." He throws up a Stop-sign hand. "We have no idea how she'll react. You don't know what her history is."

"She'll be fine, Ben. Promise."

"You can't promise, you don't know."

He's right. But so am I. "She'll be fine."

"Shit and double shit. You'd better be right." He disappears into the indoor arena.

I retrieve Toby's tack and go find my black rescue pony. She looks up from her hay and watches as I enter her stall. She no longer tries to become one with the back wall when someone enters. That's progress. Hopefully enough progress that she'll shine in her first lesson.

Hope checks my pockets, familiar with my treat-hiding spots. She's quiet while I brush her and even rewards me with a neck-stretch-muzzle-twitch when I curry her withers. She opens easily for the bit and holds still while I fasten the buckles on the bridle. She doesn't even flinch when I position the saddle on her back. I run my hand down her side. She's put on a couple of pounds but she still has a long way to go.

"Aren't you the perfect lady," I coo at her. I give her a pat and walk around to attach the girth to the billets. She's much skinnier than Toby so I slip the girth to the last hole. With my right hand on her haunches, I walk back to her left side and reach under her belly for the girth. It barely reaches the second hold. There's no way I misjudged by that much. I take a step back and watch as my pony deflates by a girth size.

"You're no novice, are you?" I laugh. I take a step forward and she blows up like an anorexic puffer fish. "Oh yeah, you're good."

I lead her out of the stall and into the indoor arena. I'll walk her with the distractions of the other lesson to see how she does.

"Okay if I join in?" I ask Ben when the pony and I reach the middle of the ring. "Hey, check out her party trick."

I take a step away and the girth loosens to the point you can almost see daylight. Then a step forward and the daylight disappears.

"She's going to be a fun one," Ben says, giving Hope a pat on the neck. She ducks her head and shifts away from Ben. Not a big move but just enough to remind us both of where she came from.

"Oh, baby." I hug her head and slip her another treat. Who cares if she has a bit in her mouth. This pony deserves love and rewards.

I mount and walk around the ring, keeping my distance from the lesson kids. After riding Wally, being on Hope feels like being at the kids' table. But she has a smooth walk with a surprisingly long stride.

My therapy student turns out to be an eight-year-old autistic boy. He takes one look at Hope, squeals, breaks from his adult, and rushes to hug her. Ben and I both tense and I grab for the bridle but Hope doesn't flinch. She lowers her head enough for Aaron to give her more hugs.

My rescue pony is ready to rescue kids.

Two hours later, I walk back to the barn behind a grumpy pony and his crankier rider.

"What happened there?" Ben watches the procession.

"I made him work." I hold up the pair of spurs. "Jillian allows him to use these. He doesn't use his legs, just slams his heels into that pony's sides. The mom warned me the pony is lazy and stubborn and 'just plain awful.' It's not the pony who's lazy and awful, though."

Ben laughs then mumbles an "uh-oh" when the kid's mother storms into the barn.

She thumps to a stop in front of me, her hands pushing into the fat on her hips. "Matty is beside himself over that lesson. How dare you treat him like that."

Even though she wasn't asking me a question, I steel myself to respond. "First of all I didn't 'treat him like that.' I was teaching him to ride, which, unless I'm mistaken, is what he's here for."

"He's been riding with Jillian for a year and knows how to ride perfectly well."

"Look, Ms. . . ." I hesitate.

"Thomson," she supplies with a shift of hip rolls.

"Look, Ms. Thomson, I'm sorry my teaching style doesn't suit you. I'm only filling in for Jillian tonight. Matty has pretty good basics, but in my opinion he's not riding the best he could be. Once we took the spurs off and he started using his legs, the pony's attitude changed dramatically."

She blinks at me as though trying to decide if I'm on to

something or totally out of line. Apparently unable to decide, she huffs and walks off in search of her pouting child.

"Nicely done," Ben says.

"Yeah well, I don't think I'll be getting a holiday card from her."

"Probably not. I've watched them a few times. That child is a spoiled brat. You know they paid a fortune for that pony. And completely ruined him."

"How can Jillian allow that?"

"Just told you: because they paid a fortune for that pony. They pay for three lessons a week and go to every show possible. She charges nicely for coaching fees at the shows, by the way. She lets him do what he wants, which works because they don't want to hear the truth."

"You mean that the kid is a shitty rider?"

He laughs again. "Yeah, that. I think you're the first person who ever made him work."

"No wonder he hates me. He's going to be sore tomorrow. And even crankier. Glad I won't be here next time they come to the barn."

Ben's expression turns serious. "Tomorrow?"

I nod.

"Why?"

"Clinging to that last crazy straw of my professional life, I guess."

"You're sure?"

I nod again.

"That wasn't one of your more decisive nods."

I smile. "Sorry."

Before he can push further, Tony walks up and grabs the halter on Jack's stall. "You should move before I get back with devil goat."

"Good idea." Ben takes a few steps toward the tack room, then turns and adds, "You've got an hour to clean up, Emma. I'm taking you out to dinner."

I smile at Ben and reach for the halter. "I'll get him, Tony."

He squints at me, the halter suspended between us. Finally he releases the soft leather into my outstretched hand and mumbles, "Crazy lady."

I walk out of the barn in search of my charges—a geriatric horse with a limp and a geriatric goat with an attitude.

Jack is standing at the fence, head hanging, watching my approach. He nickers as I get close and flaps his lips in his equine hello.

I wrap my arms around his neck. "I hate leaving you again."

"Hey," I yell as I'm jerked into the fence. Jukebox has my jacket in his teeth and is looking at me through the fence slats, his beady eyes daring me to play tug-of-war with him.

Jack pulls back and nips at the goat's rear end. Juke releases my jacket, rounds his back, and hops in a circle, bleating goat obscenities at me.

Free to move without fear of losing a chunk of my jacket, I take a step back and rub the black horse's head. "Thanks, bud."

He rests his muzzle on my shoulder, his warm breath tickling my neck. "Do you think I'm doing the right thing going back?"

Jack's head gets heavier on my shoulder. "Are you falling asleep while I'm talking to you?" I twist my head to look at him. His eyes are closed. "Typical." I snake my arm under his throatlatch and rub behind his ear. He grunts and leans into my hand.

"Come on, let's go for a walk." I put his halter on and swing the gate open, standing as close to the fence as possible to stay out of Jukebox's flight path. But instead of following the goat to the barn, I lead Jack toward the outdoor arena. Jukebox bleats and hops to catch up, giving me attitude for trying to lose him.

At the entrance to the arena I stop. Jack twists his head and taps my chest with his muzzle as though saying, "It's okay, we've got this." I rest my hand on the crest of his neck and together we walk to the mounting block. I tie the loose end of the lead rope to the ring on the back of the halter and take the three steps up.

The pounding of my heartbeat in my ears is louder than even the goat's protests. Sixteen years of regret and heartbreak propel me forward and I slide onto Jack's back. I'm holding my breath. Why am I holding my breath?

Jack turns his head and lips the toe of my boot while Jukebox hops around us, agitated at the change in routine.

I nudge Jack's side with my heels and close my eyes as the familiar movement transports my body sixteen years. Years of riding this horse in my dreams can't compare with this moment.

We take the path away from the stable, around the perimeter of the property, toward the pond. This was our cool-down, wanna-be-alone path. The fingers of my left hand weave into Jack's mane. A cold wind nips at us but I might as well be in a bubble of warmth.

Each step away from the barn draws me deeper into the past. The first time I came to Jumping Frog Farm, I was eight and desperately needed a place where I could belong, where I could escape from the darkness of my family. This guy—I pat the black horse under me—showed me the way out of the shadows.

We reach the edge of the pond. Jack halts and drops his head to grab at a juicy patch of grass. I lean back until I'm lying down, looking up into the afternoon sun. Jack's body warms my back and the insides of my legs, and the sun offers a tepid ray to thaw my face. I'm fourteen, lying like this on Jack, Jilli is next to me on Tolstoy. Our horses graze and we are, just are. No heavy discussions, no deadlines to worry about, no life-shattering secrets to unravel.

I turn my head but Jilli and Tolstoy aren't next to us. I'm not fourteen. Jilli isn't my best friend. Jack isn't the spunky show horse he used to be. Tolstoy is dead. And deadlines and secrets are gnawing at my insides.

Jack shifts and I sit up. Staring at us from the edge of the woods is a deer. Jack doesn't move, the deer doesn't move. The goat, on the other hand, works himself into a tizzy, bleating and hoping and spinning and strutting. When he gets too close, Jack gives him a gentle nip on the haunches.

Jack whinnies, the vibration rattling through my legs to my

upper body. The deer lifts its head and turns our way, then leaps into the woods.

"What did you say to him?" I lean down and wrap my arms around Jack's neck. Another, deeper whinny travels through my limbs, straight to my heart. "You may be right."

Jack starts a slow walk back in the direction of the barn. With each step, I'm more sure. This guy is showing me the way out of the shadows again. Each stride bringing me closer to home.

40

I spent most of the night turning from one side to the other. Beast attacked my foot after multiple complaints went unheeded. The dreams were as restless as my waking fantasies.

In one dream, I'm pushing the black pony into the elevator of my apartment building. The uptight woman with tight brown curls and beige cashmere twinset from the floor above asks if I have a poop bag with me.

In another dream, Jukebox is standing in my closet, my favorite Ferragamo boots shredded, the heel of the left boot hanging from the side of his mouth like a cigar.

And then there was the dream where I'm riding Jack. We cross a dry creek but the path leading up the hill is blocked by a herd of deer. I turn Jack around and we walk upstream where my mom is sitting on a fallen log. She waves and I wave back.

I extract my leg from under the cat and get out of bed. I only have a few more hours before my flight, it's pointless wasting them fighting insane dreams. I need to talk to Jillian and say my good-byes even though I'm pretty sure I don't want them to be good-byes.

I change into jeans and a sweater, stuff my nightgown into the suitcase, and prop it by the door. Beast struts up to it and pretends to spray it. I can't disagree with that sentiment.

Tony is well into his morning routine when I get downstairs

and Ben is lunging an uncooperative bay mare. This one has a nasty habit of diving to the outside of the circle and pulling whoever is lunging her off-balance. Yesterday she almost succeeded in tossing me face-first into a manure pile.

I stop at the entrance to the arena. "Hey, Ben, have you seen Jillian?"

He looks at me in disbelief. "You're looking for her after yesterday's blow-up? Are you nuts?"

"Probably. But I have to talk to her."

"She was headed for the jumper ring last time I saw her. If you're not back in an hour, I'm calling the paramedics."

I smile despite the hammering in my chest.

She's there, sitting on a fake brick wall jump. She crosses her arms in a coming-close-will-be-your-dumbest-move-yet. And it probably is. Except this discussion has been on hold for sixteen years.

"It's time we talked." I perch on the jump next to her, keeping a body length between us.

She shifts and for a heartbeat I think she's going to leave. She doesn't. She doesn't even respond.

Okay, we're going with the silent treatment. Been a while since we've done that.

"I didn't come back to hurt you, Jilli. I'm sorry if my being here is hard on you, but I'm not sorry I returned."

"Is this where I'm supposed to thank you for coming to our rescue?" Her voice is low, tired, resigned.

"I didn't rescue anyone but that little black pony."

"I bet Grandma and Grandpa will disagree."

I don't know how to answer that so I shift direction. "Remember all those dreams and plans we made for this place?"

"We were kids."

I turn. The jump wobbles and we both grab at the base to steady it. "Dreams aren't exclusive to kids. It's lonely without them and lonelier without someone to share them with."

She bites her lower lip and looks off as though assessing the property in front of us. "Yeah, we had dreams and plans and hopes and all that other bullshit kid fluff. But this life isn't as shiny and wonderful as you think it is."

Did I think it was shiny and wonderful? Yes. At least compared to the life I'd been living.

"Why didn't you leave if you don't like it here?"

She laughs and the air between us seems to freeze. "I did and failed. Leaving wasn't a realistic option. I was never going anywhere. When you left, it was clear who was going to be successful. You had the rich father, the fancy boarding school. You got to travel all over the world and go to an uptight college. You got to be a big shot, big-city girl."

Her words tumble in my brain, grinding against one another in their search for dominance.

"You could have gone to college, done something else."

"Sure."

I twist, unsure if she exhaled or spoke.

Her shoulder pops up, a halfhearted shrug. "I didn't have a fairy godmother looking out for me. Maybe we were both Cinderellas at first, but fairy godmommy only had eyes for you. Poor Emma. We all took care of poor Emma. And look at you, poor Emma is wearing the glass slipper."

We both look at the dusty paddock boots I'm wearing.

"That's what you think? That my life is perfect? High profile, fancy? Far from it."

"Poor Emma. Guess that explains it."

"Explains what?"

"Why you're back, looking for someone else's life to glom on to. Guess money and success can't buy you out of the loneliness pit, can they?"

Loneliness. Lonely. Alone.

The pixels of truth I'd started seeing are now crystal clear. Jillian Winn collected people. Not because she liked them but because she needed them. She needed to be the center of attention. The passion that drove her was being in the spotlight. The fear that ruled her was that someone would outshine her.

And in her eyes, my bulb had been, and still was, too bright.

"You're right, money and success only get you so much. It's what's in here that gets you the real reward." I tap my chest. "My life growing up was lonely but I never was. I had you and Simon and Rena, and Jack. You became the family I needed. Rena wasn't my fairy godmother. She never put me ahead of you. You put me there because it suited your needs. All I wanted was to feel like I belonged."

"Because my family was so damn great?" She snorts.

"It was better than mine."

She puts her hands on the jump and locks her elbows, the movement pitching her body forward as though trying to dodge out of the path of the thought.

"I wasn't trying to steal your spotlight."

"Wow. Don't we think a lot of ourselves?" She whistles through clenched teeth.

For sixteen years I wondered what it would be like to see Jillian again. What I would say to her. Whether we'd be able to pick up our friendship. But now I see that our friendship hadn't really been what I'd wanted it to be for a few years before that disastrous day. Maybe it had never been what I'd imagined it to be.

"My family life sucked, but one thing my father did give me was the strength to stand on my own. Don't mistake being alone for loneliness. If you want to see what *that* looks like, take a long hard look in the mirror."

I look at the woman next to me and try to imagine the nine-year-old girl I became friends with, the eleven-year-old girl whom I shared my naïve hopes with, the teenager I envied.

If only that young me could have seen what I'm looking at now. Maybe I would have known better than to walk into that trailer; hopefully I would have known enough not to let her drive that day. But I didn't. At the time, I wanted to believe in the friend I thought I had. I didn't want to believe she was capable of such brilliant self-destruction.

For sixteen years I held on to a pebble of hope that one day Jillian and I would find our way back into each other's lives. That maybe, possibly, one of those childhood dreams was still alive.

"I don't want your life, Jilli. And neither do you."

I turn and walk out of the arena and down the long gravel path to the barn. I reach into the pocket of my jeans and palm the rock the sun picked out for me yesterday. By the time I reach Jack's paddock, I'm bubbling with renewed energy. Maybe not a gift from the forest spirits but definitely inspired by them. And I guess, in a way, Jillian is my discarded antler.

41

I wrap the sweater as snug as it'll go around me. It's colder today. Winter isn't far away.

It hadn't felt as cold when I marched out to talk to Jillian. Or maybe it had, and I'd been fueled by adrenaline antifreeze.

Three weeks ago, my only mission was to get in, sign papers, and get the hell out. I'd been curious in a scared-of-the-horror-movie way about Jumping Frog Farm and the people I'd left behind. People who'd once been my family.

I took one hell of a detour to get onto the crunchy path I'm about to take. I shiver and tuck my hands into the sleeves of the sweater.

Jukebox bleats when he catches sight of me.

"Are you saying hello or telling me to piss off?"

He bleats again, then bounces off, head and tail high.

"Piss off it is."

I watch the goat make a spectacle of himself with the big yellow ball while Jack grazes, shifting to avoid a collision.

Jack and Juke lift their heads a second before I hear the crunch of gravel. The sound continues past, slow, steady. She isn't going to say a word and she isn't going to stop. When her steps sound far enough away, I allow myself to look.

Her head is down, jacket pulled tight, shoulders rounded. It's

not the purposeful march I associate with her. Or the I-don't-
want-you-here stomp I've seen so much of during the last few
weeks.

Did I overstep?

No. I should have been strong enough to say those things
years ago. Maybe it would have helped us both. And now I have
to be strong enough to do what's right for me.

I give Jack a last kiss on the muzzle, return Juke's evil eye, and
walk back to the apartment above the barn. It's nothing like the
apartment I've lived in the last four years and nothing like where
I always envisioned myself, but it's exactly where I feel most at
home.

The black cat meows from the top of the stairs, telling me to
hurry. The moment the door is open, he tumbles in, then turns
to pretend-spray the door as though it wronged him. I trail him
past the galley kitchen and sit on the couch. Beast assesses the
space next to me, then hops up and settles into a circle, his back
pressed against my thigh.

I fire up my laptop, fingers flying with purpose. When I'm
done with the e-mail, I sit back and reread. The cursor blinks
happily, waiting for me to finish, to send, to commit.

I pull my father's sketch pad out of my bag and flip through
the now-familiar drawings until I reach my favorite. It's a render-
ing of a woman, her profile partially obscured by long, curly
hair. One spiral has popped loose and trails the curve of her
cheek. She looks young but he's captured a moment of emotional
age. What could have caused those lines at the corner of her eye,
the slight pull at the edge of her mouth? Who was she? Was she
sad? Worried?

I've stared at this image so many times over the last couple of
weeks. There are hints of me in the slope of her nose and the slant
of her eyes. But the cheekbones are different and her mouth is
fuller. I lay the photograph of Mom sitting on the lake-house
porch next to the drawing. It's her mouth and cheekbones, but
the nose isn't as straight and the eyes are more almond.

Is she a real person or what you saw clearest from the two of us?

An incoming e-mail pings. Instinctively my eyes jump to the screen and my fingers click it open. This ingrained reaction will be tough to break.

Howard. My former assistant, turned manager. *Trade show went well. New boss is quite the performer. Thought you'd be curious to hear. When are you returning?*

"I'm not." The answer falls loud and final in the stillness of the room. Beast lifts his head and blinks at me, then draws his paw over his head, shutting me out.

I type a quick response, not answering his question. Then I hit Send on my resignation.

"No going back now, is there?" I rub the cat's chin and he purrs in response.

"Hey, Emma." Ben knocks on the door to the apartment. "Are you decent? Can I come in?"

"It's unlocked. And yes, I'm decent."

He cracks the door open and peers through splayed fingers.

"Really? Why would I lie about that?"

He grins. "A man can always hope."

I toss a throw pillow at him but can't help laughing at the look on his face.

"Seriously though, Rena and Simon have asked for a meeting and they'd like you there."

"With . . ." Dread sucker punches the lighthearted moment.

"Jillian and Tony are in there with them."

"Shit. Any idea what this is about?"

"We'll find out in a minute."

I follow him down the stairs and into the barn office. Rena sits in her usual throne behind the desk, with Simon in his spot on the couch. Jillian slumps in the chair in front of the desk, head down, arms crossed. Her hair hangs loose, obscuring her face. Though she's slouching, her body twangs with the tightness of a taut rubber band.

Tony leans against the back wall and, from the look on his face, wishes he could melt straight through that wall. Simon gestures for me to sit. Ben perches on the armrest next to me.

The office feels stuffy with anxiety. I wish I could stand next to Tony and disappear through the portal with him.

Simon is the first to wade into the murky waters ahead. "Jillian has decided to take a little time off from teaching and running the stable. Ben, I'd like for you to take on more of the barn management."

I notice Jillian shifting in the chair, the slightest of moves, fingers balling the fabric of her shirt into her fist.

I wonder if Rena and Simon know about my discussion with her. I wonder if taking time off was her decision.

Ben nods, keeping his eyes on his feet.

"Emma, you've been a tremendous help and we're grateful for what you've done for the therapeutic program." He meets Rena's eyes and the tenderness glues me to the couch. I remember the first time I saw them look at each other that way. It's the look that says you'd do anything for the other person, that she means the world to you.

Maybe my father had looked at Mom like that. Maybe he'd even looked at me like that. I'll never know for sure.

"You all already know that the doctor has told me to scale back." Rena's voice is shaky and she pushes a mug with pens in it to the side of the computer, then pulls it to the front of the screen, then to the other side.

Simon watches the path of the mug. His lips purse and I can almost hear the rumbling of the words inside his head.

She releases a breath and her already small frame shrinks into the oversize leather chair. "Emma, will you reconsider going back? As the primary donor of the therapeutic program, I believe you should be the one to run it."

"Run it?" My tongue feels like a giant cotton ball. Half an hour ago I was giddy with the idea of working with Rena if she'd still have me. Now I'm terrified at the opportunity she's handed me.

"It wasn't really a suggestion from the doctor. It was more of an order." She studies her hands, picks at a ripped nail on her left hand.

The silence in the office is deafening.

Tell them. What are you waiting for?

"I . . ." Jillian winces and the words catch in my throat. Staying is the right decision for me, probably even the best decision for Rena, and undoubtedly the wrong decision for Jillian.

But the need to please my friend at any expense died the day she chose to end our friendship.

"I'll stay. I am staying. I sent my resignation before Ben came to get me. I realized this morning that I can't go back."

Rena mouths *thank you.* Simon pats my knee, then stands and tips his head for Rena to follow. Ben squeezes my shoulder and pushes off the armrest. Tony gives me a wink and melts through the door on Ben's heels.

And just like that, there are two left. Jilli looks up and our eyes meet for the skip of a heartbeat. One blink and I'm not sure if it was real or imagined. She stands and turns to the door. Our eyes meet and lock. My stomach drops like a bad amusement ride.

"Oh, Jilli." I wish I could reverse time. But life doesn't work that way. We make mistakes even when we think we're protecting the other person. My father did. Rena and Simon did. I did.

"Don't." She holds up her hand, a literal exclamation mark. "I don't want your empathy or friendship. And I still don't want you here." She walks out, but not with the defiant strides from every other time she's walked away from me.

I look around the office, at my new life, familiar and foreign.

queeze. Use your legs coming out of the corner. Squeeze."
The pony switches leads behind, then does an awkward skip-step and breaks into a too-fast trot. Matty bounces like a stuffed toy before landing in a heap in the dust of the indoor arena. The pony doesn't bother to scoot away, just walks off, unconcerned. In the two weeks I've been teaching him, Matty has fallen off at least once a week.

Mrs. Thomson squeals and darts into the arena. "Matty, darling, are you okay? Oh, baby. That awful, awful pony. I'm selling him."

And every time Matty lands in the dirt, she throws around a few accusations. A noise escapes from my diaphragm.

"Not as easy as you thought it would be, is it?" Jillian is leaning against the column of the half-door into the arena a few feet from me. The bleachers behind her are empty now that the sole occupant is in the arena, clucking and dusting at her child.

"I didn't think it would be." I bristle, because I *had* thought it would be easier. Not easy, I'm not that naïve, but I hadn't expected how challenging it could be at times. I've had my share of what-did-I-do moments and corporate-life-was-so-much-easier moments. But it's also been the happiest two weeks I can remember.

"You know, they fired me."

I turn to look at her, surprised by the words as well as the matter-of-fact tone they were delivered with.

"No way."

She nods. "Yes way. They told me I had to leave and deal with 'my issues.'"

She looks at her feet; the toe of her right foot is planted into the ground while the heel pendulums left, then right. There's an insecure vulnerability to the way she's standing. How many times did I see her do this same thing? I always chalked it up to her extra-strength attitude. Now I see it for what it is and probably always was, the need for reassurance.

"I'm sorry, Jilli. I didn't mean for any of this . . ." The words catch, afraid of igniting a Jilli response.

There's no spark, no explosion. We stare at the hole her toe has made in the footing of the arena.

"They did the right thing. I needed a kick in the ass and they needed to know that it was okay to do it. I think they were always afraid of breaking me."

Mrs. Thomson lets out a lion roar, "Absolutely not," and Matty whines, "But Mom."

I turn back to Jilli. "Are you dealing with those issues?" There's no reason to tiptoe anymore.

"It's not that easy."

"Where have you been the last two weeks?"

"Talking about my *issues*." She breaks out the syllables, puckering around the "u."

"That's good."

"That's crap."

"Speaking of crap . . ." I hold up my finger in a give-me-a-minute and walk to the middle of the arena, where Matty and his mom are arguing.

"You are not to get back on that pony."

"But, Mottthhhheeerrrrrr, I want to. I actually really want to. I almost had it."

"I forbid it. And you," she swivels her upper body, the bottom half catching up as she launches into her usual ultimatum, "are never to teach my Matty again, or we're finding another stable."

I take a dusty breath, giving my brain and mouth time to confer on an appropriate response. Hopefully my brain will prevail because my mouth is about to offer to help her pack.

"That would be a shame, Mrs. Thomson." Jillian stops a few paces back, holding on to the disgruntled pony. "I watched Matty ride, and he's made a lot of progress. Emma can teach him a lot."

"Please," Matty whines. Mrs. Thomson harrumphs, then turns and stomps off, the result looking far more comical than menacing in the soft footing of the arena.

I catch Jillian hiding a smirk. I give Matty a leg up and instruct him to walk around the ring a few times so they can both catch their breath.

Jilli and I make our way back to the side of the ring, side by side, watching the dust puff under our feet. It could almost be a flashback scene in a movie, two best friends in perfect sync.

Part of me wishes it could be like that again. But it can't. And it shouldn't.

"I realized something during those endless fucking hours of therapy. I don't want this life. I never did." Her eyes latch on to mine. There's no hatred or animosity or bitterness. "I wanted what you wanted. And then I didn't want it because you wanted it. I'm not making sense, am I?"

"Actually you are. But I don't understand why."

"Why I'm making sense?" A dry laugh disrupts the semicalm.

"Why did you turn against me?"

"I was jealous."

"Of me? What was there to be jealous?"

"Your strength."

"Me?" My voice squeaks in surprise, unsettling a few pigeons in the rafters and making Matty jump in the saddle.

"Yes, you. Except no one else saw it so they coddled you. That always pissed me off. You had every reason to crumble and yet you picked yourself up, every time, and succeeded at what you were doing. Everyone liked you, you had straight A's, and you were by far the better rider. I mean look at it, your dad uproots you and moves you to hick-town after your mom tries to off herself. Then she does off herself."

I cringe.

"Sorry. That was insensitive. I'm still working on that."

After another silence, she presses forward. "You didn't have it easy at home and look at the success you've become. Me? I had every opportunity for success handed to me and the only thing I can successfully do is screw up.

"I watched you when you first came back. I hated the way you fit in around here. Even after all those years away and the way you left, you still fit. And suddenly I felt like I was the one who didn't fit. Maybe I never did."

"That's why you started drinking, to fit in?"

She nods, her mouth pulled into a tight line. She reaches for the braid and fans the ends between the fingers of her left hand, studying the ends.

A pang of sadness flashes to my core and I swallow the emotion it's pushed into my throat. How many times had I seen her do that same gesture? I rub my thumb against my ring finger. It's smooth. I haven't chewed on it in two weeks.

"Anyway, that was the past. We're adults now." She flips the rope of blond hair over her shoulder and straightens. "I realized something else. I've missed you, our friendship. I never had another girlfriend I could confide in who understood me. We can't undo the past. But do you think you'll ever be able to forgive me?"

The bubble of emotion lodges in my chest. All those fantasies about this exact conversation didn't prepare me for hearing those words actually spoken. I guess deep down, I never thought she would. Yet here we are.

And I can't find the words to respond.

I'd never been able to replace the bond, either. For all the friends I have, there's not one person who ever came close. I learned to be alone. And to be okay with being alone. My father's death has turned my life upside down. Not because I lost my only living relative, but because losing him brought me out of my "alone shell."

The discomfort of that realization is magnified by Jilli's expectation of a reply.

"Of course." I smile but neither of us is fooled.

I force the next words out. "Now that you're back, will you take on your full class load and managing the barn again?"

"I'm not coming back."

I whip around to look at her. "What? Why?"

"I can't. I guess neither one of us could go back to our former lives."

"What will you do?"

Her mouth pulls into a smile. "Switch with you. One of our regular students is a fashion designer. She has a studio in Georgetown and is willing to give me a job. Ordering supplies, fulfilling orders, booking meetings, fetching lattes. You know, high-level stuff, stuff I'm good at." She shrugs off the self-inflicted slight.

"Will you still live here?"

She releases a shaky breath. "I can't."

I nod. I understand.

"Are you going to be okay?"

Her mouth quirks into a half smile. "I think so."

She looks different. No, she looks older. Until now, I've been seeing her as a fuller version of the girl I'd last seen sixteen years ago. The changes in Simon and Rena had slapped the air out of my lungs. But Jilli was mostly the same. Until today. I match her smile. "I think so, too."

She takes a step, hesitates, and turns. "I told them the truth. About the accident. About what really happened. They knew. Even before you told them." She catches my eye. "I'm sorry, Emma. For what I allowed myself to become and for the way I've behaved. Then and now. I won't make excuses. You deserve more. Now that you're staying, do you think we'll be able to move past it, maybe start over?"

I pull my lips into a tight smile. Time stretches out. The unspoken speaks volumes.

"I get it. Well, I should get going." She steps out of the arena,
reluctant to leave.

The old twinge pokes at my insides. *Say something, fix this.*
"You'll still be coming around. I'll see you then."

"The magic of Jumping Frog Farm." She nods and she's gone.

Mrs. Thomson is still fussing at Matty at the other end of the
ring. He dismounts and pulls the sullen pony out of the arena.
His mom waddles off behind him, dusting his back as they go.

I follow, far enough behind, then slip into the lounge. I need
something warm to drink, something comforting. It's times like
this I almost miss Bruce and Howard and the corporate politics.

"Oouufff," someone grunts and I hear the scamper of hooves.
Probably that crazy goat.

I step out and collide with Jukebox. He bleats and gives me
the evil goat eye, then bounds away.

"What the hell is his problem?" I rub the top of my foot where
he stomped, no doubt on purpose.

Ben walks past in pursuit. "He's mad that Tony took Jack out
of the stall. You have a therapeutic client in the indoor, by the
way. I'll try to get the galloping kabob out of there."

"Leave him. He just wants to be with his best friend."

Ben meets my eyes.

"It's okay," I answer the unspoken question.

I make my way to the small group in the middle of the arena.
Tony is holding Jack's lead rope while a frazzled-looking woman
tries to hold a boy still a few steps away.

"Stop moving around, you'll scare the horse," she whispers
entirely too loud.

"I don't want to be here," the boy answers, his voice full with
tears. He clings to her arm and tries to hide behind her. I recognize him from a few weeks ago. He'd refused to have anything to
do with the horses.

"Hi." I squat down to his height. "I'm Emma. What's your
name?"

"Tyrone," the boy answers with little more than a whimper.

"I'm glad you're here, Tyrone. Have you ever been on a horse?"

He shakes his head, his eyes rolling left, than right, not focusing on me or Jack or even the four-legged blob standing underneath Jack's belly. Tyrone, I realize, is almost blind.

"He's . . . no," the woman says, trying to extract her arm while Tyrone clings even tighter.

I take the lead rope from Tony and urge Jack a couple of steps forward. Tyrone squeals and darts behind the lady, although he's still gripping her arm so both end up twirling in a tornado of arena dust.

"How old are you, Tyrone?"

"Ten."

"Really? Do you know this goat is also ten? His name is Jukebox." I slide a step closer to the boy and whisper conspiratorially, "He's a troublemaker. I bet you're not, though."

The boy turns his head until his eye latches on to me.

"You know, I was your age when this big horse was born. Of course, he wasn't this big back then. That was a long time ago. He's an old man now, kind of like a grandfather. Do you know your grandfather?"

Tyrone nods, then tilts his head, and I notice his left eye trying to lock on to Jack.

"Is he nice?"

Tyrone mutters, "Uh-huh."

Jack lowers his head so he's eye to eye with the trembling boy. Tyrone whimpers and grabs, but his chaperone has stepped out of range. I reach out my hand and he snaps to my side like the other half of a magnet. He's now closer to Jack than he'd intended but the alternative is to let go of an adult and he's not going to do that.

"Grandpa Jack won't hurt you."

Tyrone's eyes shift from me to the horse in front of us, back to me, and then to the door. Another whimper vibrates through his lips.

"I'll tell you a secret if you promise not to share it with anyone."

The boy quiets, waiting for a secret from an adult.

"When I was a little girl and I'd get scared or sad or lonely, I'd come talk to Jack. He always made me feel better."

"How?"

"I'll show you if you let me." I slide my arm out of his grasp until we're holding hands instead. I turn his hands over in mine so they're palms up, cupped in my own. Jack lowers his head. Through Tyrone's fingers I can feel the warm puffs of breath. The boy tenses next to me but doesn't pull away. Jack blows another breath into the outstretched hands before resting his muzzle in the hand hammock.

Tyrone's small body shudders. "He's soft."

"Right?" I whisper by his ear. "I think that's my very favorite part of a horse."

We stay like that—the horse's head resting in a boy's open palms, safely secured in an adult's hands. Jack's breathing is slow, his muzzle warm velvet. My hands are warm and protective. Nestled between us, the boy releases the death grip on his fear.

I sneak a look at Tyrone. A lone tear runs down his cheek, in complete contrast to the smile spreading across his face. He pulls his hands from mine and explores Jack's head. He grabs one of Jack's ears and bends it down. From behind I sense the movement of the woman and I lift my hand to stop her.

"Grandpa Jack," he whispers into the tube he's made of the furry ear. "I've been scared a lot. Since my grandpa went away. I want to be with my grandpa but they said I can't. They said he's dead. They sent me to live with strangers. I don't like it there but I like it here. Can I come visit you again?"

Jack leans his head into the boy's chest and Tyrone wraps his arms around the large black head, tears streaming down his face.

I stand and wipe at my eyes. I catch Tony blinking wet eyes and hear a sniffle from behind.

I pat the gentle giant's neck and return the evil stare from Jukebox.

Tyrone laughs as Jack flaps his muzzle, tickling the boy's face.

I'm not the only one who's found their second chance in the healing power of horses.